But How Are You, Really

But How Are You, Really

a novel

Ella Dawson

Dutton

DUTTON
An imprint of Penguin Random House LLC
penguinrandomhouse.com

LIBRARY OF CONGRESS CATALOGING-IN-PUBLICATION DATA
Names: Dawson, Ella 1992– author.
Title: But how are you, really: a novel / Ella Dawson.
Description: [New York]: Dutton, an imprint of Penguin Random House LLC, 2024.
Identifiers: LCCN 2023040302 (print) | LCCN 2023040303 (ebook) |
ISBN 9780593473771 (hardcover) | ISBN 9780593473788 (ebook)
Subjects: LCGFT: Romance fiction. | Bisexual fiction. | Novels.
Classification: LCC PS3604.A978585 B88 2024 (print) |
LCC PS3604.A978585 (ebook) | DDC 813/.6—dc23/eng/20230914
LC record available at https://lccn.loc.gov/2023040302
LC ebook record available at https://lccn.loc.gov/2023040303

Printed in the United States of America

1st Printing

BOOK DESIGN BY ALISON CNOCKAERT

For Tahlia, who told me to quit my job and write a book

But How Are You, Really

FROM: Hein University Reunion & Commencement Committee <rc@hein.edu>
SUBJECT: An Invitation . . .

Dear Charlotte,

My, how time flies! We can't believe it has already been five years since we graduated from Hein University. It feels like just yesterday that we received our diplomas on the President's Lawn. Some of us are still recovering from our mortarboard sunburns.

We write to you with good news: It's time to come home. We would love for you to join us at Hein for our five-year reunion on May 17–20, 2018.

Come celebrate the graduating Class of 2018 and reunite with friends on campus! Hein University is thrilled to gather graduating students and alumni together for an action-packed long weekend of programming, meals, and events. Each academic department will host open houses for returning alumni, as well as discussion panels and screenings. You can review the full schedule on the Hein Reunion & Commencement microsite. If you would like to reserve on-campus housing, double rooms have been set aside for the Class of 2013 in Randall Dormitory.

We are thrilled to announce that Roger Ludermore, CEO of *The Front End Review* and Hein Class of '81, will give the commencement address on Sunday, May 20th. As always, alumni are welcome to attend the commencement ceremony for the Class of 2018.

Lastly, remember to send Reece Krueger your updates for the 2018 edition of *Hein Magazine*! We would love to celebrate your accomplishments. Submit your updates to <rkrueger @hein.edu>.

We can't wait to see you again.

Sincerely,
Kahini Gupta, Class President '13
Luella Jackson, R&C Chair '13
Reece Krueger, Class Secretary '13

Thursday

Chapter 1

TEXT MESSAGE FROM JACKIE SLAUGHTER TO CHARLOTTE THORNE, 3:10 PM: sorry flight delayed will be there as soon as I can!!

TEXT MESSAGE FROM CHARLOTTE THORNE TO JACKIE SLAUGHTER, 3:16 PM: Can't wait to see you. Please do not make me face these people alone.

DURING THEIR SENIOR year of college, Charlotte's roommate Jackie printed a color wheel on a sheet of canvas. Each slice of the pie was labeled with an emotion: the burning crimson of *hostile*, the spiky cobalt of *depressed*, the vibrant, consuming orange of *joy*. The Feelings Chart, as they called it, hung in a place of honor on the living room wall. Whenever Charlotte crossed her arms over her chest and withdrew from a tense conversation, Jackie would point to the chart and demand, "Use your words!"

Now, standing in front of a nondescript door on the ground floor of their old dormitory, Charlotte looked at the tiny envelope in her hand embossed with the Hein University crest and realized that *déjà vu* hadn't been on the chart.

She held her breath as she unfolded the flap of the envelope. A thick metal key fell into her palm, then slid into the lock with a familiar give and tumble. Muscle memory returned like it had been days, not years, since she last lived in a dorm.

When the door swung open, her déjà vu only intensified. Her eyes swept over the high popcorn ceiling and cinder-block walls. The dull gray square contained two sets of chipped wooden furniture: narrow single beds, heavy desks, and chairs that complained against the linoleum floor. Twin dressers sat on either side of the door, and a squat bookshelf lined the far wall underneath a wide window. Every room on campus looked the same, dated and utilitarian, differentiated only by the furniture arrangement.

The smell hit her the hardest: that old fog of industrial cleaner, rubber mattresses, and spilled beer. It brought back late nights working on papers, her desk covered in coffee cups and empty bags of Doritos.

Charlotte flicked on the overhead light and listened to its fluorescent buzz, the soundtrack of her college years. Cold spread through her chest, blending indigo (*astonishment*) and a flat pale blue (*dread*). For the next four days, she was back at Hein University. Nothing whatsoever had changed, except for her.

With a grunt, Charlotte dropped her duffle bag on one of the beds. When she rolled up the blackout curtain, a thicket of trees greeted her outside. The forest helped orient her in the dorm's labyrinth of twisting hallways—this side of the building faced north. She shoved the window open, and the smell of mulch and damp leaves poured into the room.

Charlotte breathed in deep and slow. She had always preferred the earthy aroma of the suburbs. Her life in New York City smelled like humid garbage and subway exhaust. The closest she had gotten to nature since graduating was pigeon poop drying on the fire escape outside her bedroom window.

She never expected to miss living in a dormitory, least of all the reviled Randall Dormitory for freshmen, but she couldn't remember the last time she had this much space. Room 107 easily dwarfed every apartment she called home since graduation. It could fit her old place in Manhattan's Financial District, the illegal three-bedroom with the partition walls that didn't reach the ceiling. Then came the roach-infested loft in Bushwick after she lost her job at *ChompNews* . . . and the sublet in Queens with a colony of feral cats in the attic.

At least her current place in Crown Heights had a bedroom window. She lived with just one roommate—a high-strung publicist named Kit—and she didn't need to worry about her packages getting stolen in the vestibule. But the new place was still teeny: Room 107 would contain her bedroom, Kit's room, their shared kitchen-slash-living-space, and the coat closet stuffed with Kit's camping equipment.

Until Jackie arrived, Charlotte practically had a luxury SRO all to herself.

Brutalist charmer bursting with natural light! the Craigslist post would say. *Spacious square footage, complete with vintage industrial furniture! 420 friendly! NO PETS, NO IN-UNIT LAUNDRY. COMMUNAL BATHROOM SHARED WITH DIVERSE YOUNG PROFESSIONALS.*

Her phone bleated in her pocket. Her shoulders tensed at the electronic chirp. She fished a charger out of her duffle bag and plugged her phone into the outlet beside the dresser, scanning the notification.

SLACK MESSAGE FROM ROGER LUDERMORE TO CHARLOTTE THORNE, 4:47 PM: interns yelling again. what happened w HR about the quiet policy?

Charlotte swiped to dismiss the message and turned her phone upside down. As she stared at the mirror anchored to the cinder-block wall, she gave her reflection a *can you believe this* glare.

Her phone vibrated again. She reached for it reflexively but caught herself, clenching her fist. The phone stilled, only to skitter across the top of the dresser a third time.

A Roger Ludermore classic: If at first you don't get a response on

Slack, even when there is an away message up, call your assistant again and again. A piece of wisdom that would not be included in his commencement speech this weekend.

Charlotte worked at *The Front End Review*, a business and technology magazine favored by the venture capital set. It was the kind of publication most folks in her generation had heard of but few actually read, an industry-specific dinosaur behind an expensive paywall. Her petulant boss sat at its helm as CEO and editor in chief. Roger fell into the amorphous professional category of "thought leader," which as far as she could tell meant he was a rich white guy with endless opinions. Charlotte's job, as his executive assistant, was to make sure he paid his ghostwriters, showed up sober enough at his speaking engagements, and didn't murder anyone.

She performed a cost-benefit analysis of sending Roger to voicemail. If she ignored him now, she'd just have to clean up his mess later. Once upon a time she skipped answering a late-night call in an attempt to establish a healthy work-life balance. The next thing she knew, her boss was being detained by customs after trying to cross the Canadian border with his Amex instead of a passport.

With a sigh, she turned her phone over and accepted the call on speaker.

"How am I supposed to get any work done with a daycare in the kitchen?" he barked into the phone. "This is unacceptable, Charlotte. Unacceptable!"

Health insurance, she reminded herself. *You need health insurance.*

He continued: "Isn't there a closet we can shove them in? What about the East Conference Room?"

Charlotte adopted her neutral work voice. "We can't, sir."

"Why not?"

"You converted the East Conference Room into your podcasting studio."

Thin silence greeted her words. She poked at the worry lines etched into her forehead as she waited for Roger to realize that he was the one who displaced the interns.

"Are you saying this is my fault?" he finally hissed.

You need to pay your heating bill, Charlotte thought. *And your electric bill.*

"Of course not, sir. We just need to find a more permanent spot for them."

Or they could cancel Roger's vanity podcast and put the interns back in the conference room. But what did Charlotte know? She was just an assistant.

All the way in Manhattan, Roger muttered under his breath.

For the last three years, this was Charlotte's life. It infuriated and suited her in equal measure. Her boss's previous assistants hadn't lasted more than a year, but she had a knack for organizing details and managing egos.

Her salary, while not great, could certainly be worse. She knew from experience.

The line went quiet as Roger shuffled around his chrome-and-glass office. She squinted at her reflection in the mirror while his attention wandered. If she needed evidence that she wasn't a fresh-faced teenager arriving for orientation, the dead-eyed woman staring back at her offered ample proof. An early suggestion of silver started at her temples and wove through her blond hair. When she adjusted her part, she revealed an insurgent force of grays. Her skin was dull from sleep deprivation and too much time spent indoors.

Twenty-seven was still young, she knew. But she looked tired.

Charlotte pulled a tube of concealer from her purse and dabbed at the circles under her eyes.

A sharp snort burst from her cell phone speaker. She flinched and accidentally swiped the cream across her ear.

"Peter's new draft makes me sound like a guidance counselor," Roger snapped.

Charlotte sucked her teeth, fighting the urge to hang up on him.

Think of that direct deposit twice a month into your checking account. Think of how much bigger that direct deposit will be once Roger gives you his blessing to move to the art department.

"Is it too late to find a new speechwriter?" he asked. She hoped this was a rhetorical question—his commencement address was only three days away. Roger's voice sank into a playful purr. "Charlotte, why did I agree to do this?"

Because you're a narcissist who can't say no to a microphone, she wished she could say. *Because the universe is conspiring against me.*

She found a tissue in her pocket and tried to wipe the concealer out of her ear. "You've been wanting to come back to campus for a while," Charlotte reminded him gently as she turned to her duffle bag. What exactly did one wear to relive her not-so-glory days? She frowned at her mediocre packing job: a jumble of bland work clothes and clean underwear. Nothing that said *I am a successful and interesting adult now, thank you very much.*

"Hmm," Roger granted. A rare win.

Charlotte picked up a pencil skirt she wore at the office. As an undergrad, she'd have thrown on a men's button-down and a pair of ratty denim shorts. Her style as a Hein youth was *lazy-'80s-movie-heartthrob-but-gay*, combat boots and denim jackets with greasy hair and aviator sunglasses she stole from her mom. When they became friends their freshman year, Jackie called Charlotte's look "thrift store dirtbag." It was the coolest she had ever felt.

She dropped the skirt and put her blazer back on over her tank top. It smelled like sweat and Amtrak, but hopefully no one would stick their nose in her armpit. She could always take the blazer off and swing it over her shoulder like a finance bro on the subway during his evening commute.

"How's the weather up there?" Roger asked.

"It's New England in May," she said.

"So, cold and withholding."

Charlotte chuckled. An accurate description, she'd give him that. Roger could turn his charm on and off, and she fell for it more than she liked to admit.

"Aubrey will pick up your suit from the tailor tomorrow morning. It should be nice here on Sunday."

"It better be. This speech is important. The podcast still hasn't broken the charts."

Sure, because a commencement address at a liberal arts college in Massachusetts would send subscriptions to *The Ludermore Power Hour* surging.

"Of course, sir."

Her boss had become a media darling over the winter when he gave a talk about philanthropy at the World Economic Forum in Davos. His impassioned, heavily ghostwritten case for helping as many people as possible, as efficiently as possible, won him new fans in Silicon Valley. It was all bullshit, as far as Charlotte could tell, but Roger's face clogged her LinkedIn timeline for weeks after a hustle culture guru shared a clip of the speech to his millions of followers. Roger launched the podcast shortly after, eager to capitalize on the attention. Charlotte found it unlistenable, but Hein's Reunion & Commencement Committee probably hadn't gone beyond a cursory Google search before booking Roger to speak at graduation. It helped that he was a Hein alum too. Class of 1981.

She considered her sneakers. Too dusty. She replaced them with her favorite pair of loafers, the leather worn and soft.

Roger's voice flattened into a sneer. "You have a lot riding on this weekend too. Don't forget I make my recommendation for the art job on Monday."

Charlotte stiffened at the warning-slash-threat. Her thumb rose to her mouth, teeth worrying the skin at the edge of her nail.

Of course, she wouldn't forget. If everything went smoothly during the next four days, she would finally be free of Roger's petulant tyranny. The potential transfer to the art department was the only reason she hadn't told her boss to go fuck himself when he instructed her to book a train ticket so that she could live-tweet his address. Nothing else would have gotten her to come back to Hein University.

Deep breath in. Hold it. Release.

"Yes, sir," she recited in her best Siri impression. "Aubrey booked you a taxi from the train, and I'll meet you on campus when you arrive on Sunday."

"Excellent." She heard ice clatter into a glass on the other end of the line. Then the hiss of alcohol meeting the cold. Vodka, if she had to guess. "So lucky you're a Hein grad too, Charlotte. I didn't even have to get you a hotel room."

Roger laughed at his own joke as she willed him to burst into flames. The line went dead; he'd hung up.

Charlotte returned to the mirror and let out a sigh of relief. There. That worked. She could pass as *fine.* Older, but put together.

Adulthood looked nothing like she'd expected it to when she walked across the President's Lawn and received her diploma five years ago. She had four pairs of pantyhose, a roommate who communicated through rude Post-it notes, and a moderately helpful antidepressant. Whatever she'd imagined of her future, it wasn't working for a man like Roger Ludermore.

As long as no one asked her, "No, *really*, how are you?" she would get through this weekend with a guaranteed promotion and her dignity intact.

TEXT MESSAGE FROM NINA DORANTES TO CHARLOTTE THORNE, 5:03 PM: Are you here yet?

TEXT MESSAGE FROM CHARLOTTE THORNE TO NINA DORANTES, 5:08 PM: Yes, room 107. Meet you in front of Randall?

TEXT MESSAGE FROM NINA DORANTES TO CHARLOTTE THORNE, 5:18 PM: YAY

"LOOK WHO IT is," Nina boomed from her perch on a stone bench outside the dorm. "The queen of Brooklyn!" She stood to her full five foot eleven in a black jumpsuit and bright hoop earrings, her dark hair swishing in a perfect curtain, and threw her arms out for a hug. Charlotte had a moment to blink up at her before Nina squished her tight.

"Hi, Nina." Charlotte untwined herself from her ex-girlfriend's grip. "You look amazing. You're so jacked!"

"You're a sweetheart." Nina flexed a biceps. "You can thank six months in Peru for that."

Nina had just returned from a research assignment in the Amazon. Charlotte followed her adventures on Instagram, scrolling through pictures of water lilies and poison dart frogs as she waited for the subway. They hadn't talked in . . .

Oh jeez, how long has it been?

But social media made it easy to keep in touch without keeping in touch.

"You put the *bod* in *botanist*," Charlotte joked.

Nina snorted and nudged Charlotte's shoulder with her own. "You're terrible. Where's Jackie?"

"Stuck in L.A."

Nina tutted and folded her arm through Charlotte's. "You'll just have to settle for me, then."

Nina and Charlotte met during orientation at Acronym, the LGBTQIA+ program house at Hein. They fell madly in lust during a mixer for queer freshmen and transfer students, wisecracking about the baseball bros in Nina's dorm who'd already gotten in trouble for mooning the university president. Charlotte was too enchanted to be annoyed when Nina teased her about their height difference: *I'd like to kiss you, but we might need a step stool.*

Nina held herself with bulletproof confidence. Under the surface, she struggled with feeling unwelcome just as much as Charlotte did—even more so as a woman of color at a fussy New England school. But she presented a strong front, asserting her right to belong in every room, an energy that Charlotte found deeply appealing. She glommed on to Nina like a life preserver.

They delighted in flirting openly, holding hands in the cafeteria and fooling around back at Randall Dorm when Charlotte's roommate was at the gym. Charlotte didn't have to worry about her mom catching them together or explain why she returned home wearing last night's clothes. Plus, she could tag along with Nina to parties without feeling like a clueless, uninvited frosh.

And what a joy it was to be wanted . . . Charlotte liked to watch Nina from across the room and think, *That woman picked me.* Acceptance was a heady drug.

But Nina didn't just want to be wanted—she wanted a real relationship, one rooted in commitment and vulnerable conversations. Nina addressed conflict head-on and maintained healthy, firm boundaries, while Charlotte dreaded advocating for her needs. She'd only just moved out of her mother's house; dissecting her attachment style was the last thing Charlotte wanted to do. When Nina told Charlotte she wanted more, Charlotte balked.

Why her, really? Why would Nina choose her?

And college had only *just* started. Surely they were too young, and Hein was full of people for them to meet and make mistakes with. Settling down so fast had to be risky. It was better for them to stay independent, and heck, they could always change their minds.

"You're an idiot," Nina told her when Charlotte found the courage to break things off after Thanksgiving. Charlotte's hands shook, but her new ex-girlfriend rolled her eyes and patted her on the shoulder. "But that's okay. Give me three weeks of space and I'll forgive you."

That was exactly what happened, and they'd been friends ever since. Nina fell in love with Eliza, a temperamental butch in the computer science program, and they built the relationship she wanted.

Charlotte found the best friend she craved in Jackie, who worshipped Nina's sophistication from the moment they met. Charlotte and Nina had been platonic for so long that she almost forgot they used to date.

"Tell me about your fancy job!" Nina prodded.

On the walk to their class reception, Charlotte regaled Nina with the silly work anecdotes she saved for moments like this. The benefit of working for a magazine with name recognition was that people didn't expect her job at *The Front End Review* to suck, and they only wanted to hear the glamorous gossip. She started with the controversial founder of a ride-sharing app with a surprise allergy to pineapple. His tongue had swelled up to double its normal size during an interview, much to the delight of the photographer assigned to shoot his portrait.

She saved her less fashionable work stories—Roger's unrelenting phone calls, and the venture capitalist who left a spare hotel key on her desk with a vulgar note—for another time.

Preferably after several drinks.

Or never.

The Class of 2013 reception took place on the patio outside Fuller Dormitory. Fuller was a blocky brutalist building with a concrete façade and odd, thin windows. During Reunion & Commencement, older classes enjoyed professionally catered events at the beautiful, historic buildings on campus. As the youngest alumni in attendance this year, the Class of 2013 sat at the bottom of the food chain. The odds of wrangling generous donations out of the twenty-somethings, most of whom had yet to put a dent in their student loans, were low.

"At least they sprang for a keg," Nina drawled, unimpressed.

Forty or so people milled about the patio clutching plastic cups of beer and rosé. Two mobbed underclassmen in bright blue STAFF shirts tended bar on a folding table. Some industrious member of the R&C committee had strung white fairy lights between the outdoor lamps. What was meant to feel like a garden party looked more like a sad wine tasting on a glorified sidewalk, but Charlotte admired the effort.

"So this is where our four hundred dollars went." She smiled as Nina laughed.

They scanned the reception for familiar faces. A few members of their informal support group from back in the day hid in the crowd. Officially titled "Dead, Divorced, and Otherwise Disappointing Parents," the 3Ds was a clique of trauma survivors and alienated queer kids. Charlotte's homophobic mother and absent father qualified her for admission, as did Nina's controlling dad. Charlotte recognized Jio Vargas sitting on a bench with their boyfriend Matt Larsen. Amy Rosen, Nina's college roommate, chatted with a cluster of English majors.

Charlotte let out a breath she didn't realize she was holding when she detected no asshole exes in attendance. Then again, she still needed a drink before she ran the gauntlet of old friends.

Nina found her hand and towed her toward the bar. They took their place in line behind a trio of girls from the lacrosse team.

Nina's eyes narrowed as she studied the crowd. "I'm glad Eliza couldn't come. I did *not* want to see what shape she's shaved into her undercut this time."

Charlotte resisted the urge to point out that Nina's snark suggested otherwise. They must be in an off phase again. "Is she still in Cairo?"

Nina's ex-girlfriend worked for the Department of Defense doing something that Charlotte had never understood. It was a lucrative job that Nina disapproved of, which probably contributed to her irritated tone.

"Nah, she's in Dubai now. She sent me a weird WhatsApp message to get nacho fries in her honor at Terry's."

"We can do that."

"That's not the point." Nina played with her necklace, the thin gold chain catching the light.

Charlotte bit back a smile. "I'm just saying, nacho fries sound great."

"What about your love life?" Nina asked. "How are things with Merielle?"

Charlotte's smile wilted at the mention of her longest-lasting relationship since college. "Uh, nonexistent. That ended ages ago."

Her ex-girlfriend frowned. "Oh. I'm sorry. I guess it's been a while since we caught up."

An understatement, considering Merielle dumped her over a year ago. Charlotte met the cute UX designer on a dating app and enjoyed her company, but it hadn't stuck beyond the six-month mark. "It's okay. My work hours were crazy. She got sick of me canceling plans." Charlotte put on a forced smile. "Plus she lived in Queens and that's practically a long-distance relationship in New York."

Nina didn't laugh, her eyes narrowing with suspicion. Then again, she wasn't a New Yorker. That joke would have killed in Park Slope.

"Amy said she hasn't seen much of you," Nina said. "Isn't she in Brooklyn with you?"

"Fort Greene, I think. Yeah, I keep missing her book launches." Nina's former roommate was the only other member of the 3Ds who lived in New York City. Amy worked in publishing and invited Charlotte to endless author events. During their first year out of college, Charlotte would recruit a friend from work to come with her to readings at the Bluestockings Cooperative Bookstore or signings on the third floor of the Strand. Charlotte always had a blast, and it worked in Amy's favor to have cool young media people at her events.

She and Amy had never been close, but Amy made an effort to stay in touch. Charlotte genuinely liked her: her determined ambition and sunny sweet optimism. Charlotte just hadn't been free in a while—work hours, exhaustion, yadda yadda.

Charlotte shrugged. "I never have time to read anymore." That would change soon, thank goodness. Folks in the art department at *Front End* had much better work-life balance than she did. Once her transfer came through, she could have a social life again. She wouldn't have to sacrifice her happiness for much longer.

Before Nina could poke at her excuse, they reached the front of the line. Nina asked the girl tending bar for two beers.

Charlotte wedged a single into the tip jar. "I like your shirt," she told the bartender, nodding at the Reunion & Commencement staff logo on the front. The name tag beside it read *Imani* in poppy bubble letters. "I had one just like it."

"Thanks!" the underclassman chirped, her baby face rosy with exertion. Imani poured them both generous cups of a frothy IPA. "I hope you enjoy the reunion!"

Charlotte winced and took a sip. "Please keep these coming, we need fortification."

"You got it." Their new favorite bartender beamed at them before turning to the guy next in line.

Nina licked some foam off the side of her cup. "Jeez, were we ever that young?"

Drinks in hand, they beelined to the corner of the reception where Matt and Jio sat alone. The couple leapt to their feet as they approached.

"MY GIRLS!" Jio wailed. Charlotte got a brief look at their crop top and overalls before they crushed her in a bear hug. "Charlotte Thorne, I thought you were *dead*! Where have you been hiding?"

"Hi, Jio," she wheezed inside their iron grip. They let her go abruptly and engulfed Nina next.

"NINA! Did you get even taller?"

Matt chuckled at his partner's enthusiasm before extending his hand to her. Where Jio gleamed, Matt offered warm formality. "Good to see you, Charlotte."

She gave it a firm shake. "It's been too long. How's The Rock?"

Matt and Jio lived in D.C., where they both worked for nonprofits. They had an adorable French bulldog, the aforementioned The Rock, and a dozen houseplants with their own names and personality quirks. The Rock and his plant siblings were recurring guest stars on Jio's Instagram.

Charlotte loved to imagine them in their cozy co-living house. Matt and Jio met through the support group in college and fell in love immediately. Matt's parents were Disappointing—devout Mormons, they kicked him out as soon as he revealed he wasn't entirely straight. Jio's parents were Divorced but totally chill about them being nonbinary.

Charlotte had been meaning to visit them in D.C. for years, but she never got around to booking the train ticket. Leaving New York on the weekends required more energy and planning than she could summon these days.

"The Rock is an angel! Look what Matt found for him!" Jio took out their iPhone and thrust it under Nina's nose. Charlotte leaned over to watch as they swiped through pictures of a pup wearing a black turtleneck and a silver chain collar.

"That's amazing," Nina laughed.

Jio pulled on Charlotte's sleeve. "Look at this blazer!" They had yet to master their indoor voice. Their empty Solo cup probably didn't help. "You look like a capitalist! I love it!"

Her face flushed as all three of them studied her outfit. She couldn't remember the last time she'd been around this many people interested in her existence. "Uh, thank you."

"New York must be good for you," Jio said. "Do you just love it there? We barely hear from you these days!"

The back of her neck felt hot. "It's not bad," she dodged. "Work keeps me busy. I can't have a pet with my schedule. But The Rock is so cute!" She desperately tried to change the topic.

"Isn't he? I want another dog, but Matt won't let me get one!" They shoved their boyfriend's shoulder.

Matt rolled his eyes. "We can't afford another dog."

"We could if we rescued!" But Jio had already turned back to Nina. They peppered her with questions about Peru. "Did you discover any new plants? How were the bugs?"

"It's the vet bills that are the problem," Matt murmured to Charlotte. "Dogs eat weird shit off the sidewalk."

She nodded sagely. Matt looked nice—he'd styled his short brown hair into a professional-looking comb-over. Thankfully he also wore uninteresting business casual attire. As if on cue, he asked, "Are you still at *Front End*? I watched Roger Ludermore's speech from Davos. The one about effective altruism? Interesting stuff."

Here we go again.

Charlotte whipped out her safe Roger anecdotes. Matt laughed in all the right places, bless him. At the mention of a famous actor turned startup investor, Jio demanded that she start the story over, their blue eyes bright and eager.

Nina left to refill their drinks. When she returned, conversation moved on to gossip about their graduating class: who lived where, who dumped who, who sold out and took a job as a lobbyist. Charlotte stayed at the periphery, shifting her weight from foot to foot. She didn't have much intel to contribute—staying in contact with folks didn't come naturally to her.

Charlotte vaguely remembered the role she used to play in the group dynamic during their undergrad days. She and Matt were the quiet ones, but she could be relied on for a funny non sequitur and her memory for names and faces. Everyone texted her when they needed help assembling furniture or fixing a clogged sink, and she liked that. She liked to be helpful, and to talk about art or politics one-on-one with her hands deep in a practical problem. She and Jio once spent a whole afternoon discussing Beanie Babies and scarcity economics as they repainted Acronym's attic. Perched atop the dusty folding ladder, Charlotte didn't feel like the shortest and shyest member of the clique.

At parties and group hangs like this one, Charlotte was always half of a pair. Jackie made plans and Charlotte remembered them. When Jackie told an outlandish but mostly accurate story, Charlotte supplied the details she forgot.

What was the name of that Film Studies TA I hooked up with? The one whose entire personality was having the Pulp Fiction *soundtrack on vinyl?*

Ted Casella.

Teddy Casella! *Thank you, Char.*

As the group chatted at the reception, peppering their gossip with references to their new lives that she didn't understand, Charlotte felt like an actor who didn't know her lines. Five years was a long time, and the dynamic of the group had shifted without her.

Thankfully no one seemed to mind when she just listened.

"Remember Batty Lawson?" Nina said sotto voce. "From the Philosophy Society? I heard he made a fortune in Bitcoin."

Jio mimed retching into their party cup. Charlotte guffawed, and they winked at her.

Amy from the 3Ds (Dead mom, cancer) joined them. After she gave everyone the requisite hugs—and did not scold Charlotte for falling off the surface of the earth—she added her intel. "Thomas Irons lives in Tampa now," she said in a discreet murmur. "He bought a condo on the water."

"With what money?" Jio asked. "Did he go full tech bro?"

"I think he always had money. His family is from Chappaqua."

Nina plucked a dog hair from the back of Jio's crop top. "I don't remember him."

Charlotte grimaced and swirled beer around her cup. "He was tight with Ben Mead."

The name felt large in her mouth, rusty from disuse. She tried to swallow through the dryness in her throat, and then, remembering her drink, took a long pull of pilsner.

Jio winced. "*That* asshole. Is he coming?"

Rancid yellow embarrassment curdled in her throat, the way it always did when Ben's name came up around her friends. She shrugged like she hadn't given the question much thought.

In reality, she had checked the list of alumni registered for Reunion & Commencement over and over again in the weeks leading up to the event. Her ex-boyfriend's name never appeared, but she found it hard to imagine that Ben would miss the chance to come back to Hein. When they were students, he stalked across campus like he owned the place . . . which he kind of did, because his father sat on the board of trustees.

Nina gracefully changed the subject. "I think Thomas was in my coding class." She bit her lip while she searched her memory. "Did he have white-boy dreadlocks?"

"Yeah, and a perpetual smear of coke on his nose," Jio leered.

Amy giggled into her rosé.

"Yes, that's who I'm thinking of," Nina said matter-of-factly.

Charlotte didn't laugh. *Purple*, she thought as she wetted her lips. *Shame. And . . . sludge green guilt.* By the end of the night, she would have enough colors for an eye shadow palette.

Speaker feedback shrieked through their gossip. Amy hissed through her teeth as she pressed her free hand against her ear. Conversations died out as someone tapped a microphone across the patio.

Charlotte twisted to look over her shoulder in the direction of the bar. She couldn't see anything over the crowd.

"Want a boost?" Nina asked.

Charlotte glared up at her without any real malice. "Har har."

The person holding the mic hopped on top of the stone wall behind the bar. He smoothed down his jeans with his free hand as he straightened up.

Her fingers tightened on her cup until the plastic rim cracked.

"It's Reece!" Amy chirped unnecessarily. Her curly hair bounced as she stood on her tiptoes to see their class secretary through the crowd.

Bathed in the glow of the party lights, Reece Krueger's green eyes widened as he took in the crowd. Not that Charlotte could see his eye color from across the patio, but she was alarmed to discover that she remembered it: a lovely light jade like sea glass.

One side of his mouth still smiled higher than the other. *Resting happy face*, Jackie called it a million years ago.

A node of dread lodged itself in Charlotte's throat. She'd been so focused on whether Ben would attend the reunion that she forgot to worry about her *other* boy ex.

She didn't know what she felt, only that it was a dark, uneasy shade of blue.

"Good evening!" Reece said a little too loud, and the feedback hissed again. He laughed self-consciously as the alumni winced. "Sorry about that. This is, um, not my specialty."

Even from across the party, she could see Reece's smile wilt. He took a deep breath like he was steeling himself, and that millisecond of vulnerability sent her heart thundering in her chest.

"I'm Reece Krueger, your class secretary." He played with the mic cord as he spoke—a nervous tell. He and Charlotte were both fidgeters. "Welcome to Reunion and Commencement Weekend!"

The crowd applauded. Charlotte put her battered cup down on the bench and brought her hands together halfheartedly.

"I don't have remarks planned. This is supposed to be Kahini's speech, but her flight was delayed, so you've got me instead."

Someone wolf-whistled. Reece threw the corner of the party an easy grin. Charlotte could just make out the laughing face of Garrett Davis, former hockey team goalie, president of the Black Student Union, and Reece's best friend.

"I'll keep this brief," Reece continued. "We've got a great weekend planned for you. Obviously you found your way to our reception. Our class dinner is tomorrow at Beckman Hall. Tickets are still on sale."

Charlotte could barely hear him over the roaring in her ears.

He looked good. No, that was inadequate. Reece looked incredible. His dark brown hair was styled back from his face, a dramatic change from the shaggy mess of senior year. He wore the hell out of a V-neck under a knit sweater, the cozy kind popping up all over Instagram these days. She knew implicitly that the sweater was a hand-me-down from his dad.

A storage container of vivid emotions toppled over in Charlotte's mind. More swampy green *guilt.* Sunny orange *curious.* The vibrant lilac of *longing.*

Nina touched her elbow, jarring her out of her thoughts. Her ex-girlfriend raised an eyebrow. Charlotte straightened up and plastered a smile on her face.

"You can find a full list of events on the website. The R&C committee asked me to remind you that the official hashtag is #HeinRandC2018, but please don't use it to post drunk selfies. Keep it PG for the students and their families."

Garrett Davis booed at this request. Reece ignored him.

"Speaking of drunk selfies, the Lawn Party is on Saturday night." This announcement earned a cheer. Reece's responding grin seemed forced, but she doubted anyone else could tell. "You know the rules: Doors open at eight, cash bar. Alumni are welcome to join the new grads as they dance away their last night on campus. And in the morning, we'll have a picnic on the quad."

"I can't wait," Jio stage-whispered.

Charlotte chewed on her thumb, nodding automatically.

"Okay, here's the part I'm bad at." Reece took a deep breath. Her throat seized with secondhand anxiety as she watched him steady himself, his fingers gripping the microphone. The crowd waited patiently for him, and he seemed to channel their warmth as he launched into his pitch. "If you find yourself feeling the love for Hein this weekend, please consider showing it with a donation to the school. Our class has given the least to Hein's capital campaign—"

"Yeah, 'cause we're broke!" Garrett piped up, triggering a ripple of laughter. Reece's smile didn't slip, but she could see his eyes tighten.

"If you want to learn more about how to give to Hein, you can ask any of the class officers."

"Fat chance," Nina murmured. "He must be miserable up there."

Amy nodded sympathetically. "He looks great, though!"

Charlotte picked her party cup back up and took a swig.

"The Development Fund supports the whole school, from the construction of new buildings to financing need-blind admissions, which I know y'all support. So if you have that cash, show it. I'm looking at you, Batty. Fork over some of that Bitcoin." Reece grinned at his singled-out classmate, who gave a good-natured wave from the bar.

The smile on Reece's face sent Charlotte's heart lurching like the subway when some jackass pulled the emergency brake. For a moment she was a college senior again, dressed up and looking for Reece at some party. Sticky and nervous and hungry—practically starving for distraction.

Reece would smile at her when she finally found him. Like he'd been waiting for her to make up her mind and follow him out the door.

"Okay, that's enough from me. Have fun, everyone!"

Reece hopped off the stone wall, and she lost sight of him in the crowd. The noise of the party dialed up again as conversations resumed. Her friends began chatting like nothing earth-shattering had happened at all.

"Are any of you donating?" Amy asked the group. "I feel bad for him."

"I'll do it for his sake," Nina said. "They're not getting more than fifty dollars out of me."

Charlotte didn't listen. Her brain churned over Reece's big smile and the warm timbre of his voice.

He looked healthy. Filled out, better dressed, a new maturity in his posture. Strained but alert. In college, Reece only seemed serious when they were alone.

She remembered his hard stomach under her fingers, the way his muscles tightened as she breathed across his skin. His wide mouth open in a gasp, white teeth glinting. How he always knocked twice on her apartment door late at night.

Another memory followed like a bitter chaser. She cringed as she recalled the last moment she saw him at their own graduation day picnic.

In all the time she spent anticipating the reunion, she never considered what it would feel like to be around Reece again. She knew he was attending—as class secretary, he signed every email about the upcoming reunion. But any anxiety she felt when she read his name in her inbox paled in comparison to the terror of a possible encounter with Ben and the stress of preparing for Roger's commencement address. She could only deal with so much, only feel so much, before her brain went dark like a blown fuse. Reece got bumped down the priority list, just as he did in college.

Besides, she didn't have the option of backing out. Not with so much to lose at work. Roger had made it clear that she needed to be here if she wanted the art department gig, and so here she was, exes be damned.

Nina bumped her hip, jolting her out of her thoughts. "You good?"

"I'm fine." Charlotte nodded curtly to reinforce the lie. Nina didn't push.

Charlotte tried to pay attention to her friends, she really did, but her brain got stuck on Reece. Her heartbeat pulsed like radar as she tracked his party longitude and latitude. She caught glimpses of the back of his head until an amoeba of bros absorbed him. She didn't want him to see her—dreaded it, even—but some part of her needed him to be as aware of her presence as she was of his.

It didn't matter that she was now twenty-seven. It didn't matter that five years had passed since she'd last spoken to Reece, six years since she broke up with Ben, and she had lived what felt like a dozen lives since she was last on this campus. Her face burned.

She felt small and pathetic and twenty-two years old again, the same jerk who left Reece behind without saying good-bye.

In that moment, there wasn't a single thing she wouldn't trade to be back in Brooklyn alone, wearing her sweatpants and watching reality television on her laptop.

TEXT MESSAGE FROM CHARLOTTE THORNE TO JACKIE SLAUGHTER, 6:18 PM: Have you landed yet? This is awkward.
(Message not delivered.)

TEXT MESSAGE FROM CHARLOTTE THORNE TO JACKIE SLAUGHTER, 6:19 PM: Thomas Irons owns a boat now.
(Message not delivered.)

"PRIVATE INSTALLATIONS ARE where the real money is. Celebrity clients pay way more than what I made at TrackVest on the trading floor empowerment mural."

Annika Gronlund had an irritating habit of gesturing with her wine as she rattled off accomplishments. Charlotte wanted to stab herself in the eye with a paintbrush, just like she did when they had Studio Art 311 together as juniors.

"That's great," Charlotte said blandly. If this conversation continued for much longer, she might move on from impaling herself to killing Annika. But then what other white woman would paint pseudo-progressive slogans inside Amazon's warehouse?

She scanned the crowd for an escape route or a familiar face to flag down. No dice.

Annika tapped her cushion-cut diamond engagement ring against her glass. "What about you? How is your craft evolving?"

"Great!" Charlotte coughed, the lie catching in her throat like an allergy. "But I'm an assistant these days." She left out where she worked. Maybe Annika would leave her alone if she thought Charlotte wasn't worth her time.

Annika's lip curled predictably. Score one for snobbery.

"Mind if I cut in?"

Reece's voice was gentle and warm at the edges like flannel in the depths of New England winter. Charlotte's mouth went dry as she found him by her side.

She had forgotten how tall he was. He smelled divine, like coffee and linen with just a hint of nice aftershave.

"Sorry to interrupt, Annika," he said. "I'll catch you later, yeah?"

Annika blinked at them, struggling to square Reece's politeness with the firm ejection from conversation. "Oh hey, Reece. Yeah, of course!" She stalked away in search of more fertile networking opportunities.

Charlotte's cheeks burned as she rediscovered the advanced human ability of speech. "Reece. Hi." She bit back a nervous laugh. "Thank you for that."

And then Reece was looking at her, right in front of her, finally. She felt all magenta and rose.

His eyes pored over her face for a long beat before he cleared his throat. "I was hoping you'd be here." His words were refreshingly honest, no bullshit or playing coy. Confused hope sang in her chest. She had expected Reece to loathe her. She deserved it. "Jackie said she wasn't sure when you were coming."

"Oh yeah. It's kind of complicated with work." She waved her fingers with the *what can you do* exasperation Roger used at the office to convey his importance.

"Right." Reece nodded. "Are you still at *The Front End Review*?"

Charlotte blinked. How did he know where she worked? Had he been keeping up with her life on social media? She wasn't an active poster, maintaining a bare-bones Twitter presence for her career and an inactive Instagram of her old illustrations. Or maybe he asked their mutual friends about her?

Torn between flattery and embarrassment, she tried not to worry about what else he might know. "Three years now," she answered. "What about you?"

"I'm working for my mom again." He ran his hand through his

hair, which had begun to escape the hold of his styling gel. "Mostly clerical stuff, but I like it."

Reece's mother ran an animal clinic in St. Louis. During breaks from Hein, he had worked at the front desk checking in patients and selling heartworm medication. His family often fostered rescues, and Dr. Krueger kept Reece supplied with puppy pictures throughout the school year.

Charlotte smiled at the idea of Reece in a set of paw-print scrubs. The job suited him. "That must be wonderful, being around animals all day."

"Yeah!" Reece gave her a smile that didn't reach his eyes. He stuffed his hands into his pockets. She tried to think of a question that would let him change the subject, but he surprised her by leaning forward and lowering his voice. "I'm not telling people this yet, I don't want to jinx it, but I'm thinking about going back to school. There's a good vet tech program nearby."

"You want to become a veterinarian? That's amazing!" Charlotte raised her beer.

"A vet tech," he corrected her, his face a little red. "Please don't tell anyone. I'm nervous."

"What do you have to be nervous about?" This older version of Reece didn't have the brash swagger of the boy she once knew. She wasn't sure what to make of it. "Any school would be lucky to have you. You grew up in an animal hospital."

He shrugged. "My grades here kind of sucked."

Oh right. Grades. In her field she could skate by with Hein University on her résumé—goodness knows it was the only reason Roger had hired her—but technical programs cared about numbers.

"I think we both graduated in the bottom half of our year," she joked to make him feel better.

Reece stiffened. He looked over her shoulder as if in search of a back button on the conversation.

Fuck. She'd brought it up. *Graduation.*

Charlotte apologized all the time at work, even when she'd done nothing wrong. *I'm sorry that call caught you by surprise* when Roger was late to a meeting. *I'm so sorry I haven't completed that project* when her boss never assigned it in the first place. A good bullshit apology required taking full responsibility for mistakes that weren't your fault. It was a trick she'd learned while living with her mother and honed further when she dated Ben. The important part was never to mention who was really to blame.

She owed Reece an apology. A real apology, not a phony one.

Charlotte looked around. They were insulated at the side of the party, but conditions for the conversation they needed to have were far from ideal. A gaggle of lacrosse girls were doing shots out of someone's flask. Charlotte suspected her breath reeked of pilsner. Reece's face defaulted to his usual resting half smile, even as his thoughts looked miles away. He was being so goddamn nice to her.

She couldn't do it. She couldn't put the right words together. There wasn't a crowbar big enough to open that Pandora's box of regrets.

As she faltered, Reece took pity on her. "Tell me you have a fiancé and a golden retriever," he quipped.

She snorted, surprised. Then she laughed from deep in her belly. The tension between them broke like fresh snow under a boot.

"No, I have nothing," Charlotte said. She waved her hand at his raised eyebrows. "You know what I mean. I have a shitty roommate and my own pod at *Front End*."

"You have a nap pod?" he asked, poking fun.

"No, it's a desk that doesn't touch any other desks." She outlined a box with her hands, roughly four feet wide and three feet deep. "Like a cubicle but with no walls. *Front End* has an open-plan office."

He whistled. "Well, that sounds less fun."

"It's loud and always smells like someone's lunch. Whenever one person has a cold, the rest of us get it too. I used to wear noise-canceling headphones, but my boss said it made me look antisocial." Charlotte pulled a face and Reece laughed, his eyes crinkling.

"Do you like your job? You're an assistant, right?"

"To the CEO. He's actually the commencement speaker on Sunday, Roger Ludermore?" She qualified her answer to explain its misery, not to show off, but he was nonetheless jazzed.

"Dude, that's awesome!"

Charlotte grimaced. "Is it, though?"

"If Roger's as smart as everyone says, he's figured out that he's lucky to have you around." Roger was definitely not as smart as everyone said, but before Charlotte could crack a joke, Reece took her shoulder and gave her a congratulatory squeeze. Her skin hummed where he touched her and didn't let go.

As much as she wanted to be honest with him, she didn't want to shatter the glowing impression he had of her life. She'd also forgotten Reece's knack for complimenting a person so sincerely that they were temporarily disarmed. She could tell he really meant it. And it meant something to her, that he'd see her that way. Especially when the version of her he'd known in college was such a live wire. When they met in support group senior year, she still flinched at sudden movements.

That was then, and this is now, she reminded herself.

"Thanks for that. But what about you?" she asked. "Perhaps a designer doodle and a condo by the sea?"

Reece chuckled. His hand fell from her shoulder. She missed it. "You heard about Thomas's new place, huh?"

Charlotte rolled her eyes. The last time she saw Thomas Irons, he was passed out on the President's Lawn in a unicorn onesie using his balled-up graduation gown as a pillow. "Seriously, what the hell. How is *he* the most stable of all of us?"

"I don't know about 'stable,' but I ask myself that question every single day."

She gathered her nerve to ask the question she told herself she was only posing to be polite. "How are things going with Jess? Jackie mentioned her a while ago. And that you were moving in together?"

Reece's eyes fell to his sneakers. "We actually broke up a few months ago."

"Oh, I'm sorry to hear that."

Charlotte was not perfect. On occasion, stuck late at the office while Roger's meetings ran long, she stalked her exes on social media. From the pictures Reece posted on Facebook, Jess was beautiful, full stop. She had flawless skin and volunteered every weekend at the local shelter for unhoused folks. The only thing Charlotte could complain to Jackie about was her ROSÉ ALL DAY tank top in her profile picture. Even then, while Jackie agreed the shirt was cringe, they agreed that Jess made it work.

Charlotte liked Jess even more now that she wasn't Reece's girlfriend.

"It's all good." Reece shrugged. "It was a mutual thing. We figured out we were incompatible before anything got serious."

She quirked her own brow, a courtesy *are you sure?* Despite how casual he made the breakup seem, *incompatible* was a meaningful word, the vocabulary of responsibility and adulthood. You only worried about compatibility when you *were* serious about someone, when you were planning your future and factoring in that other person.

A new insecurity twitched in her chest as she realized she'd never calculated her compatibility with a partner. Not since Ben, at least, and her math had been very off. There was only so much you could do with a corrupted data set. Ever since then she hadn't been tempted to factor another person into her future, always breaking relationships off before things got too serious. Merielle came the closest to mattering, but every night they spent at bar trivia together meant at least six emails for Charlotte to answer when she got home.

Had Reece ever considered his compatibility with Charlotte? Before she bolted like a startled deer?

Reece nodded. He pulled on his collar to reveal a stretch of tan skin. "Anyway, we can talk about something other than my ex."

She didn't like the sudden stiffness in his voice. "No, it's . . ." She trailed off, searching for something to say other than *I'm glad she messed it up.* Mossy green jealousy and sunrise yellow relief warred in her chest as she read the tension in his body. Jess's loss was the rest of the world's gain. "It doesn't bother me."

Heat spread down Charlotte's neck under the intensity of his gaze. His lips parted as he took a deep breath, and for a moment it looked like he was about to say something important, something hard. Charlotte leaned forward, straining to hear his thoughts.

Suddenly, one of the lax girls shrieked and Reece jerked back. Charlotte's heart heaved. It was so transparent, how his walls went flying back up.

"Who invited a feral cat colony?" she asked, deadpan, hoping to make him laugh again. He chuckled, thank goodness. Then his attention caught on something over her shoulder.

"Hey, listen," Reece said, his voice low. "Garrett is glaring at me. I'm getting major *stop talking to your ex* eyes. This is supposed to be a boys' weekend."

"Oh, of course." Charlotte tapped the side of her empty cup. "I should go get a refill anyway. And find Nina."

"To be continued, okay?"

"Sure." Charlotte gave him her best *I do not desperately want you to stay* fake smile.

As she watched Reece return to his friends, she chewed the inside of her cheek. Dewy heat gathered in her chest and spread through her limbs, just like it had when Reece looked at her a little too long in support group. Somehow the conversation she'd been dreading was the most enjoyable one she'd had all night. She could almost pretend no time had passed at all.

Almost, but not quite. She couldn't figure out the vibe between them. Friendly, maybe even fond, but still cautious. Their conversation felt surreal, and it wasn't just that they were surrounded by judgmental acquaintances at their college reunion, or that they were older, or that this wasn't their real life anymore. Maybe it was that he was still Reece Krueger, the guy who wanted more from her at the end of senior year, and she was still Charlotte Thorne, the girl who wanted nothing from anyone at all.

Charlotte headed to the bar for a refill. Nina appeared at her side immediately, which only made her feel worse. The 3Ds must have watched their conversation from afar.

"How was that?" Nina asked, her curiosity at a low simmer.

Charlotte rolled her eyes and passed her cup to the bartender. "Another pilsner, please."

Nina blinked. "That good?"

"That's all you're getting out of me."

She patted Charlotte's head fondly. "We're about to head out for Amy's panel. Want to come?"

"Amy's on a panel?"

"English major thing at the career center. 'Hein Voices in the World' or something. They'll probably have snacks."

Charlotte wasn't sure what sucked more: that she hadn't achieved anything panel-worthy since graduating from college, or that she'd still go anywhere for free food. Or that she had botched, once again, another moment with Reece, whom she still owed an apology. Maybe Amy's panel was exactly what she needed: an excuse to sit in silence and recharge her batteries.

"Fine. Count me in."

TEXT MESSAGE FROM CHARLOTTE THORNE TO JACKIE SLAUGHTER, 7:08 PM: Reece is here.
(Message not delivered.)

Chapter 2

SLACK MESSAGE FROM ROGER LUDERMORE TO CHARLOTTE THORNE, 7:25 PM: find out who Bezos's trainer is ASAP

THE PANEL DID not have dinner, but someone from the English department had the wherewithal to at least put out cheese and crackers. While Nina scoped out seats at the back of the lecture hall, Charlotte loaded a paper plate with snacks.

She didn't recognize anyone helping themselves to Vermont cheddar and Triscuits—most of their class was still at the reception. Hein seniors and a smattering of older alumni made up the audience. The only non-senior students still on campus were the ones who stuck around to work the long weekend as R&C staff.

As the girls waited for the panel to start, Nina sipped a glass of wine and scrolled through Instagram. Charlotte checked her work email on autopilot, her thumb opening the app out of habit. Unsurprisingly, panicked messages from Roger cluttered her inbox. She skimmed them for an emergency requiring her deft hand. Her after-hours autoresponder informed Roger to contact Aubrey in her stead. She savored the thought of Aubrey dealing with Roger's ridiculous, contradictory requests.

Aubrey became Roger's second assistant six months ago when one of *Front End*'s board members asked him to find his daughter a place at the company. She wasn't Charlotte's first choice as a direct report.

In fact, Aubrey wouldn't have made it past her cover letter, which misspelled *Review*, name-dropped Mila Kunis for no apparent reason, and listed no actual work experience (unless you count "Instagram micro-influencer" and "workout class participant").

Aubrey was not the reason Charlotte hated her job, but she didn't help. Roger's interest in work had narrowed to developing his personal brand, which left Charlotte responsible for keeping the lights on at *Front End.* For nearly a year she begged Roger to hire an office manager to handle the administrative tasks requiring a dedicated professional. Charlotte already wrote his correspondence, presentations, and performance reviews for employees. She couldn't also manage his floor of the office, send packages, log his expenses, and collect his laundry.

But when Aubrey arrived in a cloud of scented oil that probably cost more than Charlotte's utility bills, she botched the simplest of tasks. She put oat milk instead of soy in his coffee and forgot to pick up his dry cleaning. Typos littered important emails. On one memorable occasion, she mistook a U.S. congresswoman for a job applicant and escorted her to an interview with the social media team.

When Charlotte appealed to HR about the nepotism involved in Aubrey's hiring, she received the corporate version of a head pat. Pauline from HR told her it was an excellent opportunity to work on her mentorship skills.

Maybe this weekend Charlotte would finally get lucky and come back from Massachusetts to find Aubrey's desk empty now that Roger had to deal with her incompetence on his own.

An executive assistant could dream.

At the front of the lecture hall, a woman draped in an elegant purple shawl stepped behind the lectern and welcomed everyone. "We're just waiting for our final panelist to arrive. Apparently, there's been a slowdown at the airport."

Indeed, an empty chair sat between Amy and the rest of the panelists. Charlotte recognized the other two alumni: a *Washington Post* columnist who graduated from Hein in the nineties, and the founder of an indie publishing house that exclusively printed Black authors. They were both featured in the glossy *Hein Magazine* printed by the alumni relations department.

"Stacked lineup," Nina said.

Charlotte swallowed a lump of cracker mush. "Amy must be nervous."

Five years ago, she and Amy received their diplomas on the same stage. They left Hein with the same awful mortarboard sunburns. Now Amy was sitting up there beside real adults, considered important, while Charlotte sat in the audience. She didn't envy Amy, and it wasn't like Charlotte's story of clinging to a job she didn't like, in an industry on the verge of falling apart, would inspire new graduates. She just wished she knew when she had fallen behind.

"Last call to grab some refreshments before we get started," the moderator called out. Nina took a cracker from Charlotte's plate.

Working for Roger looked nothing like the exciting career in media she imagined for herself as a college student. Teenage Charlotte aspired to be a *New Yorker* cartoonist, or at least an illustrator for a local newspaper. She felt on track at graduation, having secured an art internship at *ChompNews*, a millennial-driven digital magazine that published both socially conscious pop culture criticism and reported feature stories. But that didn't pan out the way Charlotte expected. Dream jobs were thin on the ground in the real world.

The assistant job at *Front End* allowed her to pay down her credit card debt and kept her in the industry, even if she wasn't working on the magazine's artwork. Every so often Charlotte considered quitting, but she never forgot how quickly financial security could disappear. Unlike her friends, she didn't have family to bail her out in the event of another layoff. There was no childhood home to move back to, no emergency loan to cover rent. Not even a Christmas card with a twenty-dollar bill.

Amy sat on that panel because she worked hard at Bloomsmith

Publishing. At twenty-six she crafted the publicity campaign for a memoir by a sexual assault survivor that helped make the book a *New York Times* bestseller. But Charlotte also knew that Amy could afford the low wages of publishing because her father was a neurologist. If he didn't pay Amy's rent directly, he at least offered a safety net. Amy's good luck didn't make her a bad person, but it gave her room to pursue her passion wholeheartedly and thrive.

How many young people Charlotte's age—without generational wealth—had stability? She would be a fool to leave Roger. She would be ungrateful.

Besides, she had a plan. The project manager role in the art department would alleviate most of her stress, and it came with a significant pay bump. Once she got away from Roger, she could refocus on her career, maybe even take on freelance illustration projects on the side. By her ten-year reunion she'd have more to show for herself.

As if on cue, Roger barged onto her screen.

SLACK MESSAGE FROM ROGER LUDERMORE TO CHARLOTTE THORNE, 7:41 PM: tell Peter to remove ALL REFERENCES to "structural inequality" from the commencement address

Nina interrupted her pity party with a gasp. Startled, Charlotte spilled wine on her jeans. "What is it?" she asked as she patted at the wet spot with a paper napkin.

Nina's face had tightened in a mask of horror. "Shit."

She followed Nina's stare to the front of the room.

The final panelist had arrived.

Her stomach seized. Charlotte clenched the damp napkin in her fist, wine leaking between her fingers.

No. Not you.

Ben Mead eased into the empty chair at the panelists' table. He gave the room a winning smirk as he shrugged off a black bomber jacket. His watch caught the light as he folded his hands together on the table—vintage, Cartier, a birthday present from his father. Charlotte had helped him get it resized downtown when it slipped off his wrist one too many times.

Her vision went dark at the edges.

Logically she knew that her ex-boyfriend couldn't see her all the way in the back row. She knew that Ben posed no threat to her onstage with dozens of eyes watching his every move. She knew that she had broken up with Ben half a decade ago, and he had no power over her.

She still felt pinned to her chair by his presence. She couldn't breathe.

"Are you okay?"

Nina's words reached Charlotte through a fog. Her nails dug into her palm as she forced herself to look away, look anywhere else but at his blond hair and his boyishly charming slouch. Her muddy memory of his face, intentionally dulled with time, sharpened into high-definition present tense. Ice blue eyes like mirrors reflecting everything she wanted to see back when she was trusting and young.

"I'm fine." The lie came easily, if not convincingly. "It's fine."

Nina hesitated, then placed a comforting hand on her knee. "We don't have to stay."

The professor moderating the panel tapped her microphone again. Charlotte's window of polite escape closed. She crossed her legs, slipping out of Nina's grasp.

My name is Charlotte Thorne, she told herself, a grounding exercise Jackie taught her years ago. *I am twenty-seven years old. I am safe here.*

When that didn't work, she counted seconds as she breathed, four beats in and five beats out.

"Okay, we're ready to get started! My name is Ade Ajibola and I'm a professor here in the English department." A smattering of polite applause, and a whoop from an undergraduate. Charlotte bit her thumbnail. "Thank you for coming to tonight's discussion with our distinguished alumni about how they have taken their Hein education out into the world."

Professor Ajibola smiled serenely at her audience, either unaware of—or politely ignoring—the tension on the panel beside her. Amy had gone brittle, her lips pursed in disapproval. Ben made himself comfortable at the table, his arm sprawled across its surface and into her personal space. Charlotte couldn't tell if he was messing with Amy deliberately or just being his usual dick self. He had a knack for asserting control over every room he entered. She swallowed, her throat tightening.

"I'm delighted to introduce our panelists," the moderator continued. "Amy Rosen is a member of the Class of 2013 and a publicity manager at Bloomsmith Publishing in New York."

Amy gave a stiff nod. She discreetly edged her chair away from Ben's. Charlotte felt a pang of gratitude for her loyalty—Amy didn't know the ugly details about their relationship, but she had enough good sense to dislike Ben on his own merit. He had a bad habit of talking over other students during class discussions, especially women.

"Ben is the host of the politics podcast *Left of the Dial*. He is also a member of the Class of 2013. What a talented year!" Ben nodded graciously. The moderator continued, "He's now studying for his master's in practical ethics at Oxford."

Nina snorted. "Ethics? Are you kidding me?"

Charlotte said nothing, too shaken to appreciate the irony. Ben preened under the attention, shrugging like his graduate work was no big deal. His false modesty only underscored the program's prestige.

They love me, she imagined him bragging to his friends tonight. *They ate that shit up.*

As Professor Ajibola introduced the rest of the panel, Ben retrieved a fountain pen from the pocket of his jacket. He spun it between his fingers as his eyes slid over the audience. Charlotte trained her attention on the moderator, refusing to get caught in the hot tar of his gaze. Pilsner and cheddar cheese threatened to make a second appearance as her throat tightened.

"Nope." Charlotte shook her head. She didn't have to do this. She was twenty-seven years old and she had left him, goddamn it. She shoved her iPhone in her pocket and knocked back the rest of her wine. "Nope, nope, nope."

Nina wordlessly took her plate. "Do you want me to come with you?"

"No, stay." Charlotte willed her voice not to break. She hunched over as she stood up, trying not to draw attention to herself. Fight-or-flight adrenaline throbbed through her fingers. "I'm fine. Tell Amy I'm sorry."

"She'll understand." Nina swung her knees aside to let her pass. "I'll text you as soon as it's over."

Charlotte crab-walked down the row. She could feel Ben's eyes following her up the aisle and out of the lecture hall, his attention a dagger at her back. But she'd choose embarrassment over listening to his achievements.

She didn't want to hear his voice. She'd only just forgotten how it sounded.

The courtyard outside the career center was deserted. She sank onto a stone bench and closed her eyes. The center of campus still smelled like fresh mulch and wet concrete. In her panic, time thinned as if junior year could reach out and grab her.

Not safe here not safe not—

Inarticulate black pain throbbed in her gut, her skin crawling.

I can't do this.

She'd been kidding herself, thinking she could fake-smile her way through this weekend without an issue. She should bail while she still had a chance. She could go back to her room, throw everything in her bag, and reschedule her Amtrak ticket. A taxi could be here in twenty minutes, thirty tops. Roger would be livid, but she could handle everything remotely, couldn't she?

Then again, how would she live-tweet his commencement address from New York? There was no live stream.

She could get a hotel room off campus and pop back here on Sunday when he arrived, skipping the reunion entirely. But she couldn't expense that, so she'd have to eat the cost, and rooms nearby had to be booked by alumni and parents of graduates. Finding a place to stay would cost a fortune.

You're spiraling, Charlotte. Pull it together.

She willed herself to breathe, drawing her legs up against her chest. "My name is Charlotte Thorne," she whispered to her knees. "I am twenty-seven years old. I live in Brooklyn. I work for *The Front End Review*."

As she reminded herself of who she was, she studied the patio under her feet. The more she repeated the anchoring words, the more color returned to the world around her. The ruddy beige of sidewalk pushed away panic's inky black. Grass grew between the cracks, stubborn streaks of green and dirty yellow. Someone had planted blue and white pansies around the courtyard to match Hein's school colors.

"My birthday is April thirtieth. My best friend is Jackie Slaughter. I am safe here."

She didn't feel safe. She wasn't safe. But maybe if she told herself often enough, she could trick herself into believing it.

Charlotte once loved it here—this school, this campus, this little town. She loved Hein University like a child loves Disney World, only she got to wake up here every single morning for four years. She never felt homesick, not for a day, not even for a minute. As other freshmen lined up in the mail room to collect care packages from their parents, Charlotte felt blissfully free. For the first time in her life, no one turned up their noses at her sketch pads or the books on feminism she smuggled home from the library. She left her dorm room whenever she wanted, and she returned whenever she damn well pleased.

When she bought two family-size bags of Cheetos at the student grocery, no one sneered at her taste. When she slept until one P.M. on a Saturday afternoon, it was no one's business but hers. And when she kissed girls, and boys, and folks who identified as neither, she had nothing to fear.

A few months into that first fall semester, she looked at her dresser and wondered what it would be like to dress for herself—not for her mother's scrutiny, not for her private high school's uniform, not even for the hipster kids down the hall. She had never liked that metallic pink pencil skirt. In fact, she had never liked skirts at all. Those espadrilles could go, and the atrocious patterned sundresses, and the cardigans, all the shit her mother bought and hung up in her closet like Charlotte was a doll and not a person.

She didn't want any of it. She was done.

Ten minutes later, a heap of clothes sat on the floor. As Charlotte considered the few items that survived the purge, a girl she vaguely recognized from downstairs popped her head through the open door. She held a cardboard box of mac and cheese. "Hi! Do you have a microwave?"

Charlotte blinked at the sudden invasion. The brunette ignored her discomfort and did a double take at the mess. "Ooo, you weeding out?"

At a loss for words, Charlotte merely nodded. She blew hair out of her face and stood still as the girl picked a pair of barely worn shorts up from the floor. The stranger cringed at the embroidered whales on the pockets. "Yikes, I see why. Hideous or not, you could make a killing reselling some of this online. These are brand name."

By the time they were done, Jackie Slaughter had helped Charlotte make two hundred dollars on eBay. They took what didn't sell to Goodwill, where Charlotte's new friend taught her how to flip through the racks quickly but methodically. She learned to identify polyester versus cotton with a simple touch, and she found a pair of black combat boots in exactly her size.

When Jackie saw her eyeing a fleece-lined denim jacket in the men's section, she forced her to try it on. "Clothes don't have a gender," Jackie insisted. "If you like it, wear it."

All told, Charlotte bought several loose men's button-down shirts and a few pairs of well-worn jeans. Plus the jacket. She wore that jacket until the elbows gave out.

College offered Charlotte more than a respected degree and a few thousand peers to learn from. It let her be herself. It let her *find* herself. Hein was the only place she'd ever felt independent and safe.

Ben changed that. Not immediately, not right away. But when their relationship was finally over, campus never felt the same. Even now, six years later.

Charlotte pressed her forehead against her knees.

Deep breath in. Deep breath out.

Of course Ben was attending the reunion. Of course he'd be a panelist. How naïve of her to imagine she could ever have Hein for herself. He was the son of a trustee, so this campus was practically his birthright. His last name was etched in marble above the doors to Mead Library.

It took her a long time to see the irony: Her ex-boyfriend had *liked* to think of her as his preppy blond trophy girlfriend from the suburbs joining him on the edge. It didn't matter that she wasn't traditional trophy material—Charlotte was shy and bisexual and helplessly afraid of sailing. Nor did it matter that Ben, the eldest son of a hedge fund manager, was hardly a rebel without a cause. The romantic tale of the leftist bad boy and the Chevy Chase, Maryland, girl-next-door flattered him and made her small. Insisting that her denim jacket wasn't warm enough, he bought her a camel designer peacoat made of virgin wool, and then elegant white snow boots lined with shearling. The more feminine she dressed for him, the better.

Now Ben was a niche podcasting celebrity to young progressives who spent too much time online. He painted himself as a hero in public while he treated women like garbage in private. No one took a closer look to see if his talking points lined up with his behavior.

Footsteps whispered through the grass surrounding the patio. Charlotte looked up to see a loose dog padding toward her on dainty paws. The fluffy animal couldn't have weighed more than twenty pounds soaking wet. It nudged her hand with its nose, a pink tongue lolling happily out of its mouth.

"Hello there," Charlotte murmured. She stroked through the dog's silky red fur to find the tag on its collar. "Misty, huh? Who do you belong to?"

Maybe she lived at one of the frats and slipped out an open door? Judging by her pristine coat and trusting nature, the dog was loved and well cared for.

Misty nuzzled against her knee, demanding pats. Charlotte obliged.

"You can hang out with me, sweetheart." She let the dog lick her hand. She probably tasted like red wine and embarrassment.

Misty's unrelenting affection made her feel grounded, the way animals always did. Mrs. Thorne showed dogs when Charlotte was little, and her prized Airedale terrier Cymbeline was the only member of the family who enjoyed Charlotte's company. Dogs never judged her for getting overwhelmed at crowded parties. One day when she felt settled enough, with a less demanding job and more financial stability, she would adopt a rescue in need of a home.

"I see you've met my girlfriend."

Reece materialized from the darkness, a leash balled up in his fist. He gave them a bemused smile. "Fancy meeting you here, Charlie," he said.

A new wave of humiliation crested over the last. How many times during college did she text Reece after a run-in with Ben, her face streaked with tear tracks and mascara? How many times did she use his warmth to chase away the cold grip of shame?

Welcome back to Hein, the universe sneered.

She said nothing as Reece squatted at her feet. "This is Misty," he continued, politely ignoring how odd she must look sitting alone outside the career center, spilled wine drying on her jeans. He gently pinched the tips of the dog's floppy ears between his fingers and hoisted them up in the air. "She's my soul mate."

Charlotte cleared her throat. "We met, but we haven't been introduced. Is she yours?"

"Garrett's. She needed a walk and I volunteered. Anything to get away from that reception." He cooed at Misty and rubbed her chin with the pads of his fingers. She closed her eyes in bliss. "Someone's gotta take care of this girl while her dad parties, and she just beelined right to you." He glanced around the deserted patio, and then at the career center behind them. "Nice place to take a break from all the fuss, huh?"

"It's a bit much." She left it at that, hoping Reece wouldn't pry. The last thing she wanted to do was admit she'd fled a panel featuring her ex-boyfriend. Especially not to Reece. "Is she allowed to be here?"

"Of course not, but Misty gets away with murder." He took the dog's face in his hands. "Who can say no to this sweet face?"

Indeed, Charlotte could not.

Misty wiggled out of Reece's hold and plopped her chin on Charlotte's knee again. Her fur felt like silk as it flowed through Charlotte's fingers. "Do you have your own yet?"

Reece eased himself down to sit on the concrete, his knees cracking. "No, not yet. Jess was allergic."

An unkind smirk pulled at the edge of Charlotte's mouth. She blamed the pilsners she had at the reception when she drawled, "No wonder it didn't work out."

He laughed without any real humor. "Yeah, I should have known. But my mom just got another Pomeranian."

"Really? How many dogs does she have now?"

Reece gave her a bleak look. "Four."

Charlotte snickered. "That's a lot of dogs."

"It's four times the amount of poop that one dog produces, yes."

"Maybe she was lonely?"

Reece grimaced. "I don't think that was it." Charlotte raised an eyebrow, and he hesitated before elaborating. "I moved back home a few months ago. Jess was the one on the lease." He started a staring contest with the dog. Misty did not seem invested in the competition, twisting around to lick Charlotte's chin.

"How's that going?" Charlotte kept her voice as neutral as possible. She didn't judge him for moving back home—between the student debt crisis, stagnant wages, and the bonkers cost of rent in most cities, it made good sense to live with family—but she knew he probably judged himself. Reece had never wanted to stay in St. Louis. She'd already assumed this was his living situation when he mentioned working at the clinic.

"The lack of privacy isn't ideal," Reece admitted. "But it's nice. I'm saving a lot of money . . ." He trailed off, giving her a nervous look.

"There's no shame in living at home. That's way smarter than the mountain of debt I took on when I moved to New York."

"Yeah, but you were just starting out," he objected. "I'm twenty-seven."

"Who cares? I bet your mom is glad to have you there with her. The dogs too."

Reece nodded, his cheeks pink. "His name is Hammer, by the way. The new Pom."

"Oh my goodness."

"He weighs four pounds, Charlie. Four pounds. *Hammer.*"

"That's just cruel."

Reece grinned and shook his head. Charlotte's face ached from smiling full and wide across her face. "Your mom is an icon," she said, trying not to fixate on how long it had been since she last grinned until her cheeks felt sore. "I aspire to that level of momitude."

"You always wanted a pug, right?" Misty wiggled her butt into Reece's lap, and he loosely wrapped his arms around her.

"Sort of." Charlotte licked her dry lips and noticed how Reece's eyes got stuck on her mouth. A rude corner of her brain enjoyed his attention. "Pugs have a lot of medical issues, so I switched my allegiance to corgis."

"Corgis can be mean," Reece warned her. "They're aloof. Very fluffy butts, though."

She nodded soberly at his advice. "My hours are too rough for me to get a dog right now. And my roommate Kit isn't really a dog person."

"Kit sucks," Reece said decisively, despite never having met Kit, or heard of her, before.

Charlotte snorted. "Kit does suck."

"I always thought you and Jackie would wind up living together again. You guys are so close."

"If only!" Resentment snuck into Charlotte's voice as she elaborated. "We were going to move to Brooklyn together, but then she got that job in L.A."

A very good job in public radio, Charlotte reminded herself. A very good job in public radio that Jackie quit a few months later, frustrated by the amount of unpaid overtime she was asked to do, but still. In her industry, Jackie had to go where the jobs were.

Life in New York would be so much easier with her best friend by her side, but Charlotte knew she shouldn't be bitter. Besides, Los Angeles agreed with Jackie. The warm ocean air softened the abrasive edges of her big personality, and if she ever got sick of working in public radio, podcast startups were hiring like crazy out there.

Reece didn't comment on her tone. "Is she here yet? I haven't seen her."

"No, her flight got delayed. The weather."

He frowned. His eyes drifted back to the spilled wine on her thigh, and her fingers clenched around the lip of the bench. "So you're flying solo?"

"I've got people." She nodded toward the building behind her. "Amy and Nina are inside."

He tilted his head and tried to read her face. His concern was so obvious that she shrank away. "I needed some air," she explained. "Too much to drink, I think."

It wasn't a lie. She didn't look forward to standing up again.

"We're heading back to Randall if you want to tag along," he offered. "I'm handing Misty off to Garrett in the lounge."

She reached out to stroke Misty's fur back from her eyes. The pup gave her wrist a hearty lick.

Charlotte would follow Reece anywhere he wanted to go. She wanted to talk about dogs and his family and what he did in St. Louis for fun, who he was now.

Plus, she knew that if she was left alone, every shitty memory of Ben would pounce and drag her down into the concrete. The late nights sitting outside her apartment building with Ben's accusations echoing in her mind. The tinny sound of his voice pouring out of an iPhone speaker: *You idiot, you ruin everything.*

"I bet the vending machine still has Oreos," Reece coaxed. His voice was silky smooth, incongruous with the childish invitation.

"Let me check my texts," Charlotte hedged.

SLACK MESSAGE FROM ROGER LUDERMORE TO CHARLOTTE THORNE, 8:08 PM: what's the password to dropbox

SLACK MESSAGE FROM ROGER LUDERMORE TO CHARLOTTE THORNE, 8:13 PM: need it now

TEXT MESSAGE FROM NINA DORANTES TO CHARLOTTE THORNE, 8:16 PM: Are you ok?

Still nothing from Jackie.

Misty sneezed. Her tiny face scrunched up and her whole body shuddered with the force of it. Reece laughed. He swept the dog up into his arms like an overgrown baby. "You got the sniffles, little one?" he cooed, his voice dark honey. "You're okay, Uncle Reece has got you."

That answered that question. There was no way she could choose answering Roger's Slack messages over snack time with the cutest dog uncle on campus. Charlotte slid her phone back into her pocket. "Fine. But those Oreos are on you. I used my last dollar as a tip."

REECE HAD ALL the good gossip. On their way back to the dorm, he filled Charlotte in on the life updates of Hein's bro population. Reece's best friend Garrett was still single but deeply devoted to Misty. His freshman-year roommate had started a monthly subscription box that sent you beauty products based on your astrological sign.

They paused outside Rosenberg Hall, a stunning Châteauesque building with brick walls and dark-shingled turrets that housed the psychology department. Misty was unimpressed by the 1880s architecture and took a leisurely pee on the granite front steps.

Charlotte searched her memory for the name of the third bro in his tight friend group. "How's Liam?"

"He's good! He'll be here tomorrow." Misty tugged him into a brisk walk, and Charlotte loped along to keep up. "He got married last year."

"Excuse me?" Charlotte didn't know Liam all that well, but he was hardly her pick for the first husband in the clique. Future weed brownie distributor, maybe.

Reece laughed at the shocked expression on her face. "I know, I know. He reconnected with his high school sweetheart at a reunion. A year later, bam, I was picking out a rice cooker at Williams Sonoma."

"That's nuts." A startling number of their classmates were making progress in the direction of marriage. She wouldn't be surprised if an invitation for Matt and Jio's nuptials arrived in her mailbox soon, assuming they didn't dismiss that kind of legal commitment as buying into the hetero-patriarchal wedding industrial complex.

"Good for him," she marveled.

They'd made it back to Randall. She held the door open so that Misty could race inside the lobby, with Reece quick on her heels. Sound ricocheted toward them from the lounge down the hall, and she winced, covering her ears with her hands automatically.

"Sounds like the party relocated," Reece said. "Let me get her back to Garrett and then we'll get snacks."

Charlotte followed him to the lounge but hesitated on the threshold. By the looks of it, the after-party had been in full swing for a while. Maybe forty people drank and howled at each other in the cavernous room. Former art majors mingled with engineers. Batty the crypto-millionaire stirred jungle juice in a plastic tub for anyone brave enough to dip in a party cup.

Garrett stood beside the beer pong competition with some other folks from the Black Student Union. She watched as Reece handed Misty's leash back to him.

Reece murmured something to Garrett, who gave him a sharp look before glancing around the room. When his eyes landed on her, his mouth immediately pulled into a scowl. Garrett's message was crystal clear. Reece might have forgiven her, but to Garrett, she would always be the jerk who broke his best friend's heart.

Charlotte stood up straight and clasped her hands behind her back. If Garrett wanted to hold a grudge, he could knock himself out.

Reece broke off the conversation and headed back toward her, a deceptively placid smile on his face.

"Everything okay?" she asked.

He nodded, his smile becoming authentic once again as he reached her side. "Snack time?"

"Absolutely."

To Charlotte's delight, the shitty vending machine in the ground-floor laundry room had been replaced by a brand-new model with a card reader and three different kinds of Oreos. Reece fed crumpled dollar bills into the machine as she debated Double Stuf versus Golden.

"Screw it, I'm honoring tradition," she announced before pressing the code for the originals.

"Hell yeah." Reece fished the cookies out of the drop tray and handed them over. "You're sharing those, by the way."

"Of course." She helped herself to a cookie as he punched in his own selection and bent down to retrieve it: Famous Amos chocolate chip. "Good choice."

Reece bowed his head like a falsely modest director winning an award. "Thank you, I have excellent taste." He leaned his shoulder against the vending machine and peeled open his cookie pack. "Obviously," he added, nodding in her direction.

Charlotte rolled her eyes but smiled despite herself. She couldn't tell if his flirtation was intentional or just kindness, and she wasn't sure if she wanted to know anyway. Good thing she had a master's degree in emotional compartmentalization.

Besides, she suspected he was just babysitting her until Jackie arrived.

She broke an Oreo in half and scraped the frosting off with her teeth, ravenous. Mid-chew, she offered him the other half. He raised an eyebrow but accepted the cookie.

"I'm part raccoon," she explained after swallowing. "No dinner."

"Ah." Reece peered into his own bag and shook it. "Is it just me or did there used to be more of these in here?"

"Capitalism is a scam," Charlotte said around a mouthful of chocolate mush. He laughed and she covered her mouth with her hand. "Sorry."

"Don't apologize. You have great manners for a raccoon." Reece offered her his bag and she plucked out a chocolate chip cookie as gracefully as she could manage.

"So," he started, his voice gentle but serious. "How are you, really?"

Charlotte chewed her cookie slowly, grateful for the excuse not to answer right away. She could lie. It wouldn't be hard. She could tell him about the celebrity founder and the pineapple allergy and the promotion Roger held over her head. She could overpronounce the consonants of *The Front End Review* and flash her teeth and swagger away with some excuse about how Slack messages don't stop in the city that never sleeps.

But she couldn't lie to Reece. She didn't want to. Something about how attentively he looked at her made her want to tell him everything that had happened in the last five years—the ugly bits that didn't make the small-talk supercut of postgrad life.

She wanted to tell him about the broken radiator in her apartment that her landlord assured her worked just fine.

She wanted to tell him how much she hated wearing skirts and dresses to work, but Roger insisted on a "classic" dress code.

She wanted to tell him that her insurance didn't cover mental health services, and she couldn't afford a therapist.

She wanted to tell him how hard it was to be so far from Jackie.

She wanted to tell him the truth about Ben, the real truth, the way he'd eaten her up until there wasn't any of her left when she met Reece.

Most of all, she wanted to tell him how she felt right now. How mad she was at herself for treating him like shit. How annoyed she was that he looked fresh off some influencer's feed. How much she missed his kindness and never once realized it until right now, this very minute.

"Not great," she said.

The truth of those words ached. She'd admitted it to herself before in quiet, fleeting moments: standing cramped between strangers on the subway who shoved their backpacks into her spine and ran over her toes with their bikes; watching her favorite queer bar close permanently because the rent had gone up again; listening to Roger pontificate about how millennials just didn't know the value of hard work as she answered his emails.

And yet she was so, so lucky, and that made it worse. What right did she have to complain? How could she want more when this was what she had always wanted? A job in media that paid a living wage, decent enough healthcare, a room of her own in an apartment with a roommate who didn't steal, at least. In another year, she'd finally pay off her debt. If she got this promotion, maybe she could get her own place.

Her career in media kept moving backward as layoff after layoff forced thousands of talented applicants to fight over fewer and fewer jobs, but she lived in the best city in the world, where you could bump into Jake Gyllenhaal on the sidewalk next to a pile of trash bags taller than an SUV.

But those incredible New York City moments—the ones that supposedly made the cost and the stress worth it—had become fewer and farther between as time went on. She couldn't remember the last time she went dancing at Cubbyhole, or wandered through a museum, or read a book in Prospect Park. All she could think of was paying through the nose for grocery delivery because she couldn't carry her boxes of La Croix all the way from Key Food.

On most days she felt like she never left that crowded subway car during rush hour, surrounded by strangers unwilling to let her through to the doors. With each new lease she signed, each year that passed without real progress in her career, the oxygen bled out of her life a little more.

"I'm not doing great," she repeated, this time for herself.

She forced a self-deprecating smile for his benefit, already worried that she'd gone too far, said too much.

But there was no pity on Reece's face, just concern. He took both her shoulders in his big hands. The urge to step forward and press her face against his chest nearly overwhelmed her. She knew he could wrap her up in his arms and insulate her from all this dread. He'd done it before.

"The good thing is you look amazing," he said. She snorted, startled out of her misery, and he grinned at her. "Seriously, it's not fair! You have Disney Princess hair, what is this?"

Reece caught one of her curls between his fingers and held it up to the light. She felt a strange thrill at the sight of her gold and silver strands held in his grasp.

"The gray works for you. It's beautiful."

"Thank you." She shoved her fist into Reece's chest and he took a step back, laughing as he let go. "Flatterer."

Reece gave her that open, joyful smile she'd never forgotten, the one just for her. Laugh lines, white teeth, the edge of his gaze soft with awe. His round cheeks crunched his eyes into bright jade beads, and a single dimple appeared beside his mouth. She wanted to poke her finger into it. She wanted to run screaming in the opposite direction. Her heart cracked open and leaked sunshine into her chest.

She wanted him. She wanted the way she felt right now, the way Reece made her feel when he looked at her just like that.

Warm. She wanted his warmth.

But she didn't deserve it. How could she even think she did?

"Reece, I—" she started, and then tripped on a stutter. "I'm so sorry."

Reece frowned, concerned. "For what?"

"You know what. For how I behaved at graduation."

She cringed at the inadequacy of her words. *How I behaved.*

"Charlie, you don't have to—" Reece interrupted.

She put up a hand. "I *do* have to. I was a jerk and I'm sorry for not—" Oh god, how should she put it? She'd owed him this apology for five years and never took the time to practice. "For not being more considerate of your feelings."

She was proud of herself for a fleeting moment before she noticed Reece's face pinching.

Damn. *Feelings* sounded so after-school-special, patronizing. She'd always been garbage at conversations like this, conversations that mattered.

"For not considering *you*," she revised. "I was wrapped up in my own bullshit when we were hooking up and I shouldn't have left campus without saying good-bye."

"We really don't need to talk about this." Reece crinkled his empty wrapper in his hands.

"Reece." She desperately wished he would look at her, but his eyes were fixed on the carpet.

"Seriously, Charlie." He sighed. "It was pretty clear that you were still hung up on Ben. It's on me that I wanted more from you."

Charlotte flinched at the sound of Ben's name in Reece's mouth. "I wasn't *hung up* on Ben." She uselessly fluttered her hands, at a loss for words. "I was *recovering* from him. From . . . the whole relationship."

Reece grimaced. "Right, recovering. Got it."

Her face burned with humiliation. Reece didn't know what happened because she never told him, and now she couldn't fathom a neat summary. It felt so raw, Ben twirling a pen as he lounged at the front of the lecture hall, a memory made flesh after years of losing its color.

"Is he coming this weekend?" Finally Reece looked at her again, only now Charlotte wished he wouldn't.

"Who, Ben?" she said. "Yeah, he's here."

His face darkened. "Cool cool cool."

Charlotte realized in a rush that he assumed they were still in contact. "We're not— We don't *talk*."

"You don't need to explain." Reece ran a hand through his hair again and a few more strands fell into his eyes. Agitation came off him in waves. "I'm sorry, I'm being a jerk," he said. He took a step back, putting his hands up. "This is none of my business."

"But it *is* your business!" she blurted out.

He raised an eyebrow at her tone. Charlotte didn't care. She couldn't look away from his face, tight with confusion and hurt. She needed him to understand that she really was sorry that she'd failed him. And that there was so much he didn't know, so much that she never told him, that explained her behavior.

She'd never wanted to hurt Reece. She'd never meant for any of this to happen.

He took a deep breath. "Thank you for the apology. I appreciate it." Instead of getting huffy like he might have done as a student, this new and improved Reece centered himself with practiced patience.

His eyes met hers, guarded under the fluorescent lights. Despite his intentional calm, there was so much in his gaze that she couldn't read. "I'm sorry too," Reece added. "This was something really great, before it wasn't."

She couldn't look away from his stare, laced with sincerity and more dangerous emotions she didn't dare name. She suddenly remembered the moment she noticed Reece's rich laugh for the first time at the 3Ds support group. She remembered watching him thunder across the ice at a hockey game while Jio cheered beside her in the bleachers. She remembered her breathless gasp as he looked up at her while his mouth pressed against her inner thigh.

Something really great.

Once upon a time they clawed at each other, struggling to stay silent at the back of Mead Library during finals week. Desperate to touch and be touched, back when they were young and ravenous and stupid, their futures unbound, the taste of freedom in their throats.

Their relationship *was* something great, a firecracker burning bright and fast in the damp spring air. She also remembered that it was her fault they'd walked away with their fingers singed.

"It was great," she agreed.

Before it wasn't.

Charlotte studied him. Reece had changed in little ways too. She recognized the new wariness on his face. Stubble clung to his jawline, softer than it used to be.

His eyes were on her mouth again. Was the sexual tension between them just her imagination, another trick of déjà vu? Did he feel the same trapdoor sensation of falling headfirst into the past? He held her gaze a little too long, she was almost sure.

Charlotte licked her bottom lip, her own nervous tell, and Reece started and looked away.

"You know what'll cheer you up?" Reece asked, unaware of the desire thawing in her chest. "Pong." He adopted a cocky smile, his eyebrows waggling.

Charlotte groaned and shook her head. "No way."

"You know you want to show those soccer pricks how it's done." Even when he used his low, seductive voice, Reece's eyes sparkled with humor. "Let's be twenty-one again. Let's pretend Barack Obama is still president. We can play with water."

"Reece . . ."

"Let's go back in time, Charlie."

It was the perfect invitation. Reece might as well have read her mind. She wanted to go back to those humid nights in his backyard when they licked away each other's anxiety.

And god, did she want to say yes. She wanted to stand side by side with him at the end of that table and razz each other when they missed the easy shots. She wanted to goof around and slide her hand into the back pocket of his jeans.

But the idea of going back to that lounge, stuffed to the brim with noise and alcohol and people she used to know, was too much. She wasn't used to the aggressive noise and blur of college parties. Even at her most confident, she'd never been a social butterfly. Especially now, when Ben could emerge from any corner, his knowing stare pinning her feet to the floor as her mind slid back in time.

"I think I'm done for the day," Charlotte admitted. "It's been kind of a rough one."

Reece picked up on her dark energy. His head tilted to the side, all platonic concern once again. Whatever he saw on her face, it was enough for him to know she didn't want to be convinced. "Okay. It's only Thursday. We have plenty of time."

Great. Three more days of this.

A sharp laugh ricocheted down the stairwell behind them, making Charlotte flinch. She knew he noticed by the way he stepped toward her automatically, like he wanted to protect her from the sound. "Let me walk you home," he suggested.

She searched his offer for innuendo, but he exuded Older Brother Energy, the words innocent. She frowned, burying her disappointment (a deep, impenetrable blue). Her feelings were tomorrow's problem. She'd deal with them later.

"Okay," she said. "I'm on this floor. Room 107."

The farther away they walked, the dimmer the noise from upstairs became. Her brain quieted like it always did when she left a crowded space.

She followed Reece down the long, winding hallway. Because they were partially underground, fluorescent lights kept the dorm's ground floor brightly lit at all hours. The harsh white glow and the lack of windows to the outside world made it feel suspended in time. Déjà vu returned: It could be the August morning nine years ago when her classmates first arrived on campus and moved into identical cinder-block suites, two kids to a room. Only the silence reminded Charlotte that she was an adult who was not where she was supposed to be.

She didn't want to go back to her room. She wasn't ready to lie in her narrow bed unable to sleep, taunted by insecurities. She didn't want to imagine what Ben thought of her swift retreat at the career center, or wonder if Reece's jokes were flirtation or just kindness. Nor did she want to scroll through Roger's email inbox to distract herself from the success of her peers. Even if she did calm down enough to drift off, Ben's taunting, braggy voice would follow her into her dreams. She couldn't be alone in that cinder-block box with her feelings, with this longing and fear and humiliation. Not just yet.

Without thinking, Charlotte stopped walking. Reece noticed she wasn't following him and turned around. For a moment he just looked at her, leaned against a wall and angled toward him, a dare in her posture. Her skin felt hot as she watched his stare move from her lips to the pale arch of her neck to the slight curve of her breasts.

Her body coursed with adrenaline and cheap beer. She trembled. She felt prone, available. She wanted the distraction only he could offer her.

Let's go back in time, Charlie. Was this what he had in mind?

Reece blinked. He didn't walk away but something stopped him from coming closer, some hesitation she wasn't privy to but could imagine easily enough. There were plenty of reasons why their hooking up was a bad idea. Not that long ago he fell for her, and she just let him fall.

This school belonged to her once too. Before she met Ben and lost herself, before their breakup turned campus into a haunted house of repressed trauma. She loved the vivid colors: the bright white marble of the library and the emerald green of the quad. Returning to campus after summer break had always felt like this, a mad rush of belonging and possibility as a new semester started. It welcomed her home and wrapped her up in its vivid palette.

This school taught her how to love herself for the first time. It hurt like hell to lose that feeling of belonging, but Reece had patched the wound.

He closed the distance between them. "Charlie," he exhaled, standing close enough to touch. Desire surged up her spine like an electric shock.

She wasn't imagining it, she knew that now. He used to look at her just like this, the two of them dancing to MGMT in his backyard, horny and drunk.

Twenty-two and hers for the taking. Twenty-seven and afraid of her, even as she knew that he wouldn't walk away from this.

Remember that first night at Acronym when you went down on me in the bathroom, she wanted to ask, or demand. *Remember how much you used to want this.*

She turned her hands behind her and flattened her palms to the cinder block. She'd gone molten inside, speechless and pink. This had the ache of history. She knew exactly how brutal and tender it would be. This was college lust, no-tomorrow lust, take-me-here-and-kiss-me-hard-and-do-it-*now* lust. She'd honestly forgotten what this felt like.

Manhattan felt very far away, the map of her responsible adult life smudged. She couldn't imagine the stack of Roger's correspondence waiting on her desk. Everything that happened since graduation had been an interruption, a commercial break. She was not a cog fetching kombucha for billionaires who wanted to solve the problems of her generation without asking for their permission.

She slipped into the life of that girl again, the one she'd forgotten, the one she'd been before Roger and Brooklyn and Ben. Charlie Thorne, *thorny bitch,* torn jeans from Goodwill and peroxide from the box. Portraits to draw and term papers to draft and injustices to fight. She felt herself again, alive and dark and electric.

Reece still stared at her, the picture of pure want. She could tell that he was just barely holding on. She could step forward, take what she wanted and meet no protest. She knew exactly what would happen, how he'd grab her hips in his big hands and open her up. How he'd gasp her name. Reece always said her name with a certain tremor of worship.

His hands hung empty at his side, fingers twitching.

Let's go back in time, Charlie.

Her phone trilled in her back pocket. Reece jerked, his hand curling into a fist. He frowned as she reached for the device on impulse, her fingers prepared to swipe and accept the call. She squinted through the haze of her arousal and read Roger's name on the screen.

She sent it to voicemail, but the spell was broken. Charlotte licked her dry lips. Reece's face had closed to her again.

Heating bill electric bill wifi bill health insurance dental insurance credit card bill art department transfer you idiot you disgrace—

What was she doing? She had so much riding on this weekend, she couldn't afford to get distracted. She couldn't afford to be anything but fine.

"Let me walk you home," Reece said again.

When they reached her door, he pulled her up against him, forcing her onto her tiptoes. His face pressed against her bare neck as her hands rose to grab his shoulders. It was so much more than a hug. This was a desperate cling of *if only* and *I want.* He clutched her so tightly that she thought she might faint.

His breath caught on her neck while they clung to each other, his mouth a little open.

When he let her go, she could practically taste him, chocolate chip cookies and flavored seltzer. But just as suddenly, he stepped back. Then he turned and walked away.

She waited for him to glance over his shoulder, to steal one last look at her before he fled, but he didn't. Reece disappeared into the stairwell, and she heard his feet hit the steps all the way to the third floor.

Charlotte wanted to sink against the door and down to the carpet. She wanted to wallow in this feeling, this abstract painting of blood-red attraction and violet regret. She wanted to go over every detail of being in his arms again.

Instead, she fished out her keys and opened the door to her and Jackie's room. She toed out of her shoes and felt her way through the darkness to her twin XL bed. She crawled between the sheets provided by the R&C committee and shuddered with shame and unfulfilled want.

She was here to work. That's all.

Her phone screamed in her hands again. Seeing Roger's face on the display, she shoved off the covers and threw the device across the room. It hit the wall with a satisfying smack before falling to the floor, the screen threaded with lightning cracks.

SLACK MESSAGE FROM ROGER LUDERMORE TO CHARLOTTE THORNE, 11:13 PM: found the dropbox password

TEXT MESSAGE FROM JACKIE SLAUGHTER TO CHARLOTTE THORNE, 1:02 AM: I HAVE LANDED. HEIN UNIVERSITY, GET READY.

TEXT MESSAGE FROM JACKIE SLAUGHTER TO CHARLOTTE THORNE, 1:03 AM: WOW I'm just getting all of your texts!! sorry my phone died and I packed my charger in my suitcase like a DOOFUS

TEXT MESSAGE FROM JACKIE SLAUGHTER TO CHARLOTTE THORNE, 1:04 AM: of course Reece is there, he's our class secretary you goober

TEXT MESSAGE FROM JACKIE SLAUGHTER TO CHARLOTTE THORNE, 1:05 AM: I'll bet my entire 401k that Thomas accidentally sinks that boat

Friday

Chapter 3

SLACK MESSAGE FROM ROGER LUDERMORE TO CHARLOTTE THORNE, 6:06 AM: did you reorder business cards

SLACK MESSAGE FROM ROGER LUDERMORE TO CHARLOTTE THORNE, 7:31 AM: I wanted cream cards not eggshell

TEXT MESSAGE FROM JACKIE SLAUGHTER TO CHARLOTTE THORNE, 9:25 AM: you awake yet? I'm getting McDonalds!

"CHAAAARRRLOTTE!"

A hand rumpled her hair. Fingernails lightly scratched her scalp. The scent of greasy food wafted through her subconscious.

"It's ten A.M.," Jackie purred. "Time to get up and hang out with me!"

Charlotte jolted awake to find her best friend perched on the side of the bed, her hair trapped in a messy topknot. Frizzy brown tendrils kissed her forehead. Charlotte hadn't seen Jackie since Thanksgiving, and she looked reassuringly herself—cozy but alert.

Charlotte lunged at her and dragged her down onto the mattress. She mushed her nose against Jackie's back and took a big whiff: sugary perfume and just a hint of fried food. "Oh my god, *finally.*"

Jackie poked her on the nose. "Boop! I got you this. Go on, drink up." She retrieved a Gatorade from the bookshelf that served as a bedside table.

Charlotte dragged herself upright and took the bottle. She screwed off the top and reluctantly took a sip. "Ugh, thanks, I hate it."

"You're welcome. There's McDonald's on the desk when you're ready."

She blinked the sleep from her eyes and enjoyed the strange familiarity of sitting in a crappy dorm bed with her best friend, one of them in pajamas, the other bursting with energy. In their four years at Hein, they'd done exactly this thousands of times: in Charlotte's freshman-year double that she shared with an elusive chem student, and then in the two-bedroom suite she and Jackie shared sophomore year in Fuller Dorm. They lived together for three years at Hein, learning each other's quirks and boundaries by heart, except the semester Jackie spent studying abroad in Paris. It was a strange miracle that they got along as well as they did, with their opposing personalities. Aside from the occasional fight about whose turn it was to clean out the mini fridge—*Your takeout is spawning alien life, Char*—they got along swimmingly.

Charlotte considered meeting Jackie to be the best thing that ever happened to her. Most of the time, at least.

Jackie leapt off the bed to fuss with her suitcase, flinging clothes everywhere, tank tops and boots and cute going-out jackets tossed haphazardly across the linoleum. She picked up a mound of shirts, refolding and organizing them on a bookshelf as she told Charlotte about her travel. "Hertz had already released my car because they're awful, but lucky me, they only had a convertible left! So we are driving in style this weekend."

Charlotte crawled down the bed and snatched the McDonald's bag into her lap. Grease leached through the paper wrapper.

Hell yes, hash browns.

"Thank you for this, I didn't eat dinner last night."

"We can go to Stop and Shop for snacks." Jackie moved on to sorting her pants. She rolled up a pair of familiar leggings with HEIN

UNIVERSITY stitched down the leg in blue. "I am too old for cheap beer, so we'll get booze too." She placed the leggings roll on a shelf beside a pyramid of balled-up socks.

Around a mouthful of potato, Charlotte garbled, "I don't think you packed enough clothes."

"It's not all to wear. The clothing swap is tomorrow."

Every year a senior hosted a big swap meet for graduating students to unload clothes they no longer wanted as they prepared to leave campus. Unclaimed items were donated to a nearby shelter.

"They still do that?" Charlotte asked.

"It's in the schedule as an official R&C event! So cool, right?" Jackie preened. "They even have a lounge reserved. When it was my turn to host, everyone just threw their stuff on our living room floor."

Charlotte smiled. "I remember." Jackie had a knack for spotting potential through the chaos, from a vintage skirt buried under piles of used clothing to a new friend looking shyly through the accessories table. Jackie's extroversion overwhelmed Charlotte sometimes, but her life was all the better for it.

"You're coming, right?" Jackie fixed her with a hopeful stare. "We can treasure hunt like we used to."

Charlotte ate the last of her hash brown as she thought through the weekend ahead. Tomorrow should be quiet. Roger wouldn't arrive on campus until Sunday morning, so she had time. "I wouldn't miss it," she promised.

Jackie threw her a wide grin. "Good." Then she turned back to her luggage, setting aside a pile to bring to the swap.

While Jackie puttered, Charlotte grabbed her iPhone from the bookshelf. She winced at the cracked screen. It wasn't too bad: She could still read the avalanche of notifications from Roger. She could probably make the phone last another six months if she didn't drop it again.

"You have an accident or something?" Jackie asked, nodding at the damage.

Charlotte threw the empty hash brown wrapper at her. Jackie swatted it away with an expert hand.

"How are you even awake right now? You must be exhausted," Charlotte asked.

Aerial assault eliminated, Jackie resumed lining up bottles of nail polish on the bookshelf: red, mint green, black, a clear top coat with flecks of silver glitter. Charlotte eyed her own unpainted toes and resolved to give them a cleanup. Maybe a nice burning red to express her sexual frustration.

"I slept on the plane, and don't change the subject."

She cringed. Unbidden, the memory of Reece standing across from her in the hallway returned to her. The heat in his eyes, the way his jaw went slack . . . every inch of her skin alive with awareness of his body near hers.

And then there was Ben at the front of the lecture hall, eyes narrowed as he took in the room.

"Yesterday was eventful." Charlotte gingerly lay back down and threw her arm over her face.

The comforting sounds of Jackie's movement about the room stilled. "Do you have something to share with the class, Charlotte Thorne?"

Jackie was the closest thing Charlotte knew to actual family. Her best friend had the dubious honor of guarding her secrets. But some things were too complex and embarrassing to admit, even to Jackie. She didn't know how to explain the tunnel-vision panic she felt at the career center when Ben took center stage, not after all these years. Nor did she want to share the gravitational pull she felt toward Reece, that selfish urge to distract herself with his smile. She didn't know if she was ready for Jackie's shrewd analysis of her friends' love lives.

"Roger's freaking out about his commencement address," she said instead.

Jackie groaned. "That scumbag. Is he still calling at all hours?"

"That's what I get paid for." Charlotte sat up and took another swig of the Gatorade. "I don't know how this speech is going to go; he's not a great fit for Hein's student body. I still can't believe he went here."

"I can't believe he's gonna be on campus. Can I meet him?" Jackie's grin was devilish.

The idea of Jackie berating Charlotte's narcissist megamillionaire boss threatened to break her brain. "For the sake of my job, absolutely not."

Jackie pouted. "You're no fun. We gotta get you out of there anyway."

Her best friend loved to talk about how much Charlotte needed to quit her job. Jackie also liked to quit new jobs at the first inconvenience, so, as much as she loved her, Charlotte didn't put much stock in her advice.

She skimmed Roger's latest emails: more back-and-forth with the speechwriter, forwarded instructions from Hein's R&C committee about social media coverage of the commencement ceremony, a reminder to reserve a taxi to pick up Roger at the train station. She cc'ed Aubrey into the thread about transportation and closed the app.

Jackie threw a clean towel on the bed. "Put your phone away and go take a shower, I want to get moving."

Charlotte clambered out of bed. "Crap, I forgot to pack shower shoes."

Jackie kicked a cheap pair of black flip-flops across the linoleum floor. "Me too. Bought these at CVS this morning en route here."

"You have lived like five lives today."

"I ran errands, you lazy bitch. Please go shower, you smell like a frat house."

SLACK MESSAGE FROM ROGER LUDERMORE TO CHARLOTTE THORNE, 12:20 PM: need Tim Cook's email address

CHARLOTTE DID FEEL better after a shower. She'd long suspected that her state of mind was tethered to the cleanliness of her hair: When it was a greasy, tangled mess, she felt cranky and out of sorts.

Ben once told her she should shave it all off, that maybe then she'd be less of a pain in the ass. She bought the infamous jar of Manic Panic as a rare protest against his bullshit. Instead of a funky lilac, her hair wound up a startling silver, almost white. As Jackie said when she helped her rinse the dye in their bathroom sink, "Mistakes were made."

Her (now naturally graying) hair air-dried in the wind as Jackie raced them across town. She would have a new set of knots to untangle when they got back to campus, but the rush of fresh air across her face felt divine. It'd been ages since she'd driven somewhere. The occasional Uber she sprang for in the city rarely went faster than fifteen miles an hour on the traffic-clogged streets.

"You're like a dog," Jackie teased as Charlotte stuck her entire head above the windshield. She laughed and the wind snatched the sound away.

"What are you thinking today?" Jackie chattered on. "I want to sit on the quad and see who looks terrible."

"Liam got married."

"Hockey team Liam? To who?"

"High school sweetheart."

Her best friend shook her head as she processed the new information. "Straight people. Who else is here?"

"Matt and Jio drove up from D.C., they're still adorable. Amy's killing it at work. Nina is super in shape, I think she could break me in half."

"Did Eliza make it?"

"Nah, she couldn't fly back from Dubai."

"Thank god, I can only handle so many pining exes this weekend."

Jackie gave her a wry grin and Charlotte shoved her in the shoulder. "Hey, don't strike the driver!"

"How's dating in L.A. going?"

"I'm swiping left on that question." Jackie changed lanes and signaled to turn into the grocery store parking lot. "It's cool, I wanted to be single for the reunion."

"Ew, why?" Charlotte wrinkled her nose. "You know everyone in our year, and the seniors look like *babies.* You will not believe how tiny they are."

Jackie pulled across the boulevard and eased into a space by the front door. She shrugged as she put the top back up on the car. "Maybe there'll be some wise lesbian in her thirties who wants to adopt a baby gay. I don't know. I'm down for whatever."

That captured their entire friendship. Jackie was down for whatever and always had snacks, while Charlotte made skeptical jokes and passed out early.

"Besides," Jackie added. "I don't plan on spending the reunion prying you away from your phone."

Charlotte rolled her eyes as she grabbed her purse from the floor. "I'm not engaging with that." No matter how many times she reminded Jackie that this weekend was technically a business trip for her, it didn't seem to sink in. Hopefully there would be plenty of quality best-friend time in between tasks for Roger.

The grocery turned out to be a popular destination. Soon-to-be-graduates ransacked the store's selection of barbecue charcoal and hot dogs.

While Jackie went off in search of sweets, Charlotte beelined to the chips aisle.

Just as she slid a bag of popcorn into her basket, her phone started blaring. Charlotte maneuvered the basket onto her other arm and dug it out of her pocket. Roger's dead-eyed headshot stared back at her on the screen.

She held her breath as she took the call.

"Where are we on live tweets for Sunday?" her boss snarled.

Some days she admired Roger's disregard for polite greetings. Why waste energy on *is this a good time* or *how's your day going* when you could jump right into bossing around your employees?

Charlotte pinned the phone between her shoulder and her ear and grabbed a bag of Doritos from the shelf. "Just waiting on a finished draft from you, and then I can write them up. How's it going with Peter?"

Roger scoffed. "I got rid of him. He accused me of being *out of touch*." He adopted a high-pitched whine as he mocked his speechwriter's spot-on feedback. "He's all *sensitivity* this and *appropriateness of venue* that. It's fine, I can write it myself," Roger continued, working himself up. "Don't know why I bothered hiring him in the first place. I'm not Steve fucking Jobs, I can put two sentences together."

Jackie emerged from the next aisle over and gave her a searching look.

Roger, Charlotte mouthed, rolling her eyes. Jackie rolled her eyes and took the basket from Charlotte's arm.

"Get me those tweets ASAP," Roger snapped, apparently remembering the reason for his call. He hung up as suddenly as he called, leaving her staring open-mouthed at her phone.

"That looked fun," Jackie drawled.

Charlotte followed her up the aisle to the register. An exhausted cashier waved them over. Jackie set their plunder down on the counter.

"He fired his speechwriter but still expects me to draft Twitter coverage of a commencement address that does not exist." Charlotte took out her wallet. Jackie waved her off and handed her credit card to the clerk. "Let me Venmo you for half," she protested, still uncomfortable with Jackie's generosity after all these years. Jackie's love of thrifting wasn't born from financial necessity—her dad was a hot-shot attorney, and her mom was the most sought-after knee surgeon in

Westchester County. The Slaughters never made Charlotte feel like a charity case, but she winced as Jackie signed the receipt.

"Absolutely not," Jackie declared.

In the end, they stocked their dorm room with Doritos, Oreos, popcorn, party cups, and another pair of four-dollar flip-flops. Not to mention a nice bottle of gin and two bottles of tonic from the liquor store next door.

As Jackie mixed cocktails and organized a tote bag to take to the quad, a wall began to thaw in Charlotte's chest. What a delight it was to be scolded to put on sunblock by a woman who'd known her for years. Charlotte had friends from work, sure, but no one who badgered her with just the right level of affection and tough love. No one who would tell her that she smelled like ass and give her a bear hug anyway.

Charlotte changed, put her hair in a loose braid, and didn't bother with makeup. She slid on her beloved aviators.

"Do I look alive?"

Jackie smirked. "Yes. *Morning-after chic.*"

"What a coincidence, that's just the vibe I'm going for." Charlotte took a small sip of the drink Jackie handed her. "*Mmm,* this is excellent. But I can only have one." She closed her laptop and stuck it under her arm like a football.

"Are you serious with that? What, are you going to answer emails on the quad?"

Charlotte stuck out her tongue. "It's called a hotspot, babe. Those tweets aren't gonna write themselves."

SLACK MESSAGE FROM AUBREY PAGE TO CHARLOTTE THORNE, 2:25 PM: hey do u have tim cooks email rogers freaking out

BY THE LOOK of the quad, the rest of the Hein Class of 2013 had the same idea. Most of the alumni from last night's reception, plus twenty or so latecomers, sprawled across the grass on blankets and towels on loan from the R&C committee. Charlotte paused on the path to take in the view. It looked as if someone had spread a vast patchwork quilt between Hein's square of original buildings, the many hues of fabric popping against the Gothic stonework. This was the school's heart, both historically and socially. Charlotte felt all mushy as she thought of the generations of students who threw Frisbees and held rallies right here where she stood. She couldn't count the naps she took in the shade of Cauldwell Hall in between classes.

Jackie picked her way through the constellation of classmates, occasionally stopping to say hi to people she knew. Charlotte kept one eye peeled for Ben, but the black hole of his presence was nowhere to be seen. When Jackie got held up by a DJ from the college radio station, Charlotte went on ahead, locating Matt and Jio on a bedsheet.

"Hey, friends." Her knees complained as she lowered herself onto her butt. "How was the rest of your night?"

Matt moved aside a cheese plate to clear more space for her. "We went to bed early. Traveling knocked me out."

Jio emerged from behind their phone with a radiant smile. "Sorry, I was working on a post!" They waved an open palm at the gourmet spread. "Help yourself!"

Jio ran digital communications for an environmental conservation nonprofit. Charlotte initially followed the Green Earth Conservatory on Instagram as a favor, but the account delighted her. They had a knack for blending complex policy with pictures of baby pandas. A uniquely millennial career path: memeing the end of the world.

Her other half dropped down onto the blanket, knocking a handful of crackers onto the grass. Charlotte scooped them up and put them in her lap.

"Hey, losers, what's cooking?" Jackie stole one of the grass crackers and popped it in her mouth.

"Jackie baby! How's L.A.?" Jio asked.

"Everyone's really into crystals. How's D.C.?"

"Gentrified." Jio mimed vomiting, much to the horror of the wrestling bros sitting on a blanket a few feet away. Matt snickered and squeezed his partner's knee. "Eat our cheese, it's not expensive!"

The three of them talked about the D.C. restaurant scene while Charlotte dug sunblock out of their bag. The sun was strong for the end of May; she'd return to Brooklyn looking crispy if she wasn't careful. She was rubbing lotion into her elbows when Jackie nudged her in the side.

"Would you look at that, a show is starting."

Reece, Garrett, and some other bros were scoping out an area on the quad to play Frisbee. The hockey alumni had doubled down on college nostalgia. They all wore loose tank tops, the kind with the sleeves cut off. Several sported backward HU baseball caps. Garrett held a can of Miller Lite as he shooed Reece farther across the grass.

Charlotte shivered as she remembered Reece's breath against her neck last night. That was no normal good-night hug, more like a plea to be convinced. If she had grasped his collar in her fist and pulled him against her, would he let her? Would he kiss her like he used to, all teeth and crackling tension?

The littlest member of the pack abandoned her fellow bros and trotted over to their blanket. Garrett kept one eye on Misty as she settled down beside Charlotte and plopped her tiny head on her knee.

Charlotte scratched behind the dog's ears and fed her a cracker. "That's all you get," she whispered. "Don't tell your father, he doesn't like me."

Misty licked crumbs from her muzzle and blinked in conspiratorial agreement.

While Jackie stretched out on a towel, Charlotte kept herself propped up on her elbows to watch the boys play. Misty burrowed alongside her like a fluffy, uninhibited fox.

It was impossible to focus on anything besides Reece chasing the Frisbee across the quad. He caught it and chucked it to Liam, whose last name she still couldn't remember. It sailed above Liam's reaching grasp, forcing him to sprint to retrieve it. Garrett booed and Reece raised his hands in apology, a bashful smile on his face.

"So," Jackie said.

"So," Charlotte repeated.

Reece kept laughing. He bent over and rested his hands on his knees like the force of his amusement was too much to bear. She'd forgotten that he laughed like an old man, bellowing and enthusiastic. His laugh always boomed through parties like thunder.

"Can we talk about it yet?" Jackie asked.

Reece yelled instructions at Garrett. Still bent forward, the cords of muscle in his arms stood out as they supported his weight. While he wasn't the lean, toned jock of his college years, he had the same glorious forearms.

Besides, Charlotte liked his new weight. He looked less wiry now. Like he ate three solid meals a day instead of scarfing a Pop-Tart and some Red Bull on his way to afternoon labs.

"Talk about what?" she asked absently.

"Can we talk about the man you're currently fellating with your eyes?"

Charlotte whipped her head around, smacking Misty with her braid. The dog snorted before dozing off again. "Jackie, that's vile."

Her best friend watched her like a hawk through her sunglasses. "I'm not wrong."

"I don't want to *fellate* him."

Even as the denial fell from her lips, she couldn't fight the impulse to watch him gallop around. As Reece leapt in the air to catch a rogue throw, his shirt bounced up to reveal a stretch of his soft stomach. He landed effortlessly, spinning on the balls of his feet to throw the Frisbee back to Liam.

She could lie. She could brush off Jackie's accusation with some story about wanting to make amends.

But Jackie had watched their non-relationship sputter and die at close range. Who held Charlotte's hand after the graduation ceremony when everyone else hugged their moms and chased siblings across the grass? Jackie. Whose family took her to dinner at Terry's Bar to celebrate and insisted on buying her an extra bag of nachos? Jackie's family.

If there was one person in this world who saw right through her, it was Jackie Slaughter. If Charlotte tried to hide her feelings, Jackie would just shove her sideways into the grass and call her a coward before feeding her more cheese.

When Charlotte and Reece ended, Jackie aligned herself with her roommate (hoes before bros) but maintained a friendship with him over the years. They hung out whenever he visited California, buying cheap tickets to L.A. Kings games and taking selfies in the nosebleed section of the hockey stadium.

Are you sure you don't mind? Jackie texted her the first time Reece crashed on her couch.

Not at all, Charlotte told her. *He's a good dude.*

Laser-focused on building a life for herself in New York, Charlotte never asked her about him. She didn't like to think about the way she'd left things between them, and she didn't know what to do with the occasional fun fact from his Instagram: *Reece's car broke down again, Reece has a new girlfriend, Reece is growing a beard.* She could almost fool herself into thinking he was some influencer they followed on social media as opposed to the guy she rebounded with after leaving her horrible ex-boyfriend.

Now Jackie reached out to ruffle Charlotte's hair. She laughed when Charlotte slapped her hands away. "I love you very much, kiddo. Even though you don't know how to talk about your feelings."

"Jerk."

Reece danced backward across the field, his arms outstretched to catch a high throw. The Frisbee breezed past his fingers by a wide margin and he turned around to lope after it, utterly relaxed.

Jackie watched her watching Reece, her eyebrows raised.

"I just want to, like, talk about dogs with him," Charlotte admitted.

Her friend's topknot bobbed precariously as she stifled a laugh. "Yeah, I'm sure that's all you want."

It wasn't. She wanted to lick from his clavicle down to his groin.

Charlotte sat up to take a sip of her G&T. She scowled at the grass between her toes. "Last night was a shit show."

"I doubt that's true."

"No, really. I got all stressed out and he had to walk me back to my room."

Not that Reece seemed to mind. But had he kept her company out of kindness or desire? She considered how Reece ran his hand over his mouth as he stared at her, and that hug that was more than a hug. She couldn't have imagined all that sexual magnetism, even if it *had* been months since she'd gotten laid.

"There was this moment when I thought something might happen, but it just—" She fiddled with the end of her braid. "I don't know."

"What?" Jackie prompted. "What don't you know?"

"We shouldn't go there."

Jackie's eyebrows came together. "Why not?"

Charlotte shrugged. She couldn't explain how back in college, Reece felt like the solution to her problems until he created even more. When he made her laugh, she stopped hearing the grating loop of Ben's Greatest Hits in her mind. When she sat in Reece's lap with her lips at his throat, she didn't feel quite so powerless, so weak, so worthless. But when he smiled at her in the darkness, she always wondered what he could possibly see in her.

Charlotte remembered how out of control she felt last night when

Ben looked over the audience, and how much she wanted to disappear before his eyes found her.

"Seriously, why is it a bad idea?" Jackie demanded. "He's recently single, you're tragically single, what's the issue?"

Charlotte licked her thumb and rubbed a smudge of dirt off her foot.

"Earth to Charlotte. You know how many people are here to hook up with their exes?"

She set her drink down on the ground, careful not to spill. "I'm not here to screw around, I'm here to work."

Jackie scoffed. "God forbid you take a break. This is our chance to relive the best years of our lives. Maybe a solid orgasm would help you get your priorities straight."

Charlotte looked around frantically to make sure no one was listening. Jio and Matt were absorbed in Instagram again, discussing some influencer they wanted to partner with at work. The hockey bros argued over a spliff, Reece rolling his eyes as he waited for the game to resume. Misty, well, Misty would keep her secrets because she was a dog.

"I do not want to discuss the merits of sleeping with my ex," she hissed.

"We weren't discussing the merits, we were discussing the obstacle that is *you* being a *coward*." Jackie poked her in the shoulder.

Charlotte shoved her wrist away. "Would you stop?"

"If we were discussing the merits," Jackie continued, undaunted, "we would be talking about his ass, and his excellent hair, and the fact that he still looks at you like you were put on this earth just to ruin his life."

The description sent heat crawling up her neck as she remembered Reece's burning eyes, and the way her name fell from his mouth under the fluorescent lights of the hallway. "How would you know how he looks at me?" Charlotte asked, tasting guilt in her throat.

"Because he's watching us, dummy."

Charlotte's eyes found Reece on the field. He indeed watched them like a bemused dad monitoring his squabbling toddlers. He gave her a jaunty wave, and she bit the inside of her cheek before returning it. Reece smiled at her until Garrett sent the Frisbee flying toward his face and he had to duck to avoid it.

Jackie laughed and golf-clapped. "Well done, boys, well done!"

Reece bowed for them before sprinting off to retrieve the disc.

"I hate you," Charlotte whispered.

Jackie pulled the Doritos out of her tote bag. "You love me," she corrected. "Eat something, you're cranky." Charlotte obediently shoved some chips in her mouth. "Good job. Chew. Swallow. Okay, now walk me through your feelings."

"I *feel* irritated."

"Do not make me pull up the Feelings Chart on my phone."

"Oh Jesus." Charlotte threw a hand up in the air. "Fine. I'm confused. Okay? He was all flirty one minute. Then, the next, he went into platonic friend mode like I was just another drinking buddy. He didn't seem mad at me for how things ended, but then he got all prickly when Ben came up in conversation. And when we wound up alone, he looked at me . . ."

She trailed off. There was no way to describe the way Reece had stared at her last night.

"Like you were put on this earth to ruin his life," Jackie repeated.

Charlotte stroked Misty's fur. "Something like that." The pup's steady breathing helped her racing heart rate slow.

Jackie ran the tip of her index finger around the rim of her cup. "When it comes to Reece, it's probably safe to assume he's always flirting with you."

Charlotte studied Reece as best as she could from a distance. He stood still, waiting for Liam to fetch another runaway throw, his hand shielding his eyes from the sun. His threadbare tank top revealed the hard planes of his shoulders.

Another stowaway detail returned: the memory of her fingernails digging into his back. A lost night in the bathroom at a house party, her shorts on the floor, her ass at risk of falling into the sink.

"Maybe," she said. She took a deep drink of her cocktail but still felt parched.

Jackie stared at her, her expression unreadable. After a long pause, she said, "Unless it's not *his* feelings you're worried about."

Charlotte set her cocktail in the grass, a tremor in her hands. "What?"

"Maybe this isn't about Reece at all. You're surprised *you* had feelings for him in the first place. And you *still* do."

She pinched the bridge of her nose between her fingers. "You're making me sound like a dick."

"When the dick fits—"

"Do not finish that sentence."

In college her feelings for Reece were simple: pure, uncomplicated attraction. She knew he wasn't capable of being anyone's boyfriend, especially on the weekend, when he lived in the margins between hungover and trashed. He had a reputation as a respectful but restless flirt, never getting involved with a woman for more than a few weeks. Too sweet to be a fuckboy, but too gorgeous and sloppy not to break some hearts.

The first time they hooked up in some dark corner at Amy's birthday party, there was nothing romantic about it. They'd been sitting next to each other at 3Ds meetings for months, exchanging looks and keeping their small talk light outside of group discussion. Charlotte knew she wasn't ready to date again, but Reece didn't seem to want a relationship either. When he asked her to dance that night at Acronym, he made it so easy to say yes. Charlotte sank into the sensation of him: raspy stubble and searching green eyes. Her brain had no room for other thoughts. Reece left a bite mark on her neck that made her look like she'd been mauled by a bear.

Charlotte admired his broad shoulders and his ability to distract her whenever she needed it. If she invited him over on a weeknight, he showed up within twenty minutes of a text message and never slept over. He was a casual but generous hookup who prioritized her comfort and her pleasure just as much as his own, if not more—a precious rarity in college. After Ben, who whined for sex acts she wasn't comfortable exploring, she appreciated that Reece understood that *no* was a complete sentence.

Sure, she'd cared about Reece. She liked bantering with him, and communicating silently with their eyebrows during 3Ds meetings, and eating junk food together after a raucous party. He gave other members of the support group weirdly good advice, remembering minor details of their family dynamics that even Charlotte forgot. Spending time with Reece was comfortable. She didn't have to brace herself for critical comments or worry about accidentally provoking him, the way she had with Ben. She never forgot that they had no future, bound for separate lives in different cities, but that didn't mean their present hadn't been fun. And then that present became the past.

This was something really great, before it wasn't.

Maybe she'd had feelings for Reece, once upon a time. Maybe Charlotte actually liked him, and it terrified her to be vulnerable after everything Ben had put her through. But that didn't mean she felt the same way now.

Did she?

Her instincts screamed at her to change the subject. Maybe she felt a lot of things, and she didn't like it one bit. She wanted to shove those colorful, kaleidoscoping feelings in a shiny new storage container and not let them see the sun.

On the field, Reece threw his body after the Frisbee and collapsed in a heap. His laughter boomed across the quad. She watched him roll over and hold the disc aloft, victorious.

How long had it been since she'd felt as much as she did last night?

How long had it been since she felt present in her own life, alert and exposed and wanting?

Jackie watched her patiently. Misty continued to huff and pant at her side, her warmth a soothing reminder of where she was. They were the two living beings in this world least likely to judge her. And she didn't want to carry this embarrassment alone.

Charlotte picked at the dry skin around her fingernails. "Ben is here."

Jackie lurched forward, her eyes sharp. All trace of tough love vanished from her voice. "What? I thought he wasn't registered."

"He was on the English majors' panel with Amy last night. I had to leave out the back."

"That prick . . ." Jackie hissed through her teeth. "Honey, I'm so sorry. Are you okay?"

No. I'm not.

"It's fine." Charlotte addressed her answer to Misty's dark eyes. "It's been years."

It didn't feel like years when Ben sat at the front of the lecture hall, surveying the crowd like his kingdom. It felt like only days had passed since he last sneered in her face, his voice pitched low so that no one would overhear him. She was the one who initiated their breakup after eight months of agony, but Ben made sure to get the last word. He always did.

Misty licked Charlotte's palm, demonstrating that eerie canine ability to pick up on people's moods. That or Charlotte still had some brie on her hands. She rubbed Misty's long ears. Her fur was blissfully soft, like a cashmere baby sock.

"Don't let him ruin this weekend for you," Jackie urged her. "You're free of him and his entitled, nasty shit. For the first time in five years, you and I are together on campus with all our friends. We are going to have the time of our gay little lives." She tilted her head to catch Charlotte's eye. "You deserve some fun. You hear me?"

She nodded. "Yeah." Misty wriggled and curled up on her side, her ear slipping from between Charlotte's fingers.

Apparently satisfied by the interrogation-slash-therapy-session, Jackie lay back down on her towel and slid her huge sunglasses back on. "I'm going to nap now. Have fun ogling Reece."

Charlotte scrunched up her face like an angry pug, miffed by Jackie's ability to be so annoying and so correct, but her best friend waved her off. Dismissed, she dug her phone out of her bag to set up the wifi hotspot. She scowled when she saw yet more messages from Aubrey and her boss.

How the hell was she supposed to know Tim Cook's email address? Did Roger think she and good old Timmy Apple traded *The Bachelor* memes on a regular basis?

She opened her laptop and waited for Slack to load.

SLACK MESSAGE FROM CHARLOTTE THORNE TO AUBREY PAGE, 3:02 PM: I just messaged Roger, I don't have it. Tell him to look through his phone.

She skimmed her inbox for fires demanding her immediate attention, or anything from HR about the art department job. The project manager gig would utilize Charlotte's skills at herding unruly people. Keeping a detailed spreadsheet of incoming requests for art for the magazine wouldn't feed her soul, but it was better than constantly worrying about Roger tweeting something offensive. She would report to the art director, a boring but civil man named Pietre who did not call his direct reports after hours.

Matt and Jio brushed crumbs off the empty cheese platter and into the grass. Misty sniffed around for morsels to snack on. "We're going to get some water," Matt said quietly, not wanting to disturb Jackie. "Can you watch our stuff?"

Charlotte nodded. She watched as the duo walked back to Randall, Jio's arm slung around Matt's waist.

Her computer made the tock-tock notification sound.

SLACK MESSAGE FROM AUBREY PAGE TO CHARLOTTE THORNE, 3:10 PM: lol ok

How professional.

"Good news?"

Charlotte looked up from the screen. Reece stood beside her, his hands at his hips. The sun burst just over his shoulder, silhouetting him in gold. With difficulty, she averted her eyes from the rope of muscle in his shoulders. "Not exactly. My boss has separation anxiety."

Reece frowned as he sat down in the grass next to her. No, Reece didn't sit. He *sprawled*, his legs long and his feet bare, toes wiggling in the sun. He leaned his weight back on his palms, fingers spreading through the grass. This was a guy who knew how to relax.

"That sucks," Reece commiserated, his eyes bright. "Want to see a puppy?"

Charlotte pushed her computer off her lap and onto the blanket. "Always."

He took out his phone and scooted closer. His shoulder brushed hers as he scrolled through his photo roll. Charlotte bit her lip. She could smell him again, that boyish aroma of laundry and coffee, now with the earthy sheen of sweat. His posture gave no hint that he was upset about last night, or that he even remembered their close call outside her room. She was aware of every touching millimeter of skin while Reece showed no sign that their proximity even crossed his mind.

"Here we go." He turned the screen toward her. A wrinkled blob of short gray fur peered back at her. "This is Joey. He's some kind of pit bull mix."

"He is *darling*." Charlotte's hand rose to her chest, covering her heart. "How old is he, eight weeks?"

Reece swiped to another picture, this one of Joey swaddled in a blue baby blanket covered in cartoon ducklings. Charlotte cooed, a human heart-eye emoji.

"We think so. Someone left him in a box outside the clinic. Mom found him shivering in the cold. We weren't sure he would make it."

"He looks like he's thriving now. What a li'l tough guy."

"He had a respiratory infection, but he's doing okay now. We're fostering him until he finds his forever home."

Reece swiped again: In a smiling selfie, he had Joey zipped into his hoodie. The puppy licked Reece's neck, his nose a perky pink. "I like to carry him around in my sweatshirt pocket," Reece said. "Mom calls it my Joey pouch."

"Stop, you're going to kill me." She covered her face in her hands, a sigh falling from her lips. "I would die for Joey. I would lay down my life for Joey."

From between her fingers, she saw Reece's grin widen into a full just-for-Charlie classic. "He needs a mommy," he said with a shameless eyebrow waggle. "He'll love you for life."

Charlotte's heart thundered. She hadn't been subjected to the full force of Reece Krueger's charm in years. The playful glint in his eyes had grown finer with age, more roguish than boyish. "Don't tempt me," she said, color rising in her cheeks again.

His arched eyebrow clued her in that he'd picked up on her double meaning. He sat close enough to hear her breath quicken, and for a moment she wasn't sure if he'd acknowledge the frisson of attraction between them. It didn't have the heaviness of last night's dark magnetism. This felt fun and easy, their rapport laced with humor.

Jackie was right. This was undeniably flirting.

Her phone trilled with a notification.

Reece blinked like someone had turned the lights on at a dark party. Charlotte tore her eyes from his soft mouth and leaned over to squint at her computer.

SLACK MESSAGE FROM AUBREY PAGE TO CHARLOTTE THORNE, 3:26 PM: roger needs post-its

"Oh for goodness' sake."

Reece read over her shoulder as she typed furiously. "Your boss again?"

SLACK MESSAGE FROM CHARLOTTE THORNE TO AUBREY PAGE, 3:27 PM: They're in the supply closet.

"My assistant. Technically Roger's second assistant, who reports to me."

Reece frowned. "Important guy to need two assistants."

She gave him a strained look. "That's what he likes to think."

SLACK MESSAGE FROM AUBREY PAGE TO CHARLOTTE THORNE, 3:28 PM: where is that

Charlotte turned her laptop toward him. "She's worked at *Front End* for six months and doesn't know where the supply closet is."

He hummed in sympathy. "Can't she figure it out by herself?"

"You'd think so, but no."

"REECE!" Garrett watched them from the field, his arms crossed over his chest. He didn't look impressed by their tête-à-tête. "We need you, bro!"

At the sound of her owner's voice, Misty leapt to her feet and bounded across the field. Garrett leaned down and ruffled her fur, his hostility dissolving. Asshole or not, the dude loved his dog.

"Oops. Busted." Reece gave her a guilty smile.

Charlotte's heart sputtered and lurched—he was hitting on her. *Intentionally.* Otherwise what would he have to feel guilty about?

"Good luck with the Post-it crisis."

"Thanks," she said as he hopped to his feet. "And thank you for the pup talk."

Damn, his smile.

"Anytime." Then he bounded off toward his friends, the back of his shorts grass-stained. "I'm coming," he yelled at Garrett, who rolled his eyes and chucked the Frisbee in his direction.

Charlotte laughed as Reece missed the catch, and he turned to give her another clumsy bow before darting after it.

There was a snort to her right. Charlotte turned to find Jackie watching her with a blatant *I told you so* face.

"You're a goner."

Charlotte leveled her with a death glare. It did nothing to cancel out her blush. "I knew you weren't asleep."

Chapter 4

@RogerLudermore, 6:00 PM: I am honored to return to my alma mater and give the commencement address at #HeinRandC2018 this weekend. Go Falcons!

CHARLOTTE HAD NOT purchased a ticket to the Class of 2013 Reunion Banquet because she kept a close eye on her budget. Jackie chose not to attend due to the myriad of disappointing ways Hein's administration would spend her money.

"The school does not need another lacrosse field," Jackie pouted as she fished out her credit card at the dining hall.

Instead of attending the banquet, they convinced most of the members of the Dead, Divorced, and Otherwise Disappointing Parents unofficial peer support group to join them at the undergraduate cafeteria, Cauldwell Hall.

This was a masterful change of plans, in Charlotte's opinion. She made her favorite sandwich at the buffet: a BLT on rye grilled almost to a burn in a panini press. Then she loaded up her plate with fresh-baked potato chips and resolved to come back for an ice cream with Oreo crumbs. The all-you-can-eat plate was ten dollars for non-students and she intended to get her money's worth.

There *might* be Tupperware containers in Jackie's tote bag to smuggle leftovers back to the dorm. Charlotte was not at liberty to confirm this rumor.

The 3Ds took over a long table at the back of the dining hall. Charlotte dropped off her plate before doubling back for napkins and a soda. The cafeteria still used the same mud brown plastic cups designed not to break no matter how hard they were dropped—or thrown—by students. Strong nostalgia vibes.

She caught Jackie stealing one of her chips when she returned to the table. "I saw that."

"I got these to share," her best friend bartered, pushing forward a plate of fries.

"Is Reece joining us?" Nina asked as she stirred her spaghetti. Another rule of the 3Ds: If they were meeting over a meal, only comfort food was allowed. No kombucha or kale, period.

Jackie squirted an appalling amount of mustard onto her hamburger. "Nah, he's hosting the class dinner. He said he'd come through for dessert."

Amy, Jio, and Matt filled out the rest of the table, laden with plates of pizza. The six of them fell into an old pattern: Amy sat on Charlotte's other side, with Nina across from Amy. Matt settled in next to Nina, flanked by Jio, who was in prime position to eat Jackie's fries.

The 3Ds dated back to freshman year. The support group was born on the living room floor at Acronym after a disco when Matt, Charlotte, Nina, and Jio traded messy coming-out stories. It felt so good to talk shit and commiserate that the foursome ended most of their nights together, even after Nina and Charlotte broke up. As a teenager, Charlotte dreamed of conversations like this: honest and relatable and camp as hell. A strange sense of humor bloomed inside her as she basked in the safety of people who understood her.

Charlotte still listened more than she spoke, emotionally repressed and armed with a limited vocabulary for her feelings. But it helped just to learn that no family was a Norman Rockwell painting, no matter how perfect and peaceful it appeared on the surface. That was doubly true for queer millennials, whose boomer parents fell on a spectrum from tactless to cruel. Charlotte could hear her anger with her mother's homophobia in Matt's unsteady voice. She recognized her insecurity from her father's neglect in Jio's defensive humor.

When Jackie's dad had a relapse near the end of freshman year, Charlotte invited her into the fold. Then in the fall, Nina brought her roommate along after her mother passed away. The group's purview expanded to include Amy's grief, and eventually Reece's.

Jackie formalized the loose bitching circle into a real group after doing a psych project on peer-support therapy. The rules were simple: Don't be embarrassed, and don't be a dick to other members. For the most part that was all they needed. Others joined over time as word spread, but there were rarely more than six people at a meeting. They were a self-selecting bunch, most of them LGBTQIA+ and inclined to share their feelings.

The Dead, Divorced, and Otherwise Disappointing Parents support group taught Charlotte many lessons. First, it was not okay for her father to skip town when it became clear that baby Charlotte would not save her parents' marriage. Second, Charlotte was not a show dog for her mother to groom and correct and compare with other daughters at her country club. Third, abuse took many forms, from violence to control to neglect.

The support group was the closest thing Charlotte knew to acceptance. Her friends helped her see that there was nothing weak about her grief, her resentment, or her fear.

When she started dating Ben in junior year, she hoped he would join the 3Ds too. On the night they met, they stayed up until sunrise talking about their conservative families and stifling hometowns. Charlotte had expected him to be an aloof player, but Ben asked thoughtful questions about her childhood in Maryland and listened intently to her answers. He understood the Thorne family dynamics with intuitive grace, and he didn't need her to explain why she did everything she could to avoid going home between semesters. He kissed her bare shoulder and called her *strong*, and she felt that word all over her body.

Anytime she worried she had shared too much, Ben offered a parallel confession of his own. His parents were still together, but he wished they would separate for his mother's sake. Ben inspected a paint stain on Charlotte's palm as he mentioned his father's temper. She curled her fingers around his thumb, hurting for this boy and the weight he carried alone.

When she joked that she usually wouldn't hook up with someone affiliated with a fraternity, hoping to lighten the mood, Ben explained he only joined Sigma Delt because his father was a brother during his Hein days.

Even when I do whatever they tell me to do, it's still not enough, he said around four in the morning, his head in her lap and his eyes glassy.

Charlotte marveled at the delicate, almost magical intimacy of the conversation. She was grateful for his trust even as she wondered how she had earned it so quickly.

Ben laughed like he couldn't believe his own words. *I'm sorry, I shouldn't be dumping all of this on you. I know we just met, but I feel like I can be myself with you.*

I know what you mean, Charlotte said as she fell into something that seemed like love.

Her hopes were dashed during his first and only visit to Acronym. With Jackie away on study abroad, the responsibility of vetting Charlotte's beau fell to Nina. The new couple ate dim sum with her and Eliza in the backyard, and Charlotte tried not to squirm as Nina asked Ben polite but pointed questions about his politics (*leftist*), his ambitions (*congressman*) and his intentions (*I'm done with hookup culture. Aren't you, Charlotte? I think I found what I've been missing all along*).

Ben turned in a brilliant performance until the 3Ds came up in conversation. Eliza jokingly warned him that he should expect his girlfriend to bring their relationship issues to the group. Nina swatted her on the arm and laughed. *I'm sorry that I wanted their help addressing my attachment issues!*

Charlotte grinned at the girls, but Ben didn't find the joke funny. *I was raised not to air my dirty laundry*, he drawled as he stood up and collected their empty paper plates.

Nina frowned at his retreating figure, waiting until he was inside the house to raise her eyebrows. *What was that about?*

I think he's nervous, Charlotte said. *Meeting the friends is intimidating, you know? And you're not just a friend, you're my ex-girlfriend!*

She didn't admit it to Nina, but the weird comment didn't sit well with her either.

Back in his room at Sigma Delt, she asked him why he'd been so dismissive.

I just don't understand what you need a support group for when you have me, he said as he stroked his fingers up and down her arm, making her wriggle with arousal and confusion. *Besides, your mom likes me! Or she likes that I'm a boy. Problem solved.* He gave her a Cheshire-cat grin, his fingernails snagging the delicate skin at her wrist.

And so Charlotte stopped going to meetings. Not immediately, but soon. There was always something Ben wanted her to do instead: Go with him to a lax game, help him revise a political theory essay, stay in bed just a little longer, *C'mon, gorgeous, please?* Before she knew it, she rarely spent time with her friends. It was just the two of them in a claustrophobic loop: Charlotte circled from class to the dining hall to Ben's room at the frat house. She lost the group's valuable outside perspective, which in retrospect was exactly what he wanted.

Thankfully, Jackie could not be shaken off that easily. When her best friend returned from study abroad, Charlotte moved her belongings from her abandoned room in Acronym to the apartment she and Jackie shared until they graduated in 2013. It took five minutes for Jackie to figure out there was a problem.

Who are you and what have you done with Charlotte Thorne? she demanded upon seeing Charlotte's closet stocked with gifted designer threads from the Mead family. *Is that J.Crew? Have you been brainwashed?*

Their friendship nearly hadn't survived the following months. Jackie thought Ben was a phony legacy kid masquerading as an activist, and he thought she was an obnoxious hipster feminist. They were not subtle about their mutual loathing. Charlotte struggled to keep the two most important people in her life away from each other, wishing they would grow up for her sake. Jackie cooled it on the criticism when Charlotte asked her to stop, but Ben made no such effort.

She's such a snob, he said, wrinkling his nose. *She thinks she's better than me because I'm in a frat, which is so unfair.*

To avoid an argument, Charlotte spent more time with Ben than with Jackie, but still less time than he thought he deserved. When the girls did hang out, he blew up her phone with text messages and questions about when she would be done.

I know you love him, Jackie said diplomatically. *I know he's . . . charming. But this isn't the kind of relationship I imagined for you.* Charlotte didn't have a comeback for that. It wasn't what she imagined either.

The situation got worse before it got better, but Jackie never wavered. She always seemed to be waiting in the apartment when Charlotte came home, and she dropped everything to help when Charlotte was ready to ask. When the end finally came, Jackie stocked the fridge with ice cream and a box of PBR cans. She even had the grace to not say *I told you so.*

When Charlotte returned to the support group at the beginning of senior year, she found she had even less to contribute to conversation than she did before. She didn't know how to be vulnerable when she had so much to hide. Her love for Ben went in its own little storage cubby, firmly bolted shut. With such a large emotional wound suppurating in her mind, she couldn't process much of anything—not her mother's frosty disappointment that she had left Ben, not her confusing feelings for Reece, and certainly not the voice in her head telling her she was a humiliating, pathetic disaster.

Jackie gave her the Feelings Chart for Christmas that year. Charlotte turned red enough to match the designated shade for *anger*, but the communication aid did help. *I feel embarrassed*, she said when Jackie reminded her about a 3Ds meeting that afternoon.

Good job, Jackie said. *And I don't care, you're coming with me.*

Your name is Charlotte Thorne, she told her before they entered the dining hall, or Acronym, or whatever venue they'd reserved for an hour. *You are my best friend. You are safe here.* Then she kept her arm securely curled around Charlotte's shoulders just in case she lost her nerve.

Jackie squeezed her knee under the table. "You okay, Char? Still with us?"

Today, all this time later, Charlotte fought off the unexpected echoes of Ben's manipulation. For years she had kept her memories of that traumatic relationship neatly tucked away, but coming back to campus had knocked them loose.

Grief lingered like mold in a dormitory bathroom, forever fresh.

"Yeah, just thinking," she said. Jackie's concern was evident in her pinched brown eyes. "I'm glad I'm here." She hoped those simple words would communicate everything that she wanted them to.

Judging by the mushy look on Jackie's face, they did. "Me too, Char. Eat your sandwich."

Charlotte did as she was told and listened to the 3Ds catch up. She focused on the flavor and texture of each bite to ground herself. Nina's voice overlapped with Jackie's as they traded relationship misfires and pop culture obsessions. Jio berated her for not watching *Killing Eve*. Amy warned them what grief-related books weren't worth reading. As a group of mostly queer and underpaid rebels, they didn't put much stock in self-help gurus or spiritual quick fixes. Tarot cards and astrology were exceptions.

Finally, once they finished their main courses and relaxed into themselves, Jackie sat up straight. "Okay," she said. "Let's get into it. Who wants to go first?"

No one spoke up. Matt gave Jio a significant look, but Jio shook their head.

Jackie's eyes glinted as she studied each of them in turn. "Five years of bullshit? I know someone here needs to vent. Or brag!"

The stillness broke as Nina leaned forward. She smoothed her glossy black hair away from her face, tucking it behind her ears. "Fine, I'll brag. After years of trying, I finally put thousands of miles between me and my dad." They clapped. She fluttered her hand like a pageant queen accepting applause. "I know, I know. Thank you. It's a miracle."

"Is he still calling you all the time?" Jackie asked.

"He is, but reception is just *so* spotty in the Amazon." Nina flashed a cutting grin.

Charlotte couldn't blame her for being petty—Mr. Dorantes ranked in the Asshole Parent Hall of Fame. Charlotte was used to not telling her mother anything, but Nina had gone to sitcom-level lengths to hide their relationship from her overinvolved dad. At one point Charlotte crawled out the window when he dropped by Nina's (thankfully first-floor) dorm room for a surprise visit.

"Really though, the nature, the plant samples . . . it's amazing," Nina gushed. "I don't want to come back to the States when my grant ends. It's not like this is the best place to live right now anyway."

Charlotte winced while Matt nodded in understanding.

"Plus I switched to Android so Dad can't stalk me on location-sharing anymore. We Skype on the last Sunday of the month after church, and I only answer his emails once a week."

"Nice boundary-setting," Jackie said. "Good for you."

"It was a bitch and a half to get here, but worth it." Nina cracked her knuckles. "Okay, I'm done. Who's next?" She fixed Charlotte in her unwavering stare, raising a perfect eyebrow.

Charlotte looked down at her plate. She envied the relief Nina clearly felt after speaking, but there was no way she was sharing. She felt flooded enough already.

When the truth came out that Charlotte was not entirely straight, her mother didn't kick her out of the house. In the eyes of Olivia Harrington Thorne, evicting her only child would be garish and uncivilized. Her status as a single mother was scandalous enough in their Maryland suburb. Better for Charlotte to stay home and keep quiet than disappear entirely and get the neighbors talking.

And so, when Olivia found Charlotte kissing her lab partner in the driveway, she simply proceeded as if nothing had ever happened. No girlfriend, no chemistry puns, no flustered conversation about sexual fluidity over the dinner table. Olivia went on a spending spree for aggressively feminine clothes and hung them in Charlotte's closet, an unspoken demand to do a better job playing the part of straight, conservative daughter. Charlotte's queerness could not exist in their house. Charlotte played along like she always had. She didn't know what else to do. Surely if she got perfect grades, if she aced her AP tests, if she won an award for her watercolors, her mother would approve of her. If she stayed quiet, if she wore the stupid dresses, if she made an effort, her mother would do the same.

It didn't work. Her mother treated her like a tenant, and then a mouse living in the walls, and then a chipped piece of furniture that sat unused for so long it became invisible. The gap between them only grew as Charlotte left for Hein and shed her preppy camouflage. She patchworked her breaks with out-of-state internships and vacations with the Slaughters. It seemed like a détente was in the cards when she started dating Ben—her mother strongly approved of Charlotte having a boyfriend, especially one with a prestigious last name—but the momentary peace crumbled after the breakup.

How could you let a good man like that get away? Olivia hissed into the phone when Charlotte broke the news. *You were always such an ungrateful child.*

The summer before senior year, Charlotte rented a room from

some Hein grad students and worked at Terry's Bar, saving up as much money as possible and increasingly afraid for her future. By the time Charlotte graduated college, she and her mother rarely spoke.

Booth Thorne, her deadbeat diplomat father, did not know she was bisexual. He didn't know much about her at all. His only positive contribution was a clause of the divorce settlement that required him to pay for all four years of Charlotte's college education. She'd seen him in person a handful of times when his second wife reminded him of his daughter's existence and suggested that the three of them have lunch. On the bright side, he always picked up the check.

There was no point dwelling on that chapter of her past. Nothing anyone said would change the choices her parents had made. No advice could make it less infuriating and sad. She would always be estranged from her family, and she didn't need that to change. She didn't want it to.

Family was who shared their fries with you.

"Charlotte?" She looked up to find Jackie watching her, bossy group leader face in full effect. "Would you like to go next?"

She bit down on the inside of her cheek. In the past, her attendance had been enough to satisfy Jackie. Apparently that rule was no longer in effect.

"Nah. I'm good, thanks," she said. Jackie frowned, and Charlotte looked away.

Nina cleared her throat. "Let's take a break," she declared, sensing the collective need to take a beat. "We need ice cream."

"Or cake!" Jio added.

Nina gave Charlotte a searching look across the table. She nodded a perfunctory *I'm fine* before following Matt and Jio into the cafeteria.

She shook her arms out, willing the anxiety from her body. Being pressed to talk about her parents always made her edgy. She didn't want to open those boxes right now.

First she loaded up a plate with brownies and house-made Rice

Krispies Treats. Then she joined Matt at the soft serve machine. They created aesthetically unappealing but delicious sundaes with vanilla ice cream, chocolate syrup, and cookie crumbs.

"Sugar sludge," Charlotte chimed, toasting Matt with her bowl.

"Cheers," Matt said, a knowing look in his eyes.

When they got back to the table, Reece had arrived. Charlotte averted her eyes, her nerves already shot from the dinner conversation. She scattered a handful of spoons on the table for anyone who wanted a bite. Jackie grabbed a Rice Krispies Treat and dipped it into the ice cream.

"REECE'S PIECES," Jio cried.

Reece rose to hug them both. "It's been too long." He sat down next to Matt in Nina's original chair, diagonal across the table from Charlotte. She nudged the dessert plate toward him, and he took a brownie, giving her a grateful wink.

"You're right on time," Nina said. "I was talking about my dad's boundary issues."

"I don't have that problem," Reece said around a mouthful of chocolate goo. Amy winced at his dark joke, and he patted her hand on the table.

He had a smear of melted brownie above his lip. Charlotte smiled into her ice cream as he tried to lick it off.

"How's your mom?" Amy asked.

"She got another dog. Her pack of Pomeranians is now a small horde."

Matt perked up. "Do you have any pictures?"

These are my people, Charlotte thought.

Reece pulled out his iPhone. "Yeah, I have a bunch! Hold on." He swiped through his photos before handing the phone to Matt and Jio.

They immediately broke out laughing. "OH MY GOD there are so MANY," Jio gushed. "Look at their little faces!" They passed the phone to Jackie, who turned it so that Charlotte could see too: a photo of Reece's sister, Sarah, holding all four Pomeranians in her arms. They seemed displeased with the arrangement, one of them caught midwriggle with a furious scowl on his face.

"The difficult one is Hammer," Reece explained.

Charlotte chewed her thumb. Sarah had Reece's sunny grin, disproportionately large compared to the rest of her face. The siblings shared the same friendly quality, something about their thrown-back shoulders and rosy cheeks. They were comfortable in their own skin.

Jackie passed the phone to Amy and Nina. "Can your mom keep up with four dogs?"

"Yeah, she's fine," Reece said. "If they were bigger it would be a problem, but four Poms aren't much more difficult than three." He didn't mention that he lived at home, and Charlotte didn't bring it up.

"How's Sarah?" she asked instead. From what Charlotte remembered, Reece's sister must be a young adult by now. She swallowed a fresh clot of guilt and hoped her discomfort didn't show on her face.

Reece took his phone back from Nina. "She's good! She's studying engineering." Jio whistled, and Reece smiled. "Yeah, she was always smarter than me."

"Do you want to talk about anything?" Jackie asked, sitting up straight again. Their leader believed in using body language to create a safe environment for sharing. Charlotte found it more sweet than authoritative.

"I miss my dad," Reece said matter-of-factly. "I wish he could come to Sarah's graduation. I wish he could tell me what to do with my life."

Reece spoke with the calm of someone who'd been riding the grief rodeo for over a decade. Mr. Krueger passed away after a long battle with cancer while Reece was in high school. Reece spent most of college trying to find solid ground again. The hockey team gave him structure, but he spent off-seasons alternating his all-nighters between the science building and the loudest party he could find. Amy brought him to a 3Ds meeting after they met at the student counseling center as juniors.

It took another few months for Charlotte to cross his path—he joined the support group during her attendance lapse. When she arrived early for her first meeting post-Ben, Reece bounded into the room a few minutes later. He clung to a cup of coffee, fresh stubble disguising the sharp cut of his jaw.

She already knew who he was. Everyone knew Reece Krueger—Hein University was tiny, making Reece a big jock fish in a small liberal arts pond. Handsome midwestern hockey players did not go unnoticed. Especially handsome midwestern hockey players who made oat pancakes and margaritas in the morning for their one-night stands.

Besides, Charlotte doubted he remembered her, but they lived in the same dorm their freshman year. Their paths crossed occasionally in the laundry room. She remembered his next-door neighbor complaining about the thinness of their shared wall.

Other than that, they didn't run in the same circles. She expected him to nod and take a seat across the room. Instead, Reece gave her a breezy "Hello!" and sat down next to her. With the discretion of a curious golden retriever, he peered at her iPad on the table. She'd been working on a portrait for the school paper before he interrupted. Under her stylus, an angular face returned his stare. "That's Annika, right? Annika Gronlund?"

Charlotte glanced at her draft, with its unfinished nose and missing eyes. She'd been drawing her classmate from memory, so it wasn't like he'd seen a reference photo. "Yeah," Charlotte said, giving the bro beside her a second look. "I illustrate the op-eds."

Reece nodded, satisfied. "Thought so. Her bangs are spot-on."

He sipped his coffee as she resumed her sketch, her shoulders unfolding as she relaxed. It was impossible to feel uncomfortable around him for long. They shared a cozy silence until the rest of the group arrived.

When Reece took the seat beside her at the next meeting, he brought her a cup of coffee.

Charlotte wished she'd been there for Reece's first 3Ds meeting. If it hadn't been for Ben, she would have met him so much earlier.

"I'm seeing a great new therapist who specializes in grief and addiction," he continued, bringing Charlotte back to the present. "Now I have a whole bunch of healthy, boring coping mechanisms."

"How was the anniversary this year?" Amy asked.

"Eh, weird. People kind of forgot." Reece broke off another corner of his brownie and popped it in his mouth. He chewed it contemplatively. "I drove up to see Sarah and we got dinner. She doesn't remember him as well as I do. Sometimes I feel guilty, like I got all the good memories."

Charlotte envied Reece's ability to articulate his emotions. He did so without embarrassment or fear, like he was commenting on the changing seasons. Some of it resulted from practice—she knew Reece had worked hard to build those skills in therapy. But mostly it was just who he was. The man sitting across from her seemed dialed in to himself in a way few twenty-somethings were.

"I know that's not my fault," Reece continued. "But you know how it is."

"And your mom?" Jackie asked.

"She went on a cruise that week. Her book club friends planned a whole trip."

Jio laughed. "Did she bring the dogs?"

Reece dropped his gaze to the ice cream, but Charlotte didn't think anyone else noticed. "I watched them," he said without elaborating.

She wanted to reach across the table and take his hand. But she fought the urge, knowing that would (a) arouse suspicion, and (b) be super weird.

Amy giggled. "I can't imagine you walking four Pomeranians."

"It's not easy. I'm fencing in the backyard so they can romp around."

Charlotte enjoyed the image of Reece wearing a tool belt as he hammered a wooden beam into the ground. His forearms featured prominently in her fantasy.

"What about y'all?" Reece asked. "Has everyone already gone?"

"Just me," Nina said.

Matt cleared his throat. "I'll go." He and Jio exchanged nervous smiles. Charlotte got the impression they were psyching each other up. "For both of us, really."

She suspected what was coming. Her hunch was confirmed when Matt took his partner's hand. "We're getting married. Mostly for insurance. My plan is a lot better than Jio's."

"Saving the polar bears doesn't offer *dental*," Jio stage-whispered.

"Congratulations!" Nina cried. She lifted her soda. "To many years of happiness and clean teeth!"

Reece raised his drink too. The whole group cheersed and clinked their plastic cups. Charlotte beamed at her friends. No one deserved happiness more than Jio and Matt. Out of any couple she knew, they worked the hardest to love each other the way they deserved to be loved.

Matt nodded in gratitude for their well-wishes, but he sobered quickly. Jio squeezed his hand. "My parents are furious," he continued. "I didn't expect them to be supportive, and we're not inviting them to the wedding. But they're not letting my brother come."

Charlotte shifted in her seat. She couldn't help but notice how Reece's face twisted in confusion as he listened.

"Does Steve need their permission?" he asked.

"Kinda?" Matt frowned. "Let's just say the church wouldn't be thrilled about him participating in our heathen ritual."

"And then there's the flights," Jio added. "He's only seventeen, he can't afford a trip to D.C. on his own."

"Maybe they'll come around?" Amy asked, not quite seeming to believe her own optimism. "Steve will find a way, he's so clever."

Matt shrugged, unconvinced.

"That sucks, dude, I'm sorry," Nina said. "It really hurts when your family can't just be happy that you're happy."

Unbidden, a memory returned of her mother's grimace when Charlotte came home after her first semester at Hein, makeup-free and wearing a loose flannel and combat boots. *Get upstairs and change*, Olivia hissed, *you look like a vagrant.*

Her grip tightened on her spoon.

Reece wrapped his arm around Matt's shoulders and gave him a sideways hug. "I love you, man. You don't deserve this."

Matt nodded but didn't say more.

Jio brought the back of Matt's hand to their lips for a small kiss. Charlotte watched affection bloom in Matt's eyes. She swallowed around the lump in her throat. "Is there anything we can do?" she asked.

"Not really. We'll figure it out. And please, no presents. We don't have any space."

"What about your parents, Jio?" Jackie asked. "Are they being supportive?"

Jio rolled their eyes. "My dad gave me a long speech about how marriage is a trap, and this is the *worst* mistake of my life. But he also offered to pay for most of it, so who's to say, really?" They grinned, and Matt laughed despite himself. "We're thinking of just going to the courthouse and spending his money on a vacation."

"Where are you thinking?" Nina asked. "Might I suggest South America?" She waggled her eyebrows.

"I've never left the country," Matt mused. "Anywhere that needs a passport would be an adventure."

"You tell me if Peru starts calling your name, I'll put you up."

"You're all invited, duh," Jio promised. "We'll try to stream it on Twitch for people who can't make it. And I still need ideas for the wedding hashtag!"

"Let me know if you need a witness, I can drive over," Reece offered. "St. Louis isn't *that* far."

"Only if you bring dogs!"

Reece laughed. "We'll put Hammer in a tutu. He can be the flower pal."

The conversation turned to wedding attire and suiting trends. Charlotte zoned out, still processing the hurt in Matt's voice as he talked about his family. Matt's parents wrapped themselves in their faith as they exiled their son and kept him from seeing his younger brother. Thankfully they weren't the most tech-savvy bigots, and they didn't know Matt and Steve talked all the time on Signal.

Was it better or worse to have a sibling? What did it feel like to have someone in your family who loved you and accepted you, but who witnessed your humiliation at the hands of your parents? Would it have been easier to survive her mother's disgust if Charlotte had a brother or sister by her side? Or would that mean there was one more person to vanish when she didn't fit her family's expectations?

As Jio shared their thoughts on stitched versus glued jackets, they ran their fingertips back and forth across Matt's open palm. Matt didn't squirm or give any sign he noticed at all, just nodded at some point his fiancé made. He accepted Jio's physical affection like it was second nature, his fiancé the one person allowed beyond his proper exterior.

Charlotte wished she could ask him how he did it. Matt's parents refused to love him for who he was, and now he was marrying the love of his life.

When the 3Ds exhausted their knowledge of professional tailoring, Matt turned to Jackie. "Your turn."

Jackie sighed dramatically. She placed both her hands flat on the table. The pose reminded Charlotte of an executive building suspense before announcing a strategy shift.

"My dad has finally agreed to go to therapy."

Charlotte's heart dropped. Jackie avoided looking at her, smirking at Nina instead.

"WHAT?" Jio yelled. "How?"

"He *didn't,*" Amy gasped.

"Oh," Charlotte let out.

Mr. Slaughter was a generous, exuberant man, and a doting parent. He was also an alcoholic. He regularly attended Alcoholics Anonymous, but Charlotte knew Jackie's dad white-knuckled it at best. Periodic bouts of depression made sobriety even more of a challenge.

Mr. Slaughter was the closest thing Charlotte knew to a father figure. He helped her apply for unemployment after *ChompNews* laid her off, and he personally invited her to Thanksgiving dinner every fall. Jackie convincing him to start therapy was a major coup, the result of years of careful coaxing and pressure.

And Charlotte didn't know.

"It was all Mom," Jackie explained. "She had a tough time at work and one of her friends recommended someone. When Mom liked it, she pushed Dad to book a session with someone else in the practice. She talked him out of all that bullshit about it being self-indulgent."

The millennials around the dinner table nodded—they'd all had to convince an older relative that therapy wasn't just talking about yourself for two hundred dollars an hour. The 3Ds had to have an emergency Skype meeting after the dressing-down Nina received from her dad when she mentioned her therapist in front of their priest at mass.

Charlotte's thumb rose to her lips. She chewed her nail, noxious green guilt swirling in her stomach again. How could she have not known something this huge? Why hadn't Jackie told her?

Or had she not been listening? It'd been a while since their last FaceTime call, but they'd just spent the entire day together.

Shit.

Charlotte hadn't asked her about family. Or about work. Or anything other than a smug joke about dating apps. She'd been too distracted by her job and boy baggage to think of anything else.

In fairness, everyone else seemed shocked too. Everyone except

Reece, who had his chin propped on his hand as he took in everyone's reactions.

Interesting. Maybe she'd missed a big change in Reece's life too. She would have to ask him later.

"I'm helping him find someone who specializes in addiction," Jackie continued.

Reece raised his free hand. "Text me if you need a recommendation. I know where to look."

"Can I call you about that too?" Jio asked. "Wedding stuff is going to wreck my brain and I need to find a practice with a sliding-scale system."

Reece nodded. "Of course, anytime."

"I hope it works out for him," Nina said to Jackie. "He's a good guy. I remember when he drove up from New York with a new laptop when you spilled soda all over yours."

"You should probably get him a dude therapist," Reece recommended. "He'll have a lot of masculinity stuff to unpack."

Charlotte tried to come up with something to say, but guilt clouded her ability to think. Her best friend must have picked up on the awkward silence. Jackie gave her a small smile, code for *we'll talk about it later.*

Matt checked his watch. "Sorry to bail early, but we need to go to Mass Liquors before they close." Jio stacked their plates as Matt stood and grabbed his messenger bag. "There's a disco tonight at Acronym if anyone wants to come."

"We'll be there," Jackie said for them both. Charlotte had been looking forward to dancing at Acronym again for months, if not for several years. And goodness knew she needed to ask her best friend some actual questions tonight.

Reece groaned. "Damn, I'll be on Atwood. The hockey seniors are throwing a party and I promised Garrett I'd help corral the boys."

"We know where the straights will be." Jio poked Reece's shoulder.

Reece grinned sheepishly. "Don't rub salt in the wound. I wanna get my Carly Rae on too."

"It'll go late, it always does," Matt assured him. "Thanks for arranging this, Jackie. It was nice to hold space as a group again." He held out his hand to her, and she gave it a hearty shake.

"My pleasure! We should resurrect the group chat, maybe do regular video hangouts if anyone needs them."

"I'd like that a lot." With that, Matt took their empty plates from Jio and jutted his head toward the exit. "After you, fiancé." Jio blew the table an air-kiss before weaving through the mostly deserted tables.

Amy checked her phone for the time. "We should head out too. There's a reading at the English department and I promised my boss I'd scout for talent." She buttoned up her cardigan as Nina swept pizza crumbs from the table onto her plate.

And then there were three. Reece helped himself to a Rice Krispies Treat from the dessert plate. He pulled it apart into gooey chunks with his long fingers and devoured it bite by bite.

The girls hid their laughter as he feasted. He realized they were staring at him as he licked sugar off his palm. "What?"

"Weren't you just at dinner?" Jackie asked.

"It was all vegan food."

"Ah."

Charlotte twisted in her chair, popping a kink in her shoulder.

"Please see a chiropractor," Jackie scolded without any real malice.

She rolled her eyes. "Yes, Mom."

Reece laughed, the rich sound enveloping Charlotte in a cherry blossom glow. She noticed his eyes dip from her face to her neck, and then a little lower to her cleavage—her shirt rode down while she stretched. She shifted her shoulders to pull the fabric back up, and Reece's stare fixed on the tattered Rice Krispies Treat on the table in front of him.

Busted.

Jackie pushed back her chair. "Okay, time for Operation Leftovers. Anyone want a refill?" She grabbed their cups without waiting for an answer and strutted away, hip-checking chairs that blocked her path.

"She scares me sometimes," Reece admitted. He stuck his index finger in Charlotte's melted sundae and licked the vanilla ice cream off. It wasn't intended to be seductive, more like a child who couldn't help himself.

Still, Charlotte couldn't fight off a smile. "There's an extra spoon right here," she said, sliding one across the table.

"It's more fun this way." He leaned forward to take another swipe of her ice cream, his eyes bright. "You've already been exposed to my diseases."

What a goddamn pleasure it was to be teased by this man.

"I could have new diseases," Charlotte baited. "You don't know what I've been up to since graduation. Maybe I have swine flu."

"Oh really? Which one of us spends more time with animals, Charlie?"

"That depends. Do venture capitalists count?"

Reece's chuckle rumbled around his chest like a lion's purr. "Probably."

Charlotte nudged some of the Oreo crumbles to Reece's side of the bowl, and he finally picked up the spoon to scoop them up.

She considered the flirtatious undertone of their banter. It had been there all day, as if their horny standoff in the hallway—and their bone-crushing good-night hug—had woken it from hibernation. She didn't know how to square this playful, open Reece with the Reece who walked her home last night. If he was still interested in her, why hadn't he kissed her?

"Last night was fun," Reece said as if he'd read her mind. He kept his eyes on the ice cream, hunting for another cookie chunk.

Charlotte studied his face, but she couldn't detect any hint at what he meant. The statement was a Rorschach test, open to interpretation. She didn't know what she wanted to read in it.

No, she knew what she wanted. She just wasn't sure if she could handle it.

"Will there be beer pong at the hockey party?" she asked.

Reece's eyes flicked up to her face. She innocently spooned some ice cream into her mouth. He watched her lips move before looking over her shoulder out the window, his Adam's apple bobbing as he swallowed. "You know it's not an Atwood party without pong."

"I think I need practice," she declared. Practice with her throwing technique. Practice enjoying the company of someone so kind.

Reece spooned up another cookie chunk. "We need a team name."

"Team Hammer," Charlotte suggested.

Reece huffed, the laugh startled out of him. "Yes, that's it."

Making a good person laugh was one of the purest pleasures in life, alongside Jackie's fresh-baked pumpkin bread and finding a movie she'd always wanted to watch streaming online for free. Charlotte wasn't a loud person—she would never be the life of the party or the host of a hit podcast. Her sense of humor was quick and weird, and it only emerged around people she trusted.

"Thank you for earlier, by the way," he said. "For not mentioning I moved home."

"Oh." Charlotte dropped her spoon in the bowl and folded her arms on the table. "Of course. That's none of my business."

"Still. I appreciate it. I'm not embarrassed, I just . . ." He trailed off, his eyes narrowing. "Everyone's doing so well."

"It certainly feels that way," Charlotte admitted.

"I wish someone warned me when I volunteered to be class secretary that for the rest of my life, people would email me their accomplishments." Reece gestured with his spoon, trying to infuse his words with humor even as his insecurity bled through. "Anytime someone sells their startup, or gets married, or publishes a book, I'm the first person to know. Meanwhile I'm broke, single, and living with my mom."

Charlotte arched a blond eyebrow. "You mean Netflix hasn't optioned your miniseries?"

"What an exciting binge that would be. The 2016 episode would be one long nap."

"You could get Lexapro to sponsor it."

Reece considered the idea as he ate the last of the ice cream. *"Dachshunds and Depression: The Reece Krueger Story."*

"It could be worse. At least you still have all your hair."

That earned another booming laugh. Reece ruffled the hair at the back of his head like he was checking that it hadn't wandered off. "That's true. Not everyone here can say that. Did you see Thomas Irons?"

Charlotte widened her eyes. "Yikes, right?"

"Then again, Thomas has a speedboat and I've barely touched my student loans. I feel so behind." Reece sighed and dropped his spoon in the empty bowl. "It's like we're seeing the Instagram version of everyone's lives in person."

"Yes," she breathed. "Exactly."

She thought of every acquaintance at the reception who flashed their engagement ring or described their new business venture. They said garbage like *it's small but it's wonderful to have a place upstate* and *there's just no innovation left in the Fortune 500.* And then they feigned humility, peppering the conversation with their accomplishments before pivoting abruptly to *but how about you, how have you been?*

Everyone also spoke in precisely crafted Instagram captions.

#Blessed.

"Even I'm doing it," she said. "People ask me about *Front End* and I say, 'Oh, it's so exciting, I meet such interesting people!'" Charlotte snatched another napkin from the table and twisted it between her fingers. "You know who I meet? Rich assholes."

Reece leaned back in his chair, balancing it on two legs. "What do you wish you could say?" he asked. "What's the unfiltered version?"

She didn't need to think about it. Just like last night by the vending machine, telling Reece the truth came easier than it should have. "Not a single day goes by that I don't fantasize about lighting a fire in the supply closet."

He whistled. "Workplace arson. A classic."

Charlotte got caught up in the glint in his eyes. She lowered her voice to a deadly serious drawl. "I want to stab my boss in the neck with a box cutter."

"Vivid! What's wrong with him?"

Her face darkened. It felt like her heart was beating behind her eyes. "In HR's opinion, nothing."

The humor fell from Reece's face immediately. He settled his chair back down on all fours. When he asked the inevitable follow-up, his words came quietly. "And in your opinion?"

Reece held his breath when he focused, sucking in his cheeks without realizing it. She took in his concern, wondering at it like a clever puzzle at a museum gift shop. What should she make of it?

Reece couldn't relate to the shitty behavior of his gender, that weird Good Guy miracle of adept parenting and inner strength. Back in college he was still learning how to process his self-righteous confusion. When Jackie complained to him about so-and-so's disrespectful text messages, Reece spouted genuine but irritating exclamations like *how could he?* and *I don't understand what's wrong with these guys!*

Jackie would roll her eyes and snap that the answer was always *the patriarchy, Krueger.*

Maybe that was partly why Charlotte never told him about Ben. She didn't understand her ex's behavior, and she couldn't imagine carrying Reece's outrage on top of her shame.

But tonight, Reece remained silent as she decided what to tell him. He didn't press or pontificate. She knew intuitively that he wouldn't ask her to explain.

She chose a piece of the story, just one. “Roger’s philanthropy schtick is a smoke screen. It’s branding. Behind closed doors he’s a jackass who just doesn’t want to pay taxes.”

Reece frowned but didn’t interrupt, giving Charlotte space to decide if she wanted to share more. She took it. “He loves to rant. ‘The #MeToo movement has gone too far, millennials are so sensitive, reverse racism,’ that kind of thing.”

She closed her eyes. She thought of the bright, colorful pantsuits in her closet that she no longer wore to the office. She remembered the comments about her body that Roger made in his emails to board members that she had to read because reading his email was her *job*.

How many afternoons had she hidden in the bathroom as she hyperventilated, her hand clasped over her mouth?

Anger tightened around her throat like a fist, just as it had during a humiliating, incomprehensible meeting with HR about Roger’s conduct. *Maybe you misunderstood?* Workplace norms were slow to change, after all, and Roger was an esteemed titan of industry. She should let these things go if she wanted to survive in media. Toughen up, let it roll off her shoulders. *Take it as a compliment.*

“What bothers me the most,” Charlotte said slowly, “is that he enjoys making me uncomfortable. He acts like I’m not in the room, but he *knows* I’m there.”

Reece’s face contorted as he grappled with his reaction. One of his hands gripped the edge of the table in either anger or concern, she couldn’t tell. “You need to quit, Charlotte,” he said, his voice level.

The rage in her chest subsided into that same miserable wound she lived with most days. He spoke with such clarity, like it was really that simple. But it didn’t bother her the way Jackie’s unsolicited advice did. He wasn’t using her work situation to show off his moral outrage.

And he didn’t come from money.

“I just can’t,” she said.

“That’s the definition of a toxic workplace environment. Like, I’m not going to mansplain harassment to you, but *holy shit*.”

His unwavering support soothed the wound a little bit. He didn't need to see the emails or verify the dates involved. He just believed her.

"Thank you," she said. "Seriously. But I should be moving to another team soon."

Reece looked like he was about to say something but then thought better of it, his mouth closing into a thin line. He drummed his fingers on the table. "Okay. You know what you're doing. But if he ever fucks with you again, I will drive up to New York and use that box cutter myself."

In this current climate, she shouldn't find a man threatening workplace violence on her behalf romantic. And yet she did.

"You are a catch, you know," she said. He gave her a funny look, not buying it, but she bit her lip and barreled through her embarrassment. He deserved to know. "I mean it, Reece. You're in a transition period right now, but you'll figure it out."

God help her, his eyes actually softened. A splotch of pink appeared on his cheek. "You will too," he said. "Team Hammer, yeah?" He extended his fist for her to bump, which she did.

"Absolutely."

Jackie wove her way back to their table, her plate stacked with brownies and fruit. Charlotte reached for the tote bag on the back of Jackie's chair and took out a stack of Tupperware containers.

"Oh my god, you guys are evil geniuses," Reece said.

"We know what we're doing," Charlotte agreed, popping off the lids one by one.

Chapter 5

FROM: Roger Ludermore <rl@frontendreview.com>
SUBJECT: FWD: JULY PROFILE OF ORGASMR APP

FROM: Roger Ludermore <rl@frontendreview.com>
SUBJECT: disregard previous about orgasmr app, was a scam

CHARLOTTE TRIED NOT to blink as Jackie traced her lash line with a sharp black pencil. Her eyes watered from the strain until Jackie's face swam before her.

"Please do not stab me, I can't pull off an eye patch."

"I won't stab you if you stop whining," Jackie chided.

Charlotte missed everything about their Friday night ritual. First came makeup application as they blasted pop music—Hailee Steinfeld belted about self-love from her laptop. Next Jackie would berate her for having nothing to wear, then she'd bully Charlotte into borrowing an outfit. Last, they would replenish their cocktails and toast to the night ahead, and to the morning that felt like it would never ever come.

In college, the beginning of the night was the best part. Anything could happen at Hein: They might fall in love with a stranger, or tell the perfect joke, or have the best sex of their lives. Their giddy anticipation held a certain magic before it could be crushed by parties discovered too early or too late. Hell was other people's jungle juice.

No roommate would ever come close to Jackie. During the magical three years Charlotte lived with her, they learned about color theory and riot grrrl punk and bell hooks and mysterious UTIs. Every problem was a shared problem, and Jackie encouraged her to take up space in their home. They covered the walls of their apartment with reprints of 1970s concert posters: Debbie Harry's sultry red lipstick, Patti Smith scowling in a black leather jacket with nothing underneath, Grace Jones's sharp profile against a bright yellow background. A magnet on the fridge held up a postcard of the Clash's *London Calling* album cover.

Charlotte used their decor as inspiration. When she wasn't preoccupied with homework, she messed around with graphic design and layout. Sophomore year she created posters for Jackie's late-night radio show: *Punk Power Hour with DJ Slaughter*, aggressive pink lettering over a high-contrast black-and-white photo of Jackie behind the mic. The poster was a smash hit, and folks around campus took notice. She was asked to make urgent, eye-catching posters for Hein's Sex Education Club and obnoxious, blocky prints for student bands who paid her in meal plan points. Her artwork spoke for her all over campus. On the page she could be loud, chaotic, and colorful. It felt like Jackie's influence, or maybe Charlotte just needed her help unleashing her inner defiance.

Charlotte and Jackie were more than friends—they were sisters. They bickered like sisters too. In college they hashed out their issues directly; Jackie insisted on it. But now something was off, a crevasse Charlotte hadn't noticed until her foot stepped out into empty air.

Why didn't Jackie tell her about her dad? When did Charlotte stop knowing the important events in her best friend's life? Or was she being melodramatic? Did Jackie not tell her, or did Charlotte not ask?

"That's good news," she blurted out. "About your dad, I mean."

"Stop talking or I'll mess up," Jackie murmured. She licked her thumb to correct a smudge at the corner of Charlotte's eye. "Okay, that's done." She whipped out a mascara wand. "Next!"

Charlotte bit her lip, not sure if she should press Jackie on her deflection. Jackie had always been better at dealing with other people's problems than facing her own. Maybe she truly didn't want to discuss it. "None on my lower lashes. I don't want to be a trash panda."

"Righto, will skip. Blink?" Jackie coaxed the wand over Charlotte's upper lashes and made a satisfied noise. "Ugh, that makes such a difference. Your lashes are so light."

"Part of the whole being-blond thing, I'm afraid."

Jackie took Charlotte's jaw in her hand. She moved her head from side to side, studying her face. "I'm thinking no lipstick. Anything I put on you will just wind up all over Reece's face."

"I don't know what you're talking about."

Jackie smirked but didn't comment. "We're almost done. I'll give you a lollipop if you can sit still a little longer."

Charlotte stuck out her tongue.

"Mature," Jackie teased, but she didn't laugh. Charlotte stayed still as she smoothed a hint of pink paint across her cheeks with her fingertips. "There. You're finished."

Charlotte slid off the bed and examined her reflection in the mirror. It never failed to blow her mind how few products Jackie needed to transform her. Her face looked brighter, her eyes bigger and more vibrant. The woman staring back at her was symmetrical and poised, the makeup subtle but effective.

The exhausted woman who'd arrived on campus yesterday afternoon, harried and dusty, had vanished. She'd been replaced by a dewy blonde with big brown eyes.

"You're a miracle worker." Charlotte wiggled her eyebrows at Jackie. "What do you think?"

"Gorgeous. What are you wearing?"

"I have nothing that will impress you. Jeans and a tank top."

"And let me guess, your loafers." Jackie sighed. She turned to consider her bookshelf of options. "I can't believe you have no going-out clothes. The shoes we can't help, but at least you'll be comfortable. Here, try this on." Jackie thrust a short-sleeved button-down in her direction.

Charlotte stripped off her tank top and put on the shirt, running her hands over the linen. It looked vintage, a beachy beige with thin blue vertical stripes. She left the top three buttons undone to reveal the pale column of her throat. Her explosion of messy curls balanced out the boyishness of the fit.

"Beautiful," Jackie decided. "I want to take you sailing and name our children after the royal family."

Charlotte plucked at the collar. "I feel a bit like Taylor Swift's date on the Fourth of July."

"You should *be* so lucky to date Taylor Swift."

She turned around to face her friend. "Thank you. You know my style better than I do."

Jackie chucked her under the chin. "Correct!" Then she turned around to mull over her outfit options, fists at her hips.

Charlotte had an easier time finding her words without Jackie looking at her. It felt wrong to just drop the conversation about her dad when Jackie chose to bring him up in support group. She had to at least try.

"And I mean it about your dad," Charlotte said to her back. "I wish you'd told me."

"You've been busy," Jackie said nonchalantly. "Help me pick an outfit?"

Well, okay then.

Charlotte tried not to take the avoidance personally. She folded her arms across her chest and looked at Jackie's bookshelf of clothing. "You're going to be dancing. You'll want something that will move well."

"And that won't stink." Jackie picked up a black T-shirt with the college radio station's logo on the front. The fabric had thinned from so many washes. "Fuck it, I'm going full 2011." She paired the shirt with a high-waisted miniskirt and Converse high-tops.

Charlotte checked her phone while Jackie dressed.

"Any updates?" Jackie asked as she wiggled her ass into the skirt.

TEXT MESSAGE FROM MATT LARSEN TO CHARLOTTE THORNE, 9:07 PM: Doors are open!

TEXT MESSAGE FROM REECE KRUEGER TO CHARLOTTE THORNE, 9:09 PM: I think I'm too old for house music. don't tell anyone

Charlotte bit back a smile at the unfamiliar sight of Reece's name in her notifications. He'd fired the first volley. She bit her lip before typing her response.

TEXT MESSAGE FROM CHARLOTTE THORNE TO REECE KRUEGER, 9:12 PM: I'm telling literally everyone.

"Hellooooooo." Jackie watched her expectantly. "News?"

"Matt says the doors are open."

"Awesome." Her best friend set up shop at the mirror to work on her makeup, leaving Charlotte in her own little world on her screen.

Reece was typing . . . She watched the thinking bubble appear and expand as his text arrived.

TEXT MESSAGE FROM REECE KRUEGER TO CHARLOTTE THORNE, 9:13 PM: traitor

Delight quivered up her spine. It had been years since her college hookup days, but she remembered this dance like it was only yesterday. If someone was into you, they'd strike up a conversation between eight and ten P.M. via text, the tone deceptively chill. Over the course of the evening, they'd touch base, ask where you were, keep checking the pulse of your interest. Eventually someone suggested a place to meet up, usually neutral territory where you'd flirt and make out before relocating somewhere more private.

The fact that Reece reached out to her confirmed that this wasn't just a one-way fantasy. He was *interested.* He could have texted Jackie, his actual friend, but he'd chosen to text *her.* And god help her, he knew how to banter. Her last girlfriend, Merielle, texted like an artificial intelligence bot coded by a fourteen-year-old. And it wasn't like the gentlemen of NYC Tinder offered scintillating conversation . . .

"How do I look?" Jackie stepped back from the mirror and twirled around.

After dinner, Charlotte had brushed out Jackie's hair and woven it into a double French braid. Paired with her outfit and signature red lipstick, the hairstyle made Jackie look like a babysitter who would teach your kids about socialism but still get them to bed on time.

"You look amazing. Very sophomore year but with more self-esteem."

"I should hope so." Jackie hopped up onto the bed next to her, careful not to spill her drink. "Let's take a selfie before we sweat it off."

Charlotte closed out of her texts and handed Jackie her iPhone. "You do it, your arms are longer than mine."

Jackie took the phone without complaint. She held it aloft at a flattering angle. Charlotte smiled and willed herself to relax into this moment of happiness.

It's a Friday night. I am twenty-one. Jackie Slaughter is my best friend. We are going to a party.

There is no train ticket in my wallet. There is no Monday morning meeting to prep for. There is no text message to send my landlord about fixing the radiator.

I am safe. I am home.

Jackie took a bunch of pictures. She flicked through them and laughed. "We look like a lesbian *Odd Couple* reboot."

"We haven't aged a day," Charlotte decided. "I'll send them to you."

"Please do. Everyone on Instagram needs to see how much fun we're having. And get a new phone, that crack is terrible."

TEXT MESSAGE FROM REECE KRUEGER TO CHARLOTTE THORNE, 9:45 PM: don't tell me if they play Carly Rae at Acronym, it'll break my heart

ACRONYM OCCUPIED AN old Victorian on the south edge of campus. The house looked a little worse for wear, its paint chipped and the front path overgrown. For decades the student newspaper tracked a conspiracy theory that the administration didn't invest in Acronym's maintenance because queer alumni were less likely to donate to Hein's endowment. Every year, shingles fell from the roof like dead skin.

Students did their best to reattach shutters and freshen up the peeling paint. Baby gays like Charlotte taught themselves how to fix squeaky hinges and install new banisters. All the DIY repairs gave Acronym the look of a beloved pair of jeans, patched over and well worn.

What the house lacked in refinement, it made up for with its charm. To walk through its rooms was to visit an ad hoc museum of queer history at the university. Concert posters from Queen to Dua Lipa lined the hallways. The names of residents covered the bathroom walls, decades of signatures written in looping permanent marker. Abandoned shoes littered the entrance. A fresh pot of coffee and a snack always waited in the kitchen.

By the time Charlotte and Jackie arrived for the disco, every room at Acronym was packed. The house purred with pop music and laughter. All of the undergrads wore sequins, and alumni danced among them like they hadn't heard music since 2013.

Charlotte paused just inside the front door to breathe in the powerful nostalgia of take-out food and incense. More than any other place on campus, Acronym felt like home. While Hein University had a wonderful arts program, Charlotte chose the school for its queer community. The first time she entered the program house, eighteen years of shame and defensiveness lifted from her shoulders. At Acronym, the front door was always open, and the people were always kind.

Jackie beelined to the kitchen. Charlotte zigzagged through the crowd to catch up. They found Matt sitting on the counter beside a student she didn't recognize, most likely a senior if he was still on campus.

"Hey, ladies! Glad you could make it." Matt shook their hands in greeting, one after the other.

"Wouldn't miss it for the world!" Jackie yelled over the music. "Booze?"

He pointed to the kitchen island behind them.

Jackie immediately set about making cocktails. Charlotte turned to the student by Matt's side and extended her hand. "Hi, I'm Charlotte. She/her."

The student took her hand and shook it firmly, wide-eyed and fabulous in a green jumpsuit. A cluster of enamel pins nestled on the breast pocket, including a transgender flag and an old-fashioned video camera. "Wynn, nice to meet you. He/him is good."

"Wynn was telling me about his summer plans," Matt said. "He'll be right downstairs from me at the Human Rights Campaign, filming election spots and interviewing activists."

"No way, that's awesome." Charlotte raised her voice to make sure she could be heard over Ariana Grande blaring from the living room. "Matt's a good guy to know. He'll take care of you." She nodded in Matt's direction.

"I can tell." Wynn's eyes were a lovely blue threaded with silver. He looked at her with reverence, the way Charlotte used to stare at returning Hein alumnae. Now Charlotte was the queer adult, forging a path into the real world. Impostor syndrome licked at her loafers.

"What about you, what do you do?" Wynn asked.

"I work in media."

"Dope, where?"

"*The Front End Review*. It's mostly tech stuff, lots of Silicon Valley stories." Wynn's eyes widened even more. Charlotte took in his misplaced awe.

It didn't feel right. Acronym was a place to be honest.

She checked to see that Jackie was out of earshot before she leaned in and added, "Honestly, I hate it!"

The world didn't end. No one screamed or dropped their drinks. Wynn just laughed, nodding politely. This was small talk at a party, not an interview. No one actually cared all that much. Charlotte grinned at Wynn as the last murmurs of her anxiety quieted in her brain.

Matt watched her with what looked like pride. "Media's the worst," he said diplomatically.

Right on time, Jackie returned with cocktails. She handed one to Charlotte before turning to Matt and Wynn. "This party's wild! I had no idea so many people from our year had come out."

"It's 2018," Matt drawled. "Everyone worth knowing is gay."

Jackie took Charlotte's hand and gave it an energetic yank. "I wanna go dance!"

"Jio's out there." Matt pointed through the archway into the living room. "They were in the front last time I saw them."

Charlotte had a second to wave good-bye to Wynn and Matt

before Jackie tugged her out of the kitchen. They quickly found Jio voguing on the dance floor with a trio of delighted seniors, their red sequined blouse catching the lights.

"LADIES!" Jio screamed when they recognized the girls in the dark.

"JIO!" Jackie immediately dragged them into doing the bump. Charlotte laughed and did an unimpressive two-step beside them. She sipped her drink, just happy to be in the middle of things.

The miracle of Acronym returned to her as the night went on: The more she danced, the less she cared about how silly she looked. She threw herself into a Janelle Monáe track, rolling her shoulders and lip-syncing when she knew the lyrics.

"YEAH CHARLOTTE!" Jio yelled. They clapped as she dragged her hand back through her hair to keep it off her face. "SHOW US WHAT YOU GOT!"

The student controlling the aux cord put on ABBA's "Take a Chance on Me" and everyone started screaming. Wynn and Matt raced in from the kitchen, inexplicably wearing flower leis. Charlotte leaned down so that Wynn could guide one over her head.

Jackie tugged on its purple petals and pulled Charlotte around to face her. They giggled and did the twist. To everyone's amazement, the usually subdued Matt did a spot-on version of the Carlton.

"THAT'S MY FIANCÉ!" Jio pulled Matt down to their level for a long kiss, both of them sweating and radiating color under the disco ball.

This flavor of pure, unbridled happiness existed in the real world. Charlotte had found it in brief, magical nights at Cubbyhole and Stonewall and other gay bars in NYC. But queer college discos were a special kind of miracle, free and safe and innocent. No one touched her ass or yanked her back against his crotch by her hips. No one asked her who let her in or demanded she prove that she belonged.

She didn't need to vouch for her bisexuality; no one counted gold stars here.

Charlotte ran her fingers through her curls and let her eyes drift closed as she danced. The disco ball sent a kaleidoscope of color across her eyelids: the neon pink of freedom, the radiant orange of excitement.

Several glittering minutes or years later, her phone vibrated in her pocket. She read the incoming text, swaying from side to side as Cardi B blasted from the speakers.

TEXT MESSAGE FROM REECE KRUEGER TO CHARLOTTE THORNE, 10:51 PM: where you at? it's team hammer's time to shine!!

TEXT MESSAGE FROM CHARLOTTE THORNE TO REECE KRUEGER, 10:52 PM: Acronym! Cardi B! Sequins!

Reece sent her a GIF of three kittens wearing party hats. Her laugh spilled out of her like frothy champagne.

Jackie tapped her on the shoulder. Her eye makeup had begun to bleed, runaway mascara dusting her cheeks. "Pee break?"

Charlotte nodded. She followed her friend through the crowd and up the stairs to the second floor. Mercifully, they didn't have to wait in line for the bathroom.

As Jackie wiggled out of her tight skirt and settled on the toilet, Charlotte examined the graffiti on the walls. Thousands of names and messages sprawled across the faded wallpaper in overlapping ink.

Dante Evans, 1999.

Cherise + Tanya 4ever

We're here we're queer go fuck yourself!!

On the back of the door, just beside the lower hinge, she found her signature. *Charlotte Thorne,* the cursive letters forming a thick green vine. A rose bloomed at the tail of the *e* of "Thorne," its red petals faded with time.

A mason jar of markers still sat next to the sink. She seized a red pen and squatted on the floor to touch up the color.

Jackie flushed. "How you doing, Char?" she asked as she washed her hands.

"Wonderful." Charlotte sucked her bottom lip between her teeth as she doodled. The red wasn't the same shade as the original. She must have used a different brand way back when. This marker would have to do.

When did she draw this? End of sophomore year, probably. It took Charlotte a while to feel like she had the right to make her mark on the house. After she met Jackie, before she met Ben. That radiant window of time when she felt like she belonged somewhere at last.

"It's not too rowdy for you here?"

Charlotte shook her head. The atmosphere at Acronym never bothered her. Her brain wrote it off as an exception to her usual noise and crowd sensitivity. If anything, she wanted to blend into all this bright chaos.

Jackie peered over her shoulder at the door. "That's still there? Jeez, that's incredible."

"The whole door is intact." Charlotte popped back up on her feet. "Is yours?"

Her best friend pointed to the lip of plaster above the shower. Jackie's signature was less artistic, just a jumble of letters following a dramatic, swooping *J*. She left her mark the night she came out to her parents over the phone. Jackie said the supportive, anticlimactic conversation still deserved a symbolic memorial—after all, her parents' kind reaction didn't discount the terror she felt when she told them she was pansexual.

"You still need to design a tag for me," Jackie pouted. "You've owed me one for like a decade."

Charlotte snorted. "Seven years, tops." A fleck of glitter stuck to Jackie's cheek, and she brushed it away with the side of her thumb. "Besides, there is nothing wrong with your chicken scratch."

"Coward." Jackie turned to the mirror to fix her red lipstick. "You just don't like to draw anymore."

The accusation landed funny in Charlotte's chest. She dropped the marker back in the mason jar. "No comment."

Her phone chimed where she'd left it on the sink. Jackie glanced down at it and raised her eyebrows. "Aren't you popular. Roger again?"

"It's Reece," Charlotte said. "He wants me to join him at the hockey party."

Jackie's eyes lit up. "Then what are you waiting for?"

Charlotte could think of a million reasons not to go. The kid DJing at Acronym had great taste in dance jams. She didn't want to ditch Jackie, especially because she could tell something was off between them, though maybe she was overthinking it. Ben was out there too somewhere, strutting around campus like a peacock. And it *could* be Roger texting her next time with an important task.

"I'm here to spend time with you," Charlotte said.

Jackie folded her arms across her chest. "Sweetheart, I know that's not the reason."

"It's not a good idea." The words came out of her unsteadily. She fought the urge to grab the marker again and draw all over the counter. Flames, maybe, in pink, purple, and blue. Anything other than having this conversation.

Jackie studied her in the mirror as she neatened her braids. "Why is it not a good idea?"

The question was too large and too small to answer. Charlotte remembered the way Reece looked at her at dinner all soft and vulnerable, the way he smiled . . .

"I screwed it up the first time around."

A sly grin snuck across Jackie's face. "So you admit you want a second time around."

"I don't need you to make me feel stupid," Charlotte growled. "I already feel like an asshole."

"You're not an asshole." Her best friend extended a hand. Charlotte took it reluctantly. Jackie tugged her in front of the mirror and grabbed a Kleenex to touch up her eye makeup. "It's not your fault that Ben messed with your head so much you couldn't see straight." She swept up some runaway eyeliner, her breath spilling across Charlotte's face. She closed her eyes and let Jackie work her magic. "Besides, Reece didn't have his shit together then. That boy drank more vodka out of his thermos than water."

It was hard to reconcile the Reece attending the reunion with the Reece she knew as an undergrad. The day they met at support group, he wore hockey team sweatpants and a long-sleeve shirt she was pretty sure doubled as his pajamas. If the 3Ds got together before noon, he arrived viciously hungover, and on one occasion still drunk. At twenty-one Reece was already gorgeous, but he had a frenetic air of distraction and hunger around him like he was afraid to sit still.

It made the sex fantastic: desperate and intense and absorbing at a time when Charlotte wanted to forget herself. He always tasted like spearmint with a streak of hard liquor. He kissed with his teeth.

Now he was contained, somehow. Present and patient.

That new wisdom made him even more dangerous.

"I don't know if I can do this again," Charlotte breathed.

"Honey, you never did it in the first place." Jackie wrapped an arm around her waist and held her close. "You never let that boy matter to you. Not really."

Charlotte wasn't so sure about that. Not when she remembered the surge of emotions in her gut when he got to the reception last night, or when he walked away from her in the hallway, his fists clenched at his sides.

Her old attempt to wall Reece out of her heart had been a fool's errand all along. Somehow he wove himself through the bricks with his precise, gentle questions and his sense of adventure. Cups of coffee and late-night grins. A firm core of strength and resolve hid underneath his silly exterior, the genuine concern of a big brother.

It wasn't nothing, what she felt. She just didn't know what to call it.

Jackie shook her head. "*Charlotte.* Just let it go. It's gonna be okay."

"Are you sure?"

Jackie's palm found her back and rubbed in comforting circles. "Reece is a big kid now," her best friend reassured her. "He can handle himself."

The true question floated across Charlotte's mind in black permanent marker scrawl.

But can I?

"Besides," Jackie added, "the two of you deserve some fun."

Fun sounded amazing. Neon red and electric blue. Simple and hungry and satisfying.

Was it that simple? Could she just reach out and take what she wanted? Could she lean into the skid of reunion and actually enjoy herself, instead of crashing into a guardrail?

Yes. Yes, I can.

Charlotte took a deep breath. She didn't know why she hesitated: This moment had a strange inevitability to it.

"Okay. I'm going."

Jackie planted a wet kiss on her cheek, leaving behind a perfect print of her red lipstick. "That's my girl."

Chapter 6

IF ACRONYM PURRED, 31 Atwood roared.

The hockey house resided in the middle of Senior Housing, a cluster of streets on the east edge of campus. The micro-village included two rows of identical prewar houses bought by the university during an admissions boom. The houses were renovated to allow groups of students to live together comfortably; the bedrooms were spacious, with actual plaster walls and hardwood floors. They had no air conditioning, but that didn't matter for most of the year—seniors lucky enough to win placement on Atwood or Steele Street threw their windows open and let the babble of their lives pour out onto the road.

A hard bass line shook the windows tonight. Charlotte stood on the sidewalk in front of 31 Atwood and willed herself to breathe. No matter how hard she tried, her feet would not move toward the party.

The time warp of the reunion seized her in its disorienting grip again. She couldn't count how many nights she stood right here, gathering her courage to walk up the concrete path and meet Reece. He lived in 31 Atwood as a senior in a spacious bedroom on the second floor. Charlotte never found out what insider hack the hockey bros used to pass the house down among themselves from year to year. The tradition drove Jackie nuts, especially when they compared 31 Atwood to their dated two-bedroom apartment in Rawls Tower, the other on-campus option for upperclassmen.

Fear seized her lungs as she remembered Ben stalking through 31 Atwood as he sought out the night's It Party. When they were together, he dragged her in and out of raucous houses and dorm rooms as he searched for a gathering where he'd be treated like a campus celebrity. He got frustrated as the night went on, often blaming Charlotte as if her shyness were the reason he was never satisfied.

She never felt the same way about crowds after that: too many bodies, too much noise.

Ben didn't have friends on the hockey team, and even if he did show up at 31 Atwood tonight, it wasn't hard to hide behind a tall jock or duck into a side room. Still, Charlotte never felt safe in this corner of campus. Not then and not now.

My name is Charlotte Thorne, she reminded herself. *I am twenty-seven years old and I have not had sex in fourteen months.*

She reapplied her lip balm and shook out her hair. Then, having run out of excuses, she thrust her shoulders back and walked up the path.

The heat hit her as soon as she opened the door. Undergrads surrounded her, their faces a dark blur. Boys wore polo shirts and Hein tank tops, while girls favored crop tops and tight skirts. Athletic pennants from other colleges hung upside down on the wall in a display of disrespect.

It couldn't be further from Acronym's bright color palette of gender expression. Charlotte could smell the heterosexuality and white privilege.

The hostile vibe brought back old insecurities. At a school as small as Hein, cliques bled into each other by necessity. There just weren't enough students to create rigid rivalries between the hipsters and the jocks and the nerds. Charlotte didn't feel unwelcome at the hockey house, per se. But at a party like this, she could never be sure if she was the hunter or the hunted. The boys grossly outnumbered the girls. It was a space owned and controlled by the men of the house. She shivered as she remembered desperately searching so many rooms for someone she recognized.

Charlotte knew she was being paranoid—none of these kids would hassle an alumna—but she couldn't shrug off the party's menace. The scene felt so different now that she looked at it with adult eyes. Just entering this house as a woman meant consenting to being cornered and hit on or grabbed from behind under the guise of dancing.

The social rules that never seemed strange to her as an undergrad now seemed arcane and rude. For all of Hein University's talk about progressive values and good citizenship, its hookup culture *sucked.*

Maybe she should turn around and go back to the disco. She should have asked Reece to meet her there instead.

Her phone vibrated. She clung to it, grateful for the excuse to lean against the wall and not talk to anyone.

TEXT MESSAGE FROM REECE KRUEGER TO CHARLOTTE THORNE, 11:21 PM: We're out back!

Charlotte muscled her way to the back door and stepped out onto the deck. A group of bros she didn't recognize hovered around lines of coke on the glass patio table. She turned away quickly and headed for the stairs to the grass below.

The homes on Atwood and Steele Street backed up onto a communal yard. Students moved in packs between parties, the yard a single, pulsing organism with pockets of different music. She was in the belly of the jock beast at 31 Atwood. A dance party hosted by kids from the African Studies program shook the house next door. Hein's swim team barbecued on the other side.

Charlotte watched, hypnotized, as a woman in a one-piece swimsuit and gym shorts flipped a burger. The senior had a portrait of David Bowie tattooed on her shoulder blade, pink ink illustrating the lightning bolt across his face. With a dash of lust, Charlotte wondered if she'd ever been that cool during college.

"Charlie! Over here!"

She peeled her eyes from the girl at the grill and wheeled around. Reece waved at her from underneath a beech tree. He'd changed since dinner. Now he wore jeans and a white T-shirt that clung to his chest and shoulders. His hair crested in a perfect pompadour. The real difference was the open delight on his face, flushed and beautiful. Party Reece had arrived.

His friends Garrett and Liam perched on lower branches of the tree clutching tall boys of beer. Liam waved, while Garrett ignored her.

She ignored his prickly reception. Reece had invited her here. Garrett could deal with it.

Party Charlotte was in attendance too. Party Charlotte took no shit.

"How was the disco?" Reece asked. His voice scratched—he'd been yelling over the noise all night.

"Fabulous as ever. Lots of sequins."

"Is that where this came from?" He took one of the flowers on her lei between his thumb and index finger and rubbed its fabric petals. His knuckle brushed the skin of her throat.

"Yes." Charlotte swallowed. "But I think you need it more than I do." She took off the lei. Reece obediently tilted his head down so that she could guide it over his head. "There you go. Now you're properly dressed."

"*Hey, Reece,*" Liam yelled from the tree. "*You got lei'd!*"

"Ha ha," Reece replied with good humor. "Very original."

Garrett's glare caught her eye again. She gave him her best *who, me?* eyelash flutter. He scowled before taking a swig of his beer.

Reece, sweet summer child that he was, remained oblivious to the cold war between his two friends. "I think this brings out the color in my eyes," he said, examining the lei's petals.

Charlotte looked around hopefully. "Where's Misty?"

"She's back at the dorm. The noise is too much for her," Reece answered. "Plus we didn't want some asshole to steal her. That kind of shit happens during R&C weekend."

She snorted. Reece had a point. Theft became an issue at the end of term when seniors got drunk and reckless. Most students limited their petty larceny to borrowing a university golf cart for a joyride and then dumping it somewhere random on campus. But occasionally the property theft tilted toward the severe. She recalled watching from a distance, horrified, as Ben and Thomas dragged someone's La-Z-Boy back to their frat house during finals week.

But Ben was not at this party. *She* was at this party. She'd been personally invited, and she would enjoy it, goddamn it.

"You mentioned pong?" Charlotte reminded Reece.

"Oh right! Yeah, over here." He led her to the patio underneath the porch, where an abandoned pong table sat in disarray. "There was a whole tournament, but people went inside." He stacked up the dirty cups. Charlotte found new ones in a bag on the ground and set up two new pyramids. "I got my ass handed to me by some juniors working the reunion. Gen Z is ruthless."

"Think you can take me?" she asked. "Or should we invite Garrett and Liam to play doubles?"

"Let's play a round just us and then challenge someone."

Maybe he had noticed the rift between her and Garrett after all.

Reece fished a pair of plastic water bottles from a pack under the table. "Mind if we play with water?"

"Not at all." Charlotte took the one he extended to her. "I've had enough to drink. Do we have a ball?"

"Oh no!" Reece's mouth dropped open in panic, but his green eyes sparkled with mischief. He grinned as he plucked a Ping-Pong ball from his pocket.

"Very funny."

"Ladies first."

He tossed the ball to her. Charlotte dunked it in the rinsing cup before lining up her shot. The ball sailed neatly into the center cup on Reece's side of the table. She smirked and blew on her fingertips.

"Nice." Reece retrieved the ball and rinsed it. He splashed it around while he drank his punishment cup.

"They didn't play Carly Rae, by the way," Charlotte said. "Your heart is safely unbroken."

Reece raised an eyebrow. "I'm not so sure about that."

She gave him a funny look. Weren't they mutually pretending that they were in a suspended time zone where the events of graduation day had never happened?

"Oh?" she asked, keeping her voice neutral. "Why is that?"

He gestured to her face. "Looks like you found love at the disco." She gave him a blank look until he explained. "You have a lipstick kiss on your cheek."

"What? Oh!" Charlotte touched the lip print, her fingers coming away red. "I forgot that was there. That's just Jackie."

Reece smiled as he lined up his shot, keeping his eyes on her cups. "I'm happy for you both. What an exciting new chapter in your relationship." The ball bounced off a rim and she caught it on the rebound.

"Two queer women can be friends and not bang," Charlotte said. "I'm not her type anyway. She says I'm too bony."

Reece snorted. "That girl does not mince words."

Charlotte missed her shot. She watched Reece decide his next move, his face half in darkness underneath the porch. Stripes of light fell through the floorboards, catching his profile whenever he shifted to examine the field of play. Time had been kind to him, Charlotte decided: His skin had cleared up and his face was filled out in the right places. Even the way he stood was more grounded, less haphazard.

Stress kept his shoulders tight—his student debt, grad school, worry for his mom—but he seemed less ruled by it. He carried the pressure instead of staggering under its weight.

During college they had nothing in common: He majored in

biology while she studied sociology and art; he came from a loving, tight-knit family, and she would have spent Thanksgiving break on campus alone if Jackie hadn't dragged her to the Slaughters' house. Reece had seemed like the kind of guy who would expect nothing from her beyond the obvious. Bros usually didn't get attached. She wrote him off as a useful, attractive distraction. A partner in crime to blow off steam, to fool around, to drink too much and shield her from Ben's shadow. The noise in her head got so loud when she was alone.

Charlotte should have known better. It was obvious to her now. In college she saw only what she wanted to see: his handsome face and broad chest, and how his eyes narrowed into lust-drunk slits before she kissed him.

"Gotcha," Reece bragged as the ball splashed into one of her cups. He grinned at her, joy dancing in his eyes. "Drink up, Charlie."

She drank her water. She sank a few more shots.

"You're quiet tonight." Reece rearranged the cups into a diamond for her. "Are you okay?"

"I'm fine." And she *was* fine. She just couldn't shake the feeling that she was in the right place with the right person at the wrong time. "This weekend is intense."

"It's weird being back." Reece caught the ball when she threw it too far. "Nothing and everything has changed."

Charlotte nodded, grateful that he understood. "I keep thinking I'm in a time warp."

"I got the worst case of déjà vu when I checked in yesterday," he said. "They put me in my freshman hall. I'm like two doors down from my old room."

"Weird."

Reece sank the ball again. "It's not like I want to go back to college, my time here was brutal. I was so messed up over my dad." He raked his hand through his hair. "But living with your best friends? Sleeping until noon? Shit, I miss that."

"The real world is lonely." Charlotte bit her bottom lip as she calculated the angle of her toss.

"It doesn't have to be," Reece said. "But everyone is so busy. And I'm exhausted at the end of the day." He winced as her throw landed perfectly in one of his last remaining cups. She only needed one more shot to win. "Jeez, how are you so good at this?"

She chuckled as he fished the ball out of the cup. "I always loved beer pong. It gave me something to focus on at parties other than the noise."

He hummed in understanding as he brought the cup to his lips. She watched his throat move as he took a deep sip, his eyes never leaving her face.

Reece set the empty cup in the growing stack beside him. "Should I stop talking?" he teased. "Am I distracting you?"

Yes.

"You wish." Charlotte drummed her fingers on the edge of the table. He laughed, a stomach-deep chuckle that made her want to curl her fingers around the collar of his shirt. "I like talking to you," she said before she could think the words through.

The humor vanished from Reece's face at her rare confession. He palmed the ball as he stared at her, momentarily at a loss for words. Finally, just as she felt like she might die from humiliation, a quiet smile flitted across his mouth. "I like talking to you too," he said.

A comfortable silence fell between them as Reece lined up his next shot. He chewed the corner of his mouth and flexed his wrist back and forth. Just before he let the ball sail from his grasp, he said, "I think you just don't want people to know how fun you are."

Charlotte gulped. There was something sinful in his pronunciation of the word *fun.*

Reece kept staring at her, unconcerned as his ball bounced off the rim of a cup. "Am I wrong?"

Instead of answering, Charlotte kneeled to find the ball. It gave her a moment out of his eyeshot to hide the blush spreading across her cheeks.

Fun could mean a lot of things. For example, *fun* like him littering her thighs with bite marks when they should both be in class. *Fun* like sucking him off in the stairwell at the art studio when she needed a break from her thesis.

She pulled the ball from the crevice between tiles on the patio floor. When she stood up, she avoided his eyes. "I'm not all that fun anymore."

But she wanted to be.

Reece tutted like a daytime television therapist. "Charlie Thorne, all grown-up."

She intentionally missed her next shot, enjoying the game too much to bring it to an end. "Hard to feel grown-up here, though," she said as she watched him crouch down in pursuit of the ball, his ass delightfully firm in his jeans.

When he popped back up, he gave her a smug look that made it clear he knew she'd been staring. "What, is mediocre trap music not good enough for Miss Brooklyn?"

She stuck out her tongue instead of dignifying that with a response.

"Real mature." Reece gave her that dizzying smile again, lined with just a hint of mischief. "You know what I think?"

"What?" she asked, her voice breathy.

He stood still on the other side of the table, his palms pressed against the surface. "I think you're overdue for some grade-A collegiate *fun*."

Charlotte could only stand there, stunned, as Reece threw the ball in a perfect arc. It landed neatly in her second-to-last cup, splashing water onto the table. The next person to score would win.

His joke was an offer. There was no mistaking it. She knew the way he flirted, she *knew* this lightning-in-a-bottle chemistry. She'd stuffed the memory of it in some neglected corner of her mind under her blue cap and gown and her absurdly expensive textbooks. But it was back like a hot shock, a searing burn. She didn't know how this kind of attraction could exist with someone she hadn't touched in years.

She took the Ping-Pong ball out of the cup and whiffed the shot badly, hitting the rim of her last cup.

Reece groaned. "You're letting me win!"

"I don't know what you're talking about," she said, her voice shaking.

He squatted down, his eyes even with the table. "Just making sure it's level," he explained as she rolled her eyes.

Reece pressed down on the corner and watched the cups for any wobble. Satisfied, he stood up and cracked his knuckles. "Okay, are you ready for this? Reece's revenge? Are you watching?"

Charlotte waited patiently, her hands on her hips. "I'm ready."

She'd never felt less ready in her goddamn life.

Reece took a few steadying breaths. He feinted a throw before stepping back to recalculate his angle.

"Reece!"

"I'm going, I'm going."

After giving his arm a few experimental flexes, the ball cradled between his thumb and index finger, Reece let it go. It soared across the table before bouncing off the rim of the cup.

The ball disappeared into the grass behind her. Charlotte groaned as she lost sight of it in the darkness.

"I think that's a home run!" Reece declared.

He rounded the table to help her look for it. They wandered through the overgrown backyard, dodging partygoers and gently kicking over empty cardboard cases of beer. She struggled to keep her focus on the grass when Reece's body was suddenly so much closer to hers, the long table no longer between them.

The ball was nowhere to be found, absorbed into the chaos of someone else's party.

"Does this mean you win?" he asked.

"That's no fun." Charlotte pulled out her cell phone and turned on the flashlight. She shined the bright light at the ground and saw nothing but her loafers and Reece's sneakers.

Reece waved her concern away. "Forget it, it's just a ball."

"I want to beat you fair and square, Krueger."

"Oh, last names! Spicy."

She shoved him in the shoulder, smiling against her better judgment. He snickered, never losing his balance. He probably had fifty pounds on her. "Such aggression."

"I'm annoyed!" she cried as she turned off the light, her grin giving her away.

"No, you're not," Reece teased. He stepped closer.

All six feet of him demanded her absolute attention. The impulse to back up flared through her mind. She wasn't used to standing this close to anyone.

Was it only last night that Reece clung to her body in a smoldering hug?

But that had been unplanned, a sudden crush of limbs when they couldn't help themselves. This felt intentional. All their interactions since then had been a careful dance, a steady give-and-take.

Charlotte stood still, blinking up at him as he studied her face. That smile still played at his lips. He raised his hand and rubbed at her cheek with his thumb.

"Your kiss is smearing," he said. "We can't have you looking sloppy."

His touch was gentle, the softest pressure, a flower petal in an open palm. She held her breath as Reece examined her cheek. Then his eyes moved to her lips, parted in surprise. For a heartbeat Charlotte thought he was about to kiss her, his hand moving to cup her jaw. He looked spellbound, giving her that same look of wonder that used to make her so nervous.

His eyes met hers. "There you go," he said, licking the lipstick off his thumb. "All better."

He stepped back, just a careful foot or so. Just enough for Charlotte to mourn the loss of his heat, her mind blank. She couldn't think of anything but how he touched her with such reverence.

How long had it been since someone soothed her burning skin with their fingertips? Had anyone ever brushed their thumb against her cheek like she was something fragile, something precious?

Reece held out his hand, a muted smile on his face. "Dance with me."

Charlotte guffawed. The noise escaped her throat before she could stop it. In that instant she wanted so badly to roll her eyes and hated herself for the impulse. Five years in New York City had hardened her against public displays of earnestness. Five years of being alone hadn't helped.

The dissonance of what they felt and where they were hit her just after her cynicism. Sweaty, screaming bodies surrounded them. Students shoved each other and yelled and cried and made out like it was the end of the world, probably because it was for them. In two days they would graduate from college and be thrown into adulthood, whether or not they were ready for it.

She couldn't separate the soon-to-be-graduates from the young alumni—everyone had that same glaze of drunk mania on their faces, the same desperation to pretend that this was all there was. Two kinds of alumni returned for R&C weekend: the adults, and the adults who wanted to pretend they were twenty-one again. She could hear Liam giving a drunken TED Talk about Frank Ocean somewhere behind them, his voice growing hoarse. *Bro, seriously. He's a genius. How can you discount* Blonde? *What's wrong with you?*

Rihanna blasted from the nearest porch, clashing with 31 Atwood's trap music. Charlotte couldn't imagine anything less appropriate for this shockingly intimate moment.

"Here?" she asked, her voice nearly drowned out by the snarl of competing bass lines. "To this?"

Reece was undaunted. Charlotte marveled at his lack of

self-consciousness, how unafraid he was of his feelings. The real world hadn't changed him: Reece did whatever he wanted, no matter how much it might hurt. He turned his face toward the sun and grew in the direction of happiness.

How had he learned to do that, in spite of everything he'd gone through? Reece had experienced the worst kind of loss that Charlotte could imagine and yet he remained an open soul. Beaten up and flawed, sure, but brave.

Reece had walked away from her last night in the hallway, guarded and hungry. But here he was again, leaning into the déjà vu, one hand extended to her in the middle of so much chaos.

"Yeah, to this," Reece said. He waggled his fingers. His smile contained a promise and a question: *I will take your hand when you are ready, and only then.*

Was it just a dance? She'd come to the party thinking they might hook up, sure, but she hadn't let herself think about what that *meant.* What might happen after.

She didn't know if she could trust herself with him. Didn't he understand how much this might hurt when Sunday turned into Monday and they resumed their nine-to-five existence? This could only be a temporary slow dance down memory lane.

Her head hurt. Her heart hurt.

It was too loud here.

Temporary. This was temporary and impulsive and not real. It couldn't be anything more than a hookup.

This couldn't mean anything. This weekend was all that they would have.

At twenty-one, she wouldn't have hesitated for a second. Even last night in the hallway, she would have mauled him, bitten his lip, and drunk his desire in deep. But where she was once wild and reactive, she now only felt exhaustion.

"Are you teasing me?" she asked. Her voice quivered, betraying her nerves.

Fine, it was true: She was scared shitless, and she knew he could tell. He could read her like a damn paperback.

"Wouldn't dream of it. I'm a very serious person." His smile widened.

She reminded herself: *Reece* had texted her to come to the party, *Reece* had waved her over in the backyard. Maybe he'd even blown the game on purpose. At some point between last night and today, Reece had decided that this was what he wanted. That *she* was what he wanted.

Her self-control wavered, her fingers flexing by her side.

What about her? What did she, Charlotte Thorne, actually want?

She wanted to take his hand. She wanted to stop thinking about Sunday and how it would feel to stand alone on the train platform, duffle bag at her feet. She wanted to stop judging herself for mistakes she made on this campus years and years ago.

She wanted to just *stop.* Stop worrying about the future. Stop numbing her feelings. Stop denying herself happiness.

She wanted to have some goddamn fun.

"Come here," Reece said, soft but firm. She could see no trace of uncertainty on his face now, no shadow of the past in his eyes. There hadn't been all day, now that she thought about it.

Reece wasn't the boy she'd run away from anymore. He was a man who held his hand outstretched to her, sturdy and open. "Please dance with me, Charlie."

His *please* was a delicate key. She felt the tumblers turn and fall as she stepped forward and took his hand. His palm was warm and smooth against hers.

Reece guided her into a gentle one-two. They eased from side to side amid the roar of clashing party playlists. Their dance was not graceful but they moved together easily, muscle memory helping them read each other's movement. He lifted their hands and led her into a spin.

Joy caught her unaware, her eyes closing as she twirled and

returned to his solid ground. If people were watching, she didn't notice. She didn't care.

Reece hummed a tune under his breath, the melody drowned out by the blaring music. She would have given anything to hear it.

Charlotte stepped on an empty can and stumbled. Reece steadied her, laughing as he caught her hip in his hand. His grin softened into that dangerous, tender awe once again. It scared her a little and she stepped closer to him, hiding her warm face under his chin. For a moment he stilled, his breath hiking, but then his arms wrapped around her waist. They resumed rocking from foot to foot, the slow dance an excuse to stay this close.

Her loose fists rested against his chest and she clenched her eyes shut, waves of unfamiliar emotion cascading over her. There was want, yes, need, yes, relief, yes. Shock that he would ever want her, ever *let* her this close to him again. Desire to make herself at home in his warmth. Crimson and teal and that beautiful jade green.

Desperate to compartmentalize, she struggled not to fall into the saturated emotional depths for a boy—a man—she might not see again for another five years.

Charlotte wanted to ask what they were doing. Were they like the kids screaming and colliding around them, desperate for distraction at the end of the world? Or was this something more personal than that, something true?

Like he'd read her mind, Reece whispered her name into the softness of her hair. "Charlie?"

"Hmm?" She bit her lip, nuzzling her face into his chest. His body radiated heat. She wanted to crawl into every nook and cranny of him and absorb each degree.

Reece didn't answer right away, he just kept rocking them, one of his hands pressed flat against her back. She could feel the pressure of each finger through her blouse and longed for his touch against her skin.

Finally, he let out a puzzled laugh. "What are we doing?"

The question sounded simple. Her answer would be simple too, if this were a different time. Charlotte was realizing she'd made a mistake letting Reece go, all those years ago. For some unknown reason, she'd been given a second chance to appreciate him and soak him up, to set things right between them. She couldn't let that second chance pass her by.

But she knew she couldn't take Reece's heart home with her on Sunday. "I don't know yet," she said carefully. "I'm trying to just . . . *be* here."

Reece ended their dance and looked down at her, still cradled in his arms.

"Is that okay with you?" she asked, unsettled by his silence. Her hands loosened from their fists and flattened across his chest.

For a second she thought he might protest. She almost wanted him to.

They'd been granted a temporary stay, removed and far away from their real adult lives, and that was wonderful. But it was little more than a memory in the making, the kind to press between the pages of a scrapbook and keep safe. That could be enough for her.

Reece's beautiful mouth pulled into a frown. Whether he was disappointed in her or with the circumstances in which they'd found themselves, she had no idea.

Heat rushed to her face. He brushed his thumb across her cheek to capture an errant curl.

"Yeah," he whispered. "We're having fun." He then tightened his arms around her waist.

She knew in the moment before he kissed her that this would be difficult. She also knew that she didn't care. Charlotte had spent so much time punishing herself for not always knowing the right thing to do or the right way to express how she felt. She allowed herself this one victory, because for once she had gotten it perfectly, exactly right.

Saturday

Chapter 7

TEXT MESSAGE FROM NINA DORANTES TO CHARLOTTE THORNE, 12:02 AM: did jackie leave with you?

TEXT MESSAGE FROM NINA DORANTES TO CHARLOTTE THORNE, 12:04 AM: nvm found her!

THEIR SECOND FIRST kiss was soft and slow, just the tender pull of Reece's lips against hers. His hand slid into Charlotte's hair to bring her closer. She yielded entirely. Her body felt like it was made of spun sugar, weightless and fragile and sweet. The din of the backyard faded away until she heard nothing but his slight inhale of breath.

Reece groaned as he pulled back for a fragment of a second to rest his forehead against hers. And then another kiss, a deeper embrace that tasted like spearmint—he must have chewed gum before she arrived. She smiled against his mouth.

"What is it?" he murmured.

"Nothing," she said. "Just this."

She knew nothing but this. Nothing but Reece's soft breath spilling against her cheek. Nothing but his arms around her, her hands pressed firmly against his chest. She could feel his heart pounding against his ribs. She shuddered and he held her even closer somehow, an unconscious effort to warm her.

"Are you cold?" he asked.

Charlotte didn't know how to explain that she was the polar opposite of cold. Heat throbbed through her body like she'd never been kissed in her entire life. And she hadn't, not really, certainly not like this: not a first kiss with someone she already knew could rule her and worship her until she was a gutted mess. Reece remembered everything that she liked and knew everything that she needed.

They weren't picking up where they left off. They brought everything they learned while they were apart with them to this kiss, and to the next one.

As she struggled to form an answer, Reece pressed his lips to her neck, just below her ear.

"Oh, that's not *fair*," she whimpered.

He huffed a laugh against her skin. His teeth grazed a sensitive spot that never failed to scramble her brain.

"You don't feel cold to me," Reece teased. "But the hair on the back of your neck is standing up."

"Rude." She twined her arms around Reece's neck, hugging him close.

He dropped a gentle kiss to her shoulder before finding her lips again. Pure delight leapt in her chest.

It *was* new, the way they touched each other now. No part of her held back. No part of her was too busy battling intrusive thoughts to appreciate how Reece tasted, how he smelled, how he felt against her. Tonight she breathed him in and gave herself away in return. Reece kissed her with a smile in his mouth and that overjoyed her, even as she craved more.

Reece pulled away and she whined like a newborn kitten plucked from a fleece blanket. He chuckled, rubbing his thumb across her cheekbone. "We're in a public place," he reminded her.

Charlotte knew.

Charlotte didn't care.

She tugged the hair at the nape of his neck and he hissed through his teeth. "No one here knows who we are."

"I don't care what people think," Reece said. He stole another kiss from her, making her gasp, making her think that *private* might be an excellent idea. "But we're adults. We have other options."

She liked the dark edge to his words, a promise for the rest of the night and what it might hold. His bare skin against hers, her nails marking his back, the tangy sweetness of his sweat on her tongue. Yes, other options. She wanted those other options.

Except . . .

"Oh no," Charlotte said. "We have roommates."

His mouth went slack. In all their newfound maturity, they forgot they were still operating in the reunion's time warp. The rules were different this weekend, shower shoes and shared bedrooms.

"Shit, *Garrett*."

Garrett would definitely not be cool with getting kicked out of his room so that Reece could have sex with his ex-not-quite-girlfriend.

"Jackie?" Reece suggested.

Charlotte dug out her phone.

TEXT MESSAGE FROM CHARLOTTE THORNE TO JACKIE SLAUGHTER, 12:07 AM: Are you okay to not go back to the room for a while?

Reece kissed her forehead while she waited for Jackie's reply.

Worst-case scenario they could find a blanket and curl up under a tree. Or stuff themselves into Reece's car. Charlotte winced at the thought of a seat belt shoved into her spine. Not exactly erotic.

TEXT MESSAGE FROM JACKIE SLAUGHTER TO CHARLOTTE THORNE, 12:09 AM: sure. don't you dare touch my bed.

Thank goodness for understanding best friends *whose idea this was in the first place.*

Charlotte turned her phone to let Reece read Jackie's text.

"I'm going to bake that girl a cake," he said.

She twined her fingers through his. "Let's go."

Reece followed her through a side yard and onto Atwood Street. They rushed across the pavement. God help her, she felt giddy. Happy. Drunk off disco and Reece's eyes glinting under the streetlights.

Had she ever held his hand before? Surely she had, dozens of times, but she took the opportunity to commit his touch to memory. His hand was bigger than hers, his skin a little dry from latex gloves and sanitizer at the veterinary clinic. She wanted to buy him moisturizer. She wanted to massage the sore spots from the heel of his palm. She wanted to suck on his fingers.

My name is Charlotte Thorne and I'm taking home the hottest guy in my graduating class.

"What's so funny?" Reece asked. He gave her hand a playful tug until she turned to face him in the middle of the street. A mob of students walked around them in the opposite direction, following the noise of Atwood Street like party zombies. Charlotte and Reece stood together in the middle of the current, hands swinging intertwined between them.

"I was just thinking," she said, suddenly bashful. It felt so childish, such a reduction of who he was. That kind of thinking led her to put him in a safe, impersonal box the first time around. But it was still the truth, and Reece's crush baffled her just as much now as it did five years ago. "You could have anyone," Charlotte said. She reached up to trace his cheekbone with her thumb. Reece leaned into her touch, nuzzling his temple into her palm. "And I'm taking you home with me."

She could watch his face change colors for the rest of her life. The look Reece gave her belonged in a movie reel, not in the middle of Senior Housing.

He pulled his bottom lip between his teeth, his brow furrowing adorably. "Charlie, you are the only person who makes me blush."

Molten pink gathered like cotton candy in her rib cage. How could that possibly be true? What made her so lucky?

He hesitated, another confession caught on his tongue like he wasn't sure he was ready for it. Or if she was ready for it.

"You're the only girl I want." Reece laughed humorlessly, shocked by his own honesty. "You're the only girl I can *see.*"

He stared into her eyes with a tenderness that didn't belong amid the throng of Reunion & Commencement. She barely breathed as Reece coaxed a runaway blond curl behind her ear.

It happened in an instant. The world tilted and slid like a cruel illusion. Some of its color bled away, eaten up by creeping black fear. Charlotte's heart hammered in her chest. She closed her eyes.

Ben did that. Touched her like that. Caught her hair and eased it behind her ear after some pitch-perfect profession of love. She used to hear it as a declaration of loyalty and not a trap, not a glue patch for her wings to get stuck to.

You're the only girl for me, Charlotte. You're the only one who understands me. Just like I'm the only one for you.

For a dangerous moment her brain short-circuited, caught on the live wire of memory. Reece's words repeated and twisted, *the only girl I want.*

Her, with her shitty life and her dirty hair. Her, with a job she hated and a mother she hadn't spoken to in years. Her, dragging around emotional baggage monogrammed with her initials.

Reece was too kind, too caring. Too genuine to trust. Too good for her.

No.

Charlotte lassoed the snarl of panic and yanked it into submission. She took a deep breath and held it in her chest.

No. She wouldn't do this again. She wouldn't let echoes of her past sabotage her happiness. She had no need for the manipulations of an ex-boyfriend long since banished from her life. Even if Ben *had* slipped past her defenses for a weekend, skulking just beyond this perfect moment.

Reece's hand faltered and came to rest on her shoulder. He frowned at the terror playing out across her face. "Are you okay? You still with me?"

Charlotte nodded. He cupped her chin in his hand and studied her eyes, unconvinced.

The heat of his touch against her skin grounded her. She clutched his hand still woven through hers and made him her true north.

That broken, desperate person who Ben convinced her she was, it was bullshit. Nothing but a fun house mirror reflection of her worst fears, dangerous only when it looked just familiar enough for her to believe.

My name is Charlotte Thorne. I am twenty-seven years old. It's going to be okay. I deserve to have fun.

"I'm here," she said. "Just overstimulated."

Reece didn't ask questions. He guided her across the street and through the intersection with University Road. Charlotte let him tug her along as her brain knitted itself back together.

Just a trigger. A shard of memory that couldn't hurt her anymore.

The other side of the street was quieter. A canopy of trees hung over the sidewalk, dampening the roar. The air smelled like the suburbs again, fresh dew and newly planted sod. Her panic dissipated as spring leaves swayed and whispered around them.

"Man, it was a real bacchanal back there." Reece laughed at himself, making conversation while she put herself back together.

Charlotte felt a fresh surge of gratitude for his unflappable calm. Ever the perceptive guy, he didn't push her to explain why she shut down. She added it to the long list of reasons why she liked Reece as a person.

He didn't pry.

He sucked at pong.

He danced with her to bad music surrounded by strangers.

He looked at her like she was put on this earth to ruin his life.

He loved dogs.

"Do you go out much?" she asked.

"In St. Louis? Nah. I'm an old man now." They turned onto the path back to Randall Dorm. Gravel crunched underfoot. Reece's sneaker found a loose rock and he kicked it, sending it skittering into the underbrush.

Charlotte tucked her arm through his. She glanced up at his carefully still face—Reece looked straight ahead, his hands tucked neatly into his pockets.

"When did you quit drinking?" she asked.

Reece's jaw tightened. Before she could worry that she'd overstepped, he answered. "Not long after graduation." He licked his lips. "Binge drinking is a lot less fun when you're doing it alone."

It made sense now. Water pong at the party, no cocktail in his hand at the class reception, no alcohol on his breath when he hugged her good-bye last night. She'd suspected since Jackie's announcement at dinner when he didn't look surprised. Reece must have been giving her advice on how to support her dad.

Was that why Reece didn't kiss her in the hallway? Because she'd had too much to drink, while he was completely sober?

Charlotte frowned. She rarely drank anymore, yet the second she returned to campus, she wanted a beer. She hadn't questioned the impulse. Maybe she should have.

"Is it hard being back here? There must be triggers everywhere."

Reece sighed. "Yes and no." He unfolded their arms so that he could take her hand again, an anchor in an uncharted conversation. She hoped she was asking the right questions. "I'm not tempted to drink, but the guys have been weird about it. I think I'm a buzzkill at pregames."

She didn't know what to say to that. She'd never been privy to the private drinking rituals of bros, and she didn't want to insult his friends. "That sounds hard."

"It is what it is. They're good friends." Reece squeezed her hand. "It's not their fault they want to get wasted and I don't."

"What do you like to do instead? In St. Louis, I mean." Charlotte cringed at the question as soon as it left her lips. It was such a small-talk question, like asking him about his major as they walked back to her dorm to hook up.

If she sounded vapid to Reece, he didn't point it out. "For fun, you mean?"

"Yeah. Do you still play hockey?"

He shook his head. "Nah, I don't want to risk an injury. But I still skate sometimes at the community rink. It's meditative." As he considered his answer, he traced his thumb across her palm. She shivered, ticklish. "In the summer I bike. Trails and stuff. You have to concentrate or you go ass over handlebars."

"You mean like mountain biking?" She couldn't imagine him in the woods, dirt on his knuckles, a helmet covering his face. Reece seemed too gentle, like a golden retriever who romped around the backyard, or at most, the dog park. He wasn't an off-the-trail breed.

Reece laughed at her obvious disbelief. "What, did you forget I'm a jock?"

"*No.*" Charlotte gestured with her free hand. "It's just rugged, that's all."

"I'm not rugged?" Reece waggled his eyebrows.

She scoffed. "That's not what I mean!"

"I played hockey, remember. I could throw punches. And take them."

Charlotte shoved him in the shoulder. He laughed as he swerved off the path before easily regaining his balance and returning to her side.

"Now you take care of sick cats!" she protested. "You gel your hair!"

"Ah, so now I'm domesticated." He put his hands up. "I've gone soft."

"You were always soft," she spluttered. "*And* hard. A soft jock."

A very undergrad-Reece smirk stretched across his lips. "Tell me more about how hard I am."

Charlotte sighed, exasperated. "You are the *worst.*"

Reece wrapped his arm around her shoulders and kissed the side of her head. She snuck her hand into the back pocket of his jeans.

"Nice job copping a feel," Reece teased.

She pinched his ass in retribution.

They bickered and teased the rest of the walk back to the dorm, past the grand library with its hulking marble pillars, and the stone academic buildings fronted by manicured lawns. Charlotte noticed little of it. Hein's campus faded into a muted New England blur of green and gray behind Reece's profile, and for the first time in a long time, she relaxed.

TEXT MESSAGE FROM JACKIE SLAUGHTER TO CHARLOTTE THORNE, 12:26 AM: btw there are condoms in my makeup bag!! in the side pocket with my valtrex.

CHARLOTTE FELT A new twist of déjà vu as they walked down the hallway to her room. Everything looked exactly the same as it did last night, only now her hand was tucked neatly in the crook of Reece's arm. Her phone nestled in her back pocket on silent.

The conversation they batted back and forth during their walk fizzled out as she retrieved her keys. Reece stood just behind her. She could feel his eyes on her neck, on her hair curling and knotting where it poured down her back. He watched in silence as she slid the key into the lock. She pushed the door open, the darkness of the room yawning in front of them.

She ignored the light switch on the wall—the overhead lamp would be too bright. Reece stayed in the doorway as she crossed the room to pull up the blackout curtain and let moonlight fall across the linoleum floor.

The door clicked shut behind him. At last, they were truly alone.

Charlotte hesitated at the window. She pressed her palm to the cool glass and watched the wind move through the trees. Leaves rippled in so many shades of gray, the moon leaching them of color.

Time warp again: It felt like fall, like the possibility of a new school year beginning. Nine new months to learn and reinvent herself. Nine months to storm across campus and demand adventures.

Eighteen, nineteen, twenty, twenty-one. Immortal on a September evening, her Doc Martens muddy and her shoulders bare.

She took a deep breath, and then another.

Even with her back to him, Charlotte never lost her awareness of Reece's presence. She could hear the soft noise of his sneakers on the floor as he shifted his weight from foot to foot. He waited for her to turn around again, waited for her to be ready.

She was ready, she just needed a . . . a moment. She'd done this before—hell, she'd done this with *him* before—but tonight was something else. This ran the risk of mattering.

Reece cleared his throat. "We don't have to . . . if you don't want—"

Charlotte whirled around. She didn't want to make him worry, not for a second. She owed him that much. "No, I *want*." She laughed, the words clumsy but true. She wanted. She wanted so much more than she'd bargained for.

Reece stepped toward her once, and then again. She met him in the middle, her arms circling his waist as he took her face in his hands.

"I'm so glad you're here," she said, hungry to reassure him. They were in this together, whatever it wound up being. Even if it was temporary.

"Me too," he said.

Reece eased into a crouch on the floor before her. She placed a hand on his shoulder as he guided off her left shoe, and then her right. He didn't seem to care that her toenails weren't painted or that *(oh shit)* she hadn't shaved her legs in three days.

Another thing she'd forgotten to pack for the weekend: a razor.

Once her feet were bare, Reece untied his sneakers. He lined them up beside her loafers underneath the bed. Then he stood, his full height making her feel wonderfully small. His eyes never left hers as he took off the flower lei and hung it from the bedpost.

Then, *oh sweet mother of God,* he took the bottom of his shirt in his hands and pulled it up over his head, revealing the lush expanse of his stomach. Charlotte's stare caught on the smattering of hair that led down to the fly of his jeans.

Her mouth went dry. She skimmed her fingers down his chest, lingering on his belt buckle. Reece shuddered at her touch.

"C'mere," he muttered before seizing her at the waist and dragging her against him. Their hunger from Atwood Street returned as he drew her lower lip between his own. She groaned and held on to his shoulders, bent over by the force of his kiss.

There was nothing *soft jock* about him now. Reece kissed the way he always had—with reckless appetite.

They were well matched. Charlotte wound a hand through his belt and pulled him flush against her. She could feel his hardness against her hip. Reece hissed against her lips, and she swallowed it, smug and satisfied.

He wanted her. He wanted her desperately, she hadn't imagined it. She wasn't wrong.

Reece found the buttons of her shirt. She stepped back to let him unfasten them one by one, shivering as her skin met the night air.

"*Fuck,*" Reece stammered. He stared at her breasts in disbelief.

She'd skipped wearing a bra tonight, not really needing one. Charlotte folded her arms over her stomach. She knew her body had changed since graduation, just like his. She wasn't an insecure woman, but the last time Reece saw her naked, she still had the metabolism of a teenager.

"What?" she asked as he appraised her. She hated the defensiveness in her voice.

"You are so gorgeous." He ran his knuckle across her clavicle and down her breastbone. Then he traced a line over the small swell of her breast to the firm point of her nipple. Charlotte arched her back as her self-consciousness dissolved under his touch. "So beautiful," he continued. "I thought I remembered you, but . . ."

"I'm softer now," she said with a wry smile.

Reece kissed her, slow and deep. He pulled away to brush his nose against hers. "I like it."

Their pants followed their shirts to the floor. Undressing together wasn't awkward or clumsy; they'd done it dozens of times before.

"Shit," he said, patting the nonexistent back pocket of his underwear. "I just realized—condoms. I'm sorry."

"Don't worry." Charlotte found Jackie's dresser in the darkness. She felt her way through the makeup bag and retrieved a metallic wrapper. "Jackie has some."

She put the condoms on the bookshelf and sat down next to him on the bed. He kissed her shoulder, his movements languid.

"Should we talk about it?" she asked.

Reece leaned back against the wall. "Sure." He did some mental math as he wiggled his toes. "It's been . . . four months? Since my last STI screening. Nothing new to report." His teeth caught the moonlight, his face bare of shame or awkwardness. He gave her a playful smile as he added, "My sex life isn't thriving now that I live with my mom."

Charlotte tried to remember her last checkup. She'd gotten tested once her relationship with Merielle was over, and she didn't have much to account for since then. "My last test was in August, no positives."

She didn't need to elaborate, but she couldn't help herself. "No one to jeopardize that either."

Reece took her hand from where it rested on her knee and brought her palm to his lips. Her fingers curled inward at the just-so graze of his mouth against her skin. "How has no one in that city noticed how incredible you are?"

"I haven't really . . . been trying," she admitted, her voice a ribbon of muddled concentration and desire.

Reece tugged her across the bed to straddle his lap. "Is that so?" His mouth teased the sensitive flesh where her shoulder met her neck. She writhed unintentionally, rocking against the hard ridge of his arousal. So little separated them now, just his boxer briefs and her cotton undies.

She tried to remember his question. "Too tired from work. Not . . . interested."

It took Herculean effort to string together a sentence while Reece laved kisses against her shoulder. She deserved an award: remembered words when seduced by her ex after a dry spell.

"Hmm . . ." Reece took her shoulder in his hand and tilted her backward to find her nipple with his lips. He licked and then sucked the hard peak. Lights went out one by one in Charlotte's brain. The machinery that operated her anxiety and recollection of basic grammar whirred to a stop.

Reece grazed her nipple with his teeth before letting it go, the cold air scorching her skin. "You like that," he purred as his mouth moved to her other breast. His fingers flexed at her throat. He was gentle with her neck but the slightest pressure there brought to mind his strength. She felt herself get wetter at the thought of his hand pressing down harder.

"I do, yes," she managed.

"You have no idea," he said in between kisses, "how much I have wanted this." His hand at her hips tightened, dragging her forward in his lap. "How much I have thought about this." She held back a groan at the friction between their bodies. She rocked forward again, matching the tempo he'd started. "How much I have tried to remember . . . every . . . detail of you."

The idea of Reece scrounging for memories of their short-lived relationship was erotic and laden with meaning. Charlotte took his jaw in her hand and turned his face up to hers, not sure what to say but needing to say something. "I'm here" was what came out, a firm statement of *now* and *I'm sorry*.

She had also thought about him in the city on lonely nights when she snuck her hand under the waistband of her pajamas. She thought about his green eyes finding hers over the swell of her stomach. When she found herself stuck on some first date from hell, she remembered how Reece teased her to the brink and then watched her come apart, smug satisfaction curling his mouth.

His thumb found her pulse point, thundering at her throat. "I know," he said. "And I'm not letting you go. Not until I'm satisfied."

Then he was kissing her again. Charlotte gasped and he swallowed the sound, his nails biting into her hip. She remembered how tortured he looked last night, his restraint threatening to snap as she pressed herself against the wall. All of that tension burned through their bodies. All of that desire surged through her, finally unbridled.

This was the Reece she knew in college. *This* was the Reece she'd never forgotten—the Reece who challenged and demanded and took. This Reece bent her over a sink in the bathroom at some party and fucked her, one hand over her mouth to catch her groans. He gave as good as he got, generous and merciless.

Reece bit her lower lip and she whined. She wanted this desperately, to be taken, to be taken by *him*. She wanted him to fuck her, wanted him to fuck her and kiss her and hold her and then smile at her with his ridiculous, expressive face.

His hand moved from her hip to the waistband of her underwear, teasing the hem. She squirmed against him, forward and down, and he grunted at the friction. "Touch me," she begged against his lips. "Oh god, *please.*" She wanted his hands on her, wanted his hands against her where she was slick and hot and needy.

Reece traced her slit through the soaked cotton, his thumb finding her clit. Too much and not enough, the pressure dulled by the fabric. "More. Please, Reece."

His eyes found hers and the look he gave her—*damn* was it intense. She tried not to look away from his face as he pushed aside her underwear and eased one delicious finger into her.

An anguished noise escaped his throat, a helpless little groan of disbelief. "Charlie, you are so wet."

"I know," she panted. Her voice failed her as he stroked inside. "Since last night."

Reece moaned at that thought.

He added another finger to the one already moving in and out of her, stretching her carefully. Her eyes shuttered closed, the sensation beautiful torture. It felt incredible to be touched, to be teased and stroked and played with—his thumb found her clit and circled it, pressing down. But it wasn't enough, nothing would be enough until she had him.

Charlotte leaned her forehead against Reece's, her lips parting as she struggled to regain her voice. "Reece, I want *you.*"

"I want to make you feel good," he said. His voice shook as his control began to slip. "I want to make you come first."

Such a gentleman. She knew she would too, *easily*, if she let him. He would play her body until she was a sweaty, snarled mess of herself, boneless and overjoyed. But she wanted to feel him inside her. She wanted his restraint to break, and she wanted to watch his face as he let go.

Charlotte did her best to roll them over in the narrow bed, and she hissed as her bare skin met the cold concrete wall. Reece budged over so that she could lie down. Then he was above her, his hips nestled between her thighs. The full weight of him on top of her felt extraordinary, all of that contained power. She teased the sensitive skin above the swell of his ass with her fingertips. He arched his back as he thrust forward, his erection grinding against her.

Charlotte wedged her toe into the elastic of his boxers. "Get rid of these." He sat up to pull them off. She wiggled out of her underpants and dropped them on the floor, uninterested in some drawn-out tease. They'd danced around each other long enough.

"Come here." She stretched out her hand to him as he kneeled between her thighs. He took it and pressed a kiss to her palm, his dark eyes never leaving hers. He considered her request, studying the sheer want on her face. She was well beyond walls at this point, her defenses shattered. As he looked down at her, his breath wet and hot against her skin, she'd never felt so vulnerable in her life.

"Please." She tilted up to kiss him.

Reece pulled back a fraction of an inch, his lips brushing hers as he spoke. "Are you sure?" he asked.

Charlotte growled. "Yes, Reece, I am sure."

He grinned and moved to kneel above her, retrieving a condom from the bookshelf. He tore open the wrapper and rolled it down his length with deft fingers. As soon as he finished, she grabbed his neck and pulled him back against her body, adjusting her hips as he found her entrance.

And then—*oh*. She could feel herself stretch to take him in, her legs wrapped tight around his waist. Their bodies made so much sense.

Reece clenched his eyes shut, his mouth a grimace of bliss and desperate self-control. "Christ, you feel—" he stammered, resting his forehead against her shoulder. "You feel *amazing*."

"So do you," Charlotte gasped. She shifted her hips and they both grunted as he hit a sensitive spot inside her. "Oh god, *yes*."

She needed more. She dug her heels into his back as they built a frantic rhythm. A bead of sweat dripped from his nose onto her cheek, and she loved it, she loved how he tasted when she licked his mouth.

Charlotte sucked at his shoulder and the sweat collecting on his neck. It made no sense, but she still wanted more, wanted as much of him as possible. When she bit down, he grabbed her hip and pressed her down into the mattress, driving into her hard. Her nails raked down his back as she cried out in pleasure-pain.

This was really happening. Hot and fast, sheets on loan from the R&C committee, her lips chapped. Reece's face was tight with strain as he held on. They were both so loud, she realized, groaning and begging and gasping as they fucked. An insane giggle escaped her, and he laughed before kissing her deeply.

"I can't believe this," she confessed when he pulled away for air.

He smiled at her. A special-edition just-for-Charlie-while-screwing-like-teenagers grin that took over his entire face. The kind of smile that ruined a girl's life.

"Me neither," he said.

Charlotte was close and he could feel it, her body clenching around him. She felt like she'd been aching for release all day and only needed a push. He wedged his hand between their bodies and found her clit, working at the sensitive bud of nerves with his thumb. The irregular pace of his touch as their hips rocked away and together only hastened her pleasure. She yanked at Reece's hair, grabbing at him for dear life.

She felt his teeth at her throat as he stroked deep inside her and she broke, the orgasm tearing through her body. She groaned, static shock and tension snapping, her arms tight around Reece's torso. The intensity sent her reeling, her heart racing madly.

Colors exploded on the inside of her eyelids, ruby red and sticky pink. The vein-blood blue of being alive.

The only thing protecting her from full emotional overload was Reece's ragged breath at her ear, an anchor in the present.

"Please, Reece," she coaxed, still twitching around him as aftershocks took her body. He groaned, his thrusts becoming even more erratic. Charlotte licked at the shell of his ear and nipped his lobe. "Please come for me. I want you to."

His fingers dug into her skin. She tilted her hips up to get him closer, the angle plunging him deeper. "Char—ah *yes*."

"I need you," she said, a plea and a promise. "I need you to come for me."

His body coiled tight and violently snapped as he came. She ached as he thrust into her once, twice, three times as he took his release. It almost hurt, her body complaining as she stretched to accommodate him. She felt the side effects of not having sex for months, the early shadow of tomorrow's soreness. But it was worth it to have Reece collapse on top of her, his face hidden in her shoulder. They were both soaked with sweat and relief.

The whole room smelled like sex and the cocktails left abandoned on the bookshelf.

She laughed, the sharp sound breaking the silence.

"What is it?" he mumbled against her skin.

Reece unstitched himself from her limbs, rolling off to lie at her side. He looked positively destroyed, the poor dear. She smoothed down his electric mess of hair, a smile playing at her lips. What a beautiful specimen of a man, hers for the evening, for the weekend.

"What does it smell like in here?" she asked as he took off the used condom and disposed of it in an empty shopping bag hanging from the bedpost.

Reece gave her a strange look before recognition flared across his face. His eyes widened. "Oh my god," he groaned. "College."

Charlotte stretched her arms above her head. Her body didn't feel like 2013. Sleepiness hit her like a brick wall. That and dehydration. A yawn snuck out of her mouth and nearly cracked her face in half.

Reece curled his fingers around her ankle. "You tired?"

She wriggled like a sleepy cat on the mattress. Charlotte liked the way his eyes tracked the curve of her breast. "Aren't you?"

The question was the wrong one. His face went still, his smile dimming. "Yeah, I guess," he said, and let go of her foot. "It's been a long day."

It startled her, how suddenly her insecurity returned. But that was her exhaustion making itself known. She shoved down her unease, refusing to read into Reece's emotional retreat. It was who-the-hell-knows-how-late at night and she hadn't come that hard in years.

"But a good day?" she asked, propping herself up on her elbows.

Her prodding worked. Reece's smile returned. "A great day."

He leaned over her. One of his hands settled at her hip again, his touch scalding. She grinned as he kissed her all slow and sated. She could have kissed him like that for hours, sleep be damned, but eventually he murmured, "I guess I should go?"

Charlotte did not want Reece to go. She wanted him to stay right where he was, above her and touching her with his large, warm hands. But Reece needed to go, because that was how they operated. That was their old rule and it had worked for both of them. Charlotte fell asleep wrapped in her hard-won solitude, and in the morning Reece could nurse his hangover in peace.

It had been years since she slept beside another person. She and Jackie shared beds when they traveled together, but splitting a king-size bed at a hotel with your best friend was a far cry from spending a night tangled up with a lover in a twin-size bed. Sleeping together was an intimate act, messy and vulnerable, even more so than sex. Skin bare, breath mingling. Aside from the logistical concerns of finding your way home in the middle of the night, Charlotte couldn't think of a reason to sleep with someone else that wasn't just to be close to them.

Being close, voluntarily close, hadn't been Charlotte's style for a long time.

The boundary made sense. It had protected her ever since Ben.

She just wasn't sure if she wanted to protect herself now.

"I should check my email," she said, instead of *stay with me.*

Reece brushed an errant curl off her forehead. He placed a kiss on her nose before sitting up and reaching for his boxers, wedged between the mattress and the wall. "And I should make sure Garrett and

Liam are still alive." The bed tipped as he stood up. She turned to lie on her side and watch him dress. "Let's hope they stayed away from the hard stuff."

"Godspeed," she drawled.

Reece wedged his feet back into his sneakers, not bothering to tie them. He hesitated when fully dressed, drumming his fingers on the bedpost.

Stay with me.

Charlotte chewed on her bottom lip to keep the words from escaping.

"We're going to the pond tomorrow." Reece's fingers tugged on the flower lei hanging at the foot of the bed. "Want to come?"

She knew it was silly to get excited about an invitation to hang out when they'd literally just had sex, but that was the college hookup scene for you. Charlotte's smile returned.

"I'd love to."

TEXT MESSAGE FROM JACKIE SLAUGHTER TO CHARLOTTE THORNE, 1:51 AM: can I come back yet??

Chapter 8

SLACK MESSAGE FROM ROGER LUDERMORE TO CHARLOTTE THORNE, 5:34 AM: tim cook can suck my dick

MUCH HAD CHANGED at Terry's Bar since Charlotte's last shift. The restaurant itself had a fresh coat of paint on the walls and a different layout for the dining tables. New artwork hung everywhere: paintings and photographs by Hein students, each with a small cream gallery label and a modest price. Biggest of all, a new food truck sat in the parking lot. By night it revved to life and served Hein students their beloved vegan hot dogs in hemp wrappers.

Charlotte sank into her favorite booth by the jukebox. At least that hadn't changed: The vinyl stuck to her hands as she scooted over to make room for Jackie.

Their waiter slapped plastic menus on the table. He nodded as Jackie ordered nacho fries to share.

"Nina and Amy must be late," Charlotte mused, plucking the menu from the waxy tabletop. She ran her fingertips over the text and hummed as she recognized the specials.

Jackie swigged her glass of water. After sufficient hydration, she burped quietly into her fist. "Nice hickey."

"Shush." Charlotte swatted away Jackie's finger as she tried to touch her neck. "I'll replace the condom."

"Don't bother, I'll load up at the health center this afternoon. I need dental dams." Jackie grabbed Charlotte's untouched water cup and poured it into her own. "Want to tell me all the juicy details?"

"No."

"Rude. We should get pancakes."

Charlotte's eyes slid over the pictures on the menu as all those details stole across her mind. She could still feel the pressure of Reece's lips at her neck. The heat of his breath against her skin. How his teeth grazed just a little, a mere suggestion of pain. She would never forget the relief and rightness of having him inside her again.

But there was no way in hell she was telling Jackie any of that. Even though this was only a casual thing for the weekend, it felt wrong to dissect it like they were bros at a keg party comparing one-night stands.

Jackie sat up straight, her palms flat on the tabletop. Charlotte looked up to see Nina and Amy cutting across the restaurant. Amy's hair was still wet, and she was fresh-faced and smiling widely. Nina looked a little worse for wear, last night's mascara smudged beneath her eyes.

"Good morning, Starshine," Nina rasped. "The earth says hello." She slid into the booth first, and Amy followed.

"Are you quoting *Hair*?" Jackie's lip curled, uncharacteristically ignoring Amy. "Do not quote show tunes at me, Dorantes."

"Forgive a girl for being cultured." Nina jutted her chin at Charlotte as she picked up a menu. Her dark eyes widened as she took in Charlotte's neck. "Is that a hickey?"

Jackie snickered.

Charlotte sighed behind her menu. "It's not up for discussion."

Amy's eyes widened. Mercifully, Nina dropped the subject and flagged down their waiter.

"How late were you out last night?" Jackie asked Nina. "I thought we were going to walk back to Randall together."

While Jackie interrogated Nina, Charlotte pulled out her phone under the table. She prayed silently that there wouldn't be any more Slack messages from Roger.

TEXT MESSAGE FROM REECE KRUEGER TO CHARLOTTE THORNE, 10:45 AM: where you at?

After a quick glance to make sure the girls weren't paying attention, she replied.

TEXT MESSAGE FROM CHARLOTTE THORNE TO REECE KRUEGER, 11:09 AM: Brunch at Terry's.

TEXT MESSAGE FROM REECE KRUEGER TO CHARLOTTE THORNE, 11:10 AM: jealous I miss his fries

TEXT MESSAGE FROM CHARLOTTE THORNE TO REECE KRUEGER, 11:10 AM: I'll bring back leftovers.

She put her phone down as their drinks and a steaming basket of chips, fries, salsa, and queso arrived. Nina made them wait so that she could take an enticing picture of their meal to send to Eliza.

"This is ridiculous," Jackie drawled, a strange twist to her voice. Charlotte gave her a look, and she softened, immediately apologetic. "Do you need a fill light?"

"That would be great, there's a shadow."

Charlotte watched as her best friend turned on her phone's flashlight and held it above their appetizer. She knew Jackie well enough to detect jealousy simmering under the surface of her words. But that would mean . . .

Oh. She bit down on her grin as she put the pieces together. Well, wasn't this a fun queer love triangle. Or was it a square? Not that Charlotte felt any ownership over Nina. Or her best friend, for that matter.

"You guys will not believe what happened last night at the a cappella party," Amy said, unaware of the drama brimming under her nose. She licked the salt off her glass, mischief glinting in her eyes.

Charlotte's phone vibrated in her lap. She bit down on a smile and zoned out while Amy shared a cappella gossip.

TEXT MESSAGE FROM REECE KRUEGER TO CHARLOTTE THORNE, 11:15 AM: come swim with me? water's freezing

TEXT MESSAGE FROM CHARLOTTE THORNE TO REECE KRUEGER, 11:16 AM: That sounds terrible.

Jackie slid the nacho fries across the table toward Charlotte. "Eat up, you must be starving."

Charlotte gave her a silencing look. She adored Nina and Amy, but she didn't want her and Reece to become a reunion rumor too. The last thing she needed was questions—or worse, *opinions*—about what it all meant. Or what they would do when the weekend ended. The only way to remain blissfully in the present was to keep their fling safe and private.

She decided the best defense was a good offense. "Amy, I want to hear more about your job. What books are you working on?" Charlotte asked as she scooped a glob of salsa onto a chip. Amy beamed at the invitation to describe her new project.

"Oh, you'd *love* the novel I'm planning the tour for right now! It's this YA thriller about lesbian werewolves."

Jackie gave her best wolfy growl, making Nina snort into her margarita.

"My department head is being so weird about promoting it," Amy continued. "He keeps saying there's no audience for queer supernatural stories."

Charlotte passed the nacho fries basket to Amy. "Has he never met a teenager?"

The meal passed quickly amid a half decade's worth of updates. They traded war stories about bad bosses and out-of-touch company leadership. In every industry they had run up against the same challenges: "entry-level" jobs that required years of prior experience, and research grants that always seemed to go to a well-connected nephew.

It didn't matter that all four worked in different fields: They shared the fear that they were scrambling their way up a down escalator. And in a cruel twist, if they got lucky enough to land those dream jobs, they turned out to be nightmares.

As Amy detailed her futile quest to get a raise, Charlotte's embarrassment about her zigzagging career began to lift. This was the real shit, the unglamorous truth of people's actual lives. The rosy Instagram filter fell away.

She wasn't the only one struggling. She wasn't the only one disappointed by how postcollege life had turned out.

"I'm starting to interview at other houses," Amy continued. "The only way to make more money is to jump around, but that means leaving behind my authors. But my manager keeps insisting there's nothing in the budget and this is how it's done."

"He sounds like Charlotte's boss," Jackie drawled. She speared a fluffy pancake and gave her a sideways look.

Oh great. Here we go again.

Nina fixed Charlotte in her steady gaze. "Yeah? What's it like at *Front End*?"

Charlotte looked at the three women around her: Nina's level stare, Jackie's frown, Amy's genuine interest. They'd already heard the celebrity-sparkled version of her life at *Front End*. She had a choice to make. She could trot out the practiced stories again, or she could let her guard down and confirm what they must already suspect: that she was full of crap.

But she didn't want another lecture. Not when Reece had sapped the stress from her body. Not when she finally felt calm.

"It's all right," she said.

Jackie sipped her Diet Coke, her eyes glinting. Amy's head tilted to the side like a puppy hearing a new sound for the first time. Nina just stirred her drink and waited.

Charlotte wet her lips and continued. "It's not what I saw myself doing, but it's a paycheck."

"Of course," Amy trilled. "It must be nice to pay the bills and work on your art on the side."

Ah. Well, that was an easy assumption to make. Why else would an artist work as an assistant other than to support her true passion? Never mind that Charlotte hadn't picked up a sketch pad in years, too exhausted in those very few hours "on the side" to even consider it. Never mind that executive assistants were skilled workers with real responsibilities, or that she might have a plan for career growth within *Front End.*

Because she did! Theoretically.

"Are you still doing portraits?" Nina asked. "You should share more of your work on Instagram, I bet people would love your political caricatures right now."

Charlotte avoided Nina's eyes, unable to lie directly to her face. "Sometimes, yeah."

Jackie put her soda down. "She's not drawing."

"*Jackie,*" Charlotte hissed. She didn't look at Nina or Amy, instead scowling at the woman beside her in the booth.

Her best friend raised her hands, palms forward. "What, am I wrong?"

"No, but . . ." Charlotte fished for words to express *mind your own business* and *stop looking at me like that.* "Priorities change, okay? Work keeps me busy."

Jackie rolled her eyes. "You mean miserable."

"Hey," Nina cut in. "Let Charlotte talk."

Chastened, Jackie snapped her mouth shut.

Nina considered Charlotte with her trademark steely gaze. "Is Jackie right?"

Charlotte rubbed her temples with her fingertips. A tension headache crept up on her, pressing at her eyes. After months of neatly tucking her feelings away each day, she wasn't used to prolonged questioning and excavation.

Jackie circled an arm behind her back and prodded at the stiff knot of muscle in Charlotte's neck. Charlotte wanted to shrug her off, annoyed, but the firm touch felt divine. Her eyes drifted closed. It made her heart ache for something she'd never known: an actual parent to hear out her woes and comfort her when the world got too mean.

She sucked in a deep breath and held it. Then she let it out slowly in a cool stream.

"I'm not drawing. And my job is hell."

For once Jackie said nothing, she just continued gently kneading Charlotte's neck with one hand. A loaded silence fell as the women took in her words. They knew how much it cost her to admit it. Charlotte kept her eyes shut, not needing to see the concern on their faces.

Finally, Nina asked, "Do you want to talk about it?"

What had Pauline in HR said? *Maybe you misunderstood? Your generation is so sensitive.*

"No."

Jackie's hand stilled on her back, her thumb resting against a knot on Charlotte's spine. Then her best friend pulled away, space opening up between them in the booth. Charlotte cringed at her obvious disappointment, but she had nothing else to say.

"Can you afford to quit?" Nina played with a napkin ring as she wondered aloud.

Charlotte had enough to cover two months' rent in her savings account if she only ate PB&Js and rice. Not exactly a freedom fund. "I'm not at that point yet."

Amy tried next. "Have you started looking for other jobs?"

Charlotte squirmed. She folded her napkin and put it on the table, mostly to have something to fidget with. "Not really? Media is competitive. There are hundreds of people applying for each position." Amy's angelic face fell. "I'm trying to move departments. There's a project manager position on the art team that I'm up for. Once I get that, I'll have more time to draw."

Jackie put her Diet Coke down with a thud. "Do you really think Roger will promote you?"

"He's not going to miss me," Charlotte drawled. Her boss frequently made comments about preferring to work with men. After all, women didn't know how to take a joke. HR deemed these remarks "colorful humor" as opposed to gender discrimination.

"But why would he let you move teams if he doesn't have to? What's in it for him?" Jackie's forehead creased as she poked holes in Charlotte's exit plan. "If he's such an asshole, why would anyone risk pissing him off to hire you?"

She blinked. She didn't have an answer for that. While Charlotte didn't expect Roger to mentor her, it never occurred to her that other departments might not want to touch her. He didn't need to actively sabotage her to hold her back.

"I'm not trying to be a jerk," Jackie said as Charlotte's face fell. "*Front End* just seems like a dead end."

Charlotte picked up her napkin and folded it into a paper strip. She looked for a way to defeat Jackie's logic and came up empty. Harsh reality checks were her best friend's specialty, and she had an irritating habit of being right. But they were coming at this from totally different directions: Jackie could afford to walk away from a dead-end job, and Charlotte couldn't.

Roger had all but promised her the project manager role if she came to Reunion & Commencement. Hadn't he?

"Let me ask a different question." Nina leaned forward. "If you do move teams at *Front End*, will you actually like working there?"

Charlotte's nose crinkled as she tried to imagine work without Roger's constant bullshit. Even if she didn't sit right outside his glass office, *Front End* was still his kingdom. Everything the team illustrated needed Roger's sign-off before going to print. He set the company's mission, the editorial theme of each issue, the hiring practices and the policies and the norms. If Charlotte worked with other queer folks, she had no way of knowing, as no one felt comfortable being out at work. *Front End* was also the whitest office she'd ever seen. A new manager wouldn't shield her from the toxic culture that Roger had created. She would never be proud to work there either.

"I don't know," Charlotte admitted for the first time.

She looked at each of her friends in turn, unable to elaborate. An ugly truth fell out of her storage box, one last scrap she'd denied until she couldn't anymore: At some point in the last few years, her burnout had morphed into something worse. She wasn't sad or lost or frustrated. The effort required to go out and have a life was exhausting to consider. Most nights she couldn't muster the energy to cook dinner, instead ordering from a rotating roster of restaurants near her apartment, which didn't exactly help her bank balance. This weekend was the first time she'd seen actual friends in months—either she worked straight through until Monday morning, or she spent her time off watching YouTube videos in an exhausted daze.

Recently she'd started to wonder what would happen if she just didn't get off the subway at her stop and instead rode it to the end of the line. Would anyone worry if she didn't show up for work? Or would her disappearance be an annoyance easily rectified by hiring some other girl fresh out of school with a bachelor's degree and untapped energy? Would anyone notice if she stopped answering texts?

If she disappeared, would anyone care at all?

Charlotte looked down at her bitten fingers. She thought she'd managed to keep a lid on her existential dread, hiding it even from herself. It was mortifying to realize her friends saw right through her.

But there were plenty of ways to signal that you were miserable, like falling out of touch with everyone you loved and sharing nothing but anticapitalist memes on your Instagram story.

Jackie pried the napkin from between Charlotte's fingers and took her hand. She squeezed it tightly, her thumb tracing her knuckles.

"It'll be okay," her best friend said. Like it was that simple.

Maybe it would be. Maybe it wouldn't.

SLACK MESSAGE FROM ROGER LUDERMORE TO CHARLOTTE THORNE, 12:11 PM: do they make yoga pants with built-in wifi

After chasing down the check and negotiating Venmo charges, Nina volunteered to put the meal on her credit card. "For the points, you know how it is," she insisted, waving Amy out of the booth so that she could take the bill to the bar.

Charlotte tagged along. She wanted to say hello to Terry. The restaurant's owner went out of his way to hire students who struggled financially but didn't qualify for Hein's work-study program. After Charlotte's mother made it clear that she was on her own after graduation, Terry let her pick up shifts during senior year.

Nina hopped onto a stool while she waited for service. Charlotte leaned against the dark wooden bar and studied the Polaroids tacked up behind the register. The fresh faces of Terry's current staff beamed back at her. Hein fashion looked the same: The vibe was a bit more androgynous than in the early twenty-teens, but students wore the same button-down flannels from Goodwill. A Black Lives Matter poster took the place of an Obama campaign sign on the side of the drinks fridge.

Nina tapped an elegant finger against Charlotte's wrist, jerking her out of her nostalgia. "Hey, you okay? That got a little intense." She jutted her chin toward their booth.

Charlotte had to put more effort than usual into her answering smile, but she got there eventually. She waggled her hand in the universal sign for *eh*. "I'm still conscious."

Nina raised a quizzical eyebrow before laughing. "You are so weird."

"You're not wrong." Charlotte drummed her fingers on the bar. She could hear Terry's voice in the kitchen, gravelly but encouraging as a Tom Petty song played on the radio. Another soundtrack of life at Hein that she still knew the notes to. If only she could record the sounds of campus and take them back to the city with her.

"This whole weekend is weird," she added.

Nina grunted and leaned forward to rest her chin on her folded arms. "I know what you mean." She didn't look unhappy, but Charlotte had always found Nina harder to read than the rest of their friends. When she wanted to, she could box up her emotions just as well as Charlotte.

"You must miss Eliza," she ventured. Her tone made it clear that Nina could take the subject or leave it.

Nina shifted on the stool and sat up straight again. Her sneakers squeaked as she bopped her feet together. "I do," she said carefully. "But, at the risk of sounding like a bitch, it's been . . . nice? Being here without her?"

Charlotte sat down on the stool next to her.

"I associate everything here with her. But I know if Eliza *were* here, the whole reunion would be wrapped up in our drama. I wouldn't appreciate seeing you and Amy. And Jackie." She peered over her shoulder at their friends. "It used to be fun, always focusing on her. Wondering if she'd text me back. If we'd leave together at the end of the night. But now all that just seems exhausting."

Charlotte remembered her excitement every time Reece texted her last night. He didn't distract her from enjoying her friends. If anything, he gave her something wonderful to look forward to, sunny potential on the horizon. She had known his texts were building to something. Reece wasn't the type to dip out if something better came along. She could trust him.

Ben, on the other hand . . . A text from her ex-boyfriend used to suck the air out of the room.

Now that she thought about it, she felt the same way when she got a Slack message from Roger.

Nina was still watching Jackie and Amy chat across the restaurant. New worry lines gathered on her forehead. "There were things I didn't notice with Eliza always around." She turned back to Charlotte. "Can I ask you something?"

Charlotte had a hunch that she knew where this was going. "Of course."

Nina frowned. She addressed her question to Charlotte's left earlobe. "Am I way off base, or is Jackie into me?"

Oh hell yes.

Charlotte bit back her glee. "She hasn't said anything to me, but it's not like she's subtle."

Immediately Nina relaxed, her teeth pearly white as she mirrored Charlotte's smile. "No, she is not." She laughed. "There's been a vibe this weekend, and y'know, when at Hein!"

There was beauty in Nina's smile, how obviously bemused she was by the situation she'd found herself in. She was changing the script. Instead of spending the weekend on campus pining for her ex-girlfriend, Nina had opened herself up to something entirely different.

Without Eliza around to pull Nina's focus, she and Jackie made a certain kind of sense. They were both unapologetic women, assertive and independent. And as adults as opposed to college babies, they were mature enough to sleep together and handle any complications that might arise the morning after. Charlotte approved.

When at Hein, indeed.

Nina gave her wrist a grateful squeeze. "Thank you, Char. I hope you get some quality time with Jackie too. I know she was excited to see you."

Charlotte smiled uneasily, thinking of her plan to spend the afternoon at the quarry with Reece. But she and Jackie would go to the clothing swap later, and then to dinner after that. They had plenty of time before Roger arrived and she had to turn back into Work Charlotte.

Nina glanced around the restaurant for a server. "Let's pay so I can go flirt."

Charlotte leaned over the counter and craned her neck to glimpse into the kitchen. She could see an elbow and the heel of an old sneaker. Laughter bubbled over the warble of the Dave Matthews Band.

"Oi, Terry!" she called out.

Terry's face popped around the corner immediately, his mouth caught midlaugh. "What? Oh snap, look who it is." The rest of Terry followed his head out of the kitchen. "I was wondering if I'd ever see you again."

Charlotte met his high five with a firm smack. "Hi, boss."

"You look great, Thorne. Long hair suits you." He looked her over fondly like a favorite uncle. "Glad to see you're not skin and bones anymore. Ready to cash out?" He swept their check and Nina's credit card from the counter and whirled around to the register in one smooth motion. "Where you living now? D.C.?"

"Brooklyn."

"Ah, good for you, kid. You workin' hard?"

She never knew if it was his soft Boston accent or his salt-and-pepper hair, but Terry exuded kindness. He was whip-smart and embedded in local politics, but he treated everyone who worked at his restaurant the same way. If you were hungry, he fed you. If you were short a few bucks, he put it on a tab that never needed to be paid. If you needed a ride home during a blizzard, he threw your bike in the back of his minivan and dropped you off at your dorm.

Charlotte sighed. "Too hard." He tutted under his breath as he slid Nina her bill to sign. "I miss it here. Best job I ever had."

"You get tired of those schmucks in New York, you come back

here. We got new merch and everything." He gestured to his blue T-shirt. It featured an anthropomorphized nacho chip wearing sunglasses. "Look at 'im," Terry boasted. "Ain't he cute?"

Nina caught Charlotte's eye, and she fought the urge to laugh.

"Adorable," she said. "Unsettling, but adorable."

"Ey, no free shirt for you with that attitude." Terry waggled his finger, but he was still grinning. "Let me get you some nachos to go, yeah? On the house." He barged back into the kitchen, already shouting orders.

Plastic plates clattered in the kitchen as they hit the floor. "Ey, ey, slow down!" Terry cried out, more alarmed than angry. "No need to rush, Rico, take it easy. Don't want you getting hurt."

"That nacho looks constipated," Nina observed. She slid her credit card back into her wallet and stood up. "Excuse me, I have wooing to do."

Chapter 9

TEXT MESSAGE FROM CHARLOTTE THORNE TO REECE KRUEGER, 1:07 PM: You still at the pond?

TEXT MESSAGE FROM REECE KRUEGER TO CHARLOTTE THORNE, 1:10 PM: yeah! bring nachos

COBALT POND WASN'T actually a pond. Decades ago, the Hein family supplemented its fortune by carving marble out of the Massachusetts landscape. Nature had taken the quarry back, filling its deep crevices with rainwater and runoff from a nearby river.

Four miles from campus on land now owned by the county, the quarry was a destination for Hein students during the warmer months of term. The water could freeze your toes off except for a handful of weeks in August, but its grassy banks were the perfect place to stretch out with coursework and a cheap bottle of wine. Generations of local kids added their graffiti tags on the marble outcroppings. Bros jumped like falling stars from the taller cliffs, shouting and spiraling through the air on their way down. Every so often alumni returned to take their engagement photos at the water's edge in the fall, the burning red leaves a perfect New England backdrop.

Today the quarry boasted a full house. Hein students and alumni scattered in small groups around the jagged edge of the quarry's mouth. A few people waded in the water despite the chill.

Jackie dropped Charlotte off on the roadside. "I'm going to take a nap while you're out, and then let's head to the clothing swap at five." She passed Charlotte a bottle of sunscreen from her tote bag. "Text me when you're on your way back, okay? We can find something fun for you to wear tonight."

"Sounds good." Charlotte popped open the sunscreen and rubbed a splotch across the bridge of her nose. "Are you sure you don't mind me ditching you? You're welcome to join us."

Jackie waved her off. "Go have fun, we have all night." She tossed over the take-out bag of nachos. "Five P.M., don't forget!"

"I won't."

After Jackie sped off, Charlotte crouched to roll up the cuffs of her jeans. The reunion committee had lucked out with the weather; today's temperature was in the midseventies. Perfect conditions to hang out at an old marble quarry with your ex and his bros after a night of sex and unspoken feelings.

She strode through the grass to the pond. A quick scan confirmed that Ben wasn't there. Maybe he'd only come to the reunion for the Thursday night panel? She wouldn't put it past him to bounce as soon as he wasn't the center of attention anymore.

A clique of proper adults—ten-year Hein alums, presumably—sat with a toddler on a faded quilt. Charlotte spotted the hockey guys on the opposite bank, a cooler open beside an old charcoal grill. Garrett stoked the flames under a bunch of burgers, an HU hockey cap backward on his head.

Misty romped toward her across the marble. Her red tail wagged like a flag on the back of a bicycle.

Charlotte kneeled to greet the pup. "Hey, honey." Misty threw herself into her arms and arranged herself on Charlotte's chest, panting happily. "Oh, you want to be carried, do you? Okay, princess."

Garrett stiffened as she approached their cookout, but he gave her a polite enough wave with the spatula. He must have resigned himself to her presence after Reece went MIA last night and returned in a good mood. "What's good? Burger?"

"I'm full, thanks. But I brought nacho fries from Terry's." She put her leftovers down on the cooler as a peace offering.

Liam sprawled in a beach chair, a baseball cap pulled down over his face. He patted blindly atop the cooler until his hand landed on the nachos. Then he pulled the bag into his lap and fed himself a chip, all without emerging from underneath the brim of his hat.

"Late night?" Charlotte asked.

Garrett flipped a patty. "Liam was foolish enough to partake in illicit drugs."

The bro in question groaned inaudibly.

Charlotte winced, unable to relate but still sympathetic. "Where's Reece?"

"He's swimming again." She followed the tip of his spatula to a head bobbing in the water.

"Jesus, he must be freezing."

Garrett shrugged. "Spare towels are by the marshmallows."

She nodded her thanks and eased Misty to the ground.

Charlotte stepped out of her loafers and sank her toes into the grass. She hadn't brought a swimsuit with her, but as far as she could tell, the bros hadn't either.

A well-worn dirt path led the way to the clifftop. She chose her footing carefully, dodging exposed roots and abandoned bottle caps. At the peak, the marble was slick and smooth against her skin. The outcropping over the water had softened underneath nearly a century of adventurous feet.

The warm air kissed her body as she stripped off her shirt and her jeans, leaving them in a heap on the stone. She ignored the voice in her head that worried over the temperature of the water and the height of the jump. Back in college she thought nothing of throwing herself off a thirty-foot cliff in her underpants and a sports bra.

Charlotte's toes found the edge of the cliff. The water was black despite the sunshine pouring across its surface—the quarry's depth ate up the light. She hugged her arms around her chest.

The impact would shock her body. She'd be freezing when she got out too; the air wasn't hot enough to dry her thick hair. She'd forgotten to bring a scrunchie.

Reece swam laps below her. He sliced through the water with even precision, performing a steady freestyle, one arm after the other. She pictured him easily as one of those elderly men in the YMCA pool at six A.M., faded swim trunks and a white towel from the front desk. Reece would always be handsome, at any age. He'd still have those crinkling green eyes when he smiled.

"Yo," she shouted down to him. Reece stopped his laps, treading water as he peered around. "Up here!"

He craned his neck. "Charlie?" For a moment he looked disoriented, but then he beamed up at her from underneath his dripping hair. "Are you gonna jump?"

She wasn't sure. Thirty feet didn't look like much from the ground, but up here . . . Reece bobbed like a tiny LEGO man in the water.

"I don't know!"

He laughed, not unkindly. "You don't have to! I can swim around and meet you in the shallows."

Because of course he would. Reece would never pressure her into doing something stupid, even if there wasn't much of a risk to it. She didn't have to do this if she didn't want to—he wouldn't think any less of her.

"How's the water?" she called down.

His barking laugh was answer enough. "Awful!"

She looked around the pond. Reece was the only person actually *in* the water. The past winter had been a rough one, no doubt freezing the quarry into a thick layer of ice. By the end of the summer the water would be pleasantly cool. Today it only hurt.

Reece treaded water as he watched her make up her mind. He didn't look cold, or maybe he just didn't care. "You get used to it," he yelled.

It was a terrible idea, but the whole point of the reunion was to do childish shit as long as no one got hurt. This was a reprieve from responsibility: no strategy, no five-year plan, no fail-safe.

Fun.

When was the last time she'd taken a risk? A real risk, not just ordering delivery at a new restaurant or experimenting with shoulder pads. Where was the brash impulsiveness she once had, the wonderful jerk who bought a box of cheap hair dye and blew off studying for finals to go to Amy's a cappella concert?

Where was the girl who refused to apologize for her identity, even in the face of her mother's disapproval?

Charlotte thought longingly of the girl she was before she graduated college. But that wasn't right either—this went further back than that. She bubble-wrapped herself after her breakup with Ben. Since graduation, she insulated herself against happiness even more. Some of what she felt was burnout, and some of it was genuine clinical depression, but most of it was just her. She let herself stagnate.

Once upon a time, Charlotte hadn't feared every risk and unknown path.

She wanted to be brave again. *Fuck*, did she want to be brave again.

Before she could consider the many ways she could injure herself, Charlotte stepped back from the cliff's edge. She rolled her head until her neck popped and cracked. Then she took a deep breath, held it, and let it go.

One foot after the other, her toes found purchase on the marble. And then she was falling, the air rushing against her bare skin. All around her was blue sky and the gentle green of the trees bordering the quarry. She could hear Reece whooping from the water below, and Liam and Garrett cheering for her in the distance.

She closed her eyes and curled in on herself, her arms coming around her knees.

If she could bottle this moment—if she could synthesize this pure, reckless courage—maybe she could find her way back to herself. Back to Charlotte Thorne, bachelor of fine arts with a minor in sociology, resident cartoonist of the school paper, master chef of microwaved noodles, shy until you got to know her, formerly preppy, bisexual weirdo.

The water seized her in its sudden, cold embrace. It broke her down and left her spluttering for oxygen. When her face met the silky air again, she coughed and fisted pond scum out of her eyes.

Then she laughed. The sound bounced off the marble and ricocheted around the quarry.

She'd forgotten the beautiful timbre of her own laughter.

AT REECE'S ENCOURAGEMENT, Charlotte handed over her buzzing iPhone. Her anxiety roared as he slid it into his backpack.

"You'll be with Roger all day tomorrow," Reece reminded her. His hand offered a tantalizing distraction on her thigh, fingers splayed across her bare skin.

She shivered on a damp towel in her underwear and Reece's shirt. He'd insisted she wear it when she started to turn blue. It was a sweet gesture, but her hair soaked the fabric through within minutes.

Charlotte gave his backpack a desperate look.

"There is no work for you to do right now," Reece reminded her.

She knew he was right. Saturday afternoon fell securely outside her office hours. Roger was, if his most recent Slack messages were anything to go off, hammered. She couldn't prepare Twitter coverage of his commencement address until he finished writing it . . . which he probably wouldn't do until he sobered up.

For years now she'd gone above and beyond what was required of her, and it had gotten her nowhere. Roger could fend for himself until he arrived on campus tomorrow. She wasn't going to let his bullshit ruin her Saturday, not when Reece sat next to her all sweaty and sunkissed. Not after that jump.

"Fine," she said. "Okay."

She chewed the skin around her thumb without even noticing she was doing it.

"Here." Reece clicked his tongue at Misty. The dog trotted over, her fur covered in dirt from a romp through the forest behind the quarry. "Hold her, she'll calm you down." He scooped Misty up and deposited her in Charlotte's lap, covering them both in dust and grime.

Charlotte laughed and brushed a dirt clod off her towel. "She's filthy."

"If only there were a large body of water where we could wash ourselves off." Reece lay back beside her, pillowing his head on his arms. "See? You look more relaxed already."

She felt more relaxed too. She didn't know if it was getting laid or relinquishing her phone or throwing herself off a thirty-foot cliff, but she did feel better. Lighter.

"I needed this," she said. "It's been a shitty few years."

Charlotte ran a spare towel through her wet hair. It was a losing battle—her thick mane absorbed anything and everything it came into contact with. Misty licked her stomach, unbothered by Charlotte's shifting around.

Reece squinted up at her. He cupped a hand over his eyes to block the sun. "Sounds like it. Want to give me the highlights since graduation?" A smile tugged at his lips, like he was aware of the question's absurdity.

She raised her eyebrows. "Where to start?"

"You moved to New York," he prompted, and gestured for her to continue.

Right. Charlotte moved to New York for her internship and the city's thriving queer scene, thinking she could reinvent herself and leave the ghosts of Hein behind. It worked, sort of, for a while.

She frowned. "I had that internship at *ChompNews*. I loved it there, great people, fun projects. It was kind of all-consuming in a gross way, but I was happy."

ChompNews was the hottest website of 2013. Their home page would link to an industry-shaking exposé about discrimination in

Hollywood alongside a quiz that told you which Pokémon was your ideal roommate. Instead of a salary or benefits, her internship in the art department paid her a stipend of a thousand dollars a month. She burned through her meager savings from waiting tables at Terry's during college, and she racked up credit card debt to afford her apartment.

The financial sacrifice seemed like it paid off when *ChompNews* hired her as a graphics assistant at the end of her internship. For a magical nine months Charlotte drew infographics about immigration policy, sustainable fashion, and queer representation in television. Her new salary barely covered her expenses, but now she had health insurance and a manager who cared about her professional growth. She played Ping-Pong with her co-workers after hours and was the first in line at their weekly catered lunches. There was even a Slack channel for LGBTQIA+ *ChompNews* employees that hosted a monthly happy hour at Stonewall. She felt like part of a family.

Plus she could doodle on the subway to and from the office, her brain bursting with ideas for political cartoons and posters, maybe even tattoos . . .

Sure, she still had debt that wasn't paid off, but for the first time it wasn't getting worse. Charlotte felt like she had a little breathing room, especially with the money she saved on groceries thanks to free bagels in the *ChompNews* kitchen every morning. Thousands of aspiring illustrators would kill to be exactly where she was. In fact, it was the kind of job she'd always dreamed about—the opportunity to use her skills to help people understand issues that really mattered.

For a brief moment she had her dream job.

And then she woke up.

"I was too junior to know what was going on, but the company was bleeding money. Like every other digital magazine, I guess. Things started to change. The energy shifted."

It started with the perks: no more free food or kombucha on tap. She dismissed it as innocuous corporate belt-tightening, the kind of budget-trimming a company did when it reached maturity. But then their healthcare policy changed, and premiums soared. Full-time staff writers were fired and replaced by freelancers.

"And then they sold the company, and tons of people got laid off."

Reece shifted on the towel next to her, sitting up to see her expression. She shrugged, knowing her experience was crappy but unremarkable. Just shy of her one-year anniversary with the company, *ChompNews* was acquired by a venture capital firm. They promised nothing would change in a bland email lauding the editorial achievements of the brand. Not long after, seventy percent of the staff was fired during a conference call, Charlotte included.

And so she put her succulents and her *ChompNews* beanie in a cardboard box and started applying for jobs. As her inbox remained silent, she nannied for frantic, beautiful moms in Park Slope and sold some of her clothes on eBay. She kept it together for a while, radically economizing on a diet of bodega noodles, passing on invitations from *ChompNews* friends to grab drinks at the local queer bar. She was stressed and scared, but not terrified. Not truly screwed.

"Then my wisdom teeth decided to ruin my life."

Reece groaned. Charlotte flashed him a humorless, toothy smile. She tapped her molars. "Yeah, great timing. No dental insurance, no sick leave, just a credit card."

"That's brutal," Reece said.

Disasters compounded one atop the other: She couldn't afford to go to the dentist for regular cleanings, and so she didn't know her wisdom teeth were impacted until she couldn't ignore the pain anymore. Then she couldn't afford a good dentist, so she had to wait for a cheap appointment to open at NYU's dental school. Even then, discount surgery still wasn't free.

She had to miss nannying for the surgery itself, and for recovery time, which meant even more money down the drain. She wasn't close with her roommates, and it wasn't like she had family she could turn to, so she had to manage by herself while loopy on painkillers. Her bad credit went from manageable to monstrous.

"Shit got ugly for a while, financially," Charlotte said. "I got desperate enough to contact the career center at Hein. And wouldn't you know it, Roger Ludermore, Class of '81, was hiring an assistant."

She didn't tell Reece about the weeks between the surgery and getting the job at *Front End.* She had trouble remembering that window of time, when it seemed like maybe she'd be better off not being alive at all. Being a human was expensive, especially in a city like New York, but relocating would cost money too—money she didn't have. She started walking everywhere, ostensibly to save money on subway fare, but really because the edge of the train platform made her nervous.

Charlotte didn't think Reece would judge her if she told him about the intrusive suicidal thoughts she had during those terrible weeks. She suspected he would understand. But her major depressive episode felt so far away under the early summer sun, and that chapter of her life was over. She would never let herself be that financially precarious again. She hated Roger, but she never, ever forgot the terror of her own mind suggesting that this could all go away if she wanted it to.

Her boss had saved her from ruin. Whatever nonsense he pulled, however miserable she became at work, it was worth it to pay down her debt and build a new foundation for herself. Every paycheck meant survival. Every holiday bonus meant security.

Front End's health insurance paid for her antidepressants.

She cleared her throat, mentally changing the subject.

Reece fished a bottled water out of the cooler. He offered it to her, but she shook her head. "Do you still draw?" he asked.

Coming from him, the question didn't smart. She wasn't sure why it didn't bother her the way it did with Jackie—maybe it was the gentleness in his voice. Reece didn't look at her with expectations of who she could be if she worked harder. He knew that simply getting by could be an accomplishment too.

Reece just let her talk, bearing witness. Sometimes you only needed someone to keep you company while you cleaned out your brain.

What had he asked? Did she still draw. There was a sketch pad in her desk drawer that she hadn't touched since she bought it years ago, but she knew that didn't count. She couldn't exactly brag about her collection of coloring books.

"I submitted to some places," she said. "But there's so much competition. I never heard anything back."

She had a sneaking feeling that Reece could read between the lines, but he didn't pry. "I loved your portraits in the paper," he said instead.

"You remember those?"

"You kidding? They were great." He tapped his knee, squinting as he thought back. "You drew one of Liam when he wrote an op-ed about the new rink. He had it taped in his locker for months. You got his eyes perfectly."

Charlotte hid her blushing face, touched by his memory. She loved sketching portraits of students who submitted opinion pieces to the student paper. It allowed her to get to know Hein's many personalities without having to introduce herself. On Wednesday and Sunday afternoons as the paper went into final layout, she holed up in the newspaper office and studied faces from the school directory. Every so often she got a complaint about an unflattering detail, but for the most part her minimalist profiles flew under the radar.

She chanced a look at Reece and found him studying her.

"I thought it was so cool, how much you did with just a few lines. You really see people," he marveled.

She fought the urge to deflect.

Take the compliment, Thorne.

"Thank you."

Reece looked proud of her, like he could see her discomfort with his praise. "I'm sorry work stuff sucks," he said, returning to their original conversation.

"It is what it is. Not everyone gets to be a *New Yorker* cartoonist." She stole the water bottle and took a sip after all, her throat dry. "What do you call someone who lives to work but hates her job?"

Reece's eyes flashed. "A worker exploited by capitalism?"

Charlotte huffed a laugh. "I was going to say a masochist."

"So you're not seeing anyone, you work for a jerk, and you don't have a dog even though you want one. Any hobbies?" His eyes twinkled at her, balancing out his snark.

"I bought myself a weighted blanket for Christmas. It feels like I'm being smothered every time I take a nap. It's great."

"I don't think napping counts as a hobby, no matter how many accessories you buy."

She stuck her tongue out at him. "What about you? What's your postgrad life story?"

Reece ran a meaty hand through his hair, sending it in all directions. "Pass."

"C'mon, you can't just ask me questions all weekend." Charlotte poked his shoulder. "Tell me about your life. I want to know."

"Buckle up, Charlie." Reece stole the water bottle back and took a swig. "I lived in St. Louis for a year, walking dogs and doing SAT tutoring and stuff. Somehow managed to sober up. Drove around listening to Death Cab feeling sorry for myself. Then I applied to business school."

Charlotte couldn't contain her surprise. "What?"

He rolled his eyes. "Yeah, I know. No idea what I was thinking. Didn't get in anywhere, obviously."

Reece filled her in on his ensuing move to Columbus for a marketing job, where he met his ex-girlfriend. Charlotte kept her face still at the mention of Jess, not sure what reaction she was entitled to as his weekend-hookup-ex-person.

"How long were you together?" she asked.

"Two years." Reece's eyebrows did a lot of communicating for him. She watched his face contort and smooth out again. "It feels like longer because we got serious so fast. She wanted everything as soon as possible."

Charlotte didn't follow. "What do you mean?"

"Marriage, a house, kids." Reece fiddled with the cap of the water bottle, screwing it on and off and on again. "And yeah, I'd like those things someday, but now? I'm twenty-seven and broke, the country is falling apart, the world is on fire. Becoming a dad is the last thing on my mind."

"That's fair," Charlotte said.

"The more I thought about it, the less sure I was that she was the person I'd want that future with anyway. So I moved back home." He examined his hands, calloused and tanned. "I shouldn't complain," he added. "I have my car, and my health." Reece's face fell, no doubt thinking of his dad. "The city college has a good vet tech program. It'd mean more debt, but at least that's a real track, you know?"

Reece looked at her, his green eyes swimming with poorly disguised insecurity.

Charlotte wanted to wrap her arms around him and squeeze until he understood that he had nothing to be ashamed of. His life wasn't as glamorous as some of their classmates', sure, but everyone else was full of shit. She didn't care that he wasn't living in a name-brand city or making his fortune at a scammy startup. It mattered more that he was finding his own way, building a life without a cheat sheet.

She pictured Aubrey leaning back in her desk chair, filling out her fantasy bracket for *The Bachelor* while Charlotte skipped lunch to type up board meeting minutes. It wasn't fair that someone as generous as Reece struggled while people like Aubrey sailed through life on a yacht of good connections.

"What's the clinic like?" Charlotte asked, pushing her resentment aside. "Did your mom ever expand?"

"She did." His face brightened with pride. "We can board pets now, which is a good revenue stream. Sometimes I work nights to keep them company, midnight pee breaks and stuff. When we get a super nervous dog, I take 'em into the office to watch Netflix."

"I'm sure they find sci-fi very comforting."

Reece grinned. "Dogs love *Star Trek*."

"You're a doofus."

"I will not argue with you on that."

They fell into a comfortable silence as Misty licked Charlotte's hands. The sun moved out from behind a cloud and spilled across Reece's back. He groaned as it baked his skin, his head rolling forward to rest his chin on his chest. She watched the blades of his shoulders move, muscle stretching taut across bone.

A memory of last night returned, her fingertips tracing his spine. The light pressure of her touch had sent a shiver through his body, his hips canting forward to rock into her just so. Charlotte licked her lips, her throat dry for different reasons.

When would they be alone again? She couldn't kick Jackie out of their room two nights in a row.

Reece lay down on the towel. He moved to rest on his side, one hand propping up his head so that he could look at her. "How are things with your parents? Any progress?"

Charlotte frowned at the tonal shift. Her teeth found the inside of her cheek, worrying the tender skin. She shrugged with a practiced, blasé *whatever*. "My father looks me up when he's in New York on business. We go out for a nice steak dinner and talk about the stock market." He didn't laugh at her crisp enunciation. She waggled her eyebrows. "Want any investment tips? Booth Thorne has loads of 'em."

Reece's brows crinkled. She didn't know what bothered him more, that her parents made barely any effort to see her or that she called her father by his full name.

"I'm good, thanks," Reece said. "I have a Starbucks gift card that will appreciate any day now."

She snorted.

"And your mom?"

Charlotte stared at the dirt. She hated talking about her family under normal circumstances. Telling Reece felt like peeling back her skin to show him her small intestine.

He already knew her tale of queer teen neglect from support

group. But no one other than Jackie knew the mortifying details and how they all connected: her mother's homophobia, why she and Ben broke up, what had made her blow off Reece at graduation. She kept too many secrets, and this one was impossible to expose to the daylight after so long locked away.

But the door in her memory already sat ajar thanks to her return to campus. All she had to do was open it a little further. Bravery didn't always mean jumping off cliffs.

"It's been years. She's not in my life anymore, not since graduation."

She heard Reece's quiet exhale of breath, his innocent surprise. Charlotte braced herself for judgment or pity. Or worse, for him to run away screaming. He knew her family was messy, but this was top-tier fucked-up family dynamics. Charlotte's father had been functionally irrelevant for years, an unreliable pen pal on a different continent, but that was old news and not Charlotte's choice. What kind of daughter didn't speak to her mother for half a decade?

Family was everything to Reece. His dad's death created a tight unit of respect and unconditional support. The Kruegers had been to hell and back, and they adored each other. Their nuclear-family love was never, ever in doubt.

But Reece didn't say anything, and his face remained still. He caught Misty's tail and ran it through his fingers before she squirmed out of his reach.

Charlotte wrapped her arms more securely around the dog, who settled down in her lap immediately.

That raw, dark wound in her chest roared inexplicably to life, the same way it did in the lead-up to graduation. The same way it did when Ben kissed her, when the honeymoon phase of their relationship ended and loving him required hating herself.

Ben understood that wound. When she explained her parents' divorce shortly after her birth, he only nodded. He already spoke the language of a loveless home. Some wealthy families made a hobby of quiet cruelty, and Ben's parents were just like hers. It took her too long to realize he wanted to continue his father's legacy.

Charlotte took a deep breath. Before her confidence could fail her, she asked, "Can I say something that's been bothering me?"

"Yeah, please." Reece rushed to reassure her.

She didn't want to hurt his feelings, so she chose her words with care. "You were a bit snide on Thursday when . . . when I said I was recovering from my relationship with Ben."

Reece sat up on his towel, a wet lock of hair falling across his forehead. She longed to reach up and brush it back, but she braced herself for him to get defensive.

Instead, he kept his expression controlled, not letting his emotions leak out. He chose his words as deliberately as she did. "I'm sorry. Breakups are hard. I shouldn't have been dismissive."

"That's not what I mean." Charlotte ran her hand down Misty's coat, unsticking clods of dirt. The dog stared at her with those big brown puppy eyes, giving her nothing but love. "I wasn't heartbroken. I was recovering from . . . trauma, I guess?"

Reece folded his legs up to his chest and rested his chin on his knees. She had his full attention.

Charlotte took another deep breath. The word *trauma* felt self-indulgent, a Lifetime Channel for Women overstatement. She associated trauma with plane crashes and child abductions, not the obnoxious behavior of college boyfriends. It still felt like exaggerating to claim it as her own.

But she was getting ahead of herself.

Use your words, Charlotte Thorne.

"Our relationship was not great."

Reece's mouth turned into a hard line. He waited a moment before asking, "Did he hurt you?"

Charlotte concentrated on Misty as she considered her words. "Not physically."

It had been a long time since she'd talked about Ben. These days Jackie preferred to pretend Charlotte's ex-boyfriend was simply dead.

But he wasn't dead. Ben was very much alive, and successful, and maybe within a five-mile radius of this conversation. Charlotte reflexively scanned the quarry for his blond hair.

Reece seemed to figure out what she was looking for, his brow furrowing. "I always thought the guy was a snob, but I didn't know him. Do you want to tell me about it? About him?"

No.

Maybe.

Reece's face was blank. She suspected he would keep it that way.

And, well, he asked. No one ever asked.

"I can start from the beginning," Charlotte said. He nodded, and she took a deep breath. "Okay. Junior year, Jackie went to Paris for fall semester. I had to stay here to finish requirements for my sociology minor. I missed her more than I expected. Obviously, I had other friends, but we'd been inseparable for two years and I was lost without her." She gave Reece a weak smile. "Probably some codependency issues there."

"Who among us?" Reece joked, and she laughed.

The levity didn't last. She ran a fingernail along the soft skin of her thumb, the sharp bite grounding her. "That's when I met Ben," she continued. "He was intense. I've never known anyone like him."

She liked it in the beginning. Ben Mead didn't do anything by halves. With Jackie away on study abroad, Charlotte's world hollowed out, and Ben leapt in to fill the void. He saw her standing off to the side at a party for the newspaper staff, and he chatted her up, remembering a portrait she'd drawn of him. When they went home together that night she assumed it was a one-night stand. But as sunlight crept into his bedroom at the Sigma Delt frat house, he tucked her hair behind her ear and said, *This is something real. I already know.*

When she got back to her room at Acronym the next day, a

bouquet of roses waited for her on the mat. On Friday, he took her out for Thai food off campus. *I'm a feminist,* he told her as he dropped a metal credit card on top of the check. *But as long as there's a wage gap, men should pay for dinner.*

They talked about everything: the future of journalism, her favorite classic movie posters, his political ambitions, their families. After years of campus hookup culture, everyone competing to care the least, Ben's seriousness disarmed her. It scared her a little too, but Ben assured her that was her fear of commitment talking.

It's not your fault you don't know what love looks like, he said. *Your parents didn't teach you.*

And then there were the Faber-Castell colored pencils as a one-month anniversary present, and Thanksgiving with his family in Tahoe. She got swept away. Finally Charlotte got to experience the kind of love that Nina and Eliza had, the Technicolor joy she always worried she wasn't born to feel. Ben didn't just create space for her in his world; he made her its center. He wasn't afraid to want her. To show up for her. To know everything about her.

But as the first snow fell on the eaves of Acronym, Ben's intensity showed a different side.

"I guess you could say he was clingy." Her thumb returned to her mouth, her teeth snagging a torn cuticle. An old fear returned that she was exaggerating, or that she misunderstood Ben's behavior. It wasn't like she had much relationship experience to compare him to. She'd had partners before and since Ben, but none that felt that serious, that intense. It was hard not to see him as her only Real Relationship.

Charlotte did her best to set her doubt aside. Jackie told her again and again that her feelings mattered and that she wasn't making it up. She couldn't smear Ben's reputation in the privacy of her own mind.

"No, it was worse than that," she said. "He was controlling and manipulative. When I told him I needed more alone time, he said I was being selfish. If I told him he hurt my feelings, he said I was too sensitive. He could turn every conversation around and make me the bad guy."

Her throat tightened and she stopped for a second to breathe. The wound in her chest smarted and ached. Ben's words sounded crisp and new, burned into her memory.

You're so pathetic, Charlotte. Christ, what's wrong with you?

"He made me feel crazy," she breathed.

Reece recaptured Misty's tail and rolled her fur between his fingers, listening in silence.

"I should have seen through it. I *did* see through it. But he told me I didn't know what a real relationship was because of my parents. That I was lucky he was so patient and understanding. And I believed him."

That hurt more than Ben's words: She felt complicit in his behavior. Every so often she stirred as if from a deep sleep and saw their relationship clearly, only to get sucked back in again. She didn't want to know. Finally, someone had chosen her. Finally, she was ready to be chosen. Finally, someone loved her, and it felt so good when it didn't feel horrible.

The illusion of their relationship took more work to maintain when it had a witness. "Jackie saw right through it," Charlotte said. "When she got back from Paris in January, she just . . . she hated him. But I didn't want to hear it, you know? I loved him and Jackie didn't know him. That's what I told myself."

Charlotte expected embarrassment to slow her down, but it was a relief to tell Reece the truth. He didn't rush to condemn Ben's behavior or ask her insensitive questions. There was no *why didn't you listen to her* or *how could you have been so naïve.* Or worse, *why didn't you just leave.* His face revealed the occasional flare of outrage or concern, but he didn't make her story about himself and his feelings. He knew she needed to keep going until she was done.

"Ben told me she didn't support our relationship, and that she was judgmental and pushy." Charlotte took a ragged breath, ashamed of her betrayal. "I found myself agreeing with him."

"Jackie *is* judgmental and pushy," Reece granted.

Charlotte nodded. "Yeah, she can be. So I didn't see it as an isolation tactic, I was just like, sure, my best friend is kind of abrasive. But it wasn't only her. He would go on about how jealous Nina was of our relationship, and how weird the support group was. He cut me off from everyone."

"That's hard to see when you're in the middle of it." Reece placed his hand palm up on the towel next to her. She considered it but couldn't take it, not wanting to be touched right now. To his credit, he didn't react to her subtle rejection. "How did it end, if you don't mind me asking?"

"I don't mind," she said, surprised to find she meant it. The more she spoke, the easier it was to keep going. "We were in this cycle. He would do something shitty, and I would either take it, or go back to my place to get away from him. If he sensed I wasn't going to let it go, he would start crying about how he didn't want to turn into his asshole father, and he needed my help to be a better man."

That line usually worked on her. Who could understand not wanting to become your parents better than her, the only daughter of Booth and Olivia Harrington Thorne? It mattered that he knew he had to change, that he wanted to change. In her heart of hearts, she had desperately wanted her mother to want to change too.

I want to do better, Charlotte. I want to deserve you. Please don't give up on me. You know how much I love you, right?

She was in too deep to recognize Ben's pleas for help as another manipulation.

But then the cycle was interrupted.

"One night in the spring, we had this fight."

It wasn't even a big fight, just another stupid fight in a long line of stupid fights. Could you even call it a fight when only one person raised their voice? When only one person cried?

She'd tried to get a stain out of his shirt and accidentally made it worse. Charlotte and Jackie had moved into an apartment in Rawls

Tower when she got back from Paris, and Ben came over to pick up the shirt before a Sigma Delt formal event.

You idiot, look what you've done. Do you know how expensive this is? This is Italian linen.

Charlotte rubbed at her eyes. She wasn't crying but they itched, that tension headache threatening to return.

"Ben thought we were alone, but Jackie was in her room. She recorded us on her phone through the wall. You remember how thin the walls were in that building?"

Charlotte threw Reece a nervous look, and he nodded at the rhetorical question.

"After he left, she played the fight back for me."

Thank goodness for her best friend. Charlotte would always feel indebted to her, no matter what distance grew between them, because sometimes she wondered if she would be dead if it weren't for Jackie. How much would Ben's abuse have escalated without Jackie's intervention? How much more of herself would she have lost if she'd stayed with him?

Charlotte trained her focus on the smooth surface of the quarry and the gentle sway of the grass in the breeze.

I'm safe. It's over. This happened years ago.

Even here, the past had a way of bleeding into the present. Ben's voice crackled out of Jackie's iPhone, dangerously tight. Her ex never lost his temper. He wielded it with expert precision.

"She made me listen to him call me an idiot and a bitch and a spoiled brat, all because of a *shirt*."

Reece clenched his fist on the towel.

"And I just . . . kept apologizing."

The memory caught in her throat like a shard of glass. She sounded terrified on the recording, groveling for forgiveness over a fabric stain. Her biggest fear in that moment was that he would walk out the front door. That Ben would leave and she'd be alone again, forgotten and replaced by some other girl.

That hurt more than anything Ben could ever say. When she saw their relationship from the outside, she didn't recognize herself. What happened to the girl who repaired Acronym's roof as a freshman after watching a shingling tutorial on YouTube? Where had the Charlotte gone who found a room-and-board-inclusive internship in Boston so that she wouldn't spend the summer before junior year with her mother? When did she swap out her combat boots for bougie ballet flats from Ben's mother?

She used to be so capable. She used to be strong.

Two years at Hein taught Charlotte to value her authentic self. Ben destroyed that progress in just a few months.

"It still took me a while to break up with him after that, and he didn't take it well. I told him outside the library so he couldn't make a scene in public, but he still threw a classic Ben Mead tantrum. He sent me batshit text messages until I blocked him. I barely left the apartment, I was so worried I'd bump into him. And even when it was over, it wasn't over." She laughed humorlessly. "He told everyone at the paper that he dumped me, and that I was having a nervous breakdown and he just couldn't help me anymore. When that version of the story didn't catch on, he tried to convince people I cheated on him with Jackie. It was so fucked up."

Her chest felt tight, and she realized she was holding her breath as she spoke. She inhaled slowly and then let it out.

Her heart broke twice that spring: once when she understood her boyfriend didn't really love her, and again when Hein morphed from safe haven to enemy territory. Everywhere felt like Ben's turf: the newspaper office, the student gym where he played tennis every other day, the dining hall at the heart of campus. Even the library felt dangerous, bearing his last name at the entryway. Charlotte skulked from Rawls Tower to classes and back again. She and Jackie cooked most of their meals at home or walked to Terry's.

Summer break was a blessing: She focused on her thesis and bartending at the restaurant. But the panic attacks started in the fall.

"There's so much about senior year that I don't remember," Charlotte said. "It's a blur."

"Trauma," Reece recalled.

Charlotte picked at her nails. "Yeah. Trauma."

She still struggled not to blame herself for falling for Ben. The scar tissue of their relationship would take years to heal, no matter how many books she read about love-bombing and gaslighting. And when she looked back at senior year, she understood why her brain scorched with terror anytime Reece said something too kind. It made no sense to her when he wanted more from her than sex.

How could a man so good want to be with someone like her, someone weak enough to love a monster like Ben? How could Reece want such a disaster? Why would anyone choose her?

Charlotte remembered Reece standing with his family after the commencement ceremony, his arm around his little sister's shoulders. Reece had asked her weeks before if she would meet them at the picnic, and she agreed. She even looked forward to it. Charlotte wanted to shake the hand of the mother strong enough to carry her family through tragedy while running her own business. She wanted to hug the little sister she had heard so much about in support group.

Then graduation day finally arrived and Charlotte found herself alone. She didn't have parents to hug her, or doting grandparents to gush over her internship at *ChompNews*, or aunts and uncles to hustle them all together for a group picture. No one came to celebrate her accomplishments. She felt Ben's words all over again, a year after their breakup: *You're so pathetic, Charlotte. Christ, what's wrong with you?*

When the agreed-upon time came for her to meet the Kruegers, Charlotte just couldn't do it. She saw them across the quad and turned the opposite direction. His affection for her made no sense, a rose extended to a wood chipper. Maybe Reece couldn't see it, but his family would. She was the last girl who a mother would choose for her son.

Reece broke the silence. "That must have been a lot to process."

"I didn't trust myself for a long time after that," Charlotte confessed.

There was a sheen of understanding in Reece's gaze. He connected the dots without her needing to explain.

Let's go back in time, Charlie.

"I'm proud of you for leaving him," Reece said. "I hope that's not weird for me to say."

Shame crawled up her esophagus like acid reflux. "Thank you," Charlotte said, wishing she were an easier person to love.

Reece was quiet as he considered the implications of what she had shared. Misty sniffed the air and sprang out of her lap to disappear into the grass, on the hunt for some unlucky animal. Charlotte felt strangely bereft without her.

"I'm sorry I wasn't more supportive," Reece said at last. "I had no idea what you were going through."

Charlotte waved off his apology. "How could you? *I* didn't know."

"But I never asked. I was too busy dealing with my own shit to help."

"Oh stop," Charlotte huffed. "You were so kind to me, Reece. And I kept thinking, What's the catch? When is he going to tear off his face and reveal that he's a psycho too?"

"I probably freaked you out when I got attached." He kept his voice level, but she could still hear the embarrassment lurking in his words.

"You did, a little," Charlotte said. "But that wasn't your fault. You were just trying to get to know me, and my dumb trauma brain saw that as a threat." She laughed at herself. "Which is ridiculous because you are literally the nicest person I have ever met."

"Aww, stop." Reece flashed her that big smile she loved. This time when he extended his hand to her, she took it. His fingers were sticky with sweat and fresh sunblock, but so were hers. They were equally messy.

Charlotte found herself speaking before she'd fully processed the words. Another confession tumbling out of her mouth after the others. "I like talking to you."

Reece smiled again. A private one this time, like he'd figured out a puzzle. "You said that last night."

She rolled her eyes, flustered. "It's still true."

They fell quiet again, processing. Reece pressed a kiss to her wrist, and then to her palm. She finally reached out to smooth his hair back into place, a few droplets of pond water trickling down the side of his nose.

He found his words again before she did. She realized he'd been avoiding her eyes as he gathered his thoughts. "I always thought you . . ." Hurt made his voice choppy and he trailed off. Charlotte combed his hair with her fingers until he continued. "I heard the rumor that he broke up with you, and I thought you wanted him back. And that I wasn't good enough." He forced a self-deprecating smile. "There's no building on campus with my name on it."

Rosewood affection and reseda guilt bloomed in her chest. Charlotte cupped his chin in her hand, forcing him to look her in the eyes. "I'm so mad at myself for making you feel that way for a second, Reece." He gave her a thin smile. She gave his chin a gentle shake. "No, I'm serious. You were never the problem, ever. I just wasn't ready for you then."

They both heard it at the same time. Reece blinked but didn't say anything as Charlotte realized what she'd let slip.

Then implied a *now*.

Charlotte hit her vulnerability limit. Self-consciousness crawled across her skin like a cold sweat. She let go of Reece's face, her hands dropping to her lap.

He recognized the wall going up and didn't try to stop it. Maybe it was too much for him too, their hearts exposed to the elements after all this time apart. They had barely twenty-four hours left together, and where could this possibly go when there was so much distance between them in the real world? The deeper this went, the harder it would be to walk away.

"Thank you for telling me," Reece said.

She bit her lip as anxiety garbled her brain. "Thank you for listening," she said. Words were woefully inadequate, failing her yet again. She met his gaze with as much courage as she could gather.

Reece's brow knitted together as he read her face. Then, just as her stomach began to squirm again, he leaned over and kissed her forehead.

That was enough of five years ago, Charlotte decided. Enough of anything before today.

Chapter 10

3 MISSED CALLS FROM ROGER LUDERMORE

REECE'S JEEP WAS messy with boy paraphernalia: Empty bottles of Gatorade rolled across the floor, along with lint rollers, a gym bag bursting with laundry, and what looked like a stuffed plush sheep in the trunk. In the back seat with Liam and Misty, Charlotte watched the dog immediately start sniffing every crevice of the car.

"She smells the Poms," Reece explained as they drove back to campus. He caught Charlotte's eye in the rearview mirror. "She'll settle down."

Garrett twisted in his seat to hand Misty a treat from a plastic bag. She took it obediently, her pink tongue giving his palm a thorough cleaning. "Misty loves the car," he cooed like a proud papa.

"Put on some tunes." Liam emerged from his groggy stupor to hand his iPhone to Garrett, who plugged in the aux cord. Tropical indie pop pumped through the car.

Charlotte rolled down her window and tilted her face into the breeze. It was a short trip back to campus and she let the music and the boys' idle chatter drift by her.

"There's a pregame in Batty's room tonight," Garrett said. "I figure we hit that up before heading down to the Lawn. Then the after-party on Atwood."

Tonight was the big party on the President's Lawn, where alumni and undergrads blew off steam on the night before graduation. Charlotte barely remembered her own class's Lawn Party—her last night on campus was an ugly haze of gin and self-loathing. As an undergrad, she probably spent five minutes under the massive white tent before storming off to sulk alone.

Charlotte shook the memory away. The Lawn Party was another experience that demanded a do-over, this time with no drama and lots of dancing. There was always a better-than-average DJ and a cash bar run by actual bartenders, not just students from the R&C committee. Hopefully it'd be like last night's disco at Acronym, only with Reece beside her. She'd finally get the Hein farewell she deserved.

Misty crawled across Liam's lap to sniff at the window. He patiently hugged her around the waist so that she could stick her muzzle into the wind without tumbling to a pavement-related death.

"What're you up to tonight, Charlie?" Reece watched her reflection in the mirror again.

"Eyes on the road, Krueger," she commanded, and he smirked but obliged. "There's a pregame in Nina's room. She's somewhere on the second floor. I'm sure you're all welcome if you want to drop by. She's making funfetti-tinis."

"What's a funfetti-tini?" Liam enunciated every syllable with relish.

Charlotte smiled—the third bro in Reece's trio was quite fun when he was conscious. "Cream soda mixed with cupcake-flavored vodka."

Garrett gagged in the front seat.

"It's gross," she granted. "We'll probably have a sip for nostalgia's sake, wonder out loud how we ever drank such garbage, and then go back to beer."

Reece palmed the steering wheel as he turned into the campus parking lot. "You have arrived at your final destination. Please remember to take all personal belongings with you."

Charlotte made sure Misty was safely installed in Liam's arms before she opened the door. Reece fell into step beside her on the long flight of stairs to the rear entrance of Randall. He pressed his hand to the small of her back as she climbed the crumbling stone steps. The chivalrous gesture must have been automatic for him, but even the suggestion of his fingers against her body made her wish they were alone. It would be hours before she could revel in his touch again.

"I still can't believe you drove all the way from Missouri," she said, shaking off her horniness. "How long did it take?"

"I think like twenty hours on the road, with a stopover at my aunt's place in Philly." Reece shrugged. "It was nice. I love road trips. They give you time to think, time to listen to podcasts . . ." His thumb rubbed at the small of her back. "Time to mentally prepare yourself to see your ex."

"Touché," Charlotte said, a little embarrassed.

"I'm just teasing you." Reece slid his hand into her back pocket. The gesture was wonderfully possessive, and it drew her hip closer to his. His lowered his voice and asked, "What are you up to now?"

Before she could read his face, he stepped back to hold the door open. She let Liam and Garrett pass by as she considered her answer. The boys continued into the stairwell and up to the third floor where they were staying, leaving them alone.

Reece was staring at her mouth. It took a great deal of concentration to remember he'd asked her a direct question.

"Jackie hasn't texted me back. She must be asleep." Reece nodded at the underlying message of her words: *My room is occupied.* "And I need to get the pond scum out of my hair." She smelled more like Misty than was typically considered attractive by polite society.

"A shower sounds amazing." Reece ran a hand through his own hair. A disloyal cowlick sprang up at the back of his skull. "We have spare towels if you don't want to wake her up."

Charlotte's skin warmed as she picked up on the subtext of Reece's offer. "Are you suggesting what I think you're suggesting?"

Reece studied the pink glow spreading across her chest. "I don't know what you're talking about, Charlie."

"Yeah, sure you don't." She rolled her eyes, her face hot. "Lead the way, Krueger."

Reece and Garrett's room was just as chaotic as the Jeep. What looked like an entire Target men's section had exploded on Reece's side. Misty curled up on a foam pad under Garrett's lofted bed, chewing a bully stick.

Liam and Garrett were in the middle of a heated debate about a playlist. They didn't look up from Garrett's computer when the door opened. Reece grabbed two towels from a huge pile on the bookshelf as Charlotte hesitated in the doorway.

"How did you guys get so many towels?" she asked.

"Garrett has an in on the R&C committee," Reece explained. She gave him a disapproving look, and he laughed. "Nothing creepy. His sister is a junior."

"Oh awesome, I didn't know."

"Gov major," Garrett supplied without looking up from the laptop. "Imani's going to be a senator someday."

"Right on," Charlotte said.

Reece picked up a hairbrush and a travel kit of toiletries. He tossed her the brush and folded the towels under his arm.

She began the arduous process of brushing out her wet snarls as she followed him down the hallway.

The third floor had a communal bathroom that served the entire hall. She looked around at the floor-to-ceiling brown tile and thought longingly of her shower shoes downstairs.

Reece staked out the last stall. He lined up his products on the shelf and shucked off his shorts. After he turned the water on, he peered back at her from behind the plastic curtain. "Come on in, Charlie. Water's warm."

Well, when at Hein.

Charlotte kicked off her loafers and put them on a bench outside the stall. Then she wriggled out of her clothes, the denim of her jeans sticking to her legs. They were the only people in the bathroom, so she peeled off her underwear and sports bra before hopping into the stall behind him.

The sight of Reece standing in the shower killed any hesitation she felt about bathing with someone else in public. The water ran down his body like a blessing. It slid in tendrils from his hair and along the back of his neck. Droplets arced between his shoulder blades and down to the ripe swell of his ass.

Charlotte had to admit it: She was an ass woman. She wanted to bite down on his firm cheek.

Reece made room for her under the showerhead. She shivered with delight as the hot water kissed her face. He handed her a little bottle of hotel shampoo. "You go first, you'll take longer."

She squirted a splatter onto her palm and rubbed it across her scalp, staying under the water to let it foam. Then she stepped back and let him wash and rinse. The soapy water trailed down his chest and caught in the thicket of hair beneath the V of his hips.

"See something you like?" Reece licked water from his lips as he smiled.

"No comment."

"Your turn, rinse."

The water felt divine on the knots in her shoulders. She coaxed the shampoo out of her hair and rolled her head from side to side on her neck. "You sore?" Reece asked, his face pink. From the hot water, of course.

"Just my neck," she said. She took the conditioner from his hand and lathered it through her mane. "Nothing new. It's from sitting at a desk all day."

"You're not . . . from last night?" Concern suited him well, endearing worry lines at the corners of his eyes. He would look at her just like that at the end of a hard day at work, putting on a pot of tea to boil as she told him about Roger's latest ego trip. Reece radiated Boyfriend Energy.

You don't get to keep him, you ninny. You're just having fun.

Charlotte stepped forward and backed him up against the tile. "I'm fine." She trailed her hand down his neck and chest to the soft expanse of his stomach. His abs tightened underneath his belly, a low hiss escaping his throat.

She kissed him first this time, deep and unhurried. She ran her tongue along his lower lip and he opened for her. His lips smelled like the coming summer, sunscreen and the earthy flavor of Cobalt Pond. She moaned and Reece caught the noise, weaving his hands through her wet hair.

The sensual moment ended when his fingers got stuck in a knot. She winced, jerking back automatically. "Oh god, I'm sorry!" Reece blurted out. "Are you okay?"

"Happens all the time," she said, rubbing the smarting spot on her scalp. "Just give me a second."

Regretfully, she returned to the task of combing the conditioner through her hair with her fingers.

Reece watched the water cascade down her body, unbothered by the break. If anything he got harder as he watched a droplet pool at her nipple and fall to the floor like dew from a flower petal. He swallowed, his Adam's apple bobbing. She didn't have any room to doubt his feelings, he was so transparent and unapologetic.

"Okay," Charlotte said when she was satisfied with the state of her hair.

Reece was on her in a heartbeat. He knitted himself to her, one knee nudging between her thighs as he crushed her against the shower stall. She wrapped her arms around him, fully submitting to public indecency. It had been nearly impossible to keep her hands off him in front of the guys all afternoon. All she wanted to do was crawl into his lap and rub herself against him like a sexually frustrated freshman.

His lips tore from her mouth to ravage her neck, licking and then sucking hard. Reece created a path of inflamed, red destruction from just below her ear to her breasts and then down her stomach. Charlotte's heart leapt into her throat as he settled on his knees below her on the tile.

"You're going to get knee fungus," she blurted out.

Reece huffed a laugh, his hands coming to rest on her hips. "I'll survive." He nosed against her inner thigh, encouraging her to spread her legs for him. When she widened her stance, he groaned. "I've wanted to do this all day." He stroked across her wet folds with his fingers before leaning forward to kiss the tender hood of her clit.

Charlotte tried not to cry out but she failed, the sound echoing across the tile. She managed to hold in her next wail when his tongue traced her seam and delved inside for a taste. She grabbed his hair, wobbling on her feet. "Reece, I—*oh.*"

He guided her leg over his shoulder. She held on to the top of the shower stall, splayed open for his exploration.

"You taste incredible." Reece slid a finger into her heat, and then another. She shuddered around him, the combination of his words and his touch sending waves of pleasure through her body.

His tongue was indefatigable, lapping and pressing against her clit until she couldn't keep her eyes open—and she really wanted to, she wanted to watch the determination on his lovely, angular face.

Reece watched her quiver and shake. His eyes were dark and eager, sending an additional thrill of lust up her spine. A third finger joined the first two and she wanted to scream, she wanted—she could explode with how much she *wanted.*

She wanted to come. She wanted to fuck. She wanted Reece. She wanted him because he was gorgeous and kind and very, very sweet. She wanted to know all of him—his secrets and his weird phobias and his favorite foods and the way he talked to himself when he thought he was alone. She wanted to know all the things she didn't bother with in college, the details that made someone a person. She wanted his full story.

She wanted to tell him that this wasn't the plan, it really wasn't, but she'd never been good at plans anyway. All her best-laid plans were disasters and maybe what she really wanted was to start over from scratch. To be as fresh and open-ended as the hungover graduates who tomorrow would doze under the sun as Roger droned on about his own success. She wanted to seize her diploma and do it all over again, do it right.

Reece bit her inner thigh. He never slowed the unforgiving thrust of his fingers inside her even as he took a break to breathe. She grunted at the pain, her arousal dripping down her legs with the water. When Reece's tongue teased her clit, she could feel herself tensing and bracing, reaching the brink.

She'd never been so aware of her smarting skin and her tensing spine and her hungry, gushing need across Reece's face. She could see the sheen of her pleasure on his mouth and cheeks and something about how *filthy* that was pushed her over the edge, her entire body quaking.

Reece didn't stop, tightening his hold on her hips as he lapped her up. He only relented when she moaned, overly sensitive, and began to slide down the wall.

"I gotcha," he murmured. He stood in one smooth motion to catch her and hold her steady. "I gotcha."

Charlotte yanked him down to her height for a kiss, desperate to taste herself on his lips. Desperate to commit this moment to memory. She shook under the hot rush of the shower and the aftershock of her orgasm.

Reece laughed into her mouth as her fingers scrambled against his slick back, wanting him closer but unable to find purchase. "Easy, Charlie," he murmured, guiding her back against the wall once more.

She changed tactics and drove her hand into his wet hair, fingers pressing against his skull. If she kissed him hard enough, surely she could swallow him up and keep him with her forever.

You don't get to keep him. He's not yours.

The door to the bathroom swung open, its metal knob slamming into the tile. Giggles bounced off the walls, a conversation in progress. Charlotte stilled against Reece, her wide eyes finding his.

"We should go before we run out of hot water," he whispered, his lips finding the shell of her ear.

She shuddered, arching her neck as his breath met her damp skin. "You go first," she said. "I'll see you later tonight?"

Reece pressed a kiss to her neck, and then another to her shoulder. "Definitely."

He stepped back to kiss her properly one last time, and then he winked and stepped around the shower curtain. He wrapped himself in a towel before giving her a jaunty wave and leaving the stall.

Charlotte locked the door behind him and slithered back into the shower. She stayed under the hot water until her legs stopped wobbling, still feeling ravenous and shaky. The image of Reece's hungry mouth between her thighs wouldn't let her go and she curled her fingers around the top of the stall, letting the shower beat against her back. She breathed in the steam and held it in her chest.

The girls left the bathroom, banging the door into the wall again on their way out. Charlotte turned off the water and shook out her hair. She did her best to squeeze out the excess water as she coiled her hair into a thick rope.

The bathroom was blissfully empty when she left the stall. Her iPhone sat on top of her clothes, returned to her possession like a magic trick. When she picked it up, a deluge of notifications swam across the screen, all from Roger.

1 NEW VOICEMAIL FROM ROGER LUDERMORE,
4:41 PM

Her reprieve was over.

Charlotte padded barefoot into the hallway and down the stairs, wincing as her feet went from clean-ish tile to grungy carpet to rubber steps. She pinned her cell phone between her cheek and shoulder as she listened to Roger's message.

By the time it was over, she stood frozen in front of her dorm room.

"I don't know where the fuck you are, but something's come up, so I'm gonna need you to write my speech. Use Peter's notes, whatever, you already know what I want to say. Get it to me by midnight. Don't make me sound like a pussy. And remember, Charlotte—I give my recommendation to the art department on Monday."

Shit.

She checked the time—4:50 P.M. That gave her seven hours to come up with an entire commencement address if she skipped the clothing swap, dinner, Nina's pregame, and the Lawn Party.

She would make this work, she had to. If she started now, she could work through dinner and bang out a mediocre draft by nine. It didn't have to be good, it just had to be . . . vaguely commencement-address-shaped. Roger would rewrite it anyway, he just needed a template.

She could do this. She wrote his tweets, didn't she? This was just. . . . several hundred tweets.

Jackie would understand if she skipped the clothing swap. They'd have the rest of the night together. If Charlotte could just explain, everything would be fine.

She quietly let herself into their room, easing the door open and shut in case Jackie was still asleep. But the covers were thrown off the other bed, clothing scattered across the floor.

Her phone trilled.

TEXT MESSAGE FROM JACKIE SLAUGHTER TO CHARLOTTE THORNE, 4:55 PM: where are you? I went early to help set up, these kids are so trendy I can't stand it. conrad hall lounge, come quick before the good stuff is gone!!!

Oh, this was not good. This was very not good.

But what could she do? She couldn't risk the department transfer.

It was her only hope of staying at *Front End* without completely losing her mind.

Wouldn't Jackie prefer she skipped the clothing swap so that they could go out tonight?

Sure, Charlotte didn't like it. But this was her *job.* And she was here to work.

TEXT MESSAGE FROM CHARLOTTE THORNE TO JACKIE SLAUGHTER 5:07 PM: Change of plans, Roger's making me write his speech for tomorrow. Heading to Mead Library to crank it out. I'm so sorry but I will see you at Nina's! We will dance it out!!

TEXT MESSAGE FROM JACKIE SLAUGHTER TO CHARLOTTE THORNE, 5:21 PM: :/

TEXT MESSAGE FROM CHARLOTTE THORNE TO JACKIE SLAUGHTER, 6:12 PM: Do you remember literally anything our commencement speaker said? I swear I have no memory of them, there's a blank void in my mind.

TEXT MESSAGE FROM JACKIE SLAUGHTER TO CHARLOTTE THORNE, 6:31 PM: no

TEXT MESSAGE FROM JACKIE SLAUGHTER TO CHARLOTTE THORNE, 7:33 PM: u gonna make it to dinner? we're getting taco bell

TEXT MESSAGE FROM CHARLOTTE THORNE TO JACKIE SLAUGHTER, 7:38 PM: Still working, I'll grab something from the vending machine.

TEXT MESSAGE FROM CHARLOTTE THORNE TO JACKIE SLAUGHTER, 9:05 PM: Finished! Where are you?

TEXT MESSAGE FROM JACKIE SLAUGHTER TO CHARLOTTE THORNE, 9:11 PM: nina's

TEXT MESSAGE FROM JACKIE SLAUGHTER TO CHARLOTTE THORNE, 9:11 PM: left something out for you

Charlotte couldn't say her commencement address was any good. She was by no means a compelling writer, and Roger Ludermore was about as far from an inspiring role model as a person could get. The draft she sent her boss was a mess of clichés, bullet points, and bland remarks borrowed from other commencement speakers, rewritten just enough to pass the smell test. It would not win any awards.

But it existed, and she turned it in well before Roger's midnight deadline.

As she unlocked the dorm room, she felt if not proud of her output, then at least gratified that she'd salvaged the rest of her evening. Jackie's text messages were clipped but not hostile, and she could work with that. Sure, Charlotte wished Jackie had waited to get ready with her, but she couldn't expect her to sit around all night in an empty dorm room. And also, yeah, Jackie's feelings were valid. She had the right to be ticked off. But they were both adults, they'd be fine. They'd been here before.

It would all be fine.

And then Charlotte saw her bed.

Jackie had laid out an entire outfit for her. A heather gray crop top with the Hein crest on the breast pocket, paired with distressed black denim overalls cut at the thighs into shorts. She'd even put out clean white ankle socks beside Charlotte's sneakers, and a pink scrunchie to tie her hair back if she needed to.

Charlotte rubbed the fabric of the shirt between her thumb and index finger. Pure cotton, never worn from the looks of it, also cropped by hand. She turned to the trash bag hooked at the end of her bed and—ah, yes. Discarded denim and gray fabric.

Jackie had made this for her.

Simple. Comfortable. Sexy but not too feminine, not complex or colorful. The perfect outfit to dance in. The perfect outfit for her.

TEXT MESSAGE FROM CHARLOTTE THORNE TO JACKIE SLAUGHTER, 9:30 PM: Thank you so much. On my way up now.

Chapter 11

AS PREDICTED, THE funfetti-tinis made Charlotte want to barf. The pink party cups Nina used to serve her monstrous creation did nothing to distract from its murky brown coloring.

Charlotte caught Jio discreetly pouring their bastardized vodka soda into Matt's party cup. They gave her a helpless shrug before declaring "Delicious, honey!" and sailed over to kiss Nina's cheek.

Jackie threw in the towel next. "I can't do it," she muttered. "I'm not strong enough."

With a polite word to Nina, Matt excused himself for the bathroom. Charlotte guessed that his funfetti-tini would soon grace the communal bathroom's sink.

"What did you guys do after brunch?" Amy asked. She perched on the edge of her bed, swinging her legs back and forth in white patterned tights. Her feet were fastened into mint green sneakers in preparation for the dance party. She looked like a life-size Polly Pocket.

Charlotte took a determined pull from her drink, awkwardness prickling at the back of her neck. Jackie plunged ahead for them both. "I took a nap," she said. "Then Jio and I went to the clothing swap and got Taco Bell."

Amy kicked her sneakers through the air. "Oh! What'd you get?"

"Gorditas, bitch."

"I meant at the swap."

Jackie waved to Charlotte's outfit like a model presenting a prize on a game show. "Am I good or what?" If she sounded a little salty, only Charlotte picked up on it.

Amy smiled benignly. "I love that top! It looks brand new."

"The school store had overstock, and this one was slightly damaged." Jackie slipped a finger behind Charlotte's neckline at the back and gave it a tug. "They sewed the tags on upside down and couldn't sell them."

When Amy turned away to ask Nina about the music, Charlotte bumped Jackie's shoulder with her own. "Thank you for the outfit. It's perfect."

"I know," Jackie said. "You're welcome." She tapped a sharp nail on her party cup, letting the silence stretch uncomfortably.

"And I really am sorry I missed the swap," Charlotte said in a low voice, her eyes fixed on Jackie's knees. "I wouldn't have gone to the quarry with Reece if I'd known I would have to work today."

Jackie sucked her teeth and shook her head. "I'm glad you're spending time with Reece. That is not what this is about."

Frustration and guilt boiled in Charlotte's stomach, mixing about as well as the cupcake vodka and cream soda. "If I could have gone to the swap, I would have. You know that."

Her best friend sighed, looking forlornly at the door. Then she straightened up and shook out her shoulders. "We're going to talk before we leave tomorrow. But not tonight, okay? Let's just have fun."

"Jackie, shouldn't we at least—"

Jackie turned and fixed her with a stern glare. "Charlotte, please hear me when I say *not right now*. This weekend isn't just about what works for your schedule. I want to enjoy the party. Okay?"

The wind went out of Charlotte's lungs. The only thing keeping her from spiraling out in guilt and panic was the fact that this *wasn't her fault*. And now their fight would loom over this evening like a dark cloud. Nothing put her in the mood to party like a prescheduled confrontation. She scowled.

Jackie gently tucked a stray curl behind Charlotte's ear, her lips pursed. Charlotte had kept her chaotic hair loose, the only statement accessory she needed. "I'm glad you left your hair down. It's so beautiful these days. The scrunchie's for dancing later, if you get sweaty."

Charlotte recognized the peace offering. She'd take it.

She closed her fingers around Jackie's wrist and gave it a careful squeeze. "Thank you."

The door swung open. They both turned to look, Charlotte's heart leaping to her throat. It was only Matt returning from the bathroom.

She hadn't heard from Reece since their fraternization in the third-floor showers. Not a text message, not even a meme. She had been too busy in the library to dwell on thoughts of him, but every time the door to the pregame opened, her hopes went up that it would be Reece standing in the hallway.

She knew she could just text Reece, but she found an odd pleasure in tormenting herself. The college thrill of the chase was something special—not knowing when and where you'd see your crush, reveling in anticipation while checking in with each other throughout the night. *What's up? Where you at? Wanna come over?*

This was even better than the undergrad game of cat and mouse. Reece wouldn't stand her up or blow her off. She didn't need to fear being abandoned at some party when a hotter girl came along. Reece was temporarily hers.

His availability scared her in college. Now she found it exhilarating. She knew who she would end the night with, and she could enjoy the in-between tension without feeling insecure.

"What about you?" Jackie asked Amy, who had been left on her own as Nina chided Matt for disappearing. "What did y'all do today?"

"Big soccer game on the quad! Then we went on a liquor run." Amy tapped the side of her party cup.

"That reminds me." Her perpetually sweet face sobered with concern. Amy patted Charlotte's knee to get her attention. Charlotte felt a tendril of dread close around her throat. "We ran into Ben."

She stiffened. So he was still here. Some optimistic part of her brain had convinced herself he was gone. He hadn't surfaced last night on Atwood, and he didn't seem to be staying in Randall.

But why would he fly in from Europe for one night? Of course he stayed for the weekend. Ben would never miss the Lawn Party.

"We didn't speak to him, because *gross*," Amy continued. "He's probably here to hang out with his frat. I saw a bunch of those Sigma Delt guys on the quad today."

Jackie settled a hand on Charlotte's shoulder and gave it a squeeze. "You're not going to see him," she promised. "There'll be hundreds of people there tonight."

"It's fine," Charlotte said. Her voice felt tight like an overstrung violin bow.

Jackie poured Charlotte a gin and tonic from the bar on the windowsill, letting her wrangle her thoughts in peace.

My name is Charlotte Thorne. I am twenty-seven years old. I work at The Front End Review. *I am safe here.*

Charlotte accepted the fresh drink and abandoned her funfettitini on the bookshelf. "Thank you for the warning," she told Amy.

Amy nodded. "I don't think exes should be allowed at reunions. They should all be like Eliza and move to Sudan."

"Dubai," Nina corrected her as she joined the group. She clambered up onto Amy's bed, careful not to spill her frothy cocktail on the bare mattress. "And I wholeheartedly agree." She gave Jackie a layered look. Then she finally took a sip of her drink and gagged. "Jesus, this is terrible. Why didn't anyone say anything?"

Jackie took her cup with an adoring smile. "I'll make you something else." She left the funfetti-monstrositini on the desk. "How about a Jack and Coke?"

"Please," Nina said.

Jio nosed their way into the circle, tugging Matt along by the belt loop. "What are we talking about?"

"Exes!" Amy chirped. She grinned at Nina, who rolled her eyes.

"Can we not?" Charlotte said delicately. What would be worse: more discussion of Ben, or for this conversation to veer in the direction of her postbrunch shower?

"Let's talk about something other than relationships," Nina decided.

"Let's talk about dogs," Charlotte suggested, and Jio nodded enthusiastically.

Jackie groaned. "Veto."

Charlotte's phone chimed.

TEXT MESSAGE FROM REECE KRUEGER TO CHARLOTTE THORNE, 10:05 PM: what's nina's room no.?

Her heart bleated with joy. Somehow it had only taken two days for her to grow impatient for his company. While she loved hanging out with old friends, the pregame felt like killing time before the evening's main event.

As much as she loathed to admit it, she was starting to miss him when he wasn't around.

"Reece is on his way," Charlotte told the group. "This is room 218, right?"

Amy nodded.

"Can we address how good he looks?" Jio said. They waggled their eyebrows at Charlotte, who pretended not to hear them as she texted him back. "Talk about a glow up, goddamn."

Jackie laughed. "Some of us may have noticed more than others."

Charlotte elbowed her in the side.

"He finally figured out what to do with all that hair." Amy touched the bangs of her own bob, imagining Reece's dark hair spilling over his forehead. "Does he seem happy to you guys? It's so hard to tell with him, he's always smiling."

"He's finding his way," Jackie demurred. Then she lowered her voice. "He finally broke up with that girl Jessica, thank god."

"Oh, HER." Jio squished up their face. "Vanilla pudding."

Charlotte leaned forward. "Did you meet her?" She wasn't eager to learn about Reece's ex-girlfriend, but she wouldn't turn down an opportunity to feel superior.

Jio laughed. "Didn't need to. I found her Insta."

The door swung open behind them. Charlotte's skin rippled with heat as Reece materialized in the hallway. His eyes immediately found her atop the bookshelf, and his mouth went slack before soaring up in a grin.

She savored the sight of him looking her over. The silent moment lasted two seconds, maybe three, but a whole conversation passed between them.

There you are.

Finally.

"Hey there!" Nina called out.

Reece tore his eyes from Charlotte's to greet his host. He gave her a brotherly squeeze. "Hey, Nina-bean."

"We weren't at all talking about your love life," Jackie said.

Charlotte's face burned. Reece looked at her over Nina's shoulder, one eyebrow yanked up toward the ceiling. "Is that so?" he asked.

"I'll get you a drink," Jackie said. "Don't touch the funfetti-tinis."

Reece moved from Nina's arms to Amy's. "Thank you for having me, Amy." He stood patiently as she fussed with his hair, still intrigued by his new cut.

Charlotte scooted over on the bookshelf to make room for him. When Reece sat down, he left a sliver of space between them for propriety's sake, but his arm brushed hers as he accepted a Coke Zero from Jackie.

"Hi," Charlotte said. She tilted her head to the side and gave him a shy smile.

"Hey." He leaned over just so to bump her shoulder with his. "Nice fit."

She proudly displayed the ragged hem. "It's a bespoke Slaughter creation."

Reece's laugh practically sparkled. He found a loose thread at the cuff of her shorts and gave it a pull, the denim whispering against her skin. "She's very talented."

Charlotte preened. "How was Batty's pregame?"

"Good. Weird. Everyone was drinking André." He took a sip of his cold soda and groaned in appreciation.

She smiled, his joy contagious. "You'd think he'd spring for Veuve Clicquot with all that crypto money."

Reece shrugged. "I guess everyone's feeling nostalgic this weekend."

"Warning: Objects in the rearview mirror may taste worse than you remember," she drawled. He laughed and clinked his can to her glass.

Nina paused the music as everyone turned to face her. "How are we feeling? Ready to head down to the party? Or should we stay here?"

"I'M READY!" Jio cheered. Amy laughed and shouted her agreement.

Charlotte eyed Reece's full soda. "Let's finish our drinks?" she suggested.

"Okay, five more minutes and then we roll." Nina pushed play on the music again. The room filled with the blare of saxophone as Carly Rae Jepsen's "Run Away with Me" blared from the tinny laptop speakers. Reece hissed his appreciation and leaned back against the wall. His thigh pressed against hers as he relaxed.

Charlotte soaked up the satisfaction of this moment. The pregame was small enough to be cozy but large enough for the room to feel full. Jackie and Jio giggled as they coaxed liquid liner across Matt's lash line. It occurred to her that this was another of those rare snapshots in time when she was exactly where she wanted to be. These people, this school, this night.

Her body never lost its awareness of Reece beside her. They had all the time in the world to enjoy this evening together: to dance and to flirt and to fool around until dawn if they could find a corner of campus to call their own.

Reece placed his free hand on his knee. His knuckles brushed the side of her thigh. She pressed her leg closer to his, a not-so-discreet Morse code of flirtation. *I missed you.*

He countered by snaking his arm behind her on the bookshelf, ostensibly to support his weight. His thumb teased the small of her back, rubbing against the thin fabric. Another message traded from skin to skin: *I can't stop thinking about you.*

She longed to rest her head on his shoulder, to kiss his cheek and nip at the sensitive shell of his ear. Instead, she contented herself with smelling his sweat and fabric softener. Wholesome perfection.

Eventually Nina declared it time to venture forth. They made a halfhearted effort to clean the room, stacking used cups and shoving them into a shopping bag to recycle in the morning.

Reece offered Charlotte his arm. "Shall we, Charlie?"

She wrapped her fingers through the crook of his elbow. "Lead on, Krueger."

The group ambled out of the dormitory and into the night. Jio and Jackie led the pack, following the booming echoes of music toward the heart of campus. The party would rage on the President's Lawn well past midnight. Even when the music finally stopped under the tent, the revelry would relocate to Senior Housing until daybreak. Every year some smartass set off illegal fireworks and added the sirens of Campus Safety to the din.

This night at the end of the world was always loud.

Charlotte shuddered, not from the cold. Reece wrapped his arm around her shoulders and folded her sideways against his chest. "That better?" he murmured into her ear, his lips brushing her hair.

She nodded.

My name is Charlotte Thorne. I am here with Reece and my friends. The graduation ceremony tomorrow isn't mine. The past is in the past.

I am where I belong.

Charlotte burrowed her hand into Reece's back pocket. "Always so handsy," he rumbled.

"My hands are cold too."

Jackie whirled around and danced backward on the dirt path. She jazz-hands-ed through the air like a deranged tour guide. "Hurry up in the back," she yelled. "No one gets left behind!"

Charlotte flipped her off. Jackie's answering laughter bounced off the dark stone of the academic buildings.

The tent was a massive white structure erected behind the university president's house. Tomorrow, R&C staff would hastily unfold rows of plastic chairs and assemble them in lines across the grass. Friends and family of the Class of 2018 would watch the hatchling adults graduate from the safety of the shade. But tonight, the tent was dedicated to the crush of writhing undergrads and alumni in varying states of intoxication. They'd been invited to an annual bacchanal of celebration, nostalgia, and denial.

Charlotte clung to Reece's arm as they stepped through the tent's flaps. The temperature rose a solid ten degrees underneath the vinyl. It overwhelmed her immediately. The layout of the venue hadn't changed: A bandstand stood along one side for the DJ booth, and a massive bar with multiple serving stations ran along the opposite edge of the party. Loose, long lines of customers waited at each station.

CONGRATULATIONS, CLASS OF 2018 was projected on the inside of the tent's roof. Colored lights cast strange hues across everyone's faces. Skull-shaking sound poured from the speakers.

Charlotte took a deep, fortifying breath against the swell of noise and memory. Reece unwound their arms and took her hand in his. The simple gesture anchored her in the sensory overload.

She gave him a shaky smile. "This is a lot."

"We can leave if you need to." Reece kept his concern discreet, murmuring the offer quietly into her ear. "Just say the word."

She knew he meant it too. If she wanted to leave, he'd turn his back on the party he drove twenty hours to attend and wouldn't complain once. Reece was that kind of man.

"I'm okay." Charlotte swallowed her nerves and nodded to where Jio and Jackie had claimed turf on the dance floor. "Let's catch up."

Reece shielded her from the din of the party and the anxiety it dredged up. His large frame cut an easy path through the crowd. Charlotte let him tug her over to their friends.

She focused on the way he held her hand—he did so like it was the most natural thing in the world. On their first go-around, she shied away from this kind of touch. Holding hands was a declarative statement at twenty-two. Sweet and territorial and public, a meaningful gesture in the world of campus hookup culture.

Tonight, she reveled in it. Her heart throbbed each time Reece peered over his shoulder to check that they hadn't been separated. When they reached their friends and his hand swung free from hers, she found the urge to grab it back.

Amy cupped her hand around her mouth. "Let's go up to the front!"

Jackie bounced on the balls of her feet at the suggestion and took Nina's hand. Charlotte waved them on—the last thing she wanted was to get closer to the speakers. The party lights glinted off Nina's gold hoop earrings before they were absorbed into the crowd, all trace of them vanishing. Strangers filled in the space the girls left behind them in an instant. Charlotte's eyes swam with color, and she sucked in a ragged breath.

Reece squeezed her hand. She held on tight, letting him tether her as the party whirled and gyrated around them. He looked perfectly at home amid all the chaos, a blissed-out smile lazing across his lips. She only needed to follow his steps, sway with his sway, and keep her eyes on his face.

The song ended and another nostalgia dance track thundered out of the speakers. Jio hissed their disapproval. "LET'S GET DRINKS!"

Charlotte peered around. They were surrounded by tall bodies—she couldn't see the bar, let alone the line.

Reece read the doubt on her face. "You two go ahead," he said, waving Jio and Matt off. He pulled her back to lean against his chest, his arms wrapping loosely around her waist. They rocked from side to side to the beat as she melted back against him.

"Thank you," she said when their friends were gone. "I really don't want to move."

"Me neither." His voice curled around her senses, low and laced with desire. "Right here is perfect."

His lips brushed her ear. She tilted her neck, nuzzling closer, her skin tingling everywhere his lips found.

Time lingered and swam. She didn't count the minutes, focusing instead on Reece's hands at her hips and the delicious grind of him against her ass. She twined her arms up to weave her fingers through his hair. When her nails grazed his scalp, he shivered despite the heat. Before long they were caked in sweat, surrounded and alone in the sauna of the dance floor.

Charlotte turned in his arms. She sought out his mouth, his breath spilling across her face. Reece's tongue traced her lips and she opened for him, licking at his teeth. He yanked her closer with a muffled curse.

What a surreal fantasy: the pink and purple lights catching Reece's profile, his breath ragged, his body against hers. Another unlikely moment stolen from the life she didn't choose. The boy who was never her boyfriend gave her *that look* under the same white tent, only this time she didn't run. She finally spoke this language.

She felt things. Her need for him was braided with lilac longing and neon red lust. Her heart rioted at the dangerous truth. She was out of shape for this kind of emotion, breathless and exhausted. She hadn't trained. She was falling apart in the first stretch of a marathon love.

I feel—

Reece was made to be loved. It wasn't just the cut of his face against the party lights. Reece was strong and funny and humble. He regulated the temperature of her anxiety like it was second nature to him. He walked four Pomeranians through the Missouri heat. He lost his dad as a teenager and still had the courage to let people into his heart, to let people matter.

He was so worthy of love and yet he never acted entitled to it, pleasantly surprised every time Charlotte touched him. He wanted nothing more than she could offer and deserved everything she had to give.

Someone bumped into her and she stumbled, tripping on her loafers. Reece caught her and kept her upright, his arms coming around her waist. One of his hands found the back of her neck, his fingers already massaging a knot at the top of her spine. She relaxed into him automatically, unable to stop herself, unable to protect herself.

"I gotcha," he said, "Are you hurt?"

"Just clumsy. And buzzed."

The crowd was a wild crush. Charlotte stayed close to Reece's solid form to avoid the bros shoving their way to the bar. She followed Reece's rhythm. His eyes were electric with happiness, infectious and fascinating. She couldn't look away, entranced by the life she saw there. The life she wanted. The life she could have had.

I feel—

The speakers blasted another one-hit wonder from the late aughts. Sweat snarled her hair. This time tomorrow she'd arrive at Grand Central utterly alone. Her future was a wide, unforgiving question mark.

But right now, at least she knew this.

She was falling for Reece Krueger.

"Reece," she said. His name twisted and caught in the blaring music.

He pulled her closer and she pressed her palm against his chest. "What?" he half yelled, leaning down to hold his ear at the level of her mouth.

"I—" She hesitated, her words inadequate.

Did people really do this? Did they just say how they felt, no prelude, no build up?

Charlotte curled her fingers around the edges of his jacket, holding on tight. "I just—"

He pulled back to study her face. Concern weighed down his brow. They weren't dancing anymore, just standing close in the midst of so many strangers. She wondered what she looked like right now; could he read her? All that love and want and fear?

This was what love was: real love, the kind baked with respect and admiration and humor. She loved who she was with him, and she loved who he was every day of his life.

I think I'm—

Reece cradled her chin in his palm. Charlotte shivered as he brushed his thumb over the soft curve of her cheekbone, an inaudible noise escaping his throat. His dark eyes swirled with emotion.

Then, almost imperceptibly, his jaw tightened. Her breath left her as understanding and something that looked like wonder spread across his face. Maybe no one else would have noticed the difference, but she did. Her heart leapt in her chest, relieved and petrified all at once.

Reece found her right hand on his chest and wrapped it in his left. "I know," he said roughly.

The raucous soundtrack of the night almost took his words from her, but she could read his lips. Charlotte clung to those two words. They were a promise and a lifeline, a miracle of second chances.

It dawned on her that everything he'd said to her in the last forty-eight hours meant the same thing.

Let me walk you home.

Please dance with me, Charlie.

I'm not letting you go. Not until I'm satisfied.

You're the only girl I can see.

Everything Reece said to her told her that he loved her. She just needed to listen to him.

"I don't want to go home," Charlotte blurted out. It was the closest she could get to making sense of this, the sudden need she felt to crawl under his skin and never, ever leave. She didn't know how to get on the train tomorrow and pretend she'd never discovered where she belonged. She'd been a fool to think this could only be a weekend—not for Reece's sake, but for her own.

Reece frowned. He rubbed his thumb across the back of her hand. "Brooklyn's not right for you," he said as he stroked her heated skin.

"It's not that." She shook her head, desperate to dislodge the fog of her emotions. "I don't want to not be *here*."

But that wasn't it either. It wasn't this campus, or this party, or even her phone on silent in her pocket. Her sense of rightness had nothing to do with the light buzz of cupcake vodka. It was Reece's touch, his eyes poring over her face, his smell swirling through her mind and making her heart scratch.

"I wish we could stay here," she added, a desperate shot in the dark. "I wish I could do it all over again."

The same color gradient of feelings she had sorted through all weekend spilled across Reece's face: the yearning in his eyes for the same, the clench of his jaw as he understood it wasn't possible, the desperation in his quickened breath to find a way regardless. Lilac and rust and crimson.

Even if he could put aside what happened five years ago, even if she could let him past her ivy-coated walls, even if they could trust each other to choose this properly and permanently . . . wanting was only half the battle. They were postgrad warriors fighting different battles. Her life was in New York. His was in Missouri.

The moment they stopped pretending this was only for a weekend, they had to abandon the blissful innocence of *now* and ask the question of *when*. When would they be together again? When would one of them gamble their life as they knew it to relocate?

Was that a risk either of them was willing to take? Would it work out, or was this yet another massive mistake?

Was this an insane conversation to have with someone you'd never even truly dated?

Reece swallowed, his throat dry. "Charlie, I—"

A bro collided with Reece's shoulder as he shoved his way to the stage. The boy's cup went sailing, dumping beer all over Reece's jeans. "Sorry!" the guy shouted before barreling onward.

"Shit." Reece winced and shook the alcohol from his leg. "This is my last pair of pants."

Charlotte blinked, still waiting for the end of his sentence. But the spell was broken, the volume on the party dialing up a notch. The crowd had gotten thicker. She took a step back as Reece bent over to brush at the spill, and bodies pressed against her from behind, nudging her sideways.

"Let's go find napkins," she suggested, claustrophobic.

He nodded, and she gestured for him to take the lead.

The party reached its zenith, with hundreds of kids crammed side by side under the tent's cover. Reece didn't take her hand this time and she toddled after him, dodging elbows and wandering hands.

They found a stack of paper napkins on the far edge of the bar. Charlotte watched uneasily as Reece blotted at the wet patch on his thigh. "I'm going to smell like PBR all night," he said ruefully. "Eau de fraternité."

Charlotte handed him a fresh napkin in exchange for the soaked wad of paper. "Didn't you know?" she asked, deadpan. "That cologne's all the rage this year."

Reece flashed a thin smile. He pressed the napkin against the stain and scanned the crowd for their friends. The party was an amorphous blob of hipsters, their intoxicated faces blurring together. As the night went on, alumni shrank away from the noise and HU's true students reclaimed the tent.

"We're never going to find them again," he said.

Charlotte studied his face in profile. The purple party lights deepened the shadows under his eyes, leaching his skin of its usual happy glow. She bit the inside of her cheek.

Me too. Charlie, I—

What was the rest of the sentence?

She hated this feeling: this anxious hunger for his attention. It was ridiculous—she wasn't a teenager clinging to the smallest hint that he still wanted her. She didn't want to regret speaking up, not when she so rarely asked for what she wanted.

But did it even matter? She knew all along that Reece's affection was a library book checked out on loan. At the end of this, she had to give him back.

"They'll pop up," she said. "Jackie will get hungry."

That earned a genuine laugh, albeit a soft one. She wanted to catch it and cup it between her fingers like a firefly.

Reece finally looked at her again, his dark eyes softening as he took in her hopeful face. The brittleness left his body and he leaned sideways against the bar, bringing him closer to her level.

It was ridiculous, how the slightest change in his body language calmed her down. His fingers toyed with the strap of her overalls, lightly tugging the denim.

"You're right," he said. "Do you want to get out of here? It's so loud."

"Oh god, please," she all but moaned.

Reece grinned at her obvious relief and stood to leave. But then his smile vanished from his face. The light went out in his eyes as he looked over her shoulder.

Charlotte watched with dread as a wave of tension rippled through his body, his posture coiling tight. "What is it?" she asked.

What had she said wrong now? Paranoia flared bright.

Reece was still looking over her shoulder, his eyes narrowing.

A waft of familiar cologne settled in around her shoulders. The true eau du fraternité, base notes of cedar and white-collar crime. The blood drained from Charlotte's face. Understanding arrived with sharp clarity.

No. Not you. Not now.

"Hey, Thorny!"

Her stomach convulsed. She knew that voice by heart. In truth, she'd never forgotten it. She heard it in her nightmares, and the dreams that woke her up guilty and ashamed at four in the morning. She suspected it would follow her to the grave.

Ben's voice was slick and deceptively light. An ex-boyfriend's taunt disguised as an old friend's inside joke.

Reece searched her face, silently asking her what to do. But there was nothing really, nothing to make this overdue collision less awful. Nothing short of going back in time to undo the worst years of her life.

Charlotte's body went rigid. The time warp was complete. Autopilot took over.

She turned around to face her ex-boyfriend. "Ben!" she cried out through the dryness in her throat. "Hi!" She sounded bubbly and shrill to her own ears, the chatter of a panicked flight attendant on a plane falling from the sky. A manic smile cracked across her mouth.

She couldn't process all of him, not as the tent pulsed with noise and movement around her. Details lodged into her brain in staggered seconds: his slicked-back helmet of blond hair; his wide leer; the humorless darkness in his eyes. Ben wore the expensive black bomber jacket and dark jeans from the panel, too stylish for a sweaty college party, or for a supposed leftist activist. Beautiful camouflage to attract and trap.

An old desire flared in her throat, that quivering urge to debase herself for his approval, or for her safety.

"I was hoping I'd see you here," Ben said in a feline purr. He took a step forward, his cologne overpowering. She couldn't step back, couldn't move at all.

"It's me!" she chirped. "How are you?"

Humiliation curdled in her gut.

"Oh, you know." The party lights glinted obscenely off his teeth. Charlotte's hands twitched at her sides. "Same old, same old. Clawing my way up the podcast charts." He winked, derision and pride dripping from his brag.

Revulsion streaked through her like the chemical aftertaste of Nina's funfetti-tinis. Her brain's last sliver of sanity urged her to run for the exit, but she couldn't move.

Her mouth was on its own, survival mode piloting solo. "Good for you!"

Ben slouched against the bar. His eyes tracked down her body and back up again, taking in her sneakers and scissor-cut crop top, the roll of her late-twenties tummy. She felt devoured and insulted all at once. It was indecent, his stare. Beads of sweat collected at the back of her neck.

He sucked the light out of the tent, and the strength from her body.

"You look ravishing," he said.

Ravishing was one of Ben's favorite compliments. He doled it out for the dress she wore at his fraternity formal, and for the Hollywood curls she painstakingly created before he greeted her at Rawls Tower. She remembered his hand loose at her throat as he kissed her shoulder, pushing her back against the door. *You look ravishing, Charlotte. My little thorn.*

Angry tears pressed against her eyes. She forced them back. His index finger traced a pattern on the bar and she felt it on her skin, running down her cheek and her neck and her chest and—

"Thanks," she blurted out. Her face was red but her chest was full of ice water. "Thank you, you look great too!"

Politeness poured out of her like vomit.

She had to get out of here. She didn't know how, she couldn't think, she couldn't—

Ben glanced over her shoulder, unimpressed and bored.

Oh god.

She forgot about Reece. She forgot about Reece and he was watching this and she had to get him out of here. She had to get out of here before she humiliated herself even further. She needed to be away from the noise and Ben's eyes on her skin and the memory of obeying this man at her own expense.

Ben's eyes flicked back to her, dismissing Reece without comment. "I thought that was you at my panel on Thursday," he drawled, leaning closer. Charlotte's skin crawled as he looked up at her from underneath his lashes, blue eyes flashing with amusement. "But you ran away too fast for me to say hello."

The knife slid in easily, not even rusty. One last insult to remind her that he once knew everything about her, and he remembered. Shame tasted like blood, like the dying scream in her throat.

"Anyway, I should get going. Thomas is finding us some party favors. It was wonderful to see you, Charlotte." He smirked at her, nothing but narcissism in his smile. His words dripped poison, diluting her consciousness.

She would burn her own name if it would leach away the sound of it in his mouth.

Time crunched and ground to a halt as Ben hugged her, his arms circling her waist. She felt her own hands rise up weakly, brushing the smooth fabric of his jacket. She got a nose full of his cologne and the fumes made her head spin. She couldn't breathe, she couldn't speak, she couldn't do anything but stand there and play dead.

And then he sauntered away, disappearing into the crowd. But he wasn't really gone. Ben was an oil spill, coating the world around him in a thick grime of self-loathing. Campus belonged to him now, again, still. Forever.

She'd been a fool to think anything had changed. She'd been a fool to think this weekend could be different. *She* hadn't changed. Ben was right.

You're so fucking pathetic, Charlotte, no wonder your family hates you, you're nothing—

Charlotte's throat flexed and tightened. Dread pumped through her bloodstream. Was she breathing? Did she want to breathe?

A hand touched her shoulder. She jerked away, twisting to face the new threat.

It was just Reece. His empty hand froze outstretched in the air. The world tilted around her as new shame joined the agony in her chest. Charlotte closed her eyes and grabbed on to the lip of the bar.

"Shit, I'm sorry, I—" Words got lodged and lost, the ribbon of her thoughts tearing.

"Are you okay?" Reece stepped forward and she shrank back. His face tightened with hurt. He looked so confused and upset and he didn't deserve it; she couldn't even look at him.

"I need to get out of here," she somehow managed. "I can't— I'm not—"

"Come with me." He wrapped his arm around her shoulders.

Charlotte shuddered, her skin crawling, but she let him guide her from the bar. She focused on her breathing, choppy and shallow.

My name is Charlotte Thorne. My name is Thorny and I am twenty-seven

Reece murmured comforting words that she didn't process. He found an exit and steered her through the tent flap into the cold air.

It's 2018 and I'm at Hein and I am

Charlotte lurched forward. Her body folded over as she threw up into the grass. Reece caught her as she stumbled, a thick arm slung around her waist to keep her upright. Her hair swung into her face. She realized she was crying when she tasted salt along with vomit.

"Oh god," she groaned, shuddering between heaves.

Reece made idle shushing noises. He collected her hair, ignoring the glaze of puke in the strands. "You're okay," he said. "It's okay, sweetheart."

Charlotte Thorne, thorny bitch, you look ravishing.

She'd thanked him. She'd *thanked* him. She asked him how he was and let him wrap his arms around her. She could still smell him on her clothes underneath the sour stench of her own weakness—

She retched again, the sickly sweet vodka and cream soda even worse on the way back up.

Reece's fingers were hot at the back of her neck. He kept massaging and pressing and she didn't want to be *touched* right now, not by anyone. Especially not him; she didn't want his attention and his concern and his fucking kindness. She swatted his hand away, unseeing.

I am Charlotte Thorne and I am nothing, I am an embarrassment. Everyone leaves, everyone sees who I am and they leave and I go back, I beg—

"Get *off* me."

She twisted out of Reece's arms. Her foot hit one of the tent posts and she lost her balance, landing hard on her knees. She groaned as her palms hit the dirt.

Reece crouched next to her, and Charlotte flinched away, more wild animal than human. "Stop it," she sneered, all raw nerves. "Stop touching me."

Reece shrank back like he'd been struck. Guilt joined the murky swarm of emotions wreaking havoc in her mind, but she couldn't deal with it, she couldn't hold his feelings alongside her own. She couldn't breathe.

Charlotte, how can you be so stupid? How do you fuck everything up? You are so annoying ravishing pathetic

The lid from the storage container labeled *Ben* was blown away, lost forever. His words came back to her without so much as a thin coat of dust. She could still feel his fingers on her cheek as he sipped pain from her lips. Was that five years ago or tonight?

Are you going to miss me, Thorny?

"Are you bleeding?" Reece again, still, his voice jagged with worry. "Charlie?"

Another voice joined the din in her mind, a crisp, feminine mid-Atlantic accent.

disgraceful

Charlotte clambered to her feet. Reece stepped forward to stabilize her and she jerked away. She couldn't look at him, couldn't let him touch her. She didn't want to see it on his face, that he finally knew how broken she was. That he finally understood why she wasn't good enough.

"I'm fine."

"Are you sure?" His green eyes were almost black in the shadows of the tent. He reached out for her again and she took a step back. "Do you want some water? Should we go back to the dorm?"

Too many questions. She couldn't think. Why did he still want to help her? Was this pity? Was he just that damn nice? Her fingers grabbed on to a rope supporting the tent post and held on tight.

"Charlotte?"

"Leave me alone. Please, just leave me alone."

Her voice wasn't the fawning, mewling plea from inside the tent. It was ice-cold and sharp as a diamond at the corners. Reece startled at her dismissal, frozen midstep with his hand outstretched. She bit down hard on the inside of her cheek. "I don't want your help. I don't need you."

She turned her back to him and started across the Lawn. She didn't have a direction, only away. Reece didn't follow.

disgraceful

Shame clung to her like gasoline.

God help her, she sounded just like her mother.

Sunday

Chapter 12

TEXT MESSAGE FROM JACKIE SLAUGHTER TO CHARLOTTE THORNE, 12:07 AM: where are u reece said u saw ben are u ok??

TEXT MESSAGE FROM JACKIE SLAUGHTER TO CHARLOTTE THORNE, 12:11 AM: charlotte answer ur phone

TEXT MESSAGE FROM CHARLOTTE THORNE TO JACKIE SLAUGHTER, 12:13 AM: I'm back at Randall.

TEXT MESSAGE FROM JACKIE SLAUGHTER TO CHARLOTTE THORNE, 12:13 AM: dont move im coming

ADRENALINE LEFT CHARLOTTE'S body in dribs and drabs. Exhaustion filled the space it left behind, purple like a bruise.

Jackie didn't ask any questions. Her best friend swaddled her in a blanket like an empanada and pulled up an old sitcom on her laptop. Snacks littered the bed. The cinder-block walls dampened the sound of the Lawn Party that rolled across campus like thunder. Charlotte was safe for now.

Even when her brain stopped lurching between the past and the present, Ben's sneering face wouldn't leave her alone.

How could she have been so naïve? Why did she think she could come back here and have a simple, productive weekend? There were no do-overs in life. This school did not belong to her. Hein University did not exist without Ben Mead. She should have listened to her gut on Thursday night and left.

"Thank you," she croaked when words returned to her. Her throat hurt. She took a sip from a water bottle Jackie bought at the vending machine. "Sorry I wrecked your night."

Jackie turned down the volume on her laptop. "You didn't. I'm so sorry about Ben."

Charlotte ignored the unnecessary apology. None of this was Jackie's doing; Charlotte was the one who should have been prepared. She'd had years to get ready for a run-in with Ben, years to think of what to say and practice it in front of the mirror and convince herself that she had no reason to be afraid. After all, she had the courage to break up with him when she was only twenty-one. How could she be even more petrified at twenty-seven?

"I didn't think he'd come near me," she admitted.

Jackie scoffed. "Ben's only joy in life is tormenting women." She pushed an empty sleeve of Oreos to the end of the bed. "Keep drinking water, you need fluids."

Charlotte did as she was told. The water helped with the nagging headache at the back of her skull. Her nausea had lifted but she felt like she'd left her kidneys on the President's Lawn.

Along with her pride.

Jackie offered her a bag of Doritos. Charlotte took a chip and nibbled at it. "I'll go kick his ass if you want. He's probably still there, smearing his bad attitude all over the place."

"It's fine." Charlotte licked orange chip crud off her fingers.

Jackie put the chips down. "Do you want me to text Reece? Let him know you're okay?"

On second thought, maybe her nausea wasn't gone.

It's me! How are you? You look great too!

She'd never wanted Reece to meet that mewling, neglected side of her. It was one thing to tell him about her abusive relationship in the sunshine of the quarry, at a moment of her choosing and firmly in the past tense. But to have him witness their toxic dynamic up close and personal? That was something else entirely.

Her skin crawled as she remembered the oily cling of Ben's stare on her skin.

"I can't believe Reece saw that," she groaned.

Jackie patted her head. "He's seen people vomit before."

Charlotte cringed. She was pretty sure she'd puked on his hands. His efforts saved her hair from the worst of it, but it still took her a few minutes bent over the bathroom sink to scrub out the stomach acid.

"That's not what I mean."

She didn't know how to explain what happened when Ben appeared. The moment she saw him, conscious thought abandoned her. It felt as if no time had passed at all. He'd summoned her younger self back from the dead.

"I told him it was good to see him," she admitted. Her words ran thick with self-loathing. "I could have told him to go fuck himself. I could have thrown a drink in his face. Instead I just . . ."

She chewed on her cuticles as the horror of that moment returned to her: the strength of his cologne, his smug expression, how quickly he dismissed Reece. Ben probably enjoyed that the most, making her twist and simper in front of an audience. The human equivalent of peeing on a woman in front of a competing male, just in case he didn't get the message.

See this girl? I broke her years ago. Have fun with what's left.

"I told him he looked *good*, Jackie. And Reece was right there, watching me grovel."

She pinched the bridge of her nose. Her eyes were dry but they throbbed in her skull, blood pumping at the back of her sockets.

Jackie put a gentle hand on Charlotte's shoulder. When she didn't flinch away, Jackie rubbed her back in slow, smooth circles.

"You know how animals have a fight-or-flight response to threats?" she asked.

Charlotte nodded meekly.

Jackie adopted the steady voice she used to lead the support group. "There's a theory that there are actually four trauma responses for humans, not two. There's also freeze and fawn." She massaged the back of Charlotte's neck. Charlotte let out a whimper as her fingers found a pressure point.

"Freeze is what it sounds like. But fawn is more complicated," Jackie continued. "It's when you comply. You try to manage the threat by agreeing with it, or by pleasing it. You literally fawn over it."

Charlotte didn't need her to spell out how the concept applied to her current situation. She mulled it over as Jackie poked and prodded her skull.

It made sense. In college, when Ben's temper boiled over, Charlotte managed him. She apologized, agreed, made herself small, all in the hopes that he would calm down and leave her alone. There was no point fighting back or running away. Her only option was to wait until his anger passed.

When they were together, she wrote it off as an opposites-attract thing: Where Ben was quick and assertive, Charlotte was careful and diplomatic. Every relationship had its give and take, its odd balancing acts. He needed someone to contain his temper. She had the strength for that person to be her. Years spent living with her mother had taught her just how to do it.

That was all bullshit, of course. But it made sense to her at the time.

Fawn response. She fawned over him. It didn't matter that she wasn't in any danger, or that Ben wasn't her boyfriend anymore. The urge to please him remained a part of her like a vestigial organ.

Charlotte shifted to rest her head in Jackie's lap. She covered her eyes with her hands to block out the glow of the laptop screen until Jackie closed it.

"It's funny," Charlotte said. "For a brief moment today, I forgot how much college sucked."

Jackie snorted. She smoothed Charlotte's hair away from her face. "It wouldn't be Hein without some repressed trauma blowing up in our faces."

Charlotte swallowed her humiliation. She focused on the comforting pressure of Jackie's fingers against her scalp. Before this weekend, she couldn't remember the last time someone held her without an agenda. Jackie's lap was warm and soft, and she was gentle when her fingers snagged in a knot.

"I really do think you should be a therapist," Charlotte said, instead of *thank you.*

Jackie huffed. "Maybe I'll have my own radio show," she said. "I can be a less problematic, gay Frasier."

"*Real Talk with Jackie Slaughter.* I'd call in."

Charlotte relaxed as Jackie played with her hair. Her body wanted to slow down and let go, fall asleep in her blanket cocoon. It had been a long day, the highs high and the lows extremely low.

"Seriously, though, you should text Reece. He's worried."

She stiffened.

And say what?

Thanks for letting me puke on you, so sorry I'm a damaged fuckup.

"He's just being polite, Jackie."

Another scoff from her best friend. "Are you kidding? That boy is infatuated with you and he's freaking out."

Charlotte remembered the silent struggle on Reece's face when she admitted she didn't want to leave the reunion. A big part of Reece wanted the same thing she did, she knew that for a fact. He was as transparent as a sheet of cling wrap.

But Reece was smart. He learned from his mistakes. Wanting her wasn't a mistake, but wanting a future with her *was.*

Maybe it was a good thing he'd seen her with Ben tonight. He needed to understand that she had nothing to offer him beyond a slow dance and no-strings-attached *fun*.

"Why do you always assume the worst of that boy?" Jackie's impatience bled through the question. Charlotte twisted to squint up at Jackie's sober face. "He's never given you one reason to doubt him."

She uncoiled herself from Jackie's lap and sat up. "Oh, I don't know," Charlotte snipped. "What's happened in my life to give me trust issues? I'm drawing a blank."

Jackie hesitated.

Charlotte could see her parsing the right way to respond. She continued before Jackie had a chance to coddle her. "Look, I know Reece isn't Ben. But he *just* got out of a serious relationship, and I doubt he wants to deal with my shit." She picked at her fingernails as she pictured the horror on Reece's face when she stumbled to the ground. She literally hit rock bottom at his feet. "The real world isn't pong and nacho fries. I'm not girlfriend material." She spat the last phrase. It felt perversely satisfying to admit it.

Ben had seen it, and Reece would discover eventually too. She didn't know how to have a real relationship. She didn't know how to fight for someone. And no one ever fought for her.

"Shut the fuck up."

Charlotte startled.

Jackie rolled her eyes, her voice a hard drawl. "I'm sorry that your ex showed up and ruined your night. He's a pig. But I'm not going to sit here and listen to the bullshit he installed in your brain. I know you don't believe that about yourself, and Reece doesn't either." Jackie's eyes narrowed. "Give me your hand."

"What?"

She snatched Charlotte's hand from her mouth and held it up to her face. "You are literally eating yourself. Do you see this?" Jackie waved her hand around by the wrist, forcing Charlotte to see her bleeding cuticles. "So you're a depressed bisexual with terrible parents. That doesn't mean you don't know how to love someone. Do you hear me?"

Charlotte stared at her, stuck between years of hurt and the dark laugh growing in her throat. She yanked her hand back and curled her nails into her palm.

Jackie barreled on. "You didn't deserve how Ben treated you. That's why you left him. And you don't deserve how your mother treated you. That's why she's not in your life. But don't you dare write off Reece. It's just another way for you to give up on yourself. And that's exactly what your mom would want you to do. And Roger, for that matter."

The urge to laugh at her best friend's tough love evaporated. "Please don't bring my job into this."

Jackie's eyes flashed. "Oh, I think we should, because you're a dumbass if you don't see the connection."

Charlotte crossed her arms over her chest, torn between desperation to avoid the conflict that had been brewing all weekend and anger that Jackie wouldn't let this go. "Please just drop it."

"No. I'm not keeping my mouth shut anymore." She'd clearly been thinking about this for a while, the words flying off her tongue. "I'm worried about you, and I'm not the only one. Nina hadn't heard from you in months. Jio said it's been over a year. Amy told me you never hang out with her anymore even though you're both in Brooklyn."

Charlotte jerked backward. They'd all talked about it, about her. When? This weekend?

Did they appoint Jackie as their official representative? Was Reece in on this too?

Her nails made painful crescents against her palm. "I've been busy."

"Too busy to call your best friend? You can't just assume we'll always pick up right where we left off." Jackie sat up on her knees. The accusation hit Charlotte in the chest. She knew Jackie was annoyed with her for being distracted, but nothing prepared her for the full force of her friend's hurt. "I swear, sometimes it's like you're choosing to be alone," Jackie added. "You have no idea what's going on in my life, but you immediately pick up the phone when Roger calls."

"Hey! I asked about your dad yesterday and you didn't want to talk about it," Charlotte shot back even as the attack shook her hard. Shame made her fingers twitch and curl into a fist.

"Because I didn't want to spend my Friday night thinking about my family." Jackie groaned and kneaded at her temples. "Damn it, I don't want to fight with you. I miss you! I haven't seen you since Thanksgiving and you spent that whole holiday answering emails. I thought this weekend would be different, but if anything, it's worse."

Charlotte's throat tightened, her anger thick enough to choke on. Didn't Jackie see she didn't have a choice? Or was she blinded by her loving parents and their Westchester County megamansion? "That isn't fair. You live on the opposite side of the country. I can't just walk down the hall to see you anymore."

"Oh come on. Do they not have FaceTime in Brooklyn?" Jackie shook her head, looking dazed. "I can't believe this. I thought the reunion would help, that coming back here together would help."

Charlotte's voice hardened. "I told you from the beginning that I only came here to work."

Jackie's eyes went wide. She began to blink rapidly, trying not to cry. Charlotte went cold as she realized the ugliness of what she'd said.

"*Only?*" Jackie laughed humorlessly. "Wow. Thanks, Charlotte. You really know how to make a girl feel special."

Her hurt landed with a thud between them on the bed. Charlotte dug at her fingers, barely noticing the blood under her nails. *I'm sorry* scrambled up her throat as she took in the betrayal on her best friend's face.

Jackie read Charlotte's guilt and she softened, changing tack. "I know that quitting *Front End* would be a huge deal," she said in her support group voice again, compartmentalizing her feelings to focus on the topic at hand. "But you're not trapped. You'll find another job. I'll help you! You just have to tell me how you *feel* every once in a while."

You're not trapped.

Charlotte's blood roared in her ears. She gaped at Jackie as flaming orange shock surged across her mind.

How could Jackie be so clueless?

Charlotte wasn't just trapped. She was on her own, all the time, forever. She had no supportive family a phone call away. She couldn't ask anyone for a loan when she was short on rent. She couldn't rely on a late-night pep talk from a loving parent.

She was *no emergency contact to list at the doctor's office* alone, *written out of the will* alone, *might as well be dead* alone.

And now she was *my best friend doesn't get it* alone too.

"What are you doing all this work for?" Jackie blurted out in the silence as Charlotte reeled. "Is this the life you want? Letting some asshole berate you twenty-four-seven? Is this really who you thought you'd be?"

And then it was back . . . the oil slick of shame as Ben leered at her. The noxious gray fumes of Roger's cruelty. The darkness of a subway tunnel.

Charlotte swallowed, licked her lips. "I'm sorry I don't have the luxury of thinking like that," she hissed. "I'm just trying to get through the day, every fucking day."

Jackie looked desperate. She floundered for something to say, her eyes darting. Finally she gasped, "You don't have to live in survival mode!"

"I don't have a choice." Charlotte's voice had turned to steel again, low and uncompromising. "I don't have a family, Jackie. I can't depend on anyone but myself."

Jackie's eyes finally brimmed over with tears. Her mouth flattened into a thin line. "You're gonna feel like a real asshole tomorrow for saying that," she said.

Goddamn it, she already did.

"I can't be here right now." Charlotte dropped from the bed and shoved her feet into her loafers.

Jackie watched open-mouthed as she grabbed her phone from its charging cradle on the dresser. "Where are you going?"

"I don't know. I'll see you later."

The heavy dorm room door slammed shut behind her, locking automatically. Charlotte realized a second too late that she forgot the keys.

TEXT MESSAGE FROM REECE KRUEGER TO CHARLOTTE THORNE, 1:17 AM: hey. just making sure you're okay?

CHARLOTTE TOOK THE long, winding footpath from the dorm to the south side of campus. The ambling route let her skirt University Road and the foot traffic to Senior Housing. It also kept her far from frat row, where Ben would retreat when he tired of the Lawn Party.

Better to stick to the dirt path and the dark.

She couldn't think. All she knew was swirling color, anger clotting red in her lungs, guilt blue-black in her throat. She tried to breathe, gathering lungfuls of oxygen and expelling them in slow exhales. It didn't help.

You worthless piece of shit.

Reece was mad at her. Now so was Jackie. Maybe Jio and Nina too, going off what Jackie said about them not hearing from her enough. She had neglected huge swaths of her life, and then tonight she'd burned whatever had survived the drought.

Jackie was wrong. Jackie was right. Charlotte hated her job, and she needed her job. She missed her friends, and her friends didn't understand her anymore.

She hated her life, and she couldn't live it any other way.

Right now she needed to be somewhere safe. Somewhere she didn't have to deal with Jackie or Ben or Reece. Somewhere free of traumatic memories or insulting advice. Somewhere she was accepted without question.

She turned the corner on University Road and headed down the row of student program houses. The front door at Acronym would be unlocked. She could pour herself a steaming cup of coffee in the kitchen. Maybe someone would go halvsies with her on a pizza.

Charlotte stopped short on the sidewalk. A man stood in front of Acronym, his hands thrust in his back pockets. He stared at the wood-frame house like a soldier preparing himself for battle, his body rigid with anxiety. It seemed she wasn't the only person on their own tonight, avoiding the crowds and battling inner demons.

The man shifted his weight onto his other foot. The beam of a streetlight caught his profile, illuminating his furrowed brow. Garrett still wore his clothes from the quarry, a loose bro tank and basketball shorts.

It didn't make sense: him, here, with *that* expression his face. She knew it deep in her soul, his frown severe as he worried over the house in front of him.

She had stumbled across a private moment of reckoning. Once upon a time as a freshman, Charlotte stood there herself, weighing her preppy clothes and fledgling queer identity against the explosive color of the LGBTQIA+ center and worrying that she wouldn't belong. Gathering the courage to ring the doorbell. Not knowing the doorbell was broken and she should knock, or better yet just let herself in.

Charlotte hesitated. Her riot of emotions quieted as she considered Reece's best friend. Should she turn around and leave him alone, pretend she'd never seen him here? Surely Garrett didn't want an audience, least of all her.

Then again, taking that first step up the path was so much easier with someone by your side.

Before she could decide, Garrett noticed her in the distance. He stiffened, his shoulders hunching. They eyed each other for an uncertain moment, their usual tension not fitting this new setting.

"Hi," Charlotte ventured. She knew better than to smile and feign a friendship that didn't exist.

Garrett didn't say anything, but he didn't move either.

After waiting a beat, she closed the distance between them, stopping a few feet away.

Still, he stayed quiet.

Charlotte mirrored his posture and turned to face the house. Even at the late hour, Acronym pulsed with life and belonging. The curtains were drawn but figures passed by the windows, silhouetted against the glow. A Mitski song flirted with the breeze from an open window.

"Quiet down here, huh?" Charlotte said. "The tent got too loud for me."

In her peripheral vision, Garrett's mouth twitched. "Hot too," he agreed. He sounded wary.

"I need coffee," she carried on, like they made small talk all the time instead of glaring at each other behind Reece's back. A Progress Pride flag fluttered on the porch railing, pleasant as a queer Norman Rockwell painting. "They always have a pot brewing in the kitchen."

Nothing from Garrett.

"I nearly started a fire junior year," she added. "Poured in too many grounds."

Garrett laughed, and then coughed. She cast him a quick glance. The tension in his shoulders relaxed somewhat, which seemed like a good sign. They formed a united front and considered the façade of the house together.

"I could use a cup of coffee." Hunger throbbed through his words, betraying years of yearning.

But when Charlotte took a step forward on the path, he didn't follow. He stayed rooted on the sidewalk, his posture ramrod straight.

"They don't check your queer bona fides at the door," Charlotte said. His eyes flicked from the house to her face, his mouth thinning. "Everyone's welcome."

Garrett sighed in a quick whoosh. With a dubious look at his ratty bro tank, he said, "I look like shit."

"No one ever threw me out for wearing J.Crew." During freshman orientation, Charlotte looked about as gay as a Vineyard Vines catalog.

His eyes shifted back and forth between her and the bright green doorway behind her. Charlotte felt lucky to watch him grapple with himself, an intimacy she'd done nothing to deserve.

"C'mon," she said. "It's just coffee."

His yearning won out. This time when she walked toward Acronym, he followed.

Garrett stopped when they crossed the threshold. She turned to check on him and found him thunderstruck as he took in the foyer, from the mountain of shoes beside the front door, to the multicolor wrapping paper taped to the walls. Someone had stolen blue-and-silver tinsel from the dining hall and wrapped it around the stair railing. It looked like a shabby dollhouse of radical queer politics, every surface loud and soft.

Years ago, she'd dragged Jackie through the front door with an earnest *Welcome home!* For Garrett, she kept it simple. "The kitchen's through here," she said after giving him time to adjust. He followed her down the hallway.

A boy sat on the counter surrounded by Thai take-out boxes. He looked up as Charlotte entered and smiled: It was Wynn, the almost-grad she met at the disco. He waved them over with his chopsticks. "Hi! Charlotte, right?"

"Hey, how are you?"

Wynn shrugged. He wore another jumpsuit, this one a deep blue color with a FEEL THE BERN button and several other pins on the pocket. "Just got back from the Lawn. Waiting for the ringing in my ears to stop," he said. "DJ Khaled isn't my vibe."

"Me neither. Mind if I make some coffee?" Charlotte nodded to the pot beside the sink.

"Help yourself." Wynn swirled his chopsticks through a box of pad thai. "Plenty of food too. You know where the plates are."

Garrett hesitated in the doorway, his hands stuffed in his pockets. Charlotte gave him an encouraging nod. "Wynn, this is Garrett."

Wynn waved as he chewed some tofu.

Charlotte pointed to a cabinet over the microwave. "Can you get some mugs down? You're taller than I am."

The direct request overrode Garrett's nerves, and he crossed the room to help.

"Hi, Garrett," Wynn trilled after swallowing. "Please eat something, I ordered way too much."

Garrett blinked as Wynn passed him some chopsticks. "Thank you." He unwrapped the paper and snapped the sticks apart. "Nice pins."

"Thanks!" Wynn pinched the fabric between his fingers and held it out so that Garrett could see his collection. Charlotte recognized a purple HE/HIM badge that her class made during a fundraiser for house repairs. Jio went a little nuts with the button maker at the student activities office. Extra pronoun buttons still lived in a shoebox in the library upstairs.

Garrett shook some noodles onto a clean plate. "Is this from Naga? Love that place."

"Yeah! I've been trying to re-create their cashew stir-fry, but I can't get the texture right. There's rice too." Wynn passed him another take-out box.

"You like to cook?" Garrett leaned against the counter beside him.

"When I have time. My friend and I want to start a YouTube channel with like, super basic tutorials. I have this great recipe for home-cooked potato chips, hang on."

Charlotte kept an eye on Garrett as she hunted down coffee

grounds. His hesitation faded amid the enthusiasm of their host's chatter. Nothing like food to make everyone feel included.

She put a fresh pot on to boil. Before long the room smelled like dark roast and spices. While she waited for it to brew, she read the notices stuck to the refrigerator. Magnets held up posters for concerts and student plays, handwritten infographics about consent and microaggressions.

Refugees are welcome here. DREAMers are welcome here. The undocumented are welcome here. First-gen students are welcome here. Survivors are welcome here.

Trans women are women.

Ban billionaires.

Thick black Sharpie underlined the idealism of Hein's current students. She traced the handwritten words on a page ripped from a zine: *Casual sex does not mean you can be casual with your partner's humanity.*

Below this startling wisdom, in all caps: *LOVE YOUR ONE-NIGHT STAND. HOOKUP CULTURE IS TOXIC.*

"Is someone making coffee?" Jio slinked into the room, rubbing their eyes. Their makeup was hopelessly smeared but they brightened as soon as they recognized her. "Char! Where've you *been*?"

"Get a mug, I put on a full pot." Charlotte nodded to where Wynn was walking Garrett through a recipe. "Jio, you know Garrett."

"Course I do!" Jio hopped up onto the counter beside the takeout. "How you doing, hun?"

They didn't bat a glittery eyelash at Garrett's abrupt appearance. She felt a surge of love for her friend.

The coffee maker dinged. Charlotte poured out four mugs as Wynn fetched oat and whole milk from the fridge. They sipped and chatted about soy sauce. Charlotte mostly listened, watching Garrett relax into the conversation. When she caught his eye accidentally, he hesitated before giving her a small nod.

She wondered what brought him here: who he was and how long he'd known. But the details weren't any of her business. Acronym was a place to come and just be. Grab a cup of coffee and dance to the disco music. Ignore your problems or organize to fight them. Pass out on a futon without being hassled.

Share as much or as little of your story as you want to share.

Jio snuggled in next to her. "Where's Reece?" they asked in a velvety whisper.

Charlotte ran a finger around the rim of her coffee cup. "Elsewhere."

"And Jackie?"

"Also elsewhere."

Jio rested their head against her shoulder, *hmm*-ing under their breath. They still looked half-asleep despite the caffeine. And why wouldn't they? They'd had a huge weekend. An engagement announcement, two dance parties, a long trip from D.C. . . .

Charlotte wrapped her arm around their shoulders and gave them a side hug. "I'm so happy for you," she said. "Seriously."

Jio straightened up, their smile returning even as they fought back a yawn. "Thanks, Char." The yawn escaped and Jio covered their mouth with their hand. When it passed, Jio rolled their eyes. "Who would have thought. Me, engaged."

Charlotte took a careful sip of her coffee. She hoped she wasn't being rude when she asked, "Are you scared?"

Jio drummed their nails on the kitchen island as they considered her question. "Of marriage? Not really." They frowned. "I'm scared of, like, money stuff. Debt. But marriage doesn't scare me. Matt's always been my future."

"You don't worry about, uh—" She hesitated. "I mean, your parents are divorced too."

Jio waved off her unasked question. "Yeah, but we're not them," they said. "I won't let us become them."

She marveled at their words. What a brave thing to say. She bit her lip, torn between jealousy and doubt.

Jio looped their arm around her waist. "I think Matt worries," they admitted, lowering their voice. "He didn't grow up with a lot of love. I still freak him out sometimes." Jio winked at her. "You may not know this, but I'm a *bit much*."

"I had no idea," she drawled, and they laughed. Their joy was infectious, and she smiled as they added some sugar to their coffee.

Her phone trilled in her pocket, announcing an incoming text. She felt the blood drain from her face, even though she knew it was probably Jackie. Or Reece, wanting to make sure she wasn't passed out on the softball field.

"Are you okay, hun?" Jio nudged her shoulder gently. "Something bothering you?"

Oh nothing. Only her shithead boss, her narcissist ex-boyfriend, her abusive mother, her furious best friend, and the guy she'd fallen for whom she would never, ever deserve.

Charlotte winced. "Lots of demons tonight."

Jio hummed under their breath again, and then looked around the kitchen. "We could have another meeting," they suggested. "This place is like the 3Ds clubhouse."

"No, it's okay—"

But Jio gave her a clever smile and turned to Wynn and Garrett. "Hey, do you guys have shitty parents?"

The boys gave them matching quizzical looks.

Jio gestured vaguely with their hand. "Controlling, unsupportive, that kind of thing."

Wynn smiled at some private joke. "Unfortunately, yes."

Jio nodded and turned to Garrett. "What about yours?"

He froze. "Uh . . . Sometimes?"

"Perfect." Jio clapped their hands once. They channeled Jackie's fearless-leader energy as they announced, "I hereby declare an emergency meeting of the Dead, Divorced, and Otherwise Disappointing Parents Unofficial Support Group."

Wynn guffawed at the announcement but leaned forward with interest. Garrett just blinked.

Charlotte hid her face in her hand, torn between embarrassment and amusement. Leave it to Jio to pressure two strangers into doing emotional labor in her hour of need. "You do not need to be part of this," she told them.

"Go ahead!" Wynn raised his coffee in a toast. "I've got nothing else to do."

Garrett gave her a little *you might as well* shrug, clearly resigned to wherever this night took him.

Satisfied by their consent, Jio turned back to Charlotte. "Okay, go on, then. What's on your mind?"

Fixed in the stares of her three companions, Charlotte tightened her grip on her mug. She could maybe imagine telling Jio the truth, but she couldn't bare her soul to Garrett. And Wynn was a total stranger.

Then again, there had to be a reason Reece kept Garrett around. Judging by where they were, he clearly had hidden depths. And she recognized Amy's wide-eyed faith in Wynn's open face.

Use your words, Charlotte Thorne!

"Okay." Charlotte put her coffee down, and then picked it back up to have something to do with her hands. "All right."

She opened her mouth.

She thought of the bracing cold of Cobalt Pond, and Jackie's pursed lips as she focused on her eyeliner. She remembered Reece's teeth grazing her neck in her twin bed, and his fingers woven through hers as he guided her through the Lawn Party. She felt the warmth that spread through her chest when he gave her that just-for-Charlie smile.

But . . . the freshly sharpened knife of Ben's white smile. Reece's face falling as he realized she wasn't who he thought she was. Jackie fighting back tears. Her vermillion self-loathing as she scrubbed bile out of her hair over the sink.

Her jaw closed with a snap.

Jio leaned against the island and propped their chin up on their palm. "Are you okay?"

She wanted to say no. She wanted to say yes. But her voice died in her throat like a snuffed candle. She set her mug down again and flattened her hands on the kitchen island.

Charlotte took a shaky breath. "I can't, Jio. I'm sorry."

Jio tucked a lock of her hair behind her ear. They made little cooing sounds under their breath, just like Reece had done as he guided her out of the tent.

Charlotte's eyes wandered to the fridge, to all those capital letters across construction paper. She turned to Wynn. "Does this place still have colored pencils?"

Chapter 13

TEXT MESSAGE FROM REECE KRUEGER TO CHARLOTTE THORNE, 2:25 AM: charlie?

ON THE WALK back to Randall, her cracked phone smugly informed her of the time: nearly four o'clock in the morning. All the coffee in the world couldn't mask the weariness in Charlotte's bones. Her feet hurt. Her head ached. Her throat was a special kind of scratchy that only came from laughing, crying, and barfing in the same evening.

But her night wasn't over yet. She had to talk to Reece.

Charlotte still didn't know what she needed to say. They'd carved out this time capsule with the unspoken agreement that it wouldn't last after the reunion. She wasn't sure what she wanted after that, or if Reece wanted to explore an *after* at all.

Even if their interest in *after* was mutual, assuming Reece could forgive her for being a bitch at the Lawn Party, they'd never known each other outside Hein's alternate reality. They'd never gone to the movies, or talked on the phone, or eaten a meal alone together. Oreos didn't count.

But she knew Reece cared about her. Even if she didn't understand why, or when, or how he had come to care for her, she could feel the truth of it in her bones.

She trusted him.

That trust allowed her to take out her phone and text him as she stood outside his dorm room. She knew Reece would text back. A man like that didn't care about people on a whim.

She just didn't know what would happen when he opened the door.

TEXT MESSAGE FROM CHARLOTTE THORNE TO REECE KRUEGER, 3:43 AM: Any chance you're still awake?

Her message hovered on her screen and then was delivered. She leaned against the wall opposite Reece and Garrett's room as she waited for an answer.

In the interim, she checked her other notifications.

TEXT MESSAGE FROM JACKIE SLAUGHTER TO CHARLOTTE THORNE, 2:51 AM: so uh I know we're fighting right now but would you mind not coming back to the room for a while

TEXT MESSAGE FROM JACKIE SLAUGHTER TO CHARLOTTE THORNE, 2:51 AM: or at all

TEXT MESSAGE FROM JACKIE SLAUGHTER TO CHARLOTTE THORNE, 2:53 AM: not because I'm mad at you but because I'm gonna bone Nina

Shit. She'd been sexiled.

Well, good for them.

TEXT MESSAGE FROM CHARLOTTE THORNE TO JACKIE SLAUGHTER, 3:43 AM: yes ma'am, you crazy kids have fun

As she sent her reply, the phone vibrated with another incoming message.

TEXT MESSAGE FROM REECE KRUEGER TO CHARLOTTE THORNE, 3:44 AM: there might be a chance

Charlotte considered Reece's tone. The text was clever but cautious, a raised eyebrow as opposed to a direct answer.

She matched his humor.

TEXT MESSAGE FROM CHARLOTTE THORNE TO REECE KRUEGER, 3:44 AM: I find myself in need of a bed to sleep in.

The typing bubble expanded and then disappeared. Then:

TEXT MESSAGE FROM REECE KRUEGER TO CHARLOTTE THORNE, 3:45 AM: is that so

TEXT MESSAGE FROM REECE KRUEGER TO CHARLOTTE THORNE, 3:45 AM: might I interest you in a twin xl

Charlotte snorted, more relieved than amused.

Thank goodness, her trust wasn't misplaced. Reece hadn't shut her out. He didn't hate her for how she behaved tonight, or for her vanishing act.

The door swung open. Reece stood with one hand looped around the doorknob, the room dark behind him.

"I thought there was someone skulking around out here."

"That's me. The skulker." She ran her hands over the front of her outfit, smoothing down the bedraggled hem of her crop top. God only knew what she looked like after the last eight hours. The dorm's fluorescent lights weren't exactly forgiving.

Reece kept his face blank. Scruff had begun to overtake his jaw, and he'd changed into pajama pants and a white henley.

"Did I wake you up?"

He shook his head. A wet lock of hair fell across his forehead, fresh from the shower.

"I got back from the Lawn like a half hour ago. Garrett's still out."

Charlotte almost told him that she'd left his roommate hunched over Wynn's laptop watching *Say Yes to the Dress* with him and Jio, but she didn't know what Reece knew about Garrett's queerness. That was between them, and it wasn't her information to share.

She waited for him to invite her in. Reece didn't move in the doorway.

In college their roles were usually reversed. If they didn't meet up at some party, Reece arrived all sweaty and buzzed at her door at the end of the night. She would let him into her apartment. He kissed down her throat until their self-consciousness bled away and they pretended not to care about each other. Just sex. Just distraction. Just release.

The old script hung over their shoulders, but carelessness didn't fit anymore. He couldn't paper over his feelings for her, and she couldn't refuse to feel anything at all. It was far too late for that.

"Listen, I'm sorry—" she started.

"Don't." Reece shook his head, that loose curl swinging across his forehead. He swiped at it as he stepped back, opening the door wider. "Just come in."

A thread of resignation ran through the invitation. Charlotte bristled but followed his instructions.

Moonlight spilled through the open blinds. Outside she could see students roaming campus, little more than dark forms lurching to their next destination.

She blinked as he closed the door.

"How are you feeling?" Reece leaned against the dresser, his arms folded across his chest.

Charlotte cleared her throat. "Oh, you know."

He tilted his head to the side and watched her squirm. The silence stretched between them. Reece made no effort to rescue her from her discomfort. It dawned on her that he wasn't going to let her wiggle out of talking about what happened at the party.

Damn it.

"Embarrassed, I guess." Her voice was hoarse, which only made her feel worse. Reece had already seen too much of her tonight.

Reece started across the room, only to stop at the foot of his bed. He looked like he wanted to touch her but didn't at the same time, restraining himself at the last moment. Instead, he gripped the footboard. "Why are you embarrassed?" he asked.

Like she hadn't thrown up on him, or acted like a coward in front of her ex, or screamed at him to leave her alone.

Where to start?

Charlotte picked the worst infraction. "I yelled at you. You were being nice, and I yelled at you."

Reece nodded grudgingly. "Yeah, you did. But you were having a panic attack and I crowded you." He said it like it was nothing, a simple misunderstanding already resolved.

Charlotte's hands fisted at her sides, nails biting into her palms. She didn't want Reece to be mad at her, but his easy dismissal didn't make any sense. "That doesn't make it okay."

"It's all right."

Reece ran his hand along the duvet. The bed was unmade—if he wasn't asleep when she arrived, he'd nearly been. The urge to apologize again rose in Charlotte's throat, but he didn't look angry. If anything, he looked sad.

Were his eyes wet? Or was the moonlight playing tricks on her?

"I'm not mad at you," he said, answering her unasked question. "I was just worried." His forehead creased with those new worry lines.

Charlotte shifted on her feet. *Worry.* It seemed to surround her this weekend: Jackie's judgmental worry, Nina's understated worry, Reece's earnest worry. She didn't know what to do with more worry. It made her skin itch.

"I'm okay." She gave him a hollow smile. "I'm fine!"

Reece's eyes trailed from her snarled hair to her dusty shoes. He shook his head, smiling despite himself. "Charlie Thorne, always fine." His words were thin, but he didn't elaborate. "Let me find you something to wear."

As Reece searched the explosion of clothes on his desk for makeshift pajamas, Charlotte focused on the simple task of getting ready for sleep. She tucked her shoes under the bed and texted Jackie that she would spend the night with Reece. She left her phone on the windowsill.

Reece gave her a clean T-shirt and a pair of boxers. He busied himself with plugging his phone in to charge as she changed. The shirt fell to just below her hips. Cartoon kittens scampered across the boxers. Charlotte balled up her clothes and put them next to her phone.

Having run out of stalling tactics, Charlotte hopped onto the mattress. She tucked herself in and scooted over to make room for him.

The bed shifted as he climbed up next to her. He avoided looking at her as he slid under the sheets.

They both knew the bed was too narrow to sleep without touching. Charlotte slowly turned to face the wall, and Reece positioned himself behind her, one arm curling around her waist. After a moment's hesitation, she wove her fingers through his and held tight.

They had never done this before. Reece's warm breath spilled across the back of her neck. The sensation was so unusual and pleasant that she blinked at the wall. Was sleep even possible like this? How did one doze off when squished against six feet of another human?

"Where did you go?" Reece murmured. As quiet as his words were, she clearly wasn't the only one wide awake.

He meant where she'd gone after the party. His heartbeat against her back, a quick but steady *thud thud, thud thud.*

"My room. And then Acronym."

Reece shifted to get more comfortable. He tucked his right arm underneath their shared pillow. Her nerves tightened as he engulfed her body in his warmth. It felt like being nestled in a padded envelope, precious cargo sent with care.

He squeezed her hand.

Little by little the tension left Charlotte's limbs as she melted in the kiln of the too-small bed. Her body craved sleep. But images from the night kept whirling through her mind: Ben's teeth flashing red in the party lights . . . Jackie pushing her to quit her job . . . Reece's eyes electric with life on the President's Lawn.

Charlotte felt like she was coming off a drug, wired and depleted all at once.

She focused on Reece's heartbeat, solid like the rhythm of an old watch.

Reece pressed his forehead to the back of her neck. She shivered at the delicate touch. "I'm sorry too," he said.

Charlotte frowned. "For what?"

Reece's fingers twitched between hers, but he didn't let go. "For not protecting you at the party."

She remembered that dreadful interaction at the bar. From her perspective, Reece had played silent witness to one of the worst moments of her life. He was an innocent bystander watching a car crash, utterly blameless. He didn't need to apologize.

"I had no idea what to do. He was sleazing all over you and I froze. I didn't want to make a scene if that wasn't what you wanted, but you obviously wanted him to leave you alone. I should have done something."

A strange emotion she couldn't identify spread through her chest. Of *course* Reece understood her behavior at the party. Of *course* he didn't think less of her for fawning over Ben. She always underestimated him.

Gratitude. This feeling was called *gratitude.* It sat butter yellow in her throat, warring with her irritation that he'd somehow found a way to blame himself.

"And then you doubled over, and I didn't know if you were sick from drinking or having a panic attack or what." Reece's fist clenched under her hand. "I couldn't do anything. I was just in the way."

If there was something Reece Krueger would never be, it was *just in the way.*

Charlotte twisted in his arms to face him. His mouth was a pained grimace. She recognized the expression from so many nights at support group: He looked the same way whenever he talked about his dad.

Helpless. A muted mauve color, sad and frail.

"I don't want to make you running into Ben about me, because it's not," he said firmly. "I just . . . wish I'd helped."

"You do help. You help *everyone.*" Charlotte curled her fingers into the collar of his shirt and gave him a shake. "You're helping Jio with the wedding, and you're helping Jackie find a therapist for her dad, and you help your mom all the time."

"Yeah, but I don't help you." Reece's eyes narrowed. "I didn't help when you were hurting senior year. I didn't help tonight."

She couldn't bear the tattered look on his face. Charlotte cupped his cheek in her palm. His lips were pillow-soft as she ran her thumb across his mouth. "Please stop. You can't help someone who doesn't want it."

Reece's eyebrows folded together, his brand-new worry lines multiplying.

Shit, that came out terribly. For the second time tonight, she was going about this all wrong. In the moments that mattered, she could never find the words to capture what she really felt.

What had she yelled at him outside the tent?

I don't want your help. I don't need you.

What she actually meant went something like . . . *I'm ashamed. I'm ashamed to let you see me like this.*

Reece's lips parted underneath her thumb, his breath wicking across her skin. Something about the image of Reece's mouth opening at her touch felt so vulnerable. He wasn't afraid to grant her access to his little soft spaces. Not right away, not all at once, but he let her in eventually. When he was ready.

His trust gave Charlotte the confidence she needed. She wanted to tell him the truth. To tell herself the truth, really.

"What I mean is that I don't know how to ask for help when I need it."

She had never put that thought into words. She'd never wanted to before. Doing so meant admitting to the kind of wound that risked defining you: the absent father, the abusive mother, the self-reliance that kept you alive even as it held you apart from people who might love you better. A thin line separated not needing help and thinking you didn't deserve it.

Understanding dawned on Reece's face. Her hand fell from his lips as he gathered her in his arms and tucked her head underneath his chin.

Reece pressed a kiss into her hair and held her tight. Strange, how absolutely herself she felt surrounded by his strength. If she wanted to move, he'd let her go in an instant, and that simple knowledge made her never want to move again. She wriggled closer and wrapped an arm around his waist. Her fingers found the bottom of his shirt and stole upward to trace his skin.

"You are wonderful," he murmured into her hair.

Charlotte held her breath. Her hand stilled its tender exploration of his back. If she'd been any other girl, she might have found his words romantic. Instead, her lungs threatened to crumple like an empty wasp's nest.

Goddamn it, enough of this. Reece had no reason to lie to her. She wanted to believe him.

"You're not a fan of compliments, are you?" Humor tipped his words, infusing them with curiosity rather than frustration. Reece shifted her in his arms so that he could see her expression. Green eyes peered at her in an invitation to explain. He wasn't criticizing her, just trying to understand.

Guilt pooled in her chest. Stupid goddamn defense mechanisms. She studied the well-past-five-o'clock shadow dusting his jaw. "I'm sorry, I— Thank you."

"But . . ." Reece prompted her.

But. Why *did* she hate compliments so much?

She supposed she didn't have the best track record with them. Ben doled out compliments like loose change, cheap and easy. On his worst days he used them as currency to balance his tab of nastiness. She wasn't pathetic, she was *brilliant.* She wasn't a stupid bitch, she was *ravishing.* A vague *you're beautiful* bought her forgiveness. Ben used praise to bail himself out.

"I'm used to them being bullshit." Charlotte pressed her palm against Reece's chest, grounding herself as she parsed her hang-ups. As much as it came as a relief to unburden herself like this, it hurt somewhere deep and vital to churn up buried soil. "Manipulative, I guess."

Reece's voice slipped an octave lower. "I'm not trying to manipulate you."

"I know you're not." She forced herself to look him in the eye. "I guess I have trouble believing it sometimes," Charlotte continued. She worried her lip between her teeth as she separated insecurity from self-awareness. On a cognitive level she could see herself clearly, more or less. But believing it wasn't easy. "Like, I know I'm smart. I work hard. People seem to really like my hair."

"Because it's beautiful," Reece growled, grasping a loose curl. He gave it a playful tug.

She gave him a weak smile, and he let go.

"It's just . . ." She sighed. "You get told often enough that you're a disgrace and eventually kindness feels like the lie."

Reece's eyes went round. Someone else might have rushed to tell her how great she was, but he lay in the silence with her.

"Your mom," he finally said, knitting the last pieces together.

She felt like she had gravel caught in her throat. "Yeah."

The secondhand anger on Reece's face was a little too much to take. She pressed her face against his neck and cuddled close. His arms closed around her automatically.

After a while, Reece combed his fingers through her tangled hair. "I'm having trouble picturing her," he mused quietly. "I don't think I saw her at graduation."

The old, dark wound in Charlotte's chest throbbed painfully. She assumed that Jackie had filled him in on the missing details of graduation, but obviously not. He still didn't know. She never told him.

"She wasn't there."

Reece's hand stilled. She could practically see the gears grinding in his brain as he processed this new information.

"What?" Reece blurted out.

Charlotte caught the collar of his shirt between her fingers, thin from so many washes. He really did use a lovely fabric softener.

Words, Charlotte Thorne. Use them.

"She was supposed to be there. I invited her as a sort of olive branch, and she agreed to come."

Charlotte planned her graduation outfit in advance. She found a Lilly Pulitzer dress made from white eyelet lace at Goodwill. Charlotte never wore Lilly Pulitzer, or lace, but it felt like fate when she saw it on the formal-wear rack. This was a dress Olivia Harrington Thorne would choose for her daughter to wear to her graduation. Pretty and feminine and preppy as hell.

She planned to wear the dress with electric blue cowboy boots borrowed from Nina, and her hair was still that hydrogen-peroxide-white bob. She would always be Charlotte Thorne, the bisexual dirtbag, but she intended for the dress to be a gesture toward compromise.

She closed her fist around Reece's shirt. "I thought if she saw me here, somewhere I belong, that I'd make more sense to her. That she would understand me better."

It was a fantasy, of course. The emotional whirlwind of the end of term made her think that anything was possible: an internship at an It Media Company, finally leaving her terrible boyfriend, reconciling with her mother. Their relationship had been fractious since her breakup with Ben, but Charlotte had so much to be proud of. She was moving to New York City and maybe she finally had her shit together, maybe she had it all figured out.

In reality, she had no reason to think her mother would change her mind. People didn't snap out of a decade of homophobia and a lifetime of neglect. Nothing in the world would close the gulf between them, no stack of cartoons published in the school paper or prestigious internship offers. No secondhand cocktail dress or picturesque New England campus.

"But she just didn't show up."

Graduation day was a brutal reminder that life didn't offer happily-ever-afters. Not for people like her.

Reece was still processing. "Did she ever explain why?"

Charlotte bit the inside of her cheek. "Yeah, she emailed me after the ceremony." And what an email it was, confusing and harsh. Charlotte remembered squinting at her phone in the bright sunlight on the quad, wondering what on earth her mother was talking about in her stilted, formal language. But when she figured it out . . .

As she remembered her mother's words, bloody anger wrapped itself around charcoal gray shame. She drew strength from the former as she continued.

"Remember when I told you that Ben spread a rumor about me? That I'd cheated on him with Jackie?" Reece nodded, not seeing the connection. "My mom was one of the people he talked to. I think he found out that you and I were hooking up, and he called her to stir up shit."

Reece's face whitened with horror. "Oh my god, I'm so sorry."

"Don't be, his psycho behavior is not your fault. He didn't like me moving on, and he lashed out through her. He knew that would hurt me the most. And my mother always adored him; she never understood why we broke up." A mirthless smile stretched across Charlotte's mouth, tight and hollow. "I guess it was easier for her to believe I was an unfaithful slut than that he was a controlling monster."

She clung to her self-righteous anger as Reece winced, praying her instincts were right and that he wouldn't judge her.

"Olivia said in her email that I was a disgrace to the family and no longer her daughter. I replied that she should go fuck herself."

Stunned, Reece blinked at her. "Damn," he whistled. "Good for you. *Fuck* her."

"Thanks," Charlotte said. "We haven't spoken since."

Over time it would hurt less. It already did hurt less. She never doubted her decision, even during the hardest moments of the last five years. It had taken twenty-two years for Charlotte to reach her limit with her mother, and she knew she had done everything possible to avoid that breaking point. She would choose being broke and alone over Olivia Harrington Thorne's emotional abuse any day of the week.

Reece exhaled in a huff. "I can't believe she fell for that guy's act."

"Honestly, I don't even care that she believed Ben. What if it had been true, you know?" Charlotte wiggled up into a sitting position, Reece's arm still looped behind her hips. "What if I *was* seeing Jackie? So what? Olivia didn't care that I supposedly cheated, she cared that it was with a woman." Her fury blended with pearly white certainty. "But I love being queer. It's one of my favorite parts of myself."

Charlotte meant it. No one ever took that away from her, not her parents, not even Ben. Her bisexuality wasn't a rebellious phase or a party trick, and it wasn't an inconvenience or an embarrassment to the people who loved her. Queerness meant joy and community and endless potential to fall in lust and love and understanding. Even if Charlotte had lost sight of that in the last few years.

"I'd rather not have my mother in my life than apologize for who I am," she said. "And I will never subject anyone I care about to her judgment."

Reece sat up beside her in the narrow bed. He had an odd look on his face, intense but soft. His smile was missing, but his eyes burned with something better: respect. She settled against his side as he wrapped his arm around her shoulders. A moment later she felt her curls stir as he pressed a kiss to her hair.

Now, wrapped up in Reece's embrace, it didn't hurt to remember that awful day. Her perspective shifted. Maybe it wasn't the day her mother had rejected her for good. Maybe it was the day she finally cut out her first abuser.

If only the decision hadn't come with collateral damage.

"I really did want to meet your family," Charlotte added. "I'm so sorry I didn't show up at the picnic. I should have at least answered your texts when you asked me where I was, or called you to explain." She licked her dry lips. "I was not my best self that day."

Reece found her chin with his hand and tipped her face up to his.

"Charlie," he murmured, his voice lush with awe. Not pity, not disgust. He looked at her with pure, undiluted tenderness. "I forgive you. And I can't understand anyone choosing not to know you."

His words spread through every inch of her, from her fingertips to her shins to the top of her head. She breathed in deep and exhaled on a staggered sigh. "Oh wow," she laughed humorlessly. "I think that's the nicest thing anyone has ever said to me."

His eyes creased as he smiled. "I'll tell you again anytime you need a reminder."

She wanted that. She wanted it so much she felt like her heart might seize. She wanted Reece's affection anytime, every day, whenever and wherever.

An emotion she hadn't felt in years fluttered inside her rib cage, begging to be released. She wanted to kiss him, wanted to press herself into all his little corners and absorb every ounce of his affection. She wanted to let go.

But something held her back.

"I keep waiting for you to . . . flinch," she confessed. "The more I say . . ."

Reece's smile slanted into an amused smirk. "Are you forgetting that we met at a support group?"

Charlotte bit her lip. "Fair point."

"My whole life changed when you came back to the 3Ds," he said. "I looked forward to sitting next to you every week."

"What do you mean?" she asked. And then, the real question that had nagged at her for years: "Why me?"

He smiled, all lopsided and self-conscious. "You made these little noises under your breath while people spoke. You rarely talked, but you hissed and grumbled and growled because you were so mad for everyone else."

Charlotte blushed. "I did?"

"Yeah, you did." He chuckled. "It was so cute, I lived for it. I had to sit next to you so I could hear you." He ran his thumb across her neck until he found her pulse point. She swallowed at the soft pressure of his hand against her fragile skin, her heart racing under his touch. "You care so much about everyone, and you get so pissed off when you see an injustice. But I don't think you apply that same care to yourself."

She licked her dry lips, overwhelmed and amazed. Reece just kept looking at her, seeing the best and worst of her, knowing her through and through.

"So no, I'm not going to run, Charlie." The humor vanished from his voice. "You don't scare me."

Her gasp escaped before she could squash it. It was better than any profession of love, more affecting than any romantic gesture. It was also the truth. She told him her secrets and he held her closer.

A frustrated moan stole from his mouth.

"What?" she whispered.

Reece clenched his eyes shut. "I'm trying not to make the same mistake twice."

Charlotte nuzzled against his neck, her eyelashes brushing his skin. Desire unspooled within her as she felt his pulse jump. "What's that?"

"Bombard you with affection and freak you out."

Her answering laugh was huskier than usual. She slithered her hand under his shirt, flattened her fingers against his back. It was ridiculously unfair how sexy she found the notches of his spine.

Reece's hand tightened at the back of her head, tugging at her hair before releasing. Pinpricks of pleasure-pain singed her scalp. Her mouth fell open in a silent gasp.

His hips rocked forward as his restraint faltered. She clung to his torso, not wanting him to stop.

"You're not going to freak me out," she promised. Pleaded, really. She grabbed for his waist and found purchase on his hip, pulled him against her again.

Delicious friction sparked between their bodies. He hissed through his teeth. "Charlie . . ."

She rolled over, bringing him with her as she turned onto her back. Reece didn't protest. He caught his weight on his left hand and pressed his palm against the mattress beside her head. He felt undeniably right between her thighs. Her knees bracketed his hips.

Reece looked down at her for a long beat, his face an open book of uncertainty and want. They'd hooked up only last night, but the energy felt different between them now. This wasn't just desire. Heavy, vulnerable longing threatened to consume Charlotte whole.

Against all odds and expectations, this mattered.

That little glimmer of fear returned.

"I'm not good at this," she blurted out.

She wasn't even sure what she meant. Intimacy? Sleeping together?

Falling in love?

Reece lowered himself onto his elbows. He studied her face with those glorious green eyes, dark pupils tracking across her bruised lips and pink cheeks. "That's okay," he murmured as he tucked her hair behind her ear. A suggestion of a smile pulled at his mouth. "You'll learn."

As they kissed, Charlotte stopped smuggling away details to remember later. She only knew sensation: the press of Reece's weight on her, the heat of his mouth moving with hers. There was no need to rush—time became irrelevant. She wove herself against his body with reverence, with permanence.

At some point after their clothes got lost in the sheets and the separation between their bodies disappeared, she understood. She didn't overthink it. She barely planned it. She just said it.

"I want this."

She couldn't see Reece's face, pressed as it was to her neck, but she could feel her words run through his body. He stopped moving even as his cock twitched within her. The muscles in his back tensed under her fingertips.

She wiggled her hips, pinned to the mattress, and then he was looking at her, all wide eyes and parted lips. Emotions swirled across his face, surprise and desire and awe.

Absurdly, Jackie's words returned to her: *Like you were put on this earth to ruin his life.*

"Charlie."

No one else called her Charlie. The way he said it, it was more than a nickname. He sounded like he was describing a miracle. *Her.*

"You have me."

And then there was no more talking.

Chapter 14

SLACK MESSAGE FROM ROGER LUDERMORE TO CHARLOTTE THORNE, 5:18 AM: penn station is disgusting

CONSCIOUSNESS BROKE THROUGH slowly. She was wedged between the wall and the burning heat of a man's sticky arms, her neck stiff and her back sore. Charlotte and Reece were a pile of awkwardly bent limbs. Her hair had gotten caught under his shoulder and he'd drooled on their shared pillow. Neither of them had slept deeply, wriggling in the stiff sheets and chasing each other's heat like lizards on a sunlit rock.

But miraculously, she felt fantastic. Exhausted, hungry, and somewhat hungover, but fantastic.

Damn. She felt *happy*. Dewy grass green and daisy yellow.

Gentle sunlight bathed the room; she guessed it was around eight in the morning. That meant they'd gotten roughly three hours of sleep? Maybe?

The memory of last night's whirlwind returned as she noticed Reece still held her hand. She squeezed it and smiled, even as the uncomfortable truth arrived: It was Sunday. They had run out of borrowed moments in the time warp.

Her lungs tightened. This precious escape from New York was over. She'd have to get a new storage box for this weekend and all its soaring, fleeting rightness. Within their magical window of honesty last night, there'd been no discussion of their impeding *after*.

And yet . . .

You have me.

Lips found her neck, soft and delicious. Reece's arm tightened around her waist. An adventurous hand found her breast. Charlotte settled back into his embrace. She could binge on his touch all night and still not have enough.

"Good morning," she said.

Reece hummed against her shoulder, not awake enough for words. He pressed his erection against her ass. She chuckled as he buried his nose in her hair.

Charlotte rolled over in the cradle of his arms. Reece in the morning belonged on a subway ad for memory foam mattresses. His eyes were puffy, his hair a mad scientist's tangle. He looked beautiful. She wanted to kiss his bee-stung lips and feed him pancakes over the Sunday crossword.

He squinted at her, his face half-smushed into the pillow. "G'mornin." He cupped her cheek in his hand and rubbed some sleep gunk from the corner of her eye with his thumb. For some reason, the gesture was terribly romantic.

"How did you sleep?" She kissed his wrist before snuggling closer. He lay on his back, and she nuzzled her head under his chin, draping herself over his chest.

"Good." He kissed her hair. "Terrible, but good." His fingers snuck under the bottom of her top to tap a pattern against her spine. She'd slept in his shirt, the white fabric a little worse for wear with their mingled sweat. They made a cursory attempt to make themselves respectable in case Garrett returned, but judging by his empty bed, they had the room to themselves all night.

"We've never done this before," Reece observed. He kept his tone light, an open-ended remark instead of a question. He could have been referring to anything, and she realized he was testing her, trying to feel her out without putting pressure on her.

Sweet little cautious muffin.

"I like it." Charlotte splayed her hand across his chest, a finger tweaking his nipple. He shuddered before closing his arms around her again, secure and soft. "You're warm."

"Is that all I'm good for? A space heater?" Teasing her again.

"A human-shaped furnace."

Reece pulled on a stray curl of her hair. "Happy to serve, Charlie."

She ran her fingers across the prickly growth on his jaw. Reece stayed still as she traced his face, his eyes tracking the movements of her hand. He was so willing to be vulnerable with her, to let her touch and look and explore his body. Affection spread through her gut and up her chest like a blush.

But . . . it was Sunday. In a matter of hours, he'd get on the highway and head west while she boarded a train.

Did Reece want to take this with them when they left campus? Surely he did, right? What else could *you have me* mean?

"Hey." Reece tapped her on the forehead. "What's happening up there?"

He read her panic better than she could. Charlotte thought longingly of the Feelings Chart. She wanted to point at her emotions instead of articulating them.

Unsure. Afraid. Needy.

She rested her chin on his sternum. She just had to be honest. It wasn't that hard.

"I don't know how to pretend this didn't happen." It wasn't exactly what she meant, but she didn't know how to explain the dread she felt when she imagined saying good-bye.

She never got over Reece the first time round, she just pushed her feelings way down deep until he returned to jar them loose. Leaving campus today would be eons worse. This time she knew what she wasn't taking with her.

Reece frowned as he studied her face. He pushed himself up to brace his weight on his elbows. "Charlie, I . . . I *can't* pretend." His voice darkened, taking on new urgency. "I won't."

She didn't need to ask what he meant.

"What do we do?" Charlotte asked.

Reece tucked her hair behind her ears. His thumb lingered at her jaw, sweeping across the sensitive skin there. "What do you want to do?"

She wanted to stay right here. She wanted to live in this hideous dorm and survive on vending machine snacks and have sex all night long. She wanted another day, another week, another month of reunion.

What would this look like in the real world? They couldn't afford to fly back and forth to visit each other. She didn't have a car, and she couldn't ask him to drive from Missouri to New York. It wasn't like she could relocate after one weekend together. Even if all of a sudden she wanted to.

She had a life in New York. She had a job, at least.

Reece waited for her to say something. Charlotte waited to know what to say.

She wanted to be with him, she just didn't know how. It was like trying to solve a puzzle when critical pieces were missing.

Her phone twitched on the windowsill, a Slack notification chirping dimly. She ignored it, only for the phone to start vibrating on a continuous loop. Reece frowned as she stretched her arm out to retrieve it.

INCOMING CALL: ROGER LUDERMORE

Her heart climbed up her throat. "It's my boss." Charlotte dismissed the call before pulling up the sea of new notifications waiting for her.

SLACK MESSAGE FROM ROGER LUDERMORE TO CHARLOTTE THORNE, 8:17 AM: why are there no fucking ubers here

“Oh shit.” The blood drained from her face.

“What is it?” Reece asked.

She sat up and frantically typed a reply, her hands shaking.

SLACK MESSAGE FROM CHARLOTTE THORNE TO ROGER LUDERMORE, 8:18 AM: Aubrey was supposed to book a cab for you. I reminded her on Friday. The town doesn’t allow ride-sharing apps.

“Shit.” Charlotte scrambled over Reece’s legs and wobbled as her feet hit the floor. She yanked her shorts up her legs. “Shit, fuck, *fuck*.”

Reece scooted up to sit against the wall and watch as she dashed around the room. “Charlie, what’s wrong?”

SLACK MESSAGE FROM ROGER LUDERMORE TO CHARLOTTE THORNE, 8:20 AM: get me to campus

She hammered out a text on her phone.

TEXT MESSAGE FROM CHARLOTTE THORNE TO JACKIE SLAUGHTER, 8:20 AM: SOS are you awake?? Need to pick up Roger!!

“Charlie?” Reece prodded her again.

She huffed as she scrolled through her email inbox. *There*. She really had forwarded Aubrey the email about travel logistics. She’d told her assistant to book the cab, she just didn’t have confirmation that Aubrey did it. Charlotte never double-checked because she shouldn’t have had to.

“Roger is stranded at the train station.” Charlotte waited for Jackie to reply, but her text message hadn't even delivered. Her best friend's cell phone must be dead again.

Reece winced as his feet met the cold linoleum floor. "Can't he find his own way here? He's an adult."

She laughed sharply. "You would think so, but no." Charlotte raced to the mirror to check her hair. She frowned at the ratty mess around her shoulders. "Do you have a rubber band or anything?"

Reece pointed to his desk, where a band held a bag of potato chips closed. "Thank you!" She pulled it off and forced her curls into a bun at the back of her neck. "God, I'm a mess."

"You look gorgeous," he said, but her face was buried in her phone again.

SLACK MESSAGE FROM ROGER LUDERMORE TO CHARLOTTE THORNE, 8:25 AM: this is unacceptable

Charlotte barely had fingernails left to chew on. "Hey, Reece?"

He raised an eyebrow at her plaintive tone. "Yes?"

"Can you give a girl a ride?"

AS REECE SPED down Route One, Charlotte grabbed empty Gatorade bottles from the back seat and dumped them into a plastic bag. The train station wasn't far from Hein's campus. She had maybe ten minutes to make the car presentable before Roger ruined her weekend. Not to mention the longer they left her boss waiting, the ruder he would be.

"I owe you big-time," she yelled over the wind roaring through the open windows. Roger had a thing about smells, and the odor of Misty's wet fur clung to the fabric seats.

"You owe me breakfast." Bulky sunglasses hid Reece's bloodshot eyes. "I'm talking large coffee, waffles, bacon, everything."

"Whatever you want." She climbed over the console and into the front seat. "He's going to talk shit about my outfit." She folded down the mirror and smoothed some flyaway strands back from her face. Charlotte didn't have anything to hide her exhaustion, but Roger would just have to deal with her lackluster appearance. "He won't be able to help himself."

"It's your college reunion," Reece said. "Does he really expect you to be dressed up?"

She licked her thumb and ran it under her eyes to catch last night's mascara. "To him it's a business trip, not a reunion."

"I can't wait to meet this charmer," Reece continued. Even running on three hours of sleep, he still radiated cheerfulness. "Should I call him Roger?"

"No. Call him Mr. Ludermore." She winced. "Actually, better to ignore him."

"Fine. I'll be the silent chauffeur." Reece nodded at the road, a serious look on his face.

Charlotte bit her lip. "Have I thanked you already?"

"Yes, you have." Reece rested his hand on her knee and gave it a squeeze. "It's seriously no big deal. And I get to meet your boss!" He said it like picking up Roger from the train station was an exciting relationship milestone and not a huge imposition.

She tried to channel his enthusiasm. "Welcome to my glamorous life," she said. "Catering to the whims of a wealthy man-child."

SLACK MESSAGE FROM RODER LUDERMORE TO CHARLOTTE THORNE, 8:54 AM: need a charger

Charlotte wilted. "Do you have an iPhone charger?"

"Back at the dorm."

"Damn."

"I'm sure he'll understand," Reece assured her. "You're doing him a favor."

Sweet, naïve Reece. She almost felt guilty subjecting him to what was coming.

When they pulled up in front of the station, Roger stood on the curb with a huge energy drink. He wore an impeccable suit, but his hair shone with grease, a telltale sign he'd also been up all night. Charlotte held her breath as he took in the beat-up Jeep. She wasn't sure she'd be able to keep her mouth shut if he insulted Reece directly.

She rolled down the window. "Good morning, Mr. Ludermore," she said in her inflectionless work voice.

Roger gave her a once-over. "You look like shit."

Reece's eyebrows rocketed up his face. She willed him to stay quiet, for his sake as well as her own.

Her boss opened the back door and threw himself into the car. He didn't bother to buckle his seat belt.

"We'll have you on campus in ten minutes," Charlotte said. She watched in the rearview mirror as he plucked a dog hair from the seat and examined it, his lip curling. He dropped it outside the open window.

"Hello, sir," Reece said, politely ignoring the dog hair fiasco.

Roger slurped from his Red Bull. After swallowing, he asked, "Who are you?"

"I'm Reece. It's an honor to meet you." Thankfully Reece was too busy navigating traffic to extend his hand for a shake—Charlotte suspected Roger would turn his nose up.

Roger nodded once before turning his attention back to her. "This is a massive fuckup, Charlotte."

Her heart seemed determined to wedge itself up her throat. She'd hoped he wouldn't berate her in front of a total stranger, but that had been naïve.

You have to pay your credit card bill.

"I'm sorry for the confusion." The apology assembled itself instantly, as if she'd never left the office. "Aubrey and I discussed your logistics, but something must have gone haywire."

"It's unprofessional to blame someone else for your mistakes," Roger said. "Charger?"

Reece threw her a concerned glance. Charlotte's cheeks flushed. "I don't have one, sir. We were in a rush to come get you."

Roger sniffed. "All you had to do was get me from point A to point B and you can't even get that right." She bit the inside of her cheek, knowing better than to defend herself.

Reece cleared his throat and took a turn hard, knocking Roger into the door. "Sorry about that!" he chirped unconvincingly.

Roger glared at him and put on his seat belt. "I hope you're enjoying your vacation," he said petulantly. "You really left us in the lurch at the office."

Charlotte fought the urge to ask what she had messed up, considering she had answered his emails all weekend. And written his stupid commencement address at the expense of spending time with her best friend. For that matter, what vacation?

"But we got on all right without you," he added.

We. Who was *we*?

"I'm glad to hear that," she said smoothly. "I'm ready to hit the ground running tomorrow morning to make sure you're prepped for the week ahead."

"Good." Roger's attention drifted from her as he stared out the window. "It wasn't a total loss. Aubrey and I had some time to get to know each other." He dug a handkerchief out of his pocket and wiped at his mouth. "Fun girl."

Charlotte gnawed at her tongue. "Quite."

"She brought me a smoothie from some place on Bleecker. It's part of this new fasting trend all the NYU students are doing."

Was Aubrey the *we* Roger spoke of? Since when did he describe himself and an assistant as part of a unit? Charlotte couldn't think of a single occasion Roger referred to her as anything other than *the girl.* "Aubrey certainly has her thumb on the pulse of things," she said.

"Yes, well." Roger sniffed again. He stretched his arm across the back of the seat, his manicured fingers scratching the pilled fabric. "We had an interesting conversation about you."

Charlotte did not like the sound of that. Aubrey was hardly her number one fan, mostly because Charlotte expected her to do her job. "Oh?"

"It sounds like her talent's being wasted," Roger drawled. "A vivacious girl like that."

What talent? Her talent recommending smoothie places and swanning around the office in Manolo Blahniks like she had no work to do?

"I see," Charlotte said. She pursed her lips and exhaled slowly, willing herself to keep it together. It was hard to get into character as a toady with Reece sitting right next to her, hearing every word of the conversation. "Aubrey is smart. But I've worked closely with her as her manager, and I—"

"About that," Roger interrupted. "We may have rushed you becoming a manager. Aubrey expressed some frustration with your style." He laughed, a pugnacious little snarl.

Charlotte's throat tightened. The moment she left town, Aubrey took advantage of the opening and knifed her in the back.

Dental insurance. Isn't it nice to have dental?

She pictured the glassy surface of Cobalt Pond, impenetrable and still. She was Charlotte Thorne, an integral *Front End* employee. She felt nothing.

Goddamn it, she would *feel nothing.*

The self-soothing mechanism didn't work. She struggled to keep sarcasm out of her voice. "I'm sorry to hear that Aubrey has issues with the way I manage her." Getting defensive wouldn't undo whatever damage Aubrey had done, but she had to speak up for herself. She couldn't just eat shit for the rest of her life, not when she knew she was right. "I met with Pauline last month for management training. She helped me set performance goals for Aubrey to meet—"

"Goals like perfect emails and fetching lunch?" He snorted. "Seems a bit trivial to me."

"Sure," Charlotte said dryly. "But assistants need to care about the details, and she doesn't."

"It's not her fault that the work is below her, Charlotte," Roger chided. "Her father's on the board, you know."

The insult smarted more than she expected it to. If he thought the work was below Aubrey, what did he think of her? Charlotte poured her heart into her work. Roger could at least pretend to respect it.

You don't do this job for respect, you do it to pay the electric bill and the heating bill and the internet bill.

"Working for you isn't menial labor, Roger." The blatant ass-kissing rotted in her mouth. Reece's eyebrows rose next to her, but still he kept quiet. She dug her nails into her palm as she debased herself. "I'm surprised Aubrey doesn't see the value of learning from you."

"Hey, now," Roger cooed, mollified by her shameless manipulation. "Don't go getting your feelings hurt. You know how much I appreciate you."

Charlotte clenched her hands together in her lap, fighting the urge to gnaw at her thumb. *Her feelings.* If she were a man, Roger wouldn't reduce this conversation to feelings. They were talking about her management style, her *job.* Three years of her professional life without a meaningful raise or a step toward a promotion.

"You'll have more time to focus on your responsibilities without Aubrey underfoot," he continued. "I transferred her to the art department."

Wait, what?

Charlotte blinked at the road as the Jeep barreled toward campus. Shock spread through her body in waves of orange static.

Roger gave Aubrey the promotion. Roger gave her unreliable, disrespectful, *product-of-blatant-nepotism* assistant the job she'd been strategizing for.

Her exit strategy, yanked away and gifted to someone's spoiled daughter.

It made no sense. Aubrey never expressed interest in the magazine's visuals. She wanted to be an influencer. Her highest ambition in life was to get paid to endorse diet gummies.

Even if she *did* want to be a project manager, Aubrey wasn't qualified. She had no patience for details. She missed the first five minutes of every meeting.

Charlotte wasn't biased, she was the girl's boss! Aubrey once asked her if Elizabeth Holmes was a SoulCycle instructor.

"I didn't know Aubrey wanted to project manage," she forced out.

Her shock must have been obvious because Roger stilled his fidgeting in the back seat. He returned her stare in the rearview mirror, his eyes narrowed. "Do we have a problem?"

She pursed her lips, willing herself to keep it together. Her temper bubbled and spat, brimming with righteous indignation and slowly mounting panic. She couldn't lose her escape route into the art department, not like this. Not to Audrey. "I'm just surprised to learn about this after the fact," she said. "As her manager—"

"I'm Aubrey's boss," Roger interrupted. "It's my decision to make, not yours."

"I just thought—"

"You thought what?" His tone brooked no disagreement. "That you'd get the job?"

Yes, she did, because he had given her every reason to think he'd give her the job as long as she did everything asked of her, as long as she sacrificed endlessly, as long as she behaved. Not that he ever put it in writing, no, of course not. Better to keep her unstable and dependent, unable to refuse.

Charlotte closed her eyes. She was the calm, smooth water of the quarry. Beautiful and unmoved, disguising her vicious chill underneath. She would not tear Roger's sweaty head from his body. She would not scream.

"Is being my assistant not good enough for you anymore?" Roger pressed on through her silence.

"That's not what I meant," Charlotte said through gritted teeth.

She searched for a professional way to push back against his slippery manipulation. "I just want to make sure I have . . . room to grow at *Front End*."

Roger scoffed. "Room to grow? There won't be another position opening up at the company for quite some time."

Charlotte couldn't help herself. "That's why I'm surprised you gave that position to Aubrey."

"Aubrey made herself essential," Roger snapped. "You have not done the same."

All illusion of self-control evaporated as Charlotte reached the end of her patience. She'd already used most of it up with the last-minute speechwriting and the fight with Jackie it had caused. She could only withstand so much. This wasn't just a bad job, it was a toxic joke.

Jackie was right. Jackie was always right. No one deserved to be treated like this. This wasn't the person Charlotte wanted to be.

She snuck a glance at Reece. He was watching her in his peripheral vision, his mouth closed so tight it almost disappeared into his face. When he saw her looking, he raised his head a fraction of an inch.

Chin up.

Charlotte twisted in her seat to face Roger head-on. "In the last three days I got sixty-eight Slack messages from you and two hundred emails from the company," she said. "I think that qualifies as essential."

For a moment it seemed like she'd won. Roger fell silent, gobsmacked by her back talk. Reece tried to hide his smirk with his right hand. Victory felt like pistachio green.

Charlotte knew she would pay dearly for pointing out how much Roger relied on her. She made him look so good, made his life so easy and seamless, that he couldn't see her value at all. If he did, it would mean coming face-to-face with how much he depended on her.

She understood it now: That was why he would never promote her, never support her growth, never let her go. He relied on her, his lowly assistant who kept his life together thanklessly, day in and day out.

It felt good to say it. Just once.

Then Roger leaned forward. His frame filled the gap between her seat and Reece's. When he wove his hand around her headrest, the heat from his fingers sent goose bumps along her neck.

All of Charlotte's confidence dissolved as he invaded her space. This close, she could smell his breath, rank with Red Bull and vodka. She shrank back into her seat but there was nowhere to go, no room to get away from him. The full force of his glare cornered her between the edge of her seat and the car door.

"I could hire a new assistant within the hour, Charlotte. Remember that." Behind Roger, Reece sat ramrod straight in the driver's seat. Anger rioted under the surface of his blank expression as he pulled the car into a campus parking lot.

Shame pooled with the fright in her stomach. She felt like she had failed both of them.

"Yes, sir," she said meekly.

"If you want to keep your job, reconsider your attitude. Stop thinking about yourself. Focus on helping *Front End* succeed. Then we can talk about your future." A speck of spittle flew from his mouth and hit her on the cheek.

Charlotte barely felt it. There was an odd disconnect, a familiar sensation of stepping backward and away. It was as if she watched the confrontation from outside her body. She saw the three of them stuffed in the narrow space of the front seat: Charlotte cowering, Reece agonizing, Roger seething. His words washed over and around her as he continued. "Aubrey got that promotion because she earned it. You haven't shown your dedication to this company. You haven't proven yourself to me. You are *nothing*."

The car came to a lurching stop. "We're here!" Reece interrupted.

Charlotte blinked, unable to move. Roger gave her a venomous look before disappearing into the back seat. "Beautiful campus. So nice to be back," he said as he opened the door and stepped into the parking lot. He slammed it shut behind him.

"What the hell was that?" Reece breathed. He hadn't taken his hands off the steering wheel, unable to move. His knuckles had turned an ugly gray from his death grip on the vinyl. A hard, frightened pounding echoed in her ears. Her heartbeat.

Nothing.

I feel nothing.

Charlotte flinched as Roger rapped his knuckles on the window. She rolled it down, her movements jerky and mechanical.

"Are you coming?" he asked.

Her voice shook. "Right behind you, sir."

Roger gave her his empty can. "You need to live-tweet from the audience," he prattled on as if their vicious conversation hadn't happened. "I wrote a new speech on the train. Your version was too soft. These kids won't know what hit them."

Her boss patted the roof of the car and stalked away. His shadow followed him across the pavement.

Charlotte closed her eyes.

My name is—

I am—

Nothing.

"Are you okay?"

Charlotte blinked. She looked at the empty Red Bull in her hand. He must have started drinking early today. Or he never stopped last night.

She dropped the can in the garbage bag at her feet. "You're going to be late for the picnic."

Reece twisted in the driver's seat to face her. "The picnic can wait. Is he like that all the time? That was insane."

My name is Charlotte Thorne. I feel nothing.

"Uh . . ." She coughed, still struggling to find words. A fog as thick as cotton had wrapped itself around her brain. "I guess. Do you have more trash?" She popped open the glove compartment and stared unseeing at the heap of documents and cheap sunglasses.

"Leave it on the floor, I'll get it later. Are you okay?"

"I'm fine."

She had to be fine. She couldn't be anything other than fine right now. She needed to get it together and go live-tweet his commencement address. Then she had to pack up her dorm room and get on the train. She had to go back to New York. She had to make it work. She had to be fine.

Reece wouldn't leave it alone. He leaned forward to catch her eye. She dug her phone out of her pocket just to have something to look at. "I'm not gonna tell you how to live your life," he said urgently, "And I know that was one conversation out of context for me. But that was awful, Charlie."

My name is Charlotte Thorne. I work at The Front End Review. *I am an executive assistant. I live in Brooklyn and I have to save up in case of an emergency.*

She tore at a cuticle, blood smearing on her palm. "No one likes their boss."

"He's not just some asshole," Reece ground out. "The way he talked to you is not normal. Jesus, he was threatening you! The way he invaded your space? I wanted to pull over and tell him to get the fuck out."

Charlotte opened the door and threw herself out of the car. Reece did the same. "I can't talk about this right now." She started across the pavement to the steps.

Reece followed her. "Any company would be lucky to hire you. You know that, right?"

She scoffed. "That's not true."

"Who says? That guy?" Reece gestured up the steps to where Roger had disappeared. "That's what he needs you to think. He has to justify treating you like shit, and make you feel like you can't leave."

Leave.

The loaded word broke through her disconnect. She felt it in her body like a violent strike of lightning. Charlotte whirled around. "Do you know how much rent costs in New York?" she demanded. His eyes widened as she got in his face, but she couldn't stop herself. She was so tired of being told what to do, of being told to quit her job like it was just that easy. "What about a MetroCard? Or a cell phone bill when you're not on a family plan?"

Reece backed up a step, raising his hands with his palms facing out. "Charlie, that's not—"

"No, please! Tell me! What am I supposed to do?" Her eyes were wet. She wanted to stop but the words kept coming, spilling out of her like vomit. She was so tired of having the same conversation again and again. "I keep waiting for you and Jackie to tell me, because I sure as hell don't know. I'm not going to win the lottery," she blurted out. "I can't leave when I have nowhere to go."

It broke something in her to say that. That smarting wound in her chest gaped, open and bloody like a fresh injury. Pain screamed in her throat, and she couldn't swallow it down, couldn't press it back, couldn't—

She didn't want to look at Reece and yet she couldn't tear her eyes away from the agony on his face. His hands twitched at his sides like he wanted to reach for her. He knew better than to try. It took everything in her not to bolt away from him, not to run up the steps and hide from this conversation in an empty dorm room.

Reece's horrified expression told her he could see all of it: everything she felt, everything she feared. She shuddered with shame and anger, resenting him for being *right there* all weekend, stubbornly present during the worst moments of her life.

She couldn't feel nothing when he looked at her like that.

He just stood there, frustrated and sad with his hands loose at his sides.

"There are so many people who love you, Charlie," he said. "We would do anything for you. You just have to ask us, remember? You have to *let* us help you."

She goggled at him, her mouth falling open as she tried to hear his words. No, they were her words thrown back at her in the bright light of day. Her brain whirred with panic and suspicion and worthlessness, and Roger's sneer and Ben's cologne and the empty space in her life where family was supposed to be.

She thought Reece understood that people left. They walked out or moved away or decided you weren't good enough. She could only depend on herself. She thought he knew that.

He kept looking at her with those big green eyes full of want and affection and, fuck, all the love that she never asked for and didn't deserve. She wanted it, all of it, but what if she asked and he said no? What if she asked and asked and asked and it was too much for him, what if she was too much for him, what if he decided he couldn't handle her and left her alone with all this agony and grief and—

Her iPhone shuddered in her hand. It began to wail her custom ringtone for Roger. She silenced it.

Commencement would start any minute now. She needed to find a spot on the President's Lawn to watch the ceremony and live-tweet from Roger's account. She didn't have a choice. She was here to work.

"I have to go. This is my job." She pressed her fingertips to the shattered glass of her iPhone, desperate to feel a pain separate from the collapsing black hole in her chest. "This is all I have."

He gaped at her, and then the disappointment she'd braced for all weekend made its appearance.

"So what, then?" he said, folding his arms over his chest. "I'll see you at the next reunion?"

She didn't have a comeback for that. Reece didn't follow her as she climbed the steps back to campus.

Chapter 15

THE COMMENCEMENT CEREMONY had already started by the time Charlotte made it to the President's Lawn. Beyond a sea of royal-blue-and-silver graduates, on a podium erected outside his mansion, the university president greeted the Class of 2018 and their families.

Roger sat beside the president with a toothy smirk on his face, tapping his foot on the floor. He had found his way to the stage without her.

Charlotte looked haggard next to the smiling families in their Sunday best. She entered the tent at the back of the crowd and sank into a folding chair by an R&C water station. As soon as she sat down, she caved in on herself and rested her forehead against her knees.

God, the way Reece stared at her before she walked away. The hurt in his eyes, the shock splitting his voice . . .

Reece let her in, held her close, made love to her and held her all night long and she ruined it. Again.

You are nothing.

Her job was a dead end. Her best friend hated her. Her relationship had failed before it could even start. This time tomorrow she'd be sitting at her desk with nothing to look forward to. Gray walls, gray blouse, gray future, gray existence.

She didn't know who she hated more, Roger or herself.

Disgraceful.

Ravishing.

Is this really who you thought you'd be?

Charlotte couldn't hear herself over the din in her mind. She couldn't remember the words to say, the grounding techniques, the colors. Her legs felt heavy, and her arms, and her head. She pressed her fingertips into the back of her neck. Her skin was wet and clammy under her hair.

Nothing.

Eventually Roger took the microphone. Charlotte didn't catch a word. She stared unseeing at the podium decked out in blue-and-silver bunting. The hues swam. She sat up and opened Twitter on her phone, but her hands shook too much to hold it steady.

". . . forty years in the industry, I learned to get my knuckles bloody . . ." Roger's self-satisfied growl wafted past her.

It was all for nothing. Years of answering his emails. Years of picking up his dry cleaning. Years of holding her tongue when he snapped at her for not laughing at his jokes. Years of smiling placidly as her morals rotted in her chest.

None of it counted.

None of it was enough.

Not the calls answered on the weekend, or the emails written late at night. Not the social life she sacrificed to meet Roger's unrelenting demands. Not the endless abuse she absorbed until her heart staggered and her breath came in heaving gasps.

You haven't proven yourself to me.

She knew his favorite cocktail and his preferred brand of undershirt. She filled his prescriptions and drafted his presentations. She cleaned his ashtray twice a day because the building janitorial staff refused to touch his office. She filled her head with meaningless facts about his life, all to prove that she was worth investing in.

All it had proven was that she served at his beck and call.

Charlotte had nothing outside this job and it still wasn't enough. She would never be enough.

". . . is war. It's a goddamn competition. Every day you gotta be the first, be the smartest, be the best . . ."

She remembered Reece's profile tightening as Roger berated her. Her stomach filled with acidic brown humiliation. It was so much worse to have a witness, to have *him* witness her degradation. Now for a second time. She couldn't ignore Roger's insults when Reece's reaction played out across his face. His horror made her reality impossible to ignore.

From now on she would see Reece's face when Roger called her *stupid.* She would see Reece's brows furrow in offense. She would see his eyes dart to her in concern. She would remember.

You haven't shown your dedication to this company.

". . . first at your desk in the morning and the last to leave at the end of the day. If you clock out before the sun sets, you're walking out on your dreams . . ."

Why had she run herself into the ground for this man? What had she sacrificed her friendships for, her community for? The chance to maybe, someday, move to another team, where she would continue to work overtime to design a magazine that did jack shit to make the world a better place? What kind of dream was that? What was all this striving for? What was she killing herself for?

Maybe Jackie was right about this too. Maybe abuse was all she knew.

Disgraceful.

For years Charlotte had sanded down her edges to try to fit the box her mother had made for her. She'd done it again with Ben, falling victim to the same dynamic because she didn't recognize his tactics. She thought she broke the cycle when she cut her mother out of her life, but here she was again. This was different; she didn't want love or validation from Roger, she held on to this job for financial security. But Roger knew that too. He knew how vulnerable she was as layoffs rattled the bones of the media industry, and he used it to exploit her. Another abuser in a line of abusers who bled her of her strength and convinced her she deserved it.

Why should she even live-tweet his grandiose bullshit? Why should she go above and beyond for a man who would never, ever notice her effort? Why should she care one iota about Roger's approval? She could never prove herself to a man who treated her like dog shit.

Sometimes the only option you had was to leave.

If you want to keep your job, you should reconsider your attitude.

Fuck that. On Monday she would start applying for jobs. When she landed something else, she would give her two weeks' notice.

Hell, she would give a week.

If in two months she still had nothing, she would quit anyway. She had to take responsibility for what was within her control. She didn't have to subject herself to this anymore.

Her friends would catch her when she fell. They kept offering to help and she didn't believe them, but why shouldn't she? Had they ever given her a reason not to trust them? Jackie fed her and dressed her and pushed her to share her feelings. Reece talked her through her anxiety and held her hair back when she puked. Jio and Matt kept telling her to stay with them in D.C.

She said so herself: She didn't know how to ask for help.

It was time for her to learn.

There are so many people who love you, Charlie.

She could figure out the details later. The math of her finances didn't matter. She couldn't afford to live like this anymore.

Charlotte blinked away unshed tears. The roaring in her ears quieted. She took another deep breath. She let it go.

She focused on her surroundings. The metal folding chair stuck to her thighs. Sunlight poured across the President's Lawn. Imani, the bartender from Thursday's class reception, stood behind the water station, still in her blue R&C shirt. The student grimaced as she listened to Roger's commencement address.

Someone had given Charlotte's boss an elaborate gown to wear over his suit. The shiny blue fabric clashed with his spray tan. His eyes bulged from his face. He must look ridiculous to the university's new graduates. She knew Roger well enough to recognize the liquored-up recklessness in how he spoke, and she'd bet the Hein kids listening could hear it too.

The energy on the President's Lawn had changed. Students exchanged whispers behind cupped hands. Parents shifted uncomfortably on their folding chairs. Imani took out her phone to record Roger's address, one hand over her mouth in horror.

Charlotte sat up straight, wondering what she'd missed.

Across the field, Roger hunched over the lectern, his blue-and-silver cap askew. "Your generation thinks you are so special," he sneered. The mic clipped to his lapel popped and hissed as it picked up the disdain in his voice.

Oh my god.

Her hand rose to her mouth too.

Roger wasn't kidding in the parking lot. His address was pure, uncensored Roger Ludermore wisdom. This time he didn't have a podcast editor to polish his dreck, and boy, had he picked the wrong audience.

Imani guffawed as she leaned against the water refill station. She pinched her fingers on her phone screen, zooming in on Roger's face as she filmed.

"You all complain when life doesn't hand you everything you want," he continued. Charlotte could see the malicious glee in his eyes all the way across the field. He was enjoying himself, ignorant of the damage he was causing. Or worse, reveling in it. "The world isn't out to get you. It doesn't care if you're a woman or gay or whatever words you all use now. The world just doesn't give a shit about you."

A shocked laugh escaped her mouth. Never in her wildest work-related fantasies did she think Roger would be reckless enough to broadcast his bigoted opinions to the world.

With a sneaking suspicion, she typed the Reunion & Commencement hashtag into Twitter. A sea of tweets from Hein grads and their parents filled her screen. Roger's name was already trending locally.

> **@Annabellecruz96:** Roger Ludermore is a sexist bigot and I can't believe Hein brought him here to speak. What an insult to one of the most diverse graduating classes in the school's history. #HeinRandC2018

> **@BLMbabycakes:** roger ludermore canceling himself in real time lmaooo #HeinRandC2018

> **@HeinULaborUnion:** Pretty sure @RogerLudermore just violated Title IX in this commencement address, y'all. @FrontEndReview #HeinRandC2018

Charlotte laughed. His Twitter notifications were already destroyed. People tagged *Front End*'s account in their tweets too, and she spared a thought for the company's social media team.

But Roger was only getting started. He knew he had lost his audience and he clearly didn't care. He fed off their disapproval the way he fed off Charlotte's discomfort at the office.

"If you want that job, offer to do it for free. Set yourself apart from the pack. Hate to break it to you kids, but no one is gonna hand you opportunities. You need to get off your entitled asses and fight."

@JustineDanielPerry: Did @RogerLudermore just tell #Hein2018 graduates to work for free?

This might be the best moment of her life.

Charlotte pulled up a new draft and did her best to remember Roger's exact wording. He wanted her to live-tweet this train wreck? She'd share quote after quote, word for goddamn word.

She was just typing out *hate to break it to you* when she caught her name.

"I was just talking to my assistant Charlotte about this."

Oh god. Oh no.

Her eyes snapped back to the stage across the Lawn. Roger's eyes held a manic glow.

"Nice girl, but nothing special," her boss confided like he was trading gossip in the executive lounge. "A few months ago, she gets all bent out of shape about her salary, thinks she deserves more. Now she's upset she didn't get a promotion."

Roger knew she was listening. He knew this was her school too. He knew and he didn't care. She was just a useful anecdote to illustrate a point. Just some entitled millennial who drafted his strategy proposals and coordinated terse lunches with his wife. Just some failure in an ill-fitting blazer with the gall to ask for an industry-standard salary. Just some girl who thought if she worked hard enough, something might finally go right for her.

Roger slouched on the lectern, one arm propped on the ledge while the other gestured aimlessly toward the sky. She could hear the peppery loathing in his voice as he delivered his advice to her in front of an audience.

"Look, honey: If you're not getting ahead at work, maybe you should ask yourself if you're the problem."

His words landed like a slap.

She shouldn't be surprised. She wasn't surprised. She understood.

All her life she had been the problem. She was her mother's problem, her shameful queer disappointment. She was Ben's problem, his weak-willed girlfriend who couldn't take a joke. And now she was Roger's problem, his pitiful, entitled, talentless assistant.

She had asked herself if she was the problem ever since her fourth birthday party, when she was too scared to play piano in front of so many adult strangers and learned that her mother's affection was conditional. She didn't need some wealthy libertarian prick to tell her to consider that *she might be the problem.*

Unheeded, the memory of Reece's voice blotted out Roger's diatribe. She saw his sleepy face in the monochrome of the dorm's early morning, his hand gentle against her face.

I can't understand anyone choosing not to know you.

She didn't deserve this.

I'll tell you again anytime you need a reminder.

She deserved so much better than this.

My name is Charlotte Thorne and I feel fucking angry.

Charlotte looked down at her phone. She toggled from Roger's Twitter account to her own, and she opened a new tweet.

@CThorne: Hey @RogerLudermore! I quit. Order your own ugly business cards, you obnoxious prick. #HeinRandC2018

A deep breath, the gleaming white of a decision made. And . . .

She hit post.

Immediately her tweet started racking up likes and retweets. A burst of laughter erupted from a group of students hunched together in the last row, presumably reading her post on someone's phone.

@BLMbabycakes: @CThorne omg!! good for you bitch!!!

@HeinULaborUnion: @CThorne Is this really Charlotte? Would love to connect.

Roger continued to rant, oblivious. He moved on to berating his audience for something else, her name mercifully absent.

As the tweet ricocheted across the President's Lawn, Charlotte waited for regret to hit her. When she reached for it, it didn't materialize. She wasn't disassociating. If anything, she felt robust and awake. She could smell the sunblock and sweat of the graduates sitting in front of her. A baby cried faintly in the distance. The sun bore down on the field and her heart beat hard and stubborn in her chest. Her phone vibrated in her hand as notifications continued to come in.

This part of her life was over. She was done taking anyone's shit.

She took another deep breath and put her phone on silent.

Then, on second thought, she turned it off.

Sunlight nearly blinded her as she emerged from the tent. Charlotte blinked through it and turned toward the quad, ready to join her friends at the picnic. She needed to talk to Reece. She needed to fight for him, really fight for her happiness and her friends and her future stretching bright and open ahead of her. For the life she wanted to build next, whether or not Reece chose to be a part of it.

She needed to apologize to Jackie too. She needed to tell her she was right.

"Thorny!"

She almost stopped. Her body wanted to respond on autopilot and turn to face him.

But that blissful sense of *done* made her laugh instead, because of course Ben Mead would track her down at her moment of victory. Anytime she reached for her freedom, her ex-boyfriend could smell it in the breeze.

Charlotte shook her head and kept walking.

"Hey, *Thorny*! Wait up!"

She heard his shoes behind her on the grass just before he grabbed her wrist. Charlotte planted her feet and pulled her arm out of his grip, but Ben only danced around her to block her path.

The musk of his cologne followed him. It couldn't hide his stale all-nighter smell. Ben was shorter than she remembered, and he hunched inward like the direct sunlight hurt him.

Charlotte rolled her eyes. "What do you want?"

Ben's smug mask slid neatly into place. "My, aren't you looking *flushed* today. Didn't get much sleep last night?"

The insult slid past her. She remembered Ben at twenty-one, his face contorting with fury as she collected her things from his bedroom at the frat house. *No one will ever love you*, he told her.

Roger used that same tone when he called her inessential. Dial it up a few octaves and you'd have her mother's accusation that she was a *disgrace* to the family.

It was a pattern. It was all a pattern. She let these selfish, vicious people into her life and she apologized and apologized and apologized.

Not today, Satan.

When she moved to get around him, he stepped sideways into her path again. "Hang on, I want to talk to you!"

She felt no fight or flight, no freeze or fawn. If anything, she felt hungry. She hadn't eaten since sneaking a bite of Wynn's leftovers at Acronym. A hot dog at the picnic sounded perfect.

"I have nothing to say to you," she said, trying one last time to dodge around him.

Ben's eyes narrowed as he stepped left to counter her. "Well, that's not very nice. I just want to catch up. Like old friends!"

"No, you don't," Charlotte said. "You don't give a damn about me. You're either here to harass me, or you want something. So what is it, Ben?"

Surprise took all the danger from his face. He goggled at her like she'd started speaking Swedish.

He really wasn't that handsome. His precious hairline had begun to recede. A bead of sweat collected at his temples—he must be boiling in that awful jacket.

All trace of smarm vanished as he changed tack. Ben sized her up like a negotiation opponent. "You work at *Front End*. With Roger Ludermore."

Not anymore, dipshit.

Charlotte considered correcting him, but her curiosity won out. "So?"

Ben stuffed his hands into his pockets. "I want to come on his podcast. As a guest."

Whatever she expected, it wasn't that.

Dear god, her ex-boyfriend was a loser.

"What?"

Ben didn't look pleased by the laughter in her voice. "I'm expanding my show to cover the economy." When she didn't react, he shifted his weight to his other foot. "Our audiences don't overlap, so we would, you know, mutually broaden our reach and stuff."

Charlotte's hair moved loose and wild around her face in the breeze. She grinned. "Aren't you supposed to be a leftist? Why would you want to talk to a rabid capitalist?"

Ben stiffened, caught off guard by her refusal to play his game. "I mean, it's all brand building—"

"No."

God, the look on his face. She'd remember it for years, the delicious shock that swept across his ratty, old-money jaw. No one told Ben Mead *no*. No one except her, apparently.

"Excuse me?" he stammered.

"No, I won't help you use Roger's podcast to build your career."

That jaw looked decidedly weak as he gaped at her. "What's your problem?"

Charlotte shrugged. "I don't have a problem. In fact, I have a lot fewer problems in my life now that you're not in it."

She wished she could bottle this feeling. Preppy pink delight, like the dresses her mother wore to the Chevy Chase Country Club.

Ben's hands fisted at his side. "Excuse me? Who do you think you are?"

She didn't like the anger streaking through his question, but she wasn't afraid of him, not out in the open like this. In public, Ben kept his voice low and his malice in check.

"I'm someone who really knows you," she said. "And I have somewhere else I need to be."

Charlotte turned on her heel and made toward the quad. Before she could take a step, Ben grabbed her elbow and yanked her backward. Her balance tilted and she nearly lost her footing on the grass.

"Hey, don't walk away from me," Ben sneered. His fingers dug into her skin as she tried to right herself. He wasn't built, but his grip was strong when it mattered.

The world clipped into stuttering microfiche around her. "Let go of me!" she snarled. Adrenaline roared through her body as she tried to shake him off.

"We got a problem here?" Garrett's deep voice jolted them both. He appeared out of nowhere to stand beside them, not quite getting in the middle. Reece's best friend looked between her and Ben like a referee bursting onto the field to settle a dispute between players.

Ben immediately let go and raised his hands in the air, looking at her like she was the difficult one, but his face was an ugly smear of fury. "Jesus, don't be so dramatic, Thorny."

Charlotte pulled her smarting arm against her chest, Ben's fingers still a white burn on her skin. Tears pressed against her eyes, emotionally stuck somewhere between horror and relief.

"What's going on?" Garrett barked, not taking his eyes off Ben's face.

"Nothing," Ben spat. He crossed his arms over his chest and glared at Charlotte. "Just a lovers' quarrel."

She rocked back a step as his words hit her like darts of tainted memory. Her voice flickered and died in her throat, tranquilized. She could hear her old words like an echo through time: *I'm so sorry Ben I didn't mean it—*

Garrett glanced at her, his face unreadable. Then he stepped between them in one seamless movement, his back to her.

"Okay, you're done." Garrett placed his hand at the center of Ben's chest and gave him a firm shove backward. "Get your goofy ass out of here."

Garrett's wide hockey player's body towered over her ex-boyfriend. Charlotte peered around his back to watch Ben splutter. "Do you know who I am?"

"Everyone knows who you are," Garrett seethed. He didn't need to raise his voice—his raised hackles were proof enough of his seriousness. "We don't care about your daddy. No one wants you here. Go home."

Charlotte's jaw dropped, but Garrett wasn't done. "You hear me? Back. The hell. Off." He punctuated each word with another shove against Ben's chest, not hard enough to hurt but enough to force him backward on impact.

Her ex looked around for backup, but he was alone. The graduation ceremony proceeded unaware of their argument as Roger wound up for some awful big finish. A few fearless graduates booed.

Only the R&C girl running the water station peered over at them. Charlotte realized in a rush why Imani looked familiar—she had Garrett's round face and elegant neck. His sister, the future senator.

Ben glanced at Charlotte, his eyes flinty, before considering the man in front of him. Garrett showed no sign of backing down.

With a huff, Ben brushed the front of his jacket like he was dusting off Garrett's prints. Then he spun on his heels and power-walked away, his head ducked as he disappeared into the tent.

Garrett turned around. He looked her over, his pale eyes wide with concern. Charlotte suddenly noticed they were a soft blue, like the forget-me-not flowers that grew in her backyard as a child. "You okay?" he asked.

Words abandoned her. Garrett had a fresh scrape on his chin. Little speckles of dried blood were already forming scabs. "What happened there?" she asked, nodding at the injury.

"Oh." He brought his fingers to his face. "Fell last night. Tried to jump off a loft bed."

She blinked. "At Acronym?"

"Yeah. I got dared."

She laughed. The scrape made him look rugged.

"What about you?" He stayed still and made no move to touch her, which she appreciated. Her brain felt like the needle had fallen off the record. "Are you okay?"

"I think I'm in shock?" she said. "Maybe?"

He frowned. "Seems like it. Let's get you some water, yeah?"

Charlotte rested her hands on her knees and reminded herself to breathe as Garrett dashed off to grab a drink at the water station. She felt light-headed as her adrenaline rush slowed.

Deep breath in. Deep breath out.

"Here." Garrett crouched down in front of her. He handed her a paper cup and she gulped down the cold water. "Do you need to sit down?"

"I'm fine," she said. He raised a bushy eyebrow and she coughed, pressing her hand to her chest. "Really, I'm okay. Thank you for—" She didn't know what to say, how to explain it.

No one ever stood up to Ben like that. Not even Jackie. No one but Garrett—and now Charlotte too.

Garrett cut her off with a firm shake of his head. "Least I could do," he said. "I was trying not to smack him."

Charlotte let out a shaky laugh. She took another sip of the water, her heart finally slowing its sprint.

"For serious, should we do something?" he asked in a low voice.

Charlotte shook her head. It wasn't worth it. The Mead family's lawyers had shielded Ben from much worse than being an aggressive prick to his ex-girlfriend in broad daylight. "Nah, there's no point. It would just blow back on us. And I think he's gone."

Garrett watched silently as she finished the water. Charlotte stood up and pushed her hair out of her face. She handed him the empty cup. "Thank you. You didn't have to do that."

He shrugged a meaty shoulder. "Yeah, I did."

Chapter 16

TEXT MESSAGE FROM JIO VARGAS TO CHARLOTTE THORNE, 9:41 AM: OH MY GOD CHARLOTTE WHAT ON EARTH!!!! QUEEEN!!! BITCH!!!! WHAT!!!!

(Message not delivered.)

THE QUAD BURST with color. Maybe it was the adrenaline surging through her body. Maybe she could fully experience her surroundings without worrying about Roger. Charlotte didn't care why the world had dialed up its saturation. She soaked up every detail.

Warm copper brick paths. Grass so green it belonged in a crayon box. The occasional flash of a blue-and-silver Hein tank top.

Charlotte could stand there for hours and count every hue. She wanted to grab a sketch pad and capture it on paper. It didn't matter that the picnic was organized exactly as it had been last time. Nothing was the same. She didn't feel abandoned or embarrassed. She felt no urge to hide. She felt . . .

excited scared nervous speechless satisfied irritated relieved

Honestly, she felt a little high.

She needed to find her friends.

A familiar bark pulled her from her thoughts. Little paws battered her calves. Charlotte leaned down to greet her loyal new friend. "Hey, Misty. How's my favorite girl?"

Misty panted up at her, tongue waggling from her mouth. She perched her tiny feet on Charlotte's thigh.

Charlotte scooped Misty up and held her like a hairy baby. "Where's your uncle?" she asked. "I have some groveling to do."

Misty didn't answer, but Charlotte already knew where to find Reece. R&C staff and class officers stood behind a long table beneath an old beech tree, roasting hot dogs and serving platters of scrambled eggs and bacon. She'd bet anything that Reece was exactly where he was supposed to be, serving tongs in hand.

"CHARLOTTE!"

She whirled around. Jio waved at her frantically from a blanket not far from the path. Matt lay stretched out on his back, his head pillowed in Jio's lap. She'd been so lost in her thoughts that she walked right past them.

"Charlotte, get OVER HERE!" Jio hissed, cell phone clutched tightly in their hand.

"What's wrong?" She crossed the grass and sank to her knees beside them. Misty wiggled out of her grasp and sniffed at Matt's hand. He ruffled her fur, unperturbed by his fiancé's panic.

"Girl, what did you do?" Jio barked a startled laugh at her, so she knew no one had died, at least.

"What are you talking about?"

Matt threw her a lifeline as he scratched under Misty's chin. "You're trending."

Charlotte's hand went immediately to her phone in her pocket, still as the dead—or the powered down. "Huh."

"*ChompNews* already wrote a story!" Jio shoved their iPhone at her. She made out the headline ROGER LUDERMORE'S COMMENCEMENT ADDRESS WAS SO F*CKED UP THAT HIS ASSISTANT QUIT ON TWITTER!

They'd found a photo of her, an ancient selfie from her Instagram. She could imagine the comments: supportive jokes from the *take this job and shove it* crowd, vicious attacks from the *pay your dues* boomers.

She pushed the phone away. "You know what? I don't even want to know."

Jio grinned and turned the screen back in their direction. They kept scrolling. "I'm so proud of you. My viral star. I'll keep an eye on the conversation for you, don't worry about it. Put it out of your head."

There were perks to having friends who worked in digital communications. "Thank you. I appreciate it. Let me know if anyone doxes me."

At long last Matt took off his sunglasses and revealed fond, bloodshot eyes. "Well done, Charlotte."

For some reason this praise from the most reserved member of the 3Ds got through to her. She let seafoam green pride fill her chest, determined to take the compliment.

"Thank you," she said.

Matt nodded once. Then he put his sunglasses back on.

She reached for Misty, needing the dog's reassuring weight on her lap. Misty licked her chin and resettled in her lap.

Jio typed furiously on their phone. "What's your Venmo?"

Charlotte frowned. "Why?"

"No reason." They gave her an innocent look, full eyelashes batting sincerely.

She sighed and decided to just trust her friend. "It's the same as my Twitter handle."

"Great, thank you." More furious typing. Then Jio made a satisfied noise and dropped their phone on the blanket. They smiled at her again, joy almost disguising the circles under their eyes. And the leftover glitter stuck to their cheekbones.

"You look wiped," Charlotte said before she could stop herself. "Did you sleep?"

"Garrett and I watched *Say Yes to the Dress* until six A.M.," Jio chirped. "He's coming to the wedding."

Oh goodness. The Vargas-Larsen wedding was turning into the Hein social event of the season. Garrett better acquire some sequined accessories, pronto.

She scanned the crowd for a familiar brown topknot. No dice. "Have you seen Jackie?"

Matt teased his fingers through Misty's furry tail. "Not yet."

"Hmm." Charlotte nodded. "If you do, tell her I'm looking for her."

SLACK MESSAGE FROM AUBREY PAGE TO CHARLOTTE THORNE, 9:53 AM: r u really quitting?? R u crazy??
(Message unread.)

JUST AS SHE'D expected, Reece stood behind the catering table under the beech tree. Charlotte watched from a distance as he served hot dogs. He smiled at each person, trading small talk and asking questions. When an elderly alumna couldn't hear him over the table, he leaned forward to speak directly in her ear. The lady patted him on the shoulder before moving on to a platter of breakfast sandwiches.

Charlotte felt pink. Eager to be next to him, nervous about what she had to say.

Reece loved her. He'd all but told her in the parking lot. *There are so many people who love you, Charlie. We would do anything for you.*

Even if he only meant it as a friend, she could work with that. It would be an honor to be Reece's friend. She would show up for him every goddamn day if that was what it took to convince him to let her be more than that.

She would never walk out on him again.

You just have to ask us.

Charlotte wove through the picnic and circled the banquet table. She picked up a spare set of tongs and eased into the spot next to Reece. "Hi there," she said.

Reece placed a hot dog on a plate outstretched in front of him. The alum who held it, midthirties if she had to guess, nodded in thanks and carried on.

"Hello," Reece said to her, sotto voce. He glanced at her, but his face gave nothing away.

A little girl, someone's daughter, stepped up next. "Can I have one?" she asked Charlotte, peering at the platter of breakfast sandwiches.

"Of course!" Charlotte exclaimed with as much fanfare as she could. She placed the sandwich onto the child's plate, brandishing her tongs like a wizard.

"Thank you." The little girl grinned and darted away.

Reece threw her a curious look. "You joining the alumni relations committee?"

"Exploring a career in catering," she explained. At his raised eyebrow, she added, "I quit my job."

That got his attention. He gawked at her, dropping the tongs on the hot dog platter. "Are you serious? Just now?"

Charlotte nodded. She didn't want to get into it, the commencement address and the tweet and the internet salivating over the spectacle of it all. Besides, Reece understood the deeper consequences beneath all of that. The freedom and financial precariousness it brought back into her life. What exactly she was escaping.

"It's a long story," she said.

For a moment Reece just looked at her. Her exhausted, fragile heart rose to her throat as she waited for him to say something. She didn't need him to be proud of her—her own pride was enough—but she wanted him to know that she had heard him. That she just needed to be ready to see it for herself, and to do something about it.

Then she saw it: not a smile, not a tear, but a single nod that said he got it. Before she could say anything else, he wrapped his arm around her shoulders and pulled her against this chest.

"Good for you," he murmured. She felt him press a firm kiss to her hair, and she melted.

"What are you going to do now?" he asked when he finally let her go.

She hadn't thought about it yet; there wasn't time. The future stretched out ahead of her in a delicious blank expanse. It didn't scare her because Reece was right: She didn't need to face this chapter of her life with a plan. She could nanny again, or freelance, and ask Terry for her old job back if other opportunities didn't arise. She wouldn't mind moving back here for a while and tending bar.

She would have time to draw. Anything she wanted—not cartoons, but maybe abstract shapes. Flowers. Mossy eyes and honey lips.

She hadn't asked herself what she wanted from her life for years. The prospect was strangely thrilling. She could run a marathon. She could learn how to do stick-and-poke tattoos. She could get super into Dungeons & Dragons.

"I don't know," she admitted. "But that's okay."

Reece nodded. "You have time to figure it out."

Charlotte watched him serve another hot dog to a thirty-something alum. "Can I ask you for another favor?"

"Does this one involve a billionaire?" He clacked his tongs together menacingly.

She laughed. "No, definitely not." Her thumb wanted to work its way to her mouth. Instead, she used her tongs to rearrange the breakfast sandwiches in neat lines. "On your way back to St. Louis . . . Could you drop me off in Brooklyn?"

Reece blinked. "I thought you were taking the train."

She looked around them, wary of the alumni milling about the table and her own dishevelment. This was hardly a romantic moment to tell him how she felt. But Reece deserved to hear it. She needed to be honest with him. He'd been waiting five years to have this conversation.

Charlotte put the tongs down and nodded toward the tree behind them. Without needing clarification, Reece pulled the apron up over his head and handed it to an R&C kid. Then he followed her to the other side of the tree and into the shade.

Shoot, she didn't know how to do this. She didn't know the words. But she had to try.

"I don't want to leave here without you," she admitted. "I don't know what comes after this. I don't know what I want my life to be. Some days I'm not even sure who I am. But I know that you are a good person—the best person, really—and I want to start there."

She couldn't tell if that was enough or too much, and in the end it didn't matter because it erupted out of her anyway. She couldn't stop talking now that she'd started, even as the words stumbled across each other.

"This weekend, I have felt so many emotions—so much more than I have felt in years, and I— The best feelings were with you. *About* you. I care about you, and I know I could care so much more if we . . . I could fall in love with you so easily that I might have already done it." She groaned and hid her face in her hands. "God, I'm so bad at this, I don't know how to say it."

Reece took her gently by the wrists and guided her hands away from her eyes. Thank goodness, he was smiling at her. He gave her the classic, just-for-Charlie megawatt special.

No, this was a limited edition.

"You're saying it just fine."

"Okay," she breathed.

His thumb found the center of her palm and rubbed in a comforting circle. Charlotte couldn't look away from his eyes, warm and green and full of emotions to match her own. They proved what she already knew: She wasn't alone in this.

"Charlie." She blinked up at him, powerless to do anything else. His hold on her hand tightened just so as he wet his lips. "I have loved you for years. I don't plan on stopping." He lifted her hand and pressed a gentle kiss to her knuckles. An altogether different smile teased her as he added, "Even if you're unemployed."

She swatted him in the side, and he laughed, pulling her closer for a lingering kiss. Then he murmured, "I think the Jeep has room for one more."

TEXT MESSAGE FROM JIO VARGAS TO CHARLOTTE THORNE, 1:15 PM: hey viral queen, you should check your venmo balance
(Message not delivered.)

TEXT MESSAGE FROM JIO VARGAS TO CHARLOTTE THORNE, 1:16 PM: idk how much money people have sent you but my tweet linking to it has over 8k likes sooooooo it might be a lot
(Message not delivered.)

TEXT MESSAGE FROM JIO VARGAS TO CHARLOTTE THORNE, 1:16 PM: you're welcome!!!!!!! 😊
(Message not delivered.)

WHEN CHARLOTTE GOT back to the dorm, the door to her room was cracked open. Thank goodness, because she still didn't have her keys. She had a feeling they were in Jackie's pocket, just waiting for her to ask for them.

Charlotte eased the door open. Her best friend kneeled on the floor beside her open suitcase, rolling her socks into neat balls. The package of Oreos sat beside her, almost empty.

"Hey, stranger," Charlotte said. "I brought breakfast."

Jackie startled. Her face was guarded when she looked up from her task, but it softened as she took in the plate of breakfast sandwiches. "Bless you, you asshole."

Charlotte sat down on the cold linoleum next to her, crossing her legs as she handed over the plate. She picked up a pair of jeans, unworn by the looks of their neat creases, and folded them. "I looked for you at the picnic."

Jackie swallowed a piece of bacon and then cleared her throat. Her lips pinched with uncharacteristic embarrassment. "Nina just left."

Charlotte didn't bother to fight a smile. "Good for you, lady killer."

"I would never kill a lady," Jackie trilled in a bastardized English accent. She thrust her chin in the air and pressed the back of her hand to her forehead with a flourish. "How dare you accuse me of such a crime!"

Charlotte laughed, but her smile faded as silence fell on the mountain of clothes in front of them. She reached for a sweatshirt and held it in her lap. She'd been thinking about this all morning but, once again, she still didn't have the right words.

Then again, an apology always started with the same two.

Jackie beat her to the punch. "What happened?"

She blinked. "Hmm?"

Her best friend gave her a sideways look. "You have a weird look on your face."

Charlotte picked up the hoodie and tucked the sleeves into the center. "Jio can send you a *Vox* explainer."

"What?"

She shook her head and put the hoodie in the suitcase. "Sorry, bad joke." Charlotte took a deep breath and held it. Then she turned to meet Jackie's eyes. "I quit my job."

Jackie's surprise bloomed like a rose, her lips parting in a delicate gasp. "You . . . you did?"

Charlotte nodded. Then, a little proud herself, she added, "On Twitter. During Roger's speech."

"What?" Jackie dropped her plate, the breakfast sandwich flopping open on the floor. "Char, you did *what*?"

"It doesn't matter." Charlotte took her friend's hand and closed it between both of her own. "You were right, Jackie. I'm sorry. I've been so self-absorbed."

Jackie goggled at her. "Yeah. You've been a shithead." But her face brightened, and her dazed smile melted the worry from Charlotte's heart. "But it's okay. I mean, I didn't know what was going on. I just wanted to help, but—"

"About that." Charlotte sat up on her heels for a moment to pull a folded page of cream construction paper out of the back pocket of her overalls. Then she turned over Jackie's hand, palm up, and placed it in her grasp. "I made this last night at Acronym."

Jackie gave her a curious look. She unfolded the page, smoothing out the creases, and turned it over. Charlotte watched as confusion and then understanding spread across Jackie's face, her jaw going slack as she took it in.

It was a color wheel. Not very colorful, though. Charlotte had ground the gray pencil to a nub, filling most of the pie slices with darker and lighter patches of ashy blank nothing—the void of her life, thick with insecurity and loneliness and shame. But lines of color as thin as embroidery thread wove through the expanse of gray: violet, tangerine, sepia, electric blue.

Gold for Nina. Metallic silver for Jio. Jade green for Reece. Burgundy red for Jackie.

Hope and affection and ambition and desire and anticipation all straining to break through, radiating from the corner of herself she kept protected. She wanted all those colors back.

"This is how I felt last night," Charlotte said. "When I stormed out, I mean. I guess it's how I've felt for a while." Jackie looked up from the sketch, her eyes wide but focused on her words. Charlotte licked her dry lips, her hand fisting where it rested on her thigh. "But I think that's starting to change now. I hope."

For once Jackie didn't say anything. She looked back at the page, at the expansive gray mess and the streaks of emotion fighting for space. Then she pulled Charlotte into a tight hug, her fingers clenching the back of her shirt.

Charlotte pressed her face against Jackie's shoulder, relief and security overwhelming her alongside a violent pang of love and gratitude. Warm burgundy red again, all Jackie Slaughter.

They sat like that for a very long time. Then they resumed packing.

"So, Baroness Slaughter," Charlotte spouted in her best attempt at the queen's English. "Pray tell, did you engage in scandalous conduct with Lady Dorantes?"

"How perfectly impertinent for you to inquire, Duchess Thorne!"

@HeinUniversity, 1:57 PM: The #HeinRandC2018 committee would like to apologize for our selection of Roger Ludermore as this year's commencement speaker. His remarks do not reflect the values of the Hein community. We hope the Class of 2018 will forgive us for this error in judgment.

TEXT MESSAGE FROM NINA DORANTES TO CHARLOTTE THORNE, 2:01 PM: I'm heading out for my flight, please forgive me for not saying good-bye. It sounds like you've had a wild twenty-four hours! Can we FaceTime this week so you can tell me all about it? If you need some cash this summer, I'd love to commission a Charlotte Thorne illustration of an orchid for my next tattoo . . .
(Message not delivered.)

TEXT MESSAGE FROM REECE KRUEGER TO CHARLOTTE THORNE, 2:15 PM: ready to hit the road?
(Message not delivered.)

EMPTY CUPS WENT in a shopping bag, dirty clothes into suitcases. Jackie stuffed the leftover snacks in a tote bag for Charlotte to take with her on the road. The ritual helped distract from their impending good-bye. Unlike almost every other time they'd packed up a dorm room together, they weren't guaranteed to see each other again at the end of the summer.

"I'll call you when I get off work tomorrow," Jackie promised. She shoved the empty Oreos package into the trash bag.

"You don't have to do that," Charlotte said. She collected their used towels and put them in a neat pile on top of her dresser. "Plus I want to be the one to call you."

Her fingers drifted automatically to her phone in her back pocket. She reminded herself again that it was off. It would probably take weeks for her to get used to living outside the radius of Roger's whims. Without his fragile ego at the forefront of her mind, she might even be able to understand her emotions.

Good timing too. The events of this weekend would take ages to process.

"I'm holding you to that," Jackie said. "We'll nail down those dates for you to come hang out in L.A. I'm buying roller skates."

Charlotte laughed at the idea of Jackie gliding down the Santa Monica boardwalk, her French braids peeking out from under a helmet. "Hard yes to L.A., soft maybe to skates."

"Maybe you can come when Nina visits too! That'll be a fun new dynamic." Jackie winked. "And next week you are . . . ?"

Charlotte repeated her marching orders. "Texting Amy about getting brunch, and calling your dad for help breaking my lease."

"Very good. The time has come for you to couch surf. We can all rotate hosting you, I'll put together a calendar." Charlotte's unease must have shown on her face because Jackie gave her a firm poke in the nose. "Do not give me that look! Let us love you! You can stay with me as long as you want, and I'm sure Reece will say the same."

It would take practice for Charlotte to be comfortable accepting help, but she had to start somewhere. "Yes, ma'am," she said. She didn't even tack on a self-deprecating joke.

"I wish I could put you in my suitcase and take you with me." Jackie held the bag open and offered it to her. "Do you think you could fit in here?"

"I'd have to become a lot more flexible very quickly," Charlotte drawled. "I wish we had more nachos."

"Go see Terry again before you hit the road." Jackie zipped the suitcase and toed on her sneakers. "Maybe he can hire you to fix his awful merch."

The room looked stark without their personal effects scattered across every flat surface. Charlotte folded up their used bedding and rolled down the blackout curtain. Once again it was just another anonymous dorm room with standard-issue furniture. The ceiling bulb wheezed overhead, casting a yellowish glow over the empty walls.

Over the decades, millions of adventures had unfolded here. Hundreds of occupants and thousands of nights. Parties and study groups and hookups and homesick phone calls and discoveries and mistakes.

Charlotte leaned against the door, her arms crossed over her chest. "Do you think it'll be like this at our ten-year?"

She expected a dark joke in response. Instead, Jackie tilted her head to the side in thought. "Yes and no. This place will be the same. Who knows who we'll be?"

The question could have been ominous, but Jackie smiled at her, and Charlotte smiled back. She knew what she meant. They were still at the beginning.

Jackie stood up and patted her pockets. "I should head out."

"Wallet, phone, charger, car keys," Charlotte chanted.

"Got it, got it, got it somewhere, got 'em."

"Did you remember your sunglasses?"

Jackie took her cheap shades out of her jacket pocket and popped them on like a headband. "Of course."

Charlotte leaned against her bare bed and wove together her emotional Kevlar. She hated good-byes. Good-byes called for something meaningful to say, some profound unburdening of the soul. What Jackie meant to her went beyond platitudes about platonic love.

There was so much she wanted to tell her, so many things she wanted to thank her for. Not just for this weekend. For nearly eight years of friendship. For kicking her ass and forcing her to stand up straight. Jackie was her hero, and the annoying big sister Charlotte never asked for. She was family.

They stood opposite each other for a quiet moment, Jackie with her suitcase and Charlotte by the bed. She studied Charlotte's face, the worry lines and the uncomfortable tightness at her mouth. "You're going to be okay, Char," her best friend promised. "You did good this weekend."

Charlotte snorted. "I puked on the President's Lawn."

Jackie wheeled her suitcase to the door. "Well, he deserves it for choosing such a shitty commencement speaker." She swung it open and stepped out into the hallway, the wheels quietly whisking from the linoleum onto the carpet.

Charlotte hovered in the doorway, biting her lip. "Thank you for everything."

They hugged. Charlotte rubbed her sleeve across her face when Jackie finally let go. "Come to L.A.," Jackie commanded. She tapped Charlotte's nose. "You hear me?"

"Yes, boss."

Jackie poked her in the nose again before she turned and started toward the lobby. "You coming?" she called back to her.

"I think I'm going to hang out here for a bit," Charlotte said. "Breathe in the nostalgia some more."

Jackie shook her head. "You're a freak." She put on her sunglasses even though the hallway boasted no natural sunlight. "Byeee!"

Charlotte watched her wheel down the corridor. They waved to each other one last time before Jackie turned the corner and left her alone.

Charlotte leaned against the closed door and sighed. Her shoulders sagged with relief. She was overdue for an introvert recharge, her brain waterlogged. This was the first time she'd been alone for hours and she appreciated the moment while it lasted.

Even now with Jackie gone, she wasn't truly alone at Hein. Music leaked under the door of the room across the hall. A crowd of people chatted in low voices the next hallway over, just around the curve in the corridor. She could hear footsteps overhead as people packed, doors swinging open and banging shut. The campus perpetually hummed with company, no matter the time or the day.

Tomorrow it would fall silent for the summer when the grads packed up and moved out, and its halls would lie dormant until students returned at the end of August. But during the school year, you were never truly alone if you didn't want to be.

College life played out in constant overlaps and gentle collisions. Her years at Hein were full of connections. Some were mundane, like listening to Phish with Terry during weekday lunch shifts. Some were complex and ugly, like her relationship with Ben. And others were the steady heartbeat of her life, vital and sustaining and rare. Jackie, Nina, Jio.

She closed her eyes and tried to separate the sounds. It calmed her to sort the footsteps above from the laughter echoing down the concrete walls. Car horns squawked in the distance as parents navigated the parking lot. Someone thundered down the stairwell to her left, their sneakers pounding on the rubber-topped steps.

Maybe she could stay like this for a few hours. Just rest her head against the door and soak up the daily soundtrack of the university before returning to Brooklyn's impersonal roar.

Charlotte didn't want to go back to college. She really didn't. She didn't want to sleep on narrow mattresses or wake up at noon or drink away her trauma. What she missed about life at Hein wasn't the parties or the gossip or even the challenging, cozy classes. She missed *this.* She missed a dorm full of people who said hello to each other while brushing their teeth at three A.M. side by side. She missed being part of a community.

She didn't want to be alone anymore, bubble-wrapped by isolation so that no one could hurt her or let her down. She wanted to look at life with the same optimism she had at age eighteen, already scarred by her family's rejection but still venturing forth to find people who understood her. She missed knowing others and being known.

She didn't want to go back in time. She *couldn't* go back, she couldn't even start over. She could only go forward.

"Charlie?"

Reece emerged from the stairwell, a backpack slung over his shoulder. He'd showered and changed into clean clothes, his damp hair shining under the fluorescent lights. That stupid single curl licked at his forehead, begging to be coaxed back into place with her fingers.

He really was so handsome, the rough cut of his jaw balanced out by his smile. She wondered again how she'd not seen his perfect imperfection before. Now there would never be a day when the sight of him walking toward her didn't send her heart racing.

Charlotte leaned against the door, her hand curled around the handle. She pressed her other hand palm-flat against its wood surface.

Reece stopped in front of her. The humor evaporated from his face as he devoured her inviting posture. They were exactly where they were on Friday night, give or take a few yards of carpet.

"Hi," she said. It was a pleasure to flirt with him like this, to tease and watch as heat flared in his green eyes. He was an open book to her now, willingly so. She understood the courage it required for him to love her so transparently. She would never take it for granted again.

"Hi," he repeated, a playful bend to the word in his mouth. He dropped his backpack on the carpet and crowded her against the door. Charlotte squirmed up to reach his mouth and he smiled, just beyond her reach. "We gotta get on the road, Charlie."

"Not fair," she whined, narrowing her eyes.

His laugh was rough and husky. Reece caught her jaw in his hand and tilted her face up to examine her. She shivered as he cataloged the purple bags under her eyes and the creases running across her forehead. One of his fingers traced her hairline, detecting the silver strands among the blond.

"You are so beautiful," he breathed, his voice thick with disbelief.

Finally he kissed her. She melted against him as his index finger traced below her chin and down her neck. She adored him. The emotion almost hurt, the force of it in her chest.

Their lips parted. He leaned his forehead against hers, eyes falling closed as he breathed unevenly. "We have to go if we want to avoid traffic," he said, his voice racked with regret.

She placed a kiss on his lips, chaste and sweet. "Reece . . ."

He opened his eyes. She nearly tumbled into them, green as sea glass. "What?"

"I meant what I said. I want to be with you. I love you."

She wished she could elaborate. She wished she could make him endless promises and keep every single one. She wished she could list the reasons why he broke through her walls and cemented himself into her foundation. His kindness, his self-awareness, his character, his plush mouth that said so many unadorned, incredible things. But her throat was thick with tears, and she wasn't as good at this as he was, goddamn it.

Instead, she kissed him again, pouring the intensity of how much she felt for him into every touch and tease of her lips against his. She gasped as he pressed her to the door. Charlotte wound her arms around his neck and reveled in his solid strength, in how much he smelled like home.

She loved him. It broke her open and gave her the strength to start over, to change and try and grow. She loved him and it scared and delighted her in equal measure.

Their lips parted. He leaned his forehead against hers, his eyes falling closed as he breathed unevenly.

"We're really doing this," he whispered against her lips, his fingers delving into her lion's mane. "I trust us to figure it out. I love you too much not to, Charlie."

They stayed like that for a long minute, his nose butting against hers, her arms circling his waist. Charlotte pressed her palm to the small of his back, just over the notches of his spine.

She deserved this kind of love. They both did.

TEXT MESSAGE FROM JACKIE SLAUGHTER TO REECE KRUEGER, 4:37 PM: hi loser, charlotte's phone is still off so I'm texting you. I think I left an earring on the bookshelf, any chance she grabbed it on her way out??

TEXT MESSAGE FROM REECE KRUEGER TO JACKIE SLAUGHTER, 4:39 PM: hi jackie! charlie's driving! she says she has it and she'll mail it to you when she finds time to go to the post office what with her very busy unemployment

TEXT MESSAGE FROM JACKIE SLAUGHTER TO REECE KRUEGER, 4:40 PM: tell her that I will mail her glitter again if I don't see that earring by the end of June. also tell her I LOVE YOU I AM SO PROUD OF YOU #GROWTH

TEXT MESSAGE FROM REECE KRUEGER TO JACKIE SLAUGHTER, 4:40 PM: she says you're an asshole and that glitter ruined kit's carpet

TEXT MESSAGE FROM JACKIE SLAUGHTER TO REECE KRUEGER, 4:41 PM: good, kit sucks.

TEXT MESSAGE FROM REECE KRUEGER TO JACKIE SLAUGHTER, 4:41 PM: lol I can't wait to meet her, I'm gonna crash at Charlie's tonight to break up the drive back to STL

TEXT MESSAGE FROM JACKIE SLAUGHTER TO REECE KRUEGER, 4:41 PM: oh I'm SURE it's JUST to take a break from driving. okay have fun being disgusting together byeeee!!!

TEXT MESSAGE FROM JACKIE SLAUGHTER TO REECE KRUEGER, 4:41 PM: don't let her get a dog!!!

TEXT MESSAGE FROM REECE KRUEGER TO JACKIE SLAUGHTER, 4:42 PM: charlie says, and I'm quoting directly here, "bitch I do what I want"

Acknowledgments

I wrote this story to deal with a whole bunch of confusing, painful, and beautiful feelings, so let's start there. Charlotte's Feelings Chart was inspired by the Feeling Wheel, created by Dr. Gloria Willcox in 1982 as a tool for recognizing and processing one's emotions. Over the years, many variations on Dr. Willcox's tool have been made; I'm a fan of Lindsay Braman's Emotion Color Wheel and Emotion Sensation Wheel. A nice, rosy pink solves many problems.

The first draft of *But How Are You, Really* was a colorless, broken-hearted mad dash with no external conflict. My brilliant agent, Jamie Carr, transformed this book from a daydream into a novel. I am so lucky to work with you and everyone at the Book Group. Thank you for understanding my voice from the day we met.

My editor, Maya Ziv, breathed nuance and depth into these beloved characters. Thank you for the kindest challenges and wisest suggestions. I'm so glad you took a chance on this newbie author. Everyone at Dutton Books deserves my gratitude.

I'm indebted to the authors who took the time to offer me advice when I was an overwhelmed young writer: in particular, Anand Giridharadas, David Biello, Kate Torgovnick May, and Mandy Len

Catron. It meant the world to me to have Real Adults take my ambition seriously and answer my questions.

To my patrons, your generosity and support allow me to write what I want to write every single day. Thank you for fighting the good fight with me.

I'm grateful for the friends who read this book in its infancy and told me to keep going. Thank you to Olivia, Austin, Lara, Emma, Micah, Diana, Lauren, Hailey, Julia, Anne, Pran, and more! And thank you to the Wesleyan crew who got me through college, my reunion, and the healing that followed: Leada, Hope, Caroline, Jack, and Ed at WesWings.

This book would not exist without my heroic soul mates and champions: Gabe Rosenberg, Courtney Liss, and Dalton Deschain. You have taught me so much about love, courage, creativity, and family. Thank you for believing in this story, and in me.

I am nothing without my endlessly supportive and proud parents, who always encouraged my writing even when it took me in zany directions. You raised me to use my voice and have never once asked me to lower it. Thank you for always welcoming me home.

Last, I would not be here without the victim and survivor community, and the loved ones who intervened when I needed help. I also turned to resources like RAINN (Rape, Abuse & Incest National Network), the National Domestic Violence Hotline, the Trevor Project, the 988 Suicide & Crisis Lifeline, and eventually a trauma-informed therapist. If you are dealing with intimate partner violence, suicidal ideation, child abuse, or addiction, I hope you can find the assistance you need in your community.

Writing this book kept me alive during the darkest period of my life. If Charlotte's story helps even one person believe that they deserve more than abuse, it will have been worth it. I believe you. Please ask for help; it is never too late to leave. You are worthy of love just as you are. Anyone who tells you otherwise does not deserve to know you.

About the Author

ELLA DAWSON is an NYC-based sex and culture critic whose work has been published by *Elle*, *Vox*, and *Women's Health*, among others. She was once internet famous for having herpes, but that's a whole other story. Ella is proudly bisexual, very anxious, and aspires to adopt a kitten. Follow her on social media and on Patreon as @brosandprose.